The House of Many Windows

The House of Many Windows

John Robert Allen

AuthorHouse™
1663 Liberty Drive
Bloomington, IN 47403
www.authorhouse.com
Phone: 1-800-839-8640

First published by AuthorHouse 09/13/2011

ISBN: 978-1-4670-3315-2 (sc)
ISBN: 978-1-4670-3314-5 (ebk)

Library of Congress Control Number: 2011916118

Printed in the United States of America

This book is printed on acid-free paper.

Chapter 1

What is a mastermind? A perfect description would be a person who is intellectually and socially capable. He would be an enterprising financier who would have to be energetic and intelligent. That person has the capability of convincing people that he is a leader and a person motivated to succeed. On Wednesday April 30, 1919, the Geneva Daily Times published an obituary that described Wallace W. Paine as the person who had the capabilities to be a mastermind.

On May 2, 1919 there were horse drawn carriages moving slowly down South Main Street accompanied by a few automobiles weaving around the slow parade of carriages. A strange and eerie atmosphere hovered over the area as people began to arrive at the beautiful mansion on Seneca Lake. There had been a death four days earlier that left the city in a state of shock. A cold pelting rain fell on the people who were arriving at 775 South Main Street. The slippery brick street had puddles that were deep and difficult to move through. Black umbrellas facing into the wind dotted the scene, which enabled people to arrive without being soaked by the rain. People were running on the sidewalk with their heads down while maneuvering around the puddles. The horses were standing quietly at the curbside in deep puddles that covered their hooves. The carriage drivers were standing at attention as the occupants left their carriages to make their way to the mansion. It was a dark and dismal day and the gray atmosphere seemed appropriate for a funeral. As the guests approached the front entrance they passed under black drapery that enshrouded the doorway. There was a somber group of men dressed in black tuxedos and top hats greeting and assisting the guests into the home. Everyone who came to the funeral had an air of importance.

James was the Paine's chauffeur. He was sent to the railroad station to greet the out of town guests. He awaited their arrival at the station standing by the 1919 Ford Maxwell. Wallace had the car special ordered and it was the newest and most up to date motorcar of its time. It was dark green with a convertible top that folded down into the back of the car. The top was made with dark gray canvas material. The interior had plush seats covered with the same greenish gray canvas that matched with the top. The car had wire spoke wheels. Wallace was one of the first people to have wheels of that sort. He was one of the founders and president of the first wire wheel company in the United States. Everyone in town knew whose automobile that was when it was seen on the street.

As the guests moved throughout the house people could be heard making comparisons of who was who and how they were associated with the deceased Wallace Paine. Underlying tensions were beginning to surface from various groups that were congregating in the corners of the house. There were comments such as, "How does that common man fit in here?" and "He was only a clerk at the local meat market" circulating throughout the house. The women were especially quiet as they were in the minority. Most women were not allowed to be involved in business or public affairs. They were only permitted to be in social situations. There were a few women in their midst that had a different reputation in the city. They were not accustomed to being directed by men. Women of that "type" were seen as a threat to the male dominated society. These were times when women were beginning to step out in society for purposes other than social gatherings. There seemed to be great tension between these women and the men who ran the affairs of the city.

Wallace W. Paine died on April 29, 1919 in his home on 775 South Main Street. He suffered from a brief illness. This was the era of the great influenza epidemic that killed thousands of people. The epidemic affected young people with symptoms of a cold and pneumonia. The infection caused the lungs to be congested with blood that ultimately suffocated the patient to death.

Prior to his illness Wallace took a trip to Buffalo. His new roadster had just arrived in the Port of Buffalo. The factory that manufactured the Ford Maxwell was located in Cleveland, Ohio. He had custom ordered the car and wanted to be the first to drive it. His orders were to have it shipped to Buffalo and he would drive the car to Geneva. His return trip took much more time than he expected. The April rains fell and chilly winds prevailed. Being the fast and driven person Wallace was he did not wear the proper attire for such weather. He developed a cold on his return trip. It took two days to drive from Buffalo over the unpaved roads. While traveling from Buffalo the rain created huge ruts in the road. Darkness prevented him from traveling in the night with such rough road conditions. Only as he approached cities would the roads be somewhat paved. He was excessively concerned about not damaging the new car. Wallace finally arrived back to Geneva physically sick and developed what was thought to be pneumonia. Wallace requested that his physician notify doctors in New York City of his condition. He thought the doctors had a better knowledge of the illness. They were notified but it would take more than a day to get to Geneva. Wallace died before the doctors arrived. His thirty-eighth birthday had been on April 1.

During the calling hours there were conflicting opinions about Wallace's personality. Some saw him as a smart businessman while others saw him as shrewd and underhanded. He was handsome with a bright sparkling face and had a "way with people." The Geneva Daily Times described him as a most promising citizen. He was alert, active, and eager to advance.

Winston Spaulding was at the funeral. He was maneuvering himself through the crowds. He was an acquaintance of the Paine's. He met Wallace in high school. Winston always seemed to appear in places that were not his style. He was a common man. Most people thought he was the groundskeeper because of his disheveled appearance. Rarely did his face look shaven or his clothes clean. As he walked around the room he had a mysterious attitude about him. He was determined to gather a group in the library to read Wallace's obituary. His voice sounded like a ghost trying to convince people of how things really were. There was a morbid atmosphere that permeated throughout the library. The room was dimly lit with a fireplace that gave off crackling sparks from the hot coals. At the end of the library were circular windows overlooking the shores of Seneca Lake. Foggy and misty skies hung over the lake as the rain fell. The wind blew across the water creating white caps that looked like ice. The waves pounded the shore with a deliberate crash as if making a statement much like that of Winston Spaulding. It was a gray and dismal day.

Doctor Samuel C. Haynes stood among the group that was listening politely to Winston Spaulding. Dr. Haynes was a medical doctor in Geneva. His work involved general medical care and had been Wallace's doctor. The work that he performed was of the highest standards. He was well known for his ability in the medical field. He had a reputation for high standards and associated with people who were like him. Winston began suggesting that some of Paine's business dealings were manipulated to be self-beneficial. He asked if anyone knew of the types of products that were imported and exported in Paine's business in New York City. No one in the group seemed to know much about the company. Someone mentioned imports from the Orient. There was no response to that information. The mere mention of connections to New York City and Buffalo made those listening uncomfortable. Everyone became uneasy and started to move away. Finally, Dr. Haynes responded in an aggravated tone. He was shocked that anyone would say such things about Wallace Paine at his funeral.

Rose Haynes was a stylish well-dressed woman. She stood among the people in the group that was listening to Spaulding. She was Dr. Haynes' wife. Everyone in the group was attempting to understand the motives of Spaulding's accusations. Was he trying to blame the dead man for something? Was he trying to expose a secretive past? Did he have plans to undermine his estate? The obituary further described Wallace as "a person who could grasp whatever opportunity came his way. He had the vision to accurately judge what it would take to make things work to his advantage." After a loud conversation from the library, more people came in to find out what was happening. Dr. Haynes became more vocal and was attempting to counteract the suggestions of Paine's wrongdoings in business and his personal life. He stood forward and leaned into Spaulding's face and said, "Wallace Paine was a mastermind. He was an individual who had a superior ability to focus, plan, and execute any situation into a profitable endeavor." Spaulding huffed and said, "You apparently were not aware of the real Wallace Paine." Rose stood motionless during the encounter. She glared at Spaulding and quietly but firmly said, "You, Mr. Spaulding have no right to pass judgments or accusations on Wallace when your behavior and past life have been less than admirable." At that she turned with the others and walked away.

As guests arrived they passed by Paine's casket and offered their sympathies to his wife Eveline. She was a stylish woman. Her demeanor was calm and collected. She wore an ankle length black silk dress with a low round neckline. It was designed to enhance her slender body. Her hair was covered with a large brimmed black veiled hat. She wore very little makeup and only a gold bracelet on her left wrist with no wedding ring on her finger. Her shoes went above the ankles and had buckles across the top. She wore black silk stockings. The heels were of moderate height, a bit higher than most women would wear for a funeral. As people spoke to her she said very little and responded with only a nod or a quick thank you. It was almost as if she was not connected to the situation or the people. Eveline exhibited refined mannerisms as people passed by. She thanked everyone for coming. She chatted briefly with the society type women of Geneva. The women who were there seemed quite comfortable with her behavior and admired her style. Some of the men wondered what she was thinking as she watched the guests move around the room. Occasionally she focused on some of the men who were congregating in other parts of the house. Her position in the room was such that she saw the encounter Winston Spaulding had with the group in the library. Eveline never gave an expression of judgment with the outburst Winston had with Doctor and Mrs. Haynes. Wallace's immediate family was standing by the casket but not too close to Eveline. It was as if they were trying to stay away from the action and were present only because they were his parents. They were discussing how shocked they were that he had died so quickly. Eveline stood far enough away from them so as not to listen to the same discussion over and over. She began to find the repetitiveness of the event to be tedious. Eveline and Wallace's parents did not communicate very much during that afternoon. It almost seemed like two separate families attending an acquaintance's funeral.

A man named Rudolph Williams stood with Eveline in the receiving line. He was Wallace's closest friend. They were business partners and had knowledge of each other's monetary and private affairs. He knew more about Wallace's background than Eveline did since she was usually excluded from important activities that the two men engaged in. Eveline often wondered what she would do if Wallace died. To her shock his death created the need to have Rudolph by her side. She had no insight into the magnitude of what her husband had been involved in. Rudolph offered to assist Eveline in any way he could because he was named the trustee in Wallace's will. Occasionally, he would whisper in her ear while they stood at the casket. Eveline never reacted to these brief comments. Rudolph was telling her who certain people were and how they had been associated with her husband.

Rudolph was tall in stature and had a muscular build. He was very precise with his mannerisms. He wore a black suit that was perfectly tailored to his lean body. There was a handkerchief in the top pocket of the coat that was correctly folded. He wore a red tie that matched the red handkerchief. He had dark brown wavy hair with piercing blue eyes. Some of the women at the funeral were intrigued by Rudolph and said he was quite dapper. He was a looker and he knew how to use those talents. He stood almost like a statue in every way perfect. Eveline would glance at him for time to time but he would give her no response. Her relationship with Rudolph appeared to be a cautious one. He was very businesslike with her and to the people paying their last respects to Wallace. As Eveline stood with Rudolph she thought how comfortable she felt with him. She knew a different side of Rudolph and liked it.

Eveline was described as a cultured young woman in her 30s. She was sporty in her attire but formal in her attitude toward life. She was a classy woman. Some of the women passed by with questionable looks and a raised eyebrow directed at Eveline. They stared at Rudolph but for different reasons. They had lust in their eyes. The women of Geneva were a very class-conscious group. They often were outspoken about women who did not fit into their social circle. They did not realize that their actions looked more like jealousy, which was evident when they met Eveline. She found their behavior to be low class and distasteful. The only way for her to handle that was to be an example of an independent woman.

Hundreds of people arrived at the funeral. There had never been so much happening in one place. Wallace Paine had made a huge mark on the City of Geneva. It was approaching 1PM and the funeral was about to begin.

Chapter 2

Rochester, New York had a population of 85,000 and was bustling with growth and enthusiasm in 1880. It had been fifteen years since the end of the Civil War. The country was still recovering from the effects and devastation of this war. The reconstruction years had its effect on Rochester and the liberation of the slaves. Rochester had been one of the centers for the Underground Railroad that had transported hundreds of slaves to safety and freedom. It had always been a city known for its involvement in social and political matters. In the mid 1800's, Susan B. Anthony, whose home was Rochester, was in the forefront for women's rights. During that same time Frederick Douglas had been campaigning for the abolition of slavery. The Erie Canal flowed through the city creating a passage to the Hudson River and New York City. The shipping industry was a big business helping to establish factories and employment for people.

Buffalo Street that later became Main Street, was the main route through Rochester. It was rough in many places with dirt and dust in the summer and mud the rest of the year. The road in the center of town was paved with bricks. Nighttime activity was limited because there were only a few gas lanterns placed at intersections. Transportation was by horse and buggy. Horses were used for single riders. Buggies and carriages were used for larger groups or merchandise. Men were usually seen in the streets conducting business. Women were not allowed on the streets. They could shop but never be seen doing business.

Saddlery and livery shops were familiar places in the city. They played a vital role in servicing the horses and carriages used in the city. As with most services there were different levels of saddlery and livery shops for different classes of people. Some people were the commoners and some were affluent. Everyone had a special shop for his or her transportation needs. George B. Paine and Sons owned a saddlery shop on this street. They catered exclusively to the well to do or as some said "the upper crust" of Rochester. It was a family owned operation. They offered the finest in comfort and style in the saddlery and carriage business. The saddles were made of the finest leather with studded decorations accessorizing them. These accessories were made of gold and silver to compliment the riders' attire. It was the man's responsibility to select the carriage and accessories. These exceptional carriages were called broughams. Women were not allowed in a shop of this type but were given the opportunity to make all the selections for the interior of the carriage. The Paine Company personalized their service by making home visits. The lady of the house could privately confer with Mr. Paine and make their selections in the comfort of their home. The company's motto was "personal service is a must."

Mr. And Mrs. Kimball ordered a carriage for social occasions and for going to church. They also ordered a basic buggy for the housekeeper and other hired hands. They would use it for groceries and supplies for the estate. Mr. Kimball owned the largest tobacco factory in Rochester. The Kimball Tobacco Factory was so successful that a statue of Mercury was erected and placed on the smokestack as a sign of power and success. It stood 21 feet tall and was the largest copperplate statue in America. George Paine and his wife were invited to the unveiling of the statue. They were special guests of the Kimball's and were escorted in the new carriage to the ceremony and party that followed.

Rochester continued to grow and so did the Paine Saddlery and Harness Company. They coordinated and supplied the fire department with harnesses needed for the first horse drawn fire equipment. Until that time men pulled the fire equipment and then had to fight the fire. This new equipment had horses do the work of pulling the wagons. The demand for custom-made accessories increased and the Paine Company moved farther out of town to 187 East Main Street. It was renamed The East Side Carriage and Saddlery Store. The aristocracy began moving farther out of town and a fancier shop was required nearer to their homes. Large mansions were being constructed on East Avenue, Main Street, and Clinton Avenue. Every aspect of life was growing and expanding which led to the need for more help in the shop. George Paine included his son Frank as an owner. Frank was glad to be a part of the business because they wanted it to remain a family operation.

Frank married Alice in early 1880. They lived at 13 South Clinton Street. They resided in a duplex near the center of downtown not far from the saddlery shop. Frank was known to work until late in the evening. When he arrived home he appeared tired and in a foul mood. When Alice tried to ask how his day was he told her it was none of her concern and that his job was a man's business. Alice being young and obedient never contradicted Frank. She found her life to be rather dull and spent her time taking care of the apartment. She usually did what Frank wanted. Women were viewed as second-rate citizens and were not allowed to be involved in outside affairs.

Frank was tall and handsome. He used his charm to its advantage. When he consulted with women on his home visits he could convince them of almost any thing and make them feel important. Alice never discussed her feelings about his business involvements with these upper class women. She wondered if these visits included more than an order for a carriage or the accessories. If the subject came up he told her that she was crazy. Alice was a small woman with fair features. She had long light brown hair and brown eyes. When she went shopping she wore her hair in a bun under a hat. Although she was 20 years old most people thought she was a girl in her teens. During her shopping trips she liked being part of the street life. She enjoyed when men gave her a wink but woman would raise an eyebrow as she smiled at them. Alice felt alive on the streets and found reasons to make her trips longer each time. During one of her shopping trips she watched society women go into the fancy shops. She felt a bit jealous as she observed them trying on hats, dresses, and bootery. She made a point to speak with these women as they left the shops with their hatboxes and bags. As time went by these women began to comment on how intriguing she was. Alice seemed to have a personality that mixed well with the "Women of Rochester." Gradually Alice and these women became friends. The day finally came when they invited Alice to have tea with them in a nearby restaurant. It became a weekly event. Alice realized that there were new things ahead for her. She was not staying at home waiting for Frank!

Chapter 3

ALICE WAS BORN IN Canada in 1860. The tale was that her mother Eva had been widowed shortly after Alice's birth. Life for Alice's mother had been difficult while living in Canada. She had very little money and difficulty finding work. She decided that life might be better for them in Rochester. She heard that jobs were easier to find because men were fighting in the Civil War. Immigration was encouraged. The need for verification of who you were or where you were coming from was nonexistent. Eva had no idea of what to expect when she arrived in Rochester with a baby. She took a room at a boarding house. Eva immediately set out looking for work. Within a few days she was hired as a full time maid for a wealthy family. The property had a small maid's quarters so she and Alice had a place to live. Eva worked as the housekeeper and supervised the other staff. She was perfect for the job. She was short and robust. Her hair was dark brown and curly. She wore a white cap that contrasted her round red cheeks. The children loved her because of her cooking, her jolly personality, and affectionate ways. It was as though they were part of the family. The adults in the family had a strong admiration for Eva and cared very much for Alice.

Alice went to the public schools in Rochester. She did well in school. She was a well-mannered young girl. Her classmates liked her because of her kind personality.

During her last year in school she met Frank at a school event. They dated for two years and were then married.

Alice continued to be involved with the women and their tea gatherings. It was no longer a question of whether she was included, it was expected that she attend these events. She had now become part of the socialite group. She blended into their conversations as if she had been "one of them" for years. Alice enjoyed this newly discovered aspect of life in Rochester. The women would discuss how they had arrived at their place in Rochester and how they preferred to live. When Alice told them how and why her mother came to Rochester they were fascinated that Alice had become such a perfect young woman. These women were older than Alice and had never had similar experiences.

The social meetings continued for months. During that time Alice learned more about the social ideals of the Rochester elite. She felt like she was being lifted to a higher level on the social ladder. Basically, her mother was a common worker and she was the maid's daughter. Many of the women knew Frank because of his successful saddlery and livery business. They loved to exchange conversation about how well he did his work and what an asset he was for the well to do. In the midst of one of the conversations Alice was asked what she thought of the idea of being a social events coordinator. It would involve organizing, preparing, and attending the social events that were held by the Women's Club. At first Alice felt taken aback because she compared this offer to what her mother did for a living. As she thought about the job she began to see that it was a way to meet and socialize with new and upper class people. She wondered what Frank would say. She justified her offer as a means of helping him find new clients. The whole idea excited her and she knew that she wanted to be an individual. She was not staying home to become a dull housewife. There were very few ways for a woman to become important in Rochester. She was to be paid a salary, given a clothing allowance, and admission to the events. This was her great opportunity. She could not wait to tell her mother and Frank. He was quite happy for her and thought it was good for her to do something she enjoyed. Eva on the other hand was not so happy. She merely stared at her and said "So you're becoming a socialite by going up the back stairway?" Alice resented her mother's remark. She tried to ignore it by telling herself that she was improving herself and her mother never did.

Alice enjoyed the job of social coordinator. It had its challenges and its benefits. She was responsible for the scheduling of luncheons, dinner parties, and theater events in various places around town. She would visit the people who were in charge of the facilities, the food preparation, and those who would set up the event. If there was entertainment she would schedule and hire the people to do the work. For Alice the best part was the actual event. All of her hard work came together. She could see its results when people were having fun and asking about the organizer of the event. She was always given the highest compliments and treated like an important person.

The weather in the autumn of 1880 was very hot and sultry. Every day the temperature would rise into the 90s. Alice was working on the special event for the opening of the Red Cross in Rochester. Rochester was the second city in the United States to have a Red Cross chapter. It was to be a citywide event. The mayor would be there for the ceremony with Clara Barton and they would give a speech. There was a parade and a luncheon planned for the day. During the speeches Alice fainted. She was taken to the doctor. The doctor informed Alice that she was pregnant. She was taken home to rest for the next few days. Frank was delighted and hoped for a boy. Alice was shocked that she was pregnant. She worried about how a baby would affect her job.

Chapter 4

On April 1, 1881, Alice gave birth to a boy. They named him Wallace. Frank and Alice felt that name was a strong and forthright name. She sensed that he was strong because he constantly moved during her pregnancy. Alice watched his determination from the day he was born. She told Frank, "A mother knows her own." Wallace lived up to that reputation throughout his entire life.

Alice continued her employment as social coordinator for the Women's Club of Rochester. Her worries of being a mother and having a job were short lived. She never wanted to give up her position. She enjoyed the contacts with "high society" women. They were pleased that she was returning to the Women's Club. Alice discussed the possibility that her mother be the nanny while she worked. She could go to work and feel comfortable that a family member was involved with the baby and not a stranger. Eva was reluctant to agree to the arrangements because she viewed it as the same job she would be leaving. The hardest part was leaving her position as the main housekeeper, a job she held for over 20 years. Frank offered her a salary and told her that she could live in their apartment with them. Eva realized that she was getting older and the strain of her housekeeping job was beginning to bother her. She gave her resignation, much to her employer's sadness, and moved into Frank and Alice's home a month after

Wallace was born. Eva began doing the types of things a grandmother would do for her grandson. She fed and cared for him as if he were a doll. She was the housekeeper for her family now. Both Alice and Frank were quite pleased with the arrangement. Eva seemed content with the work she was doing. She admitted that it was less strenuous than her previous job. On Sunday Frank's parents would come to visit the family. It gave Eva a chance to go out for the day if she wanted to. The families never had a strong relationship. Eva usually avoided contact with the Paine's because she felt they were too rich for her.

Everything was working out fine. Wallace was being cared for and healthy. Alice was busy with the Women's Club. Frank was glad that everyone had settled into a routine. One day Alice came home unexpectedly.

Occasionally, Eva would make remarks about Alice's job. She accused her of being too showy and proud of her position. She told Alice that she had a chip on her shoulder and that someone needed to knock it off. Alice was shocked that her mother would say such things to her. She could not understand why her mother was being so cruel. Alice noticed that Eva was starting to act distant towards Wallace as if he was not there. Alice tried to make other conversation. Frank came home and everyone had a pleasant dinner as if nothing was wrong. The next day everyone went about their duties. Alice tried to forget what her mother had said and passed it off as a bad day. When she came home the next day her mother would not speak to her. She totally ignored Alice. Frank arrived and Eva acted fine towards him. Alice began to think her mother was playing a game. Eva's behavior became worse as days passed. If Alice confronted her she would shrug her shoulders and walk away. Eva finally told Frank, not

Alice, that she was not happy with the arrangements of her job. She told him that she saw her daughter being too heavily involved with the rich people and not being a good mother. Alice was turning into someone she did not know. She thought Alice was having an affair because she would be out late, supposedly working. Frank tried to explain that he sometimes had the same schedule. Eva said it was all right for a man to be foot loose and fancy-free but a woman was a whore who did such things. She said that she felt those uppity women were using Alice and Wallace did not know who his parents were. Frank listened with astonishment and wondered how a mother could have such a hostile impression of her family.

Days passed and Alice began to notice that Wallace was not being cared for as well as he had been. He was not as clean as he should be. She found food that was thrown away that looked like it was barely touched. Alice confronted her mother about her observations. She asked her mother about Wallace's soiled pants and dirty body. She also confronted her about her attitude toward her and her accusations of being a whore. Alice told Eva that she wanted her son to grow up to be strong and healthy. Wallace was an inquisitive child who would tear things apart and then put them back together perfectly. He was now 3 years old. Eva said he was out of control. She told Alice that he was fat and should be on a diet. This was the reason that she had stopped feeding him so much. Alice was furious. Alice was angry when Eva accused her of being a whore again. She could not understand the reasoning behind this allegation. She told Alice she was tired of doing dirty work for such uppity people. Alice accused her mother of being jealous of the family. Eva said nothing except that she was finished!

Eva made arrangements to move back to Canada. Alice tried to convince her mother that it was a long time ago that she lived there and that life might be different now. Eva ignored that conversation saying, "I will go back to what I know." Eva left early in the morning on the train to Canada. She never saw Alice, Frank, or Wallace again.

A year later Alice received a telegram from her aunt that Eva had died. The telegram said nothing more. She was shocked and wondered if that was the reason her mother left Rochester in such a hurry. Alice wondered if her mother was sick and did not know it or did not tell. The death of her mother left so many unanswered questions. Alice blamed herself for having her mother work for them. She wondered how long her mother had been ill. No one could answer any of her questions. Her Aunt Catherine did not respond to any communication sent by Alice. It was like it had been a dream and it was over. What could possibly have happened to her mother? Her strange behavior at the end was never understood. Why did she run back to Canada instead of living in Rochester? Alice felt bad enough that she never knew her father and now she felt like she never knew her mother.

A few months passed and Alice began to let the events of her mother's death go. She returned to her usual work duties and she was now pregnant with their second child. A letter arrived from her Aunt Catherine. Alice was reluctant to open it. She wondered why it had taken so long to get to her. Catherine wrote the letter to finally explain her mother's past. As a young woman Eva had been committed to an asylum to rest and calm her nerves. She spent a few years there. Upon Eva's release from the asylum she met a man and became pregnant. Eva was living at her sister Catherine's home when Alice was born. It was never certain who her father had been with Eva saying that it was a soldier. Catherine helped Eva care for her baby. She sensed that Eva was not too attached to her child. It seemed strange to her but she never questioned it. Eva had a temper and was not easy to control when in that frame of mind. That was the reason she was committed to the asylum. Shortly after that Eva moved to the United States she would send Catherine letters from Rochester. They were very troubling to read. She admitted to Catherine that she hated her baby from the day she was conceived. Since Alice was born all she could feel was contempt for this "kid". This baby made her furious and resentful. These feelings only escalated when Alice became successful at the Women's Club. Eva felt she had never made anything of herself. Moving to Rochester did not really change Eva. The only thing that changed was Alice. She grew up and became a wife and a mother. Her husband was successful and they had an exceptionally strong and inquisitive child. While Eva was living with them she began to hate Alice even more. She told Catherine that she had thoughts of killing Alice and Wallace. They represented to her a happy family that was a life she never knew. She viewed her life as a failure. It was then that Eva decided to accuse everyone of the very thing that she was guilty of. She was trying to comfort herself. She in fact felt she was the whore and wished she could have been part of higher society. Eva knew that she must leave before she did something that would be devastating to the family.

Catherine found Eva dead in her room. She reported to the doctor that her sister had been slowing down with headaches that led to her feeling drowsy. She told him about her asylum years. The doctor asked about the family and what her life had been like. Catherine explained that her sister had been an angry person. She would do things to spite others. She felt that was why Eva ran out and became pregnant by an unknown man. The doctor recorded the information and performed an examination on Eva. During his examination he studied her fingernails and skin. He performed a test of her hair. He notified Catherine of the results that indicated the death had been by arsenic poison. The poison could be taken in small doses never to be detected and then death would come. Catherine finally told the doctor that her sister had admitted that she purchased the poison in the United States and she had intended to slowly watch her daughter and grandson die.

Alice was alone when she read the letter from her aunt. A sudden shock came over her when she read the last part about the intent to kill Wallace and herself. She sat in the living room and stared into the air. She wondered about this mentally deranged person she had invited into her home. How could she have known her mother was capable of planning such a hateful and deadly act? She was still uncertain about the story of her father.

Chapter 5

SHORTLY AFTER THE LETTER their second child was born. They named him Gregg. Having two children was a responsibility that Alice found to be a great deal of work. She realized that it was time to resign from her work as social planner. She told the women that her main focus now was to be at home to raise her family. Alice felt that part of her had died when she gave her resignation. She thought that her mother's wishes were coming true! She still felt the draw of her mother and her unanswered behavior. Whenever there was a social event being held Alice was now included as one of them. Alice had finally risen to their level and not their planner.

Wallace was five years old. He was becoming increasingly independent now that he was in kindergarten. Before he entered school he had mastered the basics of the alphabet, counting, reading and writing. Alice was a little concerned that he did not have any friends. He appeared happy to be by himself. She noticed when he interacted with his classmates that he was usually the leader and had a plan. He was good at getting kids to do what he wanted them to do. As he went into higher grades at the Rochester Free Academy the smart kids liked him. Wallace tried to model himself after his favorite teachers. He was not a follower he was a leader. He would make an effort to help anyone who needed assistance. His teachers enjoyed having him in class and always had the best to report to his mother. Alice had to be careful not to show too much pleasure in him. Gregg was different than Wallace. He had very little interest in school and the social activities attached to school. Gregg was more interested in the saddlery shop than anything else and hated school. Wallace was the first born and seemed to have all the intelligence and motivation. He was in school clubs, enjoyed music, was in school productions, and sang in the choir. His brother called him a "sissy" but those remarks only made Wallace more determined to do better than everyone else. When Wallace went to the shop he was more intrigued with the completed carriages. Even as a little kid he told his father that the decorations were going to make the carriage special and that they were for the rich people. His father would pay him to help finish the carriage decorations before the owner came for the new vehicle. Wallace always had money even as a little kid. He never refused an offer to do work. He loved odd jobs and liked making money. He had money for his hobbies and crafts. His father referred to him an "enterprising boy".

There was nothing that Wallace would not attempt to do. He loved drawing and writing. He pretended to be a draftsman and draw houses and buildings. He entered his drawings in a contest at school and won. Wallace would sketch cars, flowers, people, and anything imaginable. He would pretend to be a salesman. He used his drawings as advertisements and attached a jingle to them hoping to sell his product. Wallace was the type of kid that became bored with things other kids liked to do. As he got older his father did not understand him. He would tell Alice that Wallace must have come from another family. She did not appreciate his remark because it reminded her of her mother's "whore" accusations. Wallace sensed his father's dissatisfaction of him. He became more determined to seek out people outside of his family who would become his mentors.

Chapter 6

WALLACE WAS INTERESTED IN the current events in Rochester and throughout the country. In 1888, Eastman Kodak Company was established and the "Kodak Number One Box Camera" went on sale. Wallace begged his father to take him to the store to buy the camera. He had his own money and was one of the first people in Rochester to own such a contraption. People found it strange that a "little kid" could have a "gadget" like that. He began using it on everything. When he was using his camera people were a little skeptical of his intentions. His father did not like the idea of the camera in the house. He was fearful of what it might do. Whenever he found something that caught his eye he photographed it. Frank would avoid Wallace when he saw him with the camera. It was rather comical that this little kid could scare a big man. One day Wallace was with his father at the shop. He was taking pictures of everything that was flashy and different. Frank realized that he could use the photos as a sales gimmick by advertising photos around town. After realizing what a great idea it was he encouraged Wallace to take all the pictures he wanted. Wallace was a little confused that all of a sudden his father liked the camera. Little did Wallace know that he had already begun a lifetime of advertising success.

Everyday Wallace would walk through downtown on his way home from school. Construction wars were happening in Rochester. These were the days when men were attempting to build the tallest buildings. Everyone in town including the children knew about the Ellwanger& Barry Building and the Powers Building contest. This was front-page news that Wallace would read about every night. He would count the number of floors on each building everyday. In the late fall the Ellwanger& Barry Building was completed to a height of eight stories. Daniel Powers could never have let that be the end of the height contest! He proceeded to construct two additional floors with a mansard roof to the Powers Building. This reclaimed the title as Rochester's tallest building. The title held for five years.

The Rochester Chamber of Commerce was created in 1888. Howard H. Warner was its first president. He was Frank Paine's best friend and business associate. Frank's business was one of the first to be a member of the Chamber of Commerce. There was a grand opening celebration for the newly formed chamber. Frank was invited to be one of the dignitaries. There was a celebration held downtown and all the businesses were invited. Frank and Alice went to the event and they took Wallace. He took many pictures with his camera. When he arrived home he wrote captions and drew pictures for his make believe advertising campaign.

Advertising was intriguing to Wallace. He liked the idea of convincing people of ideas through a photo and caption rather than conversation. Being ten years old, his teachers found him to be extraordinary in his level of thinking and further in capabilities than most children his age. Wallace kept close track of Eastman Kodak Company because he was waiting for a new type of film to go on sale. They had developed the first transparent photographic film. Their advertisement stated that pictures would have more clarity. As soon as the film went on sale he bought it and began to improve his photographic ability. The new YMCA building had been completed at Court Street and South Avenue. He took pictures of the construction and the grand opening. It was one of the first places to have an indoor swimming pool. Down the street from where the Paines lived the Hahemann Hospital opened. Wallace was fascinated with this building because it was so different than a store. It was a place where people went to get better. He photographed the hospital and wrote advertisements for hospital care. Everywhere he went there was building and progress. With all this exposure to construction, Wallace started studying how buildings were designed. His interest in the development of architecture was just being born.

Transportation was changing how people traveled. Up to that time the horse and buggy, horseback, and walking were the ways people commuted. During the summer of 1889 trolley lines were expanding. The new line was built to connect Charlotte with Crescent Beach. Now people could ride the trolley from downtown Rochester to Charlotte and then on to Crescent Beach. Frank and Alice spent most Sundays during the summer at the beach. The kids loved it and Frank did not have to worry about the horse and buggy. He began to wonder what was going to happen to his livery business if transportation kept changing. As a surprise to the family Frank made reservations for a one-night stay at the Crescent Beach Hotel. The hotel was noted for its high style and gracious atmosphere. Spending a weekend at the beach hotel was the best time for the family. They had dinner in an elegant dining room.

Everyone dressed up for dinner. Alice commented on how many glasses and plates were on the tables. The starched white linens were a perfect background for the red roses on the tables. The children sat at the table like little statues on their best behavior. Their room overlooked the waters of Lake Ontario. Breakfast was served on the veranda. White wicker furniture with pink tablecloths decorated the outdoor restaurant. This was life at its grandest! As they rode the trolley back to Rochester on Monday morning Wallace thought about the weekend. He knew he liked that style of living. He promised himself that he would live like that someday.

Chapter 7

It was Christmas time and Wallace enjoyed looking in all the stores on his way home from school. He studied how the merchandise was advertised. Merchants began to display their goods in more colorful ways. The use of scenery and cloth background was a strong part of the store's advertising. Window designers were being trained in the modern techniques for advertising and attracting the buyers. A sales program was being introduced that would encourage the consumer to buy more than less of an item. The more you bought the lower the price. Buying in quantity offered the buyer a better deal for the dollar. Wallace would spend time thinking of different marketing plans. He liked slogans and jingles. A favorite of his was, "buy more save more $". He believed that these were things people would remember. After a while Alice and Frank did not pay much attention to him. They were glad he was occupied and out of trouble. His brother made fun of him and called him a dreamer. He was jealous of Wallace and thought he might feel better if he made fun of him. He had nothing in common with his brother.

On December 12 the Paine family received a huge box in the mail. Howard H. Warner who was president of the Chamber of Commerce had the gift sent to the family from the John D. Larkin Company in Buffalo, New York. John Larkin developed a modest soap factory in

Buffalo in 1875 and marketed only two items. The soaps were named "Sweet Home Soap", which was a yellow laundry soap and a toilet soap named "Crème Oatmeal". In 1881 the mail order business was in its infancy that gave people the ability to order merchandise by mail. To establish a brand identity, Elbert Hubbard, the advertising officer, inserted a picture with the company's logo into every box of soap. Hubbard's advertising and marketing tactics of offering a gift directly to customers was a new approach to sales. It was a gift to the purchaser for buying a product. He later suggested smaller size soap and coupons to be included in their combination box. The coupons could be used to redeem merchandise from the Larkin Catalog. The company began packaging household items along with their soaps hoping to increase sales. Because of Hubbard's suggestion Larkin created a large box of one hundred pieces of soap mixed with other trinkets and gifts. These gifts were mostly inexpensive spoons, pictures, handkerchiefs, kitchen utensils and a bottle of Modjeska perfume. This was marketed for the low price of six dollars. It was originally called the bargain box but in September of 1889, it became so popular that it was used for the holiday promotion as the Christmas box. The advertising slogan for the mammoth box of gifts was: "Sweet Home Family Soaps and Fine Toilet Articles." The Larkin's guaranteed lowest pricing since they were selling direct from the factory to the home. There was no wholesale or retail profit involved. The sales and advertising plan was an instant success.

Wallace had just arrived home from school when the box arrived. It was huge with gifts for every occasion. He had been studying about Buffalo in school. His teacher had been teaching the class about the development of large companies in Buffalo. Part of the lesson was the discussion of the Larkin Company being the first mail order company in America. The next day he went to school and told his teacher about the Christmas box. His teacher explained that Buffalo was growing rapidly because of the shipping industries, grain mills, steel mills, enormous railroad facilities, and manufacturing companies. The teacher showed the class a map of Buffalo explaining it had access to the Great Lakes and waterways to the east that made it a successful city.

Wallace studied the Larkin philosophy and followed their advertising campaigns in the newspaper. The Christmas box promotion drove profits to new heights. The success of the promotion was the stimulus for renaming the company. In February 1892 it became known as The Larkin Soap Company. Every year there was an innovative advertising campaign such as the Larkin Piano Lamp. It was offered as the gift for buying other merchandise. As profits soared more space was needed for the amount of orders being processed. The investors and stockholders of the company provided the money Larkin needed for the expansion. When the expansion was completed Elbert Hubbard and John Larkin continued to build the marketing strategy for the company to national recognition. In 1893 Hubbard retired from the Larkin Soap Company. He had helped his brother-in-law John Larkin build the company into a corporate power and was now leaving its future in his hands. During 1893 a nationwide economic depression occurred which became known as the Panic of 1893. Unemployment was high and several strikes were taking place throughout the industrial workforce. Many of the executives of the Larkin Company believed that Hubbard left the company because he foresaw an impending economic crisis.

Elbert Hubbard pursued other interests. He established an artisan's community in East Aurora, New York about 10 miles from Buffalo. He was the founder of the Arts and Crafts movement in the United States. He believed in minimalism and a life of simplicity. Everything in life had a function and purpose. He believed in simple and functional living that became part of his furnishing and housing designs. His motto was "With Heart and Hand." Hubbard believed hard work and a strong will made a perfect combination. The Roycroft campus in East Aurora was established to train apprentices in the art of pottery, metalwork, printing, and furniture production. Elbert Hubbard remained at the Roycroft Campus training, instructing apprentices and spreading his free spirited and artistic philosophy of life.

Chapter 8

SHORTLY BEFORE 1893 PEOPLE were feeling good about the economic state of the country. It became known as the Mauve Decade. William Henry Perkins' aniline dye allowed mauve to become a fashionable color for clothing; it was used in the newest dress designs. Most kids Wallace's age were playing sports and quitting school to work in a field or factory. Society was beginning to change. There were articles about shows coming to town or a society affair open to everyone. People were feeling free and loose. Dancing, drinking, and prostitution were part of the social scene. Private clubs were established mainly for the men to conduct business and only the rich were invited. Everywhere you went people were dressing up and going out to dance and have a high-spirited time. Mark Twain named the 1890s as "The Gilded Age" when he alluded to the seemingly profitable era that was stimulated by crime. The working classes were now able to be a part of the social scene. Hotels had ballrooms filled with people dancing and enjoying the entertainment. All the major hotels would advertise in the newspaper for the dinner and dancing events. The slogan most hotels used was "the more you drink the more fun you have". Life was on the upswing for many people. Wallace was old enough to stay at home to care for Gregg when his parents went out for the evening. He wondered what was so important that so many people were going out at night all dressed up. He would listen to the radio and hear the sounds of music from the hotels filled with people laughing and enjoying themselves. Single gentlemen were seen mingling around the bars and dance floors looking for women to have fun with. Sometimes these connections were for purposes other than dancing. Other times a dance partner was what people were looking for.

Prostitution, gambling, robberies, street fights and drug dealing caused a rise in crime. Mobsters and gangs were establishing themselves in the streets. The Rochester Police Department increased their staff to 175 officers. Their duty was to maintain order in the streets while people were going from place to place. Life was changing everywhere. The daily newspapers were constantly printing stories about the great new era of entertainment followed on the next page with all the criminal acts committed because of these good times.

There was a movement to protect the young people in the city from the wild ways of the night. In an attempt to control the junior and senior high school students the Rochester School Board banned dancing at school functions. There was a curfew set for people who were under 16 years of age. They had to be home or with an adult after 8PM. The school dances were not well attended and if a young person wanted to go out they would have an adult take them wherever they wanted to go. Some adults wanted to go out so they took their children with them, sometimes to unfavorable places.

Wallace was in high school experiencing everything that was going on in the world. He saw progress everywhere. As a teenager, it was a wild and exciting time to witness progress and new inventions. In 1895, Benz Velo invented the Duryea Motor Wagon that was the first standardized car. Wallace could not wait to show his father the article in the newspaper. He thought it was terrific that something like that could move without a horse. Frank was not nearly as impressed. He threw the paper on the floor and said, "This contraption could be the beginning of the end of his company." Wallace said nothing and walked away feeling disgusted. He thought that anything new was a way to improve life for people. As he walked away he heard his father grumble about what a know it all kid he was.

Wallace worked part time in a small printing shop. The shop printed advertisements for local businesses. Since entertainment at this time was on the flashy side the advertisements were catchy to the eye and suggestive to the mind. Wallace's job was to be the typesetter. While he set the type he would think of other ways to make the advertisements more attractive. He would suggest these ideas to the owner. At first the owner felt threatened that a young kid could have such ideas. After considering these suggestions of using some color and slogans they printed a few samples to see what it would look like. The owner took the samples to the customer to see what they thought. They were thrilled with the techniques and ordered extra advertisements. The print shop was the first to have flashy advertisements that people would remember. He gave Wallace a raise and increased his work schedule. In addition to extra money Wallace was given the job as the graphic designer.

Wallace was proud he was earning money for something he truly enjoyed. He investigated the possibilities of forming his own weekly newspaper. It was 1897 and he was old enough to begin his own business. His first step was to visit newspaper companies in the area that would help him set up his business. After his visits he realized he was not able to compete with the city papers. He decided to look at rural delivery areas. People out of the city received little if any newspapers. When Wallace told his father about his idea Frank told him that he was crazy. He was not going to support any such thing. Alice, on the other hand, thought it was a good idea and offered to help in any way she could. She told him he was capable of anything he set his mind to doing.

Wallace went to the school principal to discuss his idea. He wanted to start his business as a school project. In that way he might be free to use the school's print shop. The principal thought it was a fine idea but he would need the support of a teacher. Wallace asked Miss Holleran because she was his English teacher. She was surprised to be asked but agreed to help him. She agreed to be the editor and he could do the rest. Wallace was excited because that was exactly how he wanted it to be. He knew how much work it would entail but wanted to prove to himself that he could do it. The route was a few miles out of the downtown area. The plan was to compile all the news from the week into one paper. He named it "The Weekly Page." After discussing it with Miss Holleran they agreed to print the first edition in two weeks. He had to organize his news so it could be printed on both sides of the paper. He did not want any blank spots on the paper. Wallace got support from businesses and agreed to include their ads in the paper. These were services that were near the delivery routes. Miss Holleran was impressed with his resourcefulness and his ability to convince people to be a part of his endeavor. Frank ignored the whole process but Alice was right there to help him. She and Miss Holleran helped print the first edition. Alice accused Frank of being jealous of his son. She told him he should be proud of him and not ignore such hard work and talent. Alice was coming from a different point of view than Frank. She reminisced about her struggle to be successful years earlier with the Women's Club of Rochester and her mother's poor attitude toward her.

Wallace began delivering his weekly newspaper in the fall of 1897. His father allowed him to use one of the horse and buggies from the shop for his delivery. Wallace started with 30 customers. He made certain that every paper was placed where the customer wanted it. Wallace collected three cents each week for the paper. Sometimes people would not be able to pay for the paper. Wallace did not stop their delivery. He told them he would let them buy now and pay later. They loved it and would always make up the money they owed. The slogan for his business was "A Fair Deal Paper." which appeared under the title of the paper reminding people of what the paper stood for. The Weekly Page became more popular and people in other areas requested copies of it. Its wide circulation required a second person to help with deliveries. Alice agreed to help with the delivery so that Wallace did not have to pay another person. She liked the idea of getting out of the house. She actually made new friend when she was on her route. Sadly she thought about her mother. She still wondered why her mother could not have treated her like she treats Wallace.

"The Weekly Page" grew and prospered. The newspaper had wide circulation and received positive comments from the customers. His reputation for fairness in business was what he had hoped for. Whenever things were not going well Wallace tried to remember the people who were his mentors. They were the ones who always had a good word of encouragement. He thought about The Larkin Company and how they developed. They had uncertainties but were successful. He wanted to be a success just like the people he read about. The Eastman Kodak Corporate Office Building opened that year and the main streets of Rochester were electrified. Wallace reported about that in his paper. News about national and local events was part of his weekly reporting. He became so busy with gathering information, writing the articles, layout, and design of the paper that he hired his brother Gregg to purchase supplies and help deliver the paper. They now needed two sets of horses and buggies. Frank did not refuse Wallace when he asked for the additional transportation. He began to admire him for his efforts. Wallace became very good with delegating responsibilities. Miss Holleran never had any comments about the set up or editing of the paper. She admired Wallace and knew he was sure to be a successful man in the future. She became the bookkeeper for the business as well as the editor. It was a strange feeling for him to have his teacher work for him. Miss Holleran told Alice that she did that to make Wallace tougher. She thought it was good for him to have met his match. Miss Holleran had the reputation as a tough old broad. Alice agreed with Miss Holleran that Wallace had the ability to meet people at their level and to perform in a mature way. Alice never told him why Miss Holleran felt the way she did about him. She knew he probably realized that on his own.

Chapter 9

WALLACE WAS COMPLETING HIS last year in high school. He achieved high recognition for developing the Weekly Page. He planned to attend Mechanics Institute in Rochester and continue with the newspaper. He graduated from the Rochester City Schools with high honors as the president of his class. His friends thought he should be a politician because he was able to convince people to do almost anything and was elected the most likely to succeed. In front of the graduating class and their families he thanked those who helped him on his journey through school. He discussed the philosophy that he maintained in order to develop the newspaper. None of the other students had found success at anything and been quite so daring. He talked about the advertising ideas that he had studied long before he made them part of his newspaper operation. During his speech he announced his plan for the future of his newspaper. His marketing plan would be similar to the Larkin Plan that offered coupons to its customers when they purchased household items. When customers had accumulated a number of coupons they could redeem them for gifts from the Larkin Company. Wallace liked the idea and included coupons in his paper. He convinced his advertising merchants to offer a gift to the customers when they collected enough coupons.

The coupon idea was a great success, which led people to purchase his paper and the circulation doubled. Upon the conclusion of his speech the audience gave him a standing ovation. Miss Holleran gave the final speech to the graduates. She encouraged everyone to strive for excellence and perseverance in their future endeavors. She presented Wallace with an academic scholarship to college. His tuition to Mechanics Institute was paid for by a scholarship she submitted to The Council on Academic Excellence. Wallace was overwhelmed and could not believe she had accomplished such a feat.

After the graduation ceremony Miss Holleran and Alice discussed the profit that he had accumulated from his newspaper business. Wallace was so busy developing the paper that he never worried about the finances. Alice knew that Wallace was more interested in the plan and advertising of the paper than the finances. When they told him how much profit he had made he thought they were kidding. There was enough money left over to pay his college fees because the scholarship was to pay for the tuition. Wallace was adamant that the balance of money was to be invested in stocks. Eastman Kodak Company was in its infancy and he had been fascinated with his first camera from there. At 18 years old he was the youngest person to invest in Eastman Kodak Company stock.

Wallace enrolled in the advertising program at Mechanics Institute in September of 1899. He had to delegate more responsibilities to his brother and mother with the newspaper operation. He hired a close friend to assist in the production and circulation of the paper. The school was in downtown Rochester that enabled him to walk to his classes. After school he would go to the printing shop to plan the paper. He worked long and tiring hours. His mother brought him dinner every night. Alice never seemed to get over her own mother's behavior. She was left with so many unanswered questions. She vowed never to be like her mother. For Alice, Wallace was her first-born child and she was very protective of him. He had become a smart young man. He was not like his father Frank. Wallace had ordinary features and was short in stature. Like his father his hair was brown but he was not as handsome as Frank. Wallace was the studious type and did not place much emphasis on his appearance. Frank never understood why Wallace was different than the rest of his family. Alice was his advocate while Frank was the critical judge. Frank continued to ignore Alice's accusations about his jealousy of Wallace. Even after the graduation and discussion of money, Frank's only response was "that's nice." Frank was more concerned about his business. He felt like it was failing. There was more and more talk of something called an automobile. People wondered how it might change transportation. Life was changing everywhere you looked. Electric lights were installed on Main Street. The people who lit the oil lamps in the streets were replaced with electricity. A new form of communication came to Rochester. The telephone was installed and extended to Charlotte along the streetcar routes. People were protesting the installation of poles along the streets. The horse and buggy shops were changing and people began to look at the automobile idea. The wealthy liked the idea of a mechanism that could go by itself without the use of a horse for power. Frank never expected such changes. Now his son was in college and had a business that produced a profit that was being invested in an upcoming company. Wallace was so busy that he did not see his father's struggles and worries. For him all the changes and advancements were motivation to continue building his future. Slowly, Wallace drifts further from his father.

Chapter 10

THE TURN OF THE twentieth century was filled with progress and advancements in every facet of life. Boundless optimism and grand spirit could be felt everywhere you went. Progress was inevitable. Industrial dominance was now based on new technologies. Hydroelectric power had recently been transmitted from Niagara Falls to Buffalo giving way to limitless electrical power. With its direct access to the Great Lakes, Buffalo was set to become a major manufacturing center. It ranked as one of the largest cities in the United States, and the second largest city in New York State with nearly 400,000 people. The Pan American Exposition Company was formed to plan an event that highlighted the technological advances of the times. The goal was to create an event that would offer the world an opportunity to experience the latest inventions. Congress pledged 500,000 dollars for the Exposition in July of 1898. The designers of the exposition wanted it to be a contrast to the "White City" of Chicago's World's Columbian Exposition of 1893. There were debates and long conflicts over what the focus would be for the Buffalo event. It was decided that Buffalo's Pan-Am was to be a vibrant and brightly colored Exposition. The use of electricity was the major component that would be used to illuminate the Exposition. The designers and architects of the Pan-American hoped to create an experience that would exceed any former World's Fair. The date of May 1, 1901 was set for the completion and opening of the Exposition.

One of the goals of the Exposition was to promote an appreciation for the countries of the Americas. The United States had recently won the Spanish-American War, annexed the Philippines, and passed the Platt Amendment to the Cuban constitution. This authorized the United States to intervene in the internal affairs of Cuba. There was suspicion about the motives of the United States in Central and South America. William Buchanan was the director of the Pan-American Exposition and had been a respected former minister of Argentina. He felt it was vital to do what was necessary to overcome these suspicions. He recruited people from South and Central America to be a part of the development of the event. There were jobs for thousands of people and the result of such an Exposition would bring millions of dollars of revenue to Buffalo.

The Board of Directors began gathering information on possible sites for the Exposition. Eighteen sites were considered. The site decided upon created a violent division of the town's people because everyone wanted their land used for this event. The Rumsey family owned a majority of the property where the Exposition would be built. It would be adjacent to Delaware Park. Forest Avenue, Elmwood Avenue, and the New York Central Railroad would surround the Exposition. It was estimated that because of the railroad the Exposition was within a day's journey for over 40 million people. The Rumsey family had one condition that was to return the land to the original state when the Exposition ended. All the building and grounds were to be cleared away. Once the details were completed a board of architects was appointed. They needed to develop an outline of the Exposition. The natural beauty of Delaware Park would become the foreground before crossing the monumental welcoming bridge. Once inside the Exposition it resembled an inverted T with buildings adjacent to each other with similar dimensions and shapes. There would be eight architects designing the major buildings. The central court would have large water basins with geyser like fountains in the center. The Electric Tower would be at the end of the court representing the pinnacle of human achievement. The tower would be a symbol of what electricity could do and would be generated by Niagara Falls. The surrounding areas would consist of the Midway. These areas would be called living villages that would have displays from states and other nations. The atmosphere of the villages was designed to familiarize people with customs, habits, life-styles and clothing. Other buildings would be designed and constructed for dairy, livestock, and agricultural exhibits. These buildings and displays would show the modern methods for production of all types of products. Amusement rides gave a carnival atmosphere to the Midway. The Trip to The Moon and the Aerio-Cycle would be the most exciting on the Midway. The Trip to The Moon was designed to give the visitors a view of the moon and an opportunity to experience what going to the moon might be like. The designers researched what was known about the moon and its possibilities for visitation. The Aerio-Cycle was a large rotating circle that twirled upward to 275 feet. It would be 11 feet higher than the famous Ferris wheel of the Chicago World's Fair. It could only hold 18 people at a time but was worth the wait to be high above the Exposition and see the horizon. A stadium would be built to resemble the architecture of a stadium in Athens, Greece with a seating capacity of

12,000. The plan included restaurants and exhibits by the grand entrance of the stadium. The colors for the stadium would be light ivory-grey with a blue-green trim on the sashes and doors. Brightly colored awnings, banners, and flags surrounded the building.

As the planners worked on the details of the grounds, they wanted it to be different than the Chicago World's Fair. The theme focused on the theme of growth within Latin and South America. The architects agreed to have themes and motifs representing Spanish heritage. They incorporated decorative elements from Italy and other countries creating an eclectic style. The practice quickly was named "Free Renaissance." The elaborate decorative style of the Free Renaissance was not like the architectural style of the Chicago's White City which was stark and lacked color. The designers wanted this style to have sensuous curves, elaborate decorations, and bright colors. They felt the Exposition should be beautiful to the eye. Surrounding the design of the buildings were formal grounds, sculptures, landscape designs, and the natural surroundings. The theme of the Exposition was to celebrate the "Progress of Man." Karl Bitter was the director of sculpture and he wanted abundant statuary and fountains throughout the grounds. The plan was to have statuary representing the beginning of mankind at the entrance, followed by human development throughout the Exposition, ending at the Electric Tower. In the northern part of the Exposition were displays of man's advances in many fields of activity. The central courts displayed human progress in agriculture, manufacturing, art, intellect, and ingenuity. The Agriculture Building, Manufactures and Liberal Arts Building, and the Machinery and Transportation Building were included in that area. The highlight of his design was at the Electric

Tower. A statue of a "female figure" was placed at the top of the Electric Tower. It symbolized progress and the beginning of a new era.

Charles Turner was the director of color and worked closely with Karl Bitter. They coordinated color schemes that would enhance the period of time the sculptures represented. He began at the entrance using primitive colors. The color tones became more refined as the crowds advanced toward the court and the main displays. The climax would be the Electric Tower, which was the lightest and brightest in color. Turner created a new color to resemble the emerald-green water that cascaded over Niagara Falls. It seemed fitting to incorporate this color throughout the Exposition to represent the power coming from Niagara Falls. Both Turner and Bitter took a chance to create an atmosphere of vibrant color much different than ever before. The public would either find it novel and charming or reject it as gaudy and cheap. The risks were expensive but they succeeded in producing a pleasing environment never before presented in similar World's Fairs. The use of color and its presentation both day and night might make Chicago's White City fall to second place. The Pan-American Exposition noted for its vivid colors and schemes became Buffalo's "Rainbow City."

Chapter 11

JANUARY 1, 1900, THE turn of the 20th century, was marked by a light show in Downtown Rochester that amazed everyone who attended. Electricity was being used to feature important places and statues around the city. The main streets were now lit by electric lights giving the city the opportunity to have a nighttime parade to celebrate the beginning of a new century. Parties were everywhere with people celebrating and dancing in all the restaurants and hotels. This was a new century and progress was affecting everyone.

Wallace and Winston had been friends since high school. They decided to go out on the town. While on Main Street they watched people celebrate and carouse in the streets. The Seneca Powers Hotel was having a "New Century Party" so they decided to go inside to see what it was all about. As they walked through the lobby Wallace was impressed with the crystal chandeliers lighting the main floor. It was as if people were passing under twinkling stars. They went into the Chandelier Room and found an elegant party under way. Women were dressed in the highest style for this New Years party. They wore ruffled dresses and hats with feathers and bows that adorned their heads. Their shoes were made for parties and dancing. The men were dressed in suits and ties with slicked back hair. Some of the men were smoking cigarettes and giving intriguing stares that were quite appealing to the women. A young woman was starring at Wallace so he asked her to dance. He was taken by her style and wit. It was the Ragtime music and the two-step dance that Wallace and his dance partner enjoyed as they circled the dance floor. Winston was not as charming as Wallace so he stood amongst the crowd staring at all the action. Winston went to the bar to order a drink. While he was there he leaned on the bar resting one foot on the foot rail sipping his drink. Women strolled by him trying to attract his attention. He did not seem interested in all the festivities. Wallace was having enough fun for the both of them. When they finally arrived home Wallace was so enthralled by the night of lights and action he could barely sleep.

The next day it was time to go back to school. When Winston met him in their advertising class all Wallace could talk about was the great job the owners of the Seneca Powers Hotel had done. He had already thought of a great advertisement for the hotel and shared it with his professor. He wanted to use his idea as a project for his final grade in the advertising course. The professor wanted to know what was so good about it. Wallace had drawn a sketch for the newspaper that said, "Dine Under the Twinkle of the Starlight Chandeliers". He had sketched a drawing of large chandeliers above fancy tables surrounded by well-dressed people dining and others dancing in the background. His professor thought it was worth a try. He told Wallace that if he got his idea in print for the hotel he would pass the course with an A.

Wallace set out to contact the hotel to make an appointment with the owners. He printed a full-page ad of his idea. He included a type of print that was not used in advertising. It was script rather than conventional block print. He had a style of writing that was free flowing and distinct onto itself. He felt that the stylized writing in the advertisement would suggest an elegant and classy environment. Winston watched him create the advertisement in the print shop. He thought Wallace was crazy for thinking he could get a large hotel to agree to an advertisement like that. He told Wallace that it was too far-fetched and they would never agree to such a thing. Wallace argued that Winston had no confidence in himself, but he did, and if he did not like it he could get lost. Winston left in huff and Wallace finished his advertisement. He could not wait for Monday to meet the owners of the hotel.

Monday morning came. In his usual fashion Wallace dressed as if he were a businessman. He wore a dark blue single-breasted coat and vest with striped charcoal grey trousers, a white shirt and a narrow bow tie. He made sure his moustache and hair were carefully trimmed. His hair was combed back and close to his scalp. He wore a slight scent of after-shave. Wallace had a philosophy about time. He felt it was worth keeping. He always carried a pocket watch on a gold chain. The watch was in the pocket of his vest with the chain carefully draped out of it. Instead of carrying the advertisement in his briefcase he rolled it into a scroll similar to a blueprint. He knew it would be easier to see during the presentation. The meeting was to take place in the hotel office at 10:00AM. He made sure he arrived at 9:45AM. The hotel secretary greeted him. She gave him a judgmental look as if to question who he thought he was. Wallace politely thanked the woman and sat down waiting for 10:00A.M. Mr. Helfer appeared at exactly 10AM and shook Wallace's hand and invited him into his office. Mr. Helfer explained the hotel's plan for the future of their advertising. Wallace thought this would be a good way for him to begin by showing him who was in charge. He made up his mind that if Mr. Helfer did not like his idea he could probably convince him of another way to advertise his hotel. Wallace explained how he thought of the idea and how it could help to make the hotel stand out from all the rest. Mr. Helfer liked the compliment. Wallace was good at making people feel like they were the most important person around. After discussing his plan Mr. Helfer was eager to see what was being proposed. Wallace slowly unrolled the full-page advertisement. Mr. Helfer did not say anything but just stared at it. Wallace thought he did not like it. Finally Mr. Helfer sat back in his chair and said, "I can't believe you have such a vision for this hotel." Wallace thanked him. Mr. Helfer said, "You have given my hotel a unique style." Wallace told him that he only took what he saw and made it better through the advertisement. Mr. Helfer agreed to use the idea in the newspapers and was going to have posters printed. He felt these would be good at the railroad stations, trolley stations, and in public places around town. He discussed the possibilities of doing graphic displays such as these in the hotel directory and in travel magazines. The meeting was a success! Wallace was offered the job. Next, he had to negotiate the financial details for his work. Mr. Helfer requested a written proposal for his ideas with a financial category for payment. The meeting was set for the following Monday.

Wallace left the hotel and went directly to his professor. He was anxious to tell him about how the meeting went. The professor gave him the grade A he was promised. He was given the credit for his next class on financing advertising. The amount of credit would depend on how well he negotiated his contract with the hotel.

Winston was a lot like Wallace's father when he told both of them about his meeting. They listened with what Wallace thought was half an ear. He could not wait to get that contract going. As usual Alice was beaming with joy when she heard the news.

The population of Rochester had grown to 162,600 people. People were traveling further and faster than ever before. The use of railroads had expanded and Rochester had five different railroad lines. The trolley service was expanded and had lines further out of the city limits. There was a strange invention that looked like a buggy without the horses. George Selden had been working on a patent for compression gas engines and newspapers covered his work. Frank was interested in the development of the gas engine. He feared that would be the beginning of the end of his horse and carriage company. He reported losses in his company because people were beginning to use public transportation. However, the wealthy still used their private carriages and horses. He was hoping that this thing on wheels and no horses would only be attractive to the lower class people. In 1901 George Selden's patent was confirmed and the automobile had its beginning. He worked closely with Henry Ford and together they built a simple vehicle that moved with a gasoline-powered engine. Frank was furious that the newspapers had made such a big thing about an invention that was so uncertain. It was this same day that the news reported information about the gas vehicle that Frank had to let some of his workers go. This left Frank with only one shop. He decided that they needed to move to a more affordable home. He moved the family to 119 Park Avenue at the end of 1900 and were finally settled early in January 1901. There were not as many rooms so Alice, Frank, and the four children had to share bedrooms. Wallace was upset that everyone had to live so closely. He told his mother that when he had more money he would make sure the family would move to a better place. Frank told Wallace that it was none of his business and that they would live the way they wanted. At this point Wallace was so involved in school, his newspaper company, and now the advertising job at the hotel that he just turned and walked away.

He told Winston about the new apartment and the attitude his father gave him. Winston sided with Frank telling Wallace that he felt sorry for his father and that his father probably did not want to hear about all of his successes. Wallace told Winston that he really needed to get a better life for himself. Winston had been doing poorly in school and was even considering leaving the college. Wallace thought this was ridiculous. He told Winston that maybe he was in the wrong program. He suggested programs that were designed to help people improve themselves and not classes that teach you how to make people spend money. They were very opposite in their life goals. Winston listened to Wallace and agreed with him. He made an appointment with his counselor to change his course of studies.

Wallace's second appointment with Mr. Helfer was two days away. He had to prepare his financial proposal with his ideas for furthering the advertising campaign for the hotel. He wanted his earning to go to the new invention called the automobile. He was intrigued with Henry Ford and the gas driven engine. In his proposal he requested that his earning be deposited into a secured fund by the hotel. The only time the money could be used was when and if the automobile was finally developed. When the automobile company was established Wallace proposed that the hotel would match the same amount of money he earned. In this way Wallace and the hotel would be stockholders in an automobile company. The second part of his proposal was about how he envisioned the hotel's future for advertising and promoting the property. He thought that the same stylized logo would give the hotel it own notoriety. He proposed that everything the hotel used should have its logo imprinted on it. He included a promotional program for frequent visitors offering them a list of gifts compliments of the hotel. He used the Larkin idea and knew how successful that was. Frequent stays meant a free night or a free certificate to the restaurant or a gift. He proposed that the hotel could establish a full service salon for men and women. Guests could have their hair done or cut. The men could have their shoes shined. Women could have a complete beauty treatment with a massage service provided. He added the idea a full laundry and ironing service for the guests. In the marketing area the hotel would offer discounts for large group events and conventions. The railroad station was a few blocks away and easy access to the hotel. He would propose that the hotel have "take a ways", things guests could take home, such as, pens, note cards, and postcards of the hotel. He believed all these extras would make the hotel a prime property in Rochester.

Monday morning arrived and Wallace was ready for his first meeting to sign a contract with a major business. He was 21 years old and in the midst of a contract with the hotel. He reminded himself that you only have yourself to depend on so you better put your best foot forward and go for it. The worst that could happen would be no contract.

He knew that for every experience he had it would always have some benefit. Following this pep talk to himself he knew he was ready. He prepared himself much like he had the previous week. He was well groomed, on time, and alert. He arrived fifteen minutes early. The same secretary gave him the same attitude as last week. He smiled and sat down and waited for his appointment.

Mr. Helfer invited Wallace into the office. He was less formal than last week. This time he sensed a friendlier work relationship and felt like Mr. Helfer knew Wallace had something good to offer. After discussing how happy he was that Wallace had created a style for the hotel he asked for the financials. He presented him with a printed copy of his proposal of matching funds by both parties being used for the future of the automobile. Mr. Helfer was impressed by such insight. He barely knew of this invention. He thought to himself, here is a kid who already has it figured out. He liked the idea of matching funds and putting it into money at work. When they began discussing the promotional aspect of the hotel Wallace said, "This will make your hotel a gold mine." Mr Helfer found Wallace's personality very refreshing and confident. Mr. Helfer was in his fifties and was remembering how he behaved in his twenties. He liked Wallace's upbeat and positive attitude. After Wallace discussed his promotional ideas Mr. Helfer decided it was a deal. Wallace would be used as a consultant with a salary placed in a guaranteed fund. When the automobile was developed both parties would contribute equal funds in stocks. If the company never developed Wallace would receive his earnings with interest. He felt it was guaranteed one way or the other. Wallace left the hotel with a feeling of pride and success. He walked down Main Street looking at all the stores and new construction. He saw the new department store called McCurdy's that had just opened. It was a Philadelphia merchant who opened it to compete with the giant retailer called Sibley's. He stopped at the print shop. His newspaper was just being printed for its weekly delivery. His mother was in the shop helping to get the deliveries ready. He told Alice and his brother Gregg what had just been decided with Mr. Helfer. They congratulated him on what he had accomplished.

Chapter 12

WALLACE HAD BEEN FEATURING articles in the Weekly Page describing the development of the Exposition. He proposed a campaign for the hotel that would offer a package deal for travelers going to the Pan-American Exposition. His promotion for the hotel was to be entitled "The Seneca Powers Exposition Package." It was an all-inclusive deal that offered an overnight stay in the hotel with dinner, breakfast, and transportation to the fair by way of the New York Central Railroad. There were two types of packages offered which were a one night and a two-night package for travelers returning to Rochester on their way to their final destination. The promotion would begin on May 1 and be available until the fair's end. Wallace designed the package in hopes that people would plan on a longer trip that would give them time to tour Rochester and see the sights. He suggested to Mr. Helfer that an advertisement be placed in newspapers throughout Eastern and Southern New York for further outreach of the hotel promotion. The railroad stations displayed posters for travel opportunities. The promotion of it would begin on March 1 giving the hotel better advantage for sales.

During the spring semester Wallace began planning his trip to the Pan-American Exposition. This was something that he needed and wanted to see. He had been following the development of the Exposition so he knew it would offer him insights for the future. His philosophy was to be a leader rather than a follower. In order to accomplish this he had to be ready to move and act with confidence and a plan. There was a chart in the weekly newspaper that listed attendance at the fair. The fair had a slow start with nearly one hundred thousand attending weekly but as May ended attendance neared two hundred thousand. During the summer months the weekly attendance doubled. He wanted to go to the Exposition in early September and he invited Winston to go with him. He made arrangements to stay in a rooming house near the fair on Elmwood Avenue. He purchased the railroad tickets and admission to the fair through the hotel. Winston agreed to pay for the room. They were to leave Rochester on Thursday September 5 on the first train and arrive in Buffalo in time for the Exposition to open at 9AM. They were scheduled to return to Rochester on Friday taking the last train leaving the fair at 10PM. The weather was sultry on Thursday when Wallace and Winston walked to the train station. They were wearing casual clothing for the hot days ahead. Wallace had packed a small suitcase with just enough clothing for the next day. Winston was not as well prepared as Wallace. He took only his wallet and the clothes he wore. They wore top hats and suit jackets. Winston was tall and slender. His clothes never appeared to fit him. The pants were too short and the shoes never clean. Wallace was always well tailored. Each man had unique styles of grooming. Wallace had a trimmed full moustache. Winston wore a full beard that was not trimmed. He gave the rough guy appearance and Wallace the refined leader image. They would often remark to each other how different they were and how much they appreciated those differences. The station was crowded with people waiting to go to Buffalo.

The train arrived at 6AM. Some people took small bags on board and others checked their luggage at the baggage car. People were talking about what they expected to see at the Exposition. Everyone was interested in something different. Wallace was listening to what people's interests were and what they wanted to do at the fair. He thought about what he wanted to see and do while listening to others. He was surprised to hear that many people were more interested in the amusement and concession areas than they were about the technology and the arts buildings. Winston told him he was being too aristocratic and that he needed to have more fun. Wallace laughed and with a wink and a nudge told him he ought to be more concerned about advancements than amusements. They talked about what they wanted to do on the first day at the fair. Wallace could not wait to see the actual plan and lay out of the fair. He wanted to see the Larkin Building exhibit because he had been impressed with their advertising campaigns. He suggested that they plan their time so that they could be at the Temple of Music on Friday. President McKinley was scheduled to be there in the afternoon. Winston wanted to make sure they had time to go to the amusements. He heard about the ride that was called a Trip to the Moon supposedly it was the most exciting ride at the fair. The Aerio-Cycle and the Scenic Railway were some of the other attractions he wanted to go on too. They decided that they would visit the main Exposition grounds first and tomorrow they would go to The Midway and concession and amusement area. They would finish at the Temple of Music to see President McKinley.

The train made a few stops along the route to Buffalo. Every time new passengers came on board the excitement seemed to grow with every new discussion of what was at the fair. Many of the passengers were only going for the day. Wallace and Winston thought they were lucky to be spending two days at the fair. An elderly woman sat next to them and was listening to their conversation. She asked them if they were brothers. They laughed and said no with Wallace responding, "We are closer than that." She gave them a sweet smile and looked away. Wallace asked her if she was going to the Exposition. She said that she was. She told them that would probably be her last trip and she could not wait to see this thing called a car. She told them how she lived as a little girl with no modern conveniences. She hoped she would see the fair lit up in the evening. She doubted that the Niagara Falls could get power to the fair twenty-five miles away. Wallace said that it was true. She told him that she never thought so many things could happen so quickly. She informed them that she was born in 1825 and was now 75 years old. They both looked at her in amazement wondering what life must have been like way back then. When they asked her that question she laughed and said it was very hard. Most people did not live very long. She told them she was lucky to have been born into a rich family. Her father owned a large farm. He had slaves working the fields for him and caring for the farm animals. Winston asked her where she lived back then. She explained it was near Geneva, New York, but now she lived in Rochester. They had only heard of Geneva not really knowing much about it. She told them that they would see a tremendous amount of things happen before they were seventy-five years old. They laughed while thoroughly doubting that statement. Wallace thought he would see many things in his life. Winston sat in his seat and stared out the window. He had no plan for his life.

The conductor announced that the train was approaching the Buffalo area soon. Everyone was a buzz about the fair. People were talking faster and louder about what they were going to do. The conductor explained that the train would be arriving right at the Exposition. They could return and board the train at the same location when they were finished seeing the sights. The passengers were looking out the windows trying to see the fair in the horizon. A child spotted it first in the distance. He started yelling that he could see the big tower! People were cheering and laughing and said the train could not go fast enough now. They were finally at the Pan-American Exposition.

Chapter 13

As the train slowly approached the station platform the excitement grew. Black smoke from the engines filled the air as many trains pulled into the station from all directions. The smoke fumes were choking people from coal fires in the engines. The passengers were ready to leave the train with luggage of all sizes and shapes. Some people were only there for a day but people like Wallace and Winston were the few that felt lucky enough to have two days at The Exposition. The women with children were allowed to disembark first from the train. Children were pushing each other and fighting for their place in line. Fathers would try to control the situation but there was so much confusion that most of the time they just moved the families along as quickly as they could. There were some families that were more refined in their behavior toward each other and the other passengers. These people were obviously more familiar with the proper behavior in a crowd of excited people. You could hear music off in the distance from the Midway. The slight aroma of popcorn and sweet fragrance of angel fluff over powered the heavy smell of coal gas and smoke from the arriving and departing trains. Finally, it was time for the less excited people to leave the train. Wallace and Winston assisted the old woman that they were speaking with on the train. They asked her if she needed help getting around the fair.

She replied in a sweet but firm tone, "You boys run along. There is a lot to see here and you do not need an old woman following you around. I have gotten around for 75 years and I intend to do this on my own but thank you anyway." They got off the train and went on their way. They liked the idea of being called "boys" because they realized how exciting this fair made them feel. Wallace felt like he was walking into his future and he could not wait.

The Propylea was at the northernmost part of The Exposition. Its main purpose was to block the noise, smoke, and commotion from the trains that were coming and going to the fair. Everyone who came through that entrance praised the magnificent structure. There was a large portal with a huge tower on each side that visitors walked through. At the entrance were pergolas with vines overhead as you passed into the serene atmosphere of the fair. Straight ahead was the northern side of the impressive Electric Tower. Visitors felt as if they were walking into a dream or land of the unknown. The Electric Tower offered a backdrop for the bandstand where musical performances from around the world filled the air. The area was surrounded with sunken gardens and the scent of flowers was noticed everywhere. The ceiling of The Propylea was painted in blue to give the illusion of the sky opening up above. Strong violet hues were used for the trellis and pergolas. The sashes and doors were painted in green with gold accents. The Propylea was designed to be the entrance without intricate details. Walter Cook who was the architect succeeded in making his structure more than it was intended to be. His use of color accentuated the details of the entrance and its surroundings to create a magnificent effect.

After the visitors walked through The Propylea there were restaurants around the courtyards. There was an entrance to The Midway. When Wallace and Winston stood in the midst of the music and aromas in the air from the food being prepared they decided to have breakfast and plan their day. Winston was eager to experience the excitement of The Midway. He heard about amusements that had never been built until now. He told Wallace that this fair was going to beat the Chicago World's Fair. Wallace asked him, "What part was going to be better?" He replied, "The rides and not all those funny buildings." Wallace looked disgusted and asked him if he realized that the future was sitting right there on the fair grounds. He then looked him straight in the eye and informed him that if he wanted to be his friend he had better grow up and stop being so immature. As Wallace said that Winston knew that Wallace was right but he did not know how to behave differently. Wallace suggested they compromise so they decided to spend the first part of the day at The Midway. Winston was surprised that they were doing what he wanted to do first. Wallace knew that if he went along with Winston that the rest of the trip would be on his terms. This left Winston to wonder why he had his way right from the start. He looked at Wallace as they left the restaurant with a look of pleasure yet Wallace confused him. It was like he was in charge for a change instead of Wallace. Yet, he kept wondering why Wallace behaved that way.

As they walked into the Pan-American Midway they were given a map and description of the Midway. There were two parts with one for amusement and the other designed with villages from around the world. It was intended to show the development of man around the world. The Living Villages were first developed at the Paris Exposition in 1889. It was very popular. The idea was used at the Chicago World's Fair but was not as successful. The main reason being that the countries on display were depicted as bawdy and denigrating places. In Buffalo a variety of countries from around the world were shown. There were Mexican, Native-American, and Eskimo villages that represented North America and next the African culture was depicted in village settings. The Orient offered a unique style of culture. Egypt was represented with elephants and pharaohs with mummies near a small pyramid. The Latin and South American countries were part of the villages that were intended to be educational and help people appreciate cultures unfamiliar to Americans. When they saw countries from warm climates Winston asked what were they were going to do when it got cold in Buffalo. The people in the villages of South American and Africa were dressed in nearly nothing. Wallace told him not to worry because the fair was over November 1st. As they walked around there were concessions with food from the countries that were represented with traditional dances and demonstration of their countries. All these things were offered to enable people to sample the life of other nationalities that they could only read about prior to this visit to the fair. Even Winston who was not terribly enthused about the educational part thought it was pretty good. As Wallace walked around the villages he began to think about what he could do with some of these ideas from foreign countries. He was intrigued with the Orient. He liked the furniture and the decorations. The landscaping combined with architecture was unique. He thought it would be good to have a combination of American architecture and design mixed with the Oriental features. There was an architect that Wallace had read about in the United States who had designs similar to that. He was trying to remember who he was. The man had designs that many people found to be very different and he met with resistance from the design world. He knew it was someone who designed buildings with an oriental atmosphere. There was so much happening around them that he could not remember who it was. Winston looked at him and shook his head. He told him he was crazy and should stop trying to figure everything out.

It took about two hours to tour the villages. The day was warm and sunny at mid morning as they approached the amusement rides. They were glad they wore their top hats to keep the sun off their heads. Luckily Wallace had packed only a small leather bag with overnight items. He wondered how he would hold on to it when they went on the rides. Winston was so excited that he was jumping around people and trying to get to the Steel Loop De Loop Railway ride. Wallace was embarrassed by Winston's actions that he hung back until he was far enough away that he did not have to be seen with him. The Steel Loop De Loop Railway was like a railroad that went up and down steep hills. In the middle of the huge tangle of tracks was an enormous circular loop that the cars went around. At one point they were upside down. People were screaming and some were so scared they were crying. The little kids looked like they were scared to death. Winston was worse than a little child with his laughing, screaming and having a grand old time. Wallace was not as amused as his partner. When the ride ended Winston wanted to go again but the wait in line would be an hour. Wallace told him that he was done! When they recovered from the jostling and jolting of the Loop De Loop they went on the Merry-Go-Round. Wallace thought this was more civilized than the last one. They got to their seats in a hurry. It was a gigantic ride. There was not an empty seat so they were glad they got on first. Winston ran around to find a donkey to ride. Wallace followed and sat next to him on a huge black stallion. Wallace looked down at Winston and told him that he looked stupid on that jackass. Winston told him that all he wanted to do was ride on a big stallion. The ride began slowly. Wallace was more relaxed on this than the last ride. Winston was complaining that it was not as much fun as the last ride. All of a sudden the music started and the speed increased. As the music went faster so did the merry-go-round. It was moving so fast that you could not see where you had been. It was dizzying. Winston looked like a nomad who just left the desert. Wallace looked like he was riding up the side of a mountain sidesaddle on the stallion. He began to wonder why he ever brought Winston along and could not wait until the ride part was over. Finally, the ride slowed down after what seemed like forever. People were staggering around when they got off. Winston was so overjoyed by the ride he wanted to go again. Wallace told him if he did that was the end of their trip together. He said once was enough with all the rides.

After recovering from the spin of the merry-go-round they stopped for a drink at the soda stand. They had an ice-cold frosted root beer. It tasted so good on a warm September day. While they sat there they overheard people discussing the Aerio-Cycle. Winston remembered that he told Wallace about that ride before they even got to the Exposition. They followed the crowd through the street to the ride. It was very impressive. It had become the most popular ride. Its tower was 140 feet high which was eleven feet higher than the grand Ferris wheel of the Chicago World's Fair. It could be seen from many different points. The "walking beam" that connected the two wheels at each end was 240 feet long. Each wheel was 40 feet in diameter. The ride was like a teeter-totter. As that motion was happening the wheels would go around like a Ferris wheel. They had to wait an hour in the hot sun to ride on it. When they finally got their seat it began moving. The idea behind this ride was to fool your body with different speeds and motions going in opposite directions. It was a real thrill for Winston. The multiple motion movements thrilled him. Wallace had never seen him so out of control. He began to think that the faster the movement the worse Winston would behave. He began to wonder what the night might bring. Wallace found this ride to be equal to an eggbeater in a bowl. Wallace wondered why so many people thought this type of treatment was so much fun. He thought maybe he was missing something. They finished that ride in five minutes. Winston was geared up and Wallace was in a daze. Everyday there was a bulletin board with announcements on it. One of them listed the names of important people that were at The Pan-American Exposition. It was September 5th and Thomas Edison had been there and went on the Trip To The Moon. Governor O'Dell of New York went on that ride with Edison. Today, President William McKinley was taking the ride. Wallace read the sign and told Winston that maybe they would see the President. He hoped that they would be on the ride at the same time. Finally, Wallace seemed excited. Winston was happy about that. They arrived at the moon building. While they stood in line they looked around for any sign of important people. Then they thought the President might disguise himself. As they got closer to their turn they gave up hope that they would see him. They got their seats and it was as if they really were traveling to the moon. It was hard to believe you could feel like you were approaching something so far away. The spaceship sped through space and darkness. Kids were scared. One woman passed out and when she came to they told her she was on the moon and she passed out again. Winston thought that was hilarious. Wallace told him to shut up and behave himself. On their way back to earth Winston relaxed. Wallace thought he was tired but little did he know that Winston was angry with him. When they got outside of the building they went to some other rides that were not as much fun as the first ones. It was time for lunch. Wallace was relieved that his part of the compromise was over.

Chapter 14

During lunch Wallace studied the visitor's map. He told Winston that they could divide their time into two parts. They wanted to see the Pan-Am lit up at night so they made sure that they stayed until evening. Wallace had a good idea of where the boarding house was so he knew they could walk there in less than an hour. They each ordered foot long sausages that were smothered with onions. The aroma of charcoal made them think of a picnic. Everywhere they looked there were people strolling around. The large areas that had fountains in the middle of ponds filled with pink and yellow water lilies. The bandstands were full of musicians playing tunes from different parts of the world. When they finished their lunch they walked through Delaware Park because the main entrance to The Exposition was there. When entering the Formal Exposition grounds the people had to cross the Triumphal Bridge. They walked by four pylons that stood 149 feet tall with statues on top of each one. At that point the visitors saw and had a clear sense that the country had reached national power and glory. Wallace and Winston felt like royalty as they walked across the bridge. Everywhere you went you could hear two prominent sounds: the sound of water from the fountains and music. They were so impressed with the atmosphere that they stood and stared at the grandeur of the setting.

A horse drawn watering truck went by spraying water on the gravel to keep the dust down. Their shoes already looked like they had been walking in the desert. The Horticulture Building was to their left. They thought that would be a good place to begin. The building was accented with brilliant blue, green, rose, and yellow colors. Wallace read about the architecture as they entered the building telling Winston that it was an Italian Renaissance style. He was not interested in the style but Wallace was studying everything as they entered the building. The exhibit focused on the advancements in growing plants, harvesting, and displaying the natural surroundings. A flower show featured tropical plants and local flowers. The palms and ferns that adorned the entrance gave the illusion that you were entering a subtropical environment. Wallace was acting like a tour guide reading and describing the flowers and trees. Winston welcomed this idea because he would only have to listen. He read that huge greenhouses with newly invented temperature-controlled refrigeration were used to keep the vegetation at its proper temperature. As they proceeded through the conservatory they viewed a display of the ornamental trees, orchards, shrubs, and evergreens that were part of the local environment. On the outside there were more than 500 beds of popular flowers that were grown and used throughout the Exposition grounds. Wallace started to write down the things he wanted to remember as he went through the exhibits. He had a notebook that he used to jot things down that he wanted to remember. The first thing he was certain he wanted to do was to list the flowers he liked and write a description of them. He noticed that there were consistent things at the Pan-American. The shapes of ponds, gardens, walkways and buildings had a circular design. There were huge circular flowerbeds with one type and color of flower. He was impressed with the red canna lily beds. He drew a diagram of a shade garden with various hosta plants circling the base of a tree. There were circular ponds in the gardens with water lilies and Koi swimming in the water. At the end of the walkway was a garden with tall bluish-purple flowers. They were delphiniums given to the Exposition by Dr. Matthew D. Mann. He was a flower fancier and donated the plants from his collection. The breeze made the tall stalks of bluish-purple flowers sway and almost blend in with the colors of the sky. Wallace had many opportunities to use his camera. He was taking pictures of everything. There were only a few people using cameras. Most people were having their pictures taken by a person who would offer to take pictures for a price. Wallace was glad he did not have to do that because he had a lot he wanted to take. Winston was elected to be the camera carrier that gave him something to do. On the perimeter of the gardens a privet hedge was planted to divide the walkways from the gardens. They were neatly manicured with a rounded top. The English style gave the gardens a formal appearance. Wallace liked the natural surroundings of these gardens and would someday want these things for his home.

The Mines Building held the horticultural exhibit that dealt with the industrial aspect of growing things. There were farm displays featuring the latest machines for crushing, pulverizing, milling, and harvesting crops. When Wallace and Winston passed through the building you could smell the hay as it was cut and thrashed. The smell of fertilizer and sulfur made them think of rotten eggs. They were not as impressed with the farming aspect of plant growth as they were with the ornamental displays. Wallace believed that was for farmers and he was more interested in the beauty of the landscaping.

The Graphic Arts industry had demonstrations of papermaking, printing, engraving, and bookbinding. The printing advancements were of interest to Wallace because of his newspaper. There had been newer and faster techniques for printing the newspaper. Electricity was being used to make the printing presses work faster. The bookbinding display demonstrated how a machine could print and bind a book using half the number of people instead of former handmade book binding methods. Wallace was comparing his printing shop to the newer methods and realized that he would need to upgrade his shop when he got back to Rochester. He was thinking of expanding his newspaper circulation so these new techniques would make it possible to do more with new equipment. He took notes and wrote down the names of the companies that were represented there. Winston told him that he was crazy for trying to work on something that is only in a show. Wallace did not say anything but just shook his head. They left the exhibit and Wallace's head was spinning with ideas for what he wanted to do when he got back home.

Walking ahead of Wallace and Winston were a group of people discussing the wonderful job that the Larkin Company did on their building. A man in the group said that the company built it on their own with no financial assistance from the Exposition. Wallace overheard the woman say to her group, "It's no wonder they didn't need help, they have loads of money. They know how to promote the business." They decided that their next stop would be the Larkin building. The building was constructed at significant expense and the plaque outside said that thousands of visitors pass through everyday. That seemed hard to believe because every person received a freshly wrapped bar of their famous Mojeska soap. Once they were inside the building they saw rooms furnished with all the Larkin gifts you could receive from the coupon campaign. Wallace took pictures of the rooms and remembered the day the Christmas box was delivered to his family. He recognized the slogans and jingles of "Buy More Save More" which were so much a part of the Larkin Plan. They watched the final stages of soap making and how new technology was able to wrap each bar for the visitors. After they saw the Larkin exhibit they went to the Heinz 57 Company that was constructed to look like an Oriental Kiosk. There were woman showing the new products that were developed. The sweet pickles, tomato soup, and preserved fruits were offered as samples when they passed by. Winston thought that was a good idea since he was hungry again. They left and continued on to the Government Building. They did not want to spend much time there. The only thing they really wanted to see was the process for making money. There were displays from the patent office, post office, and the weather bureau. They found the place where the US mint had been showing the process for making coins. They watched the press and cutting machines make the indentations in the various metals. The machines were making pennies at 80 per minute and then given as souvenirs. There was a new invention that caught their eye. It was located near the patent office display. It was called an X-ray machine. Winston was like a little kid when he realized that it could take pictures of his bones. The guide said that this machine would be a miracle worker to doctors when they could not see what was wrong inside the human body. People thought it was a joke but others seemed happy to see an invention to help the medical profession. Everywhere they went they were given souvenirs of the things they saw. The bag Wallace was carrying was filling up fast with all types of stuff. He told Winston that he was going to carry the bag and he would carry the camera.

It was almost 3PM in the afternoon. The Ethnology Building was the next stop. The Exposition map described it as the study of man. It had four classifications relating to prehistoric archaeology, historical archaeology, anthropology, and ethnology connected with art. Wallace thought this was more than he wanted to know so he suggested that they pass that one up. Winston laughed and said he did not even know how to say those words. He was relieved that Wallace did not drag him through that one. They wanted to go to the Electric Tower when it was still daylight. As they approached the tower they saw fountains surrounding the base with grand open spaces giving the area an airy feeling. The water was representative of the power of Niagara Falls. At the top of the tower standing 18 feet tall was the Goddess of Light. The tower was 410 feet tall from the base to the tip of the torch that the goddess held. The tower was built to represent the pinnacle of human achievement. The Age of Electricity had now begun. The tower was an artistic triumph for the Pan-American Exposition. Winston commented on the bright blue-green color the panels of the tower had been painted. Wallace informed him that color was designed to represent the color of the water as it cascaded over Niagara Falls. There was an elevator in the center of the tower that was built by the Otis Elevator Company. For 15 cents you could ride to the top of the tower in 30 seconds. Winston acted just like he did on the amusement rides. He could not wait for the next thrill. Wallace shuddered to think what might happen on the way up. He told Winston not to get to carried away and jump over the edge. Winston looked at him as if to ask, "How stupid do you think I am?" They paid the money and rode to the top. It went so fast that they felt light headed. The view at the top was spectacular. The entire Exposition could be seen. The horizon appeared miles away and you could see Buffalo and beyond. Wallace was taking pictures from every angle he could. He had never been so high up in the air. He thought he could even see Rochester! Winston was running around hanging over the edge-trying look down on all the people who were looking up at the tower. He was waving and yelling at them but not many people paid him any attention. Wallace told him that they needed to go back down to the bottom. Winston was ready for the feeling of falling fast, as he put it. When they got to the bottom they went to the Electricity Building.

The Rand-McNally handbook described the building as greatly admired by everyone. As they walked toward the building they noticed how it was the most picturesque building of the entire fair. It was located on what was an existing street that was being used as a service road. In the handbook Wallace read that the Exposition planners decided from the beginning to leave the street undisturbed. It had a row of mature poplar trees on the side and a landscape mall was between the Electric Tower and The Electricity Building. It was one of the most appealing environments of the Pan-Am. Winston was impressed with the colors that were used to accentuate the building. He took a liking to the light yellow that was the color of the walls of the building. It was bright and inviting. Gray trimmings and green doorways were accent colors that added to the appeal. Wallace took pictures of the building and wrote notes in his journal so he would remember what the buildings looked like. He knew that he could never remember all the colors when he saw his snapshots. Winston kept telling him that it was not important to remember all that stuff. He told him to enjoy it for today and not to worry about tomorrow. Wallace had his own idea of what should be remembered.

The handbooks noted that it was the largest electrical exhibit in the country. They could not wait to see all the electrical wizardry that they had so often heard about. Thomas Edison became known as the "Wizard" with his display of a new storage battery that might be used for electric cars. The phonograph was particularly interesting with its sounds that came from an electric wheel turning in circles. As they went through the exhibits they wanted to know where they could buy these things. Everyone was saying the same thing as the level of intrigue grew while the tourists walked around. The incandescent lighting was featured throughout the building helping the displays be more vivid. The Buffalo Bell Telephone Company had a central switchboard that showed operators connecting telephone calls from far off places. As they walked around both guys were speechless. They could not believe that such things could be possible. Even more impressive to them was the transformer that was working on converting and transporting power from Niagara Falls. It was 25 miles away and one transformer would illuminate the entire Exposition in less than an hour. Wallace said," Truly amazing!"

When they left the Electricity Building daylight began to fade into evening. Little by little the lamps along the walkways were beginning to shimmer. The crowds began to look around and up at the Electric Tower. Wallace read in the handbook that this time of day was called the "Illuminating hour." It took about 90 seconds for the entire Exposition to come up to full illumination. There were two hundred thousand 8-watt bulbs used to light the Pan-Am. There was anticipation over what the fair was going to look like at night. Some kids were scared that everyone was acting like some strange phenomenon was about to begin. Winston exclaimed that it was like magic and you did not even light a match. Wallace gave him one of his dirty looks thinking how immature he was acting once again. As darkness came the Exposition became a giant fair of lights. To everyone's amazement and cheers they could actually see as if it were daytime. Some thought it was a miracle. Wallace said it was a miracle in that this would better all of mans lives. People in every direction were gazing up and down from their left to their right looking at the world of light. The old woman that Wallace and Winston sat with on the train came by. She saw them and asked if they were having a good time. They were surprised to see her again and that she remembered them. They told her they were really having fun. She told them that she never thought she would ever see the day an entire city could be so bright. She too was impressed with the fair. Before she walked off she told them to have fun tonight. They looked at each other and said, "Sure will."

By this time it was almost 11PM. They had eaten their dinner before the illumination and it was time to find the boarding house. Wallace knew it was on Elmwood Avenue. Streetcars were constantly going up and down the street. They got on a streetcar and went about 7 blocks where they found the boarding house. It was a large Victorian Style home. Winston commented that it looked like a gingerbread house. Wallace agreed that it was beautiful but not his style. They walked up to the porch that was furnished with big wicker rocking chairs. There were huge Boston ferns hanging around the edge of the porch ceiling. They eyed a double-seated swing with big puffy red pillows. There was a large straw rug on the floor. Huge striped awnings of yellow and green hung from the porch. Wallace said that it reminded him of a place where royalty might stay. He spoke into the speaking tube that was on the side of the door. Wallace said they were there as guests for the night. A deep bellowing man's voice came out of the tube that said come in. They looked at each other and walked into the vestibule. The entrance was very ornate with heavy drapes on the windows. It was lowly lit with gas lamps. Winston said in a smart tone voice, "Guess they haven't been to the Exposition yet." Wallace nudged him and told him to stop that or they might get thrown out. A large man appeared from the back that they thought might have been the kitchen. He was like a butler and a proper acting gentleman. He had on a black vest that rounded out from his chest accentuating his large stomach. He had a baldhead and a round bearded face. Winston whispered in Wallace's ear that he wondered if Santa Claus had a summer job. Wallace gave him another look of disgust and shook his head. He asked Winston if he thought everything was a joke.

They were led up the curved stairway to the third floor. The room they were to occupy was at the end of the hall. The man said that they had the last room for the night. He told them it had recently been very busy. The room was sparsely furnished and small. As the three men stood in the doorway, the butler said, "I am sorry but this room has only one bed." Then suddenly an uncomfortable feeling came over Wallace and Winston. For the first time neither of them could speak. They gave each other a glance and Wallace finally said, "We're very close friends and won't mind sharing the bed." The butler looked cautiously at them. It was a bed for one person.

Chapter 15

MORNING ARRIVED WITH SUN beaming through the windows as a warm breeze was blowing into the room. Wallace was aroused first when he smelled the aroma of coffee and fresh bread. He looked at his watch and realized that they had slept until 9AM. He was facing Winston's back when he awoke. He felt a sense of closeness and comfort as he stared at Winston's furry back. Neither one of them wore nightclothes. Wallace began thinking about how he felt about Winston. He knew that they had been friends for many years. He did not always like the way Winston behaved. He thought he was too childish at times but as he looked at his disheveled hair and dark beard, sensations came over him. He realized that he felt closer to him than he had ever felt about anyone before. It was like he did not want this time to end. Winston began to stir. Wallace moved a little so he would not appear too close. Winston rolled over and saw Wallace. He smiled and asked him how he had slept. Wallace told him that he had slept well and had never felt like this before. Winston rolled closer and told him that he was glad to hear that. Wallace thought maybe he should not have said anything but Winston told him he felt the same way. They stayed in bed for a bit longer enjoying the peaceful atmosphere. Winston too had hoped for this opportunity to show Wallace how he felt about him.

There was a knock at the door! Wallace got out of bed and pulled on his trousers. The butler stood in the doorway. He smiled and asked if they were planning on having breakfast. He looked at Wallace and saw Winston on the bed and with a coy expression turned and said, "How about a half an hour." They got ready for the day. Wallace had to shave and dress in his usual well-put together self. Winston on the other hand did not shave and put on exactly what he wore the day before. Breakfast was served in the dining room; other guests were already seated. The two guys walked in and took the last 2 seats. Everyone was discussing the Exposition and the parts they liked the best. The women were especially interested in the two of them. They thought it was very nice that two young chaps were traveling together. The men did not appear as fond of the situation as the women. The butler circulated around the table and made facial gestures toward Wallace and Winston. He sensed that the men at the table were uncomfortable. He kept asking the men if they had ever traveled with another man. They were fidgety and said they only travel with their wives. The butler said in his casual way . . . "Too bad." Wallace was having a great time listening to the conversation and watching the interaction of the breakfast group. Everyone was eager to get to the Exposition. The butler told them that the best thing to do in the morning was to go to Delaware Park. The park had beautifully landscaped walkways. There were places to take gondolas rides on the lake. The park was located in the front of the Exposition entrances. Entering the Exposition by the water route in a gondola was an impressive way to start the tour. The lakes, canals, and fountains contributed to the beautiful scenery and the spectacular Exposition in the background. He reminded them that President Mc

Kinley was going to be at the fair. He was giving a speech and having a reception line at the Temple of Music in the afternoon. Wallace told Winston that they had better get going. It was their last day and he wanted to see as much as he could before the train went back to Rochester at 9PM. They excused themselves and were carefully watched by the men as they left the room. The women told them that they wished they could go with them because they seemed like a lot of fun. The butler smiled and wished them a good day.

They walked on Elmwood Avenue to the trolley stop. They got on the trolley and took it to the corner of Delaware and Forest Avenues and on to the gondola ride that took them on a leisurely ride to the Exposition. As they approached the Exposition the water route approached a three-arched bridge of massive masonry. According to the guidebook it was named the Bridge of the Three Americas representing North, South, and Central America and was built by the city of Buffalo. Winston was busy feeding the ducks as they swam up to the gondolas while Wallace took pictures. He took pictures of the scenery around the lake because there was a different view from the boat than from the land. As the boat approached the shore, the New York State building came into view. The gondolier said they would be docking in a few minutes. The sun was reflecting off the water creating a mirror like image. The people on the gondolas all agreed that they felt it was going to be a good day; there was excitement in the air. People were dressed in their finest clothes for the visit to the Exposition. The women wore dresses and fancy hats and the men had on suits with top hats. Some people commented that the women were the smart ones because they carried an umbrella to shade themselves from the hot sun. Even the children were dressed as if they were going to church. Wallace figured it was because the President was coming today. The gondolier commented that all visitors coming to the Exposition dressed in fine clothes.

As people got off the boat they saw a large daily activity board that gave a list of the special things to see and do on that day. On the very top of the list was the announcement that President William McKinley was giving a speech at the Temple of Music at 4PM. He had given a speech yesterday to an audience that had paid extra for their admission to have a reserved seat for his speech. Today's reception was open to everyone for the organ recital so you had to get there early to get a seat. It was Friday, September 6 and this was one of the biggest highlights of the Exposition. They decided that they would go to The New York State Building first. There was a sign that gave information about the construction of the building. It was to be the only structure remaining after the fair. It had to be built to withstand many years of use. It took much longer to build than the temporary ones. Wallace read that it had more visitors than any other building at the Pan-Am. There were huge bronze doors with allegorical figures representing fields of history and ethnology on each panel. It was not as ornate as the other buildings at the Exposition. It was constructed of white marble and overlooked the lake. It was a perfect copy of the Parthenon. When Wallace and Winston toured the building they saw descriptions of United States history and displays of New York State's influence on the development of the country. When they finished with the tour it was lunchtime. The smell of a charcoal fire and sizzling food made a perfect atmosphere for a tasty lunch. Winston offered to pay for lunch, Wallace told him that was the least he could do. During lunch they decided to spend a few hours alone. Winston was going to go back to the Midway for the rides. Wallace decided to go back to see more of the Larkin Building and the home furnishings display. He wanted to see the latest inventions for the home.

After lunch they parted ways agreeing to be at the Temple of Music at 2 pm. Winston hurried off to the amusement areas. Wallace went to the home furnishings displays. He wanted to see Gustave Stickley's furniture designs. There was an entire home furnished with Rookwood pottery, cut glass from Hawkes Crystal Company, carpets from different countries, and a telephone that worked. As part of the home display there were diagrams and examples of vacuum cleaning machines, hot water heaters, and electric lighting for homes. There were displays of a modern kitchen that demonstrated how cooking could be done with a gas stove instead of wood fires and sinks with hot and cold running water. There was something there that reminded him of an icebox but it had no ice and the food stayed cool because of electricity and refrigeration. Music was coming from the parlor where a Victrola was on display playing records. The atmosphere made him feel like this was the type of home he would someday want to have. He promised himself as he went through the exhibit that he would have all these latest things for his home placed in a unique environment. He walked around for quite some time trying to see everything and remember all that was shown. Wallace took pamphlets for all the new items in the displays for his home file. He made up his mind that this was the beginning of his future and he needed to have as much information as he could to make it a reality. After the Larkin Exhibit he went to the Court of Fountains to watch people. Wallace found that watching people was a real lesson in life. He observed how people interacted with one another. He saw people who did not get along very well and he watched children take more charge of the adults than they did with themselves. Human interaction was right in front of him in every direction. He was fascinated how people reacted to the Exposition. Most of the women were impressed. Some of the men acted as if the were being dragged along like some of the kids. He could not understand how anyone could not be impressed with all the things that were there. He looked at his watch; it was almost 2PM. He walked to the Temple of Music to meet Winston. He saw him standing in the front of the entrance. There were hundreds of people waiting to get into the building for the recital. Winston told Wallace that he went to the moon again and the aerio-cycle ride. Wallace laughed and shook his head. He said, "Better you than me."

Chapter 16

THE CROWD WAS GROWING by the minute as they got in line to go into the Temple of Music. It was an enormous building. It had seating for 2,200 people. Luckily for Wallace and Winston they were at the head of the line to enter the theater. They hoped to have seats close to the front of the stage. While they were finding their seats Winston was telling Wallace about the organ that was installed in the theater. He told him that it was one of the largest in the world and it weighed 25 tons and stood 43 feet high. Winston was happy to do the reporting this time about the details of the instrument. He told Wallace that Emmons Howard and Son of Westfield, Massachusetts built the organ at a cost of $18,000. Wallace laughed and said, "It is about time something excited you other than those rides." Today J.D. Dussault of Montreal, Canada was performing on the organ. Everyday the temple was filled with joyous music coming from the largest pipe organ ever constructed. The building was built with a huge dome in the center of the ceiling. The walls were red with green bronze panels and ivory details. The dome was gold with red background and blue-green decorations to represent the color of the water cascading over Niagara Falls. The building had a sculpture at the four corners of the dome above each entrance. The statuary by Isidor Konti represented a different allegory at each entrance. There was Heroic Music, Music of the Dance, Sacred Music, and Lyric Music that was enhanced by the sculptures. It was a luxurious atmosphere for the musical world. It was known as the "Gem of the Exposition."

The excitement and noise of people talking and laughing was resonating from every part of the theater. Wallace took the guidebook from Winston and found a final paragraph about the Exposition from a speech given by President McKinley the day before. He read it to Winston, "Our lives will be better in the 20th century. Babies will live because of the infant incubator displayed on the Midway. People will be cured because of the x-ray machine in the Electricity building. The automobile in the Machinery and Transportation building will be able to take us further and faster than horses. We will live in a world made more sanitary and clean. We will be warmer in winter and cooler in summer and be able to read and work at night because of an endless supply of electricity. What a century the 20th century will be!" When he finished Winston said, "I wonder what your father will think of the automobile?" Wallace looked at him and said, "Probably not much." The chimes on the organ began to sound. It was 3PM and the concert was about to begin. The audience applauded as the organist walked out to the bench. Wallace could not believe he was actually there and he would be meeting the President of the United States. The number of things he had seen in the last two days were more than he could comprehend. He had the biggest smile on his face and glanced at Winston with a twinkle in his eye. The entire building shook when the mighty organ began. It was the loudest sound they had ever heard. It sounded like every pipe was working at once. The crowd applauded which encouraged the organist to play even better. This had to be the highlight of everyone's day!

The organ performance was magnificent with the last musical piece ending with a processional march at 4PM. When it ended President William McKinley appeared on a platform at the front of the theater. There were Secret Service people surrounding the area. President McKinley was in a cheerful mood and enjoyed the hearty applause he received when he arrived. People were standing, applauding and cheering as John C. Milburn of Buffalo motioned for people to be seated. It took minutes before the crowd settled down to hear the President's brief speech. President McKinley greeted the crowds and told them he hoped they enjoyed the Pan-American Exposition. The crowd went wild again with clapping and cheering. It took a few more minutes before his speech could continue. He told the audience that he hoped that each and every one of them would be able to go home with at least three new ideas for their future. He told them that all things come in threes. He quoted part of his speech he gave the day before. He said, "Expositions are the timekeepers of progress. They record the world's achievements. They stimulate the energy, enterprise, and intellect of the people and quicken human genius. They go into the home. They broaden and brighten the daily life of the people. They open mighty storehouses of information to the people." He thanked everyone for being a part of the Exposition and wished them well. The audience went wild with excitement and cheers could be heard all over the Exposition. Wallace was overwhelmed with all the action in the theater. Winston for a change was calmer than Wallace. The excitement was more than he could handle. Winston told him it was probably good they were going home in a few hours. He did not think Wallace could take any more excitement.

People began to line up to shake the President's hand. President McKinley was noted for shaking hands with everyone he met on his tours. Wallace and Winston were a few hundred people away from their turn. It was great thrill to actually see and met the man who runs the country. Winston said, "I wonder if he has a firm handshake?" Wallace said, "Don't make it a contest with him." Winston laughed and looked ahead. Slowly they moved closer to the platform. Wallace kept watching the President to see how he was reacting to all the different people passing by him. He smiled and bowed extending his hand. All of a sudden two gunshots were heard. The crowd became silent. The President stood still. His face seemed bewildered as if something serious had just happened. Wallace said he hoped the President was not the one who was shot. Sure enough a commotion started. Three men jumped forward to grab a man who had a handkerchief wrapped around his hand. They tackled him to the ground as the Secret Service men got hold of the man. President McKinley stepped back and fell into a chair. The crowd had just witnessed an assassination attempt on the President of the United States. Wallace could not believe he had just watched someone try to kill the President. Winston was also stunned. Within minutes confusion and pandemonium erupted in the theater. The crowd began to go wild. They realized the enormity of what had just happened. There was panic. Men were shouting and fighting while women were screaming and children were crying. People nearest the doors ran outside before a stampede began. Medical attendants were trying to enter the building to assist the wounded President. For the first time in his life Wallace felt truly scared. He was afraid they might be trampled in the stampede of frightened people. The man who shot the gun was hustled out through the rear of the theater. The medical assistants from the Exposition hospital were coming up to the front to help the President. The police were yelling for the people to try to be calm and leave the building. No one seemed to listen to anything that was being said. The screams were getting louder from people who could not see or get out of the building. One little kid was stepped on and pushed aside. The mother was on the floor trying to cover the child from people running over them. Winston got punched in the side and doubled over in pain. Wallace thought it would be a miracle if they ever get out of there.

While they were standing in the crushing crowd of frightened people four doctors came to transport the President out of the theater. Wallace just happened to notice the name badge on one of the men. For some strange reason he remembered it as Dr. Samuel Haynes. He had no reason to notice except that he was a little older than him and good looking. He did not think any more about it but watched the President being taken away. Dr. Haynes was doing more to help the President than the other doctors. Maybe he had more experience. Dr. Haynes fascinated Wallace. Winston saw him watching Dr. Haynes since they were so close to all the action. He asked him why he was staring at that man. He told Winston he did not know. As the doctors took the stretcher out of the building they passed by Wallace and Winston. Wallace still watched Dr. Haynes as he passed by. Dr. Haynes saw Wallace staring at him and smiled. There was so much happening at that time that Wallace was not sure about anything now. Slowly the crowd began to leave after the President was transported to the Exposition hospital. Wallace looked at his watch. It was now 7PM. They were hungry and scared. People were no longer enjoying any part of the Exposition. What started out as a beautiful day right from waking up with Winston had turned into a nightmare. The train going back to Rochester did not arrive for 2 more hours. They decided to go out near the train station. Maybe they could find some food and a place to sit. Everywhere they went panic had taken over.

Chapter 17

THE TRAIN STATION WAS like being in a maddening crowd or as Winston said, "It's like being in a stampede." There were people everywhere trying to find out if their train was going to be arriving on time or cancelled because of the shooting of the President. The ticket attendants were yelling at the crowds to be calm and patient. Children were screaming and running around falling over luggage and people who were resting on the floor. Wallace sat on a bench and watched how much panic and lack of control the crowd had. People were pushing and yelling at anyone who got in their way. A train pulled up to the platform. It was like a tidal wave of people trying to get on the train. People would throw their tickets at the conductor or just try to push on by. Some men started fistfights and the police came to arrest them for causing a riot. As Winston and Wallace sat there watching all the confusion, Winston said, "Boy you sure have a lot to put in your paper next week." Wallace looked at him with a distant and confused face and said, "You're right I do." He broke out of his trance, pulled out his notebook and began recording as many details as he could about what they had just experienced. Winston offered things he remembered that Wallace did not. He told Wallace that they made a good team. The lights did not seem as bright tonight as they had last night. There was a foreboding atmosphere; no longer was there laughter and gaiety. The air was still and it was a warm and humid night. The trains came and went as black smoke from the engines lingered in the air. People were coughing and choking because of the smoke as masses of people jammed into the area. The Exposition closed early because of the shooting so everyone had to leave at the same time. People resorted to using horses and buggies to get to their destination because the trains were overloaded and running behind schedule. They overheard a woman telling a group of people about her experience in front of the Temple of Music just after the shooting. She told them that she got outside just before the President was taken from the theater to the Exposition hospital. She watched the doctors pull up in a new type of vehicle. She said that it had a sign on the side of it that called it a Car Ambulance. A person in the group said she must be mistaken because horses usually pulled ambulances. She became irritated with the stranger and marched up to him and put her finger in his face and said, "This is no time to tell me what I saw. If you don't believe me that's too bad, the car is one of the new inventions and is part of the Exposition." With that remark he walked away in huff. Wallace was writing down the information about the ambulance as fast as he could. He wondered to himself if Dr. Samuel Haynes, the good-looking doctor, may have been the driver. He knew that would be a great part for his newspaper report to tell about a new way to get to a hospital. He already knew what his father was going to say about the car but figured that was going to be his problem. People kept pouring out of the fair and no one seemed to be leaving the station. It was getting more crowded by the minute. People were falling on each other and using their bags as armor to get through the crowd. An old man fell and people walked right over him until the police helped him get up. He was cut, bruised, and had broken his leg. The police took him away. Winston got excited when he thought maybe the car ambulance would come to get the man. Wallace told him that there was probably only one of those cars around. A lady heard him say that to Winston and said she had heard the same thing. It was nearing 9PM; the train to Rochester had not yet arrived. A person from the station came out and announced a new schedule for arrivals and departures. The train to Rochester was arriving at 11PM. They were told it had derailed coming from Cleveland. No one was hurt but everyone had to get off the train in a field so that the workman could get the train back on the track. They sat down and felt like they may never see home again. Mothers were sitting on the platform trying to comfort their children. Most of them were crying and the fathers were annoyed with the whole scene. Cigar and pipe smoke wafted into every part of the crowded station to make the air even more irritating to the eyes and nose. While Wallace and Winston sat on the bench the old woman they were on the train with yesterday came up to them. She looked very weary and acted as if she was going to fall down. Wallace offered his seat to her. She sat down and said it was so nice to have met such nice young gentlemen. Winston asked if they were all going on the same train. They looked at their tickets and found out that they were scheduled to leave at 11PM. They agreed to sit together when they finally got on the train. There was more information from the station office telling the people that the train had a few less passenger cars because of the derailment. They looked at each other as if to say we may all get home at different times or even different days. Now even more exhausted with the worry of getting home, combined with the panic and tempo of the crowd, they fell into complete quiet. Wallace glanced at his watch and found that it was now 11PM. He shook his head and said, "I wonder if anyone at home even knows what has happened?" They looked at him and said nothing. Wallace was still trying to get his head together about what he was going to write for his newspaper. The idea of making a supplement to his usual paper seemed appropriate in light of what had happened. He thought about the man who shot President McKinley and what made him do it. He hoped that he would find out the details tomorrow when the actual reports were given. Wallace knew that he would have to make his report different than the ones that would already be printed before his paper came out. He decided to write it first hand since he was feet away from the crime. Most reporters would only be using the information given to them from the police and the Exposition officials. Wallace knew first hand reporting was what people would pay for. Even though he was exhausted his mind had already organized this story.

At midnight the train to Rochester pulled into the station. The station workers had organized a plan that would allow people to safely board the train. Boarding the train was first offered for elderly people with a family and then families with small children. The old woman with Wallace and Winston said to them, "You boys have just become my grandsons." Winston lit up and laughed and thought that was a great idea. Wallace helped her up and they walked to the conductor. Winston followed behind with their luggage and the old woman's bag. Wallace took her by the arm and she carefully climbed onto the train. When they got in their seats, Wallace asked, "Are you okay, you seem very weak?" She smiled and devilishly said, "I was an actress when I was young. I knew I could get us on this train if I acted that way." She winked at both of them. They looked at each other and smiled. She said, "I know you boys have probably had more experiences these last two days than you ever thought." They both gave each other a look of agreement and a nudge. The train filled up fast with mostly families with children. Wallace told Winston that he was glad they had ran into the old woman. Wallace realized that neither of them had asked what their names were. He decided to ask her what her name was. She said it was Rose. Her first name was Sybil. He told her his was Wallace and that was Winston. She asked in a coy way if they were sure they were not brothers. Winston said, "We're closer than brothers." Wallace looked at him with a twinkle in his eye and shook his head.

The train left the station at 1AM. People were calming down. The passengers sat quietly relieved to be on the train to Rochester. Wallace, Winston, and Sybil sat quietly as they heard the conductor give the last call for the departure. The train began to chug and you could hear the wheels begin to slowly turn. The whistle sounded and black smoke passed over the train. Everyone watched as the train was far enough from the Exposition to see it fade into the horizon. You could hear people saying that was the most unbelievable trip ever. There had been so much to see and so much terror that it was hard to believe any of it was real. The trip to Rochester took about three hours with a few stops along the way. Some people got off in Batavia, which left more room for people spread out. Many people were sitting on others laps and on the floor. Wallace looked at his watch and it was now 2AM. He hoped they would get back to Rochester by 3AM. He settled back in his seat. Winston sat next to him with his head on Wallace's side. Sybil began to doze off also. Wallace wondered how so much could have happened in two days. He was thinking about the thrill of all the new things he had seen. He reminisced about the stay at the boarding house too. He had felt so many new things over the last two days. The train came into the Rochester area. He gave a sigh of relief and nudged Winston and told him they were almost home. He woke up and Sybil seemed ready to be there too. The train pulled into the station at 3:15AM. When they got off the train Alice was waiting for them. She heard that something terrible happened. She sat at the station for many hours. The man at the train station kept Alice updated through most of the night. She said that Frank stayed home but she could not just sit there wondering if the boys were okay. Wallace hugged her and Winston did too. They introduced Sybil to Alice. She told Alice that she was to be very proud of these young men. They were real gentlemen. Alice looked at both of them and agreed. They said their goodbyes to Sybil and walked home. All Wallace could do was talk about everything that had happened. Winston only talked about the Midway and the boarding house. Wallace worried about just how much he was going to tell about the boarding house. They walked by the hotel and Wallace wondered how well the promotion was doing for the Exposition Package. He needed to see Mr. Helfer soon about more advertising plans. Alice was busy telling Wallace about the newspaper and how they needed more help. Wallace said he knew exactly who he wanted. Alice asked who he thought of. Wallace looked at Winston and said, "You're walking next to him." Winston said, "You've got a deal."

Chapter 18

FRONT-PAGE NEWS FEATURED THE shooting of President McKinley. Wallace bought as many newspapers as he could find. He knew that every reporter would have a different version of what happened. He wanted his article to be authentic since he saw the shooting in person. He found out who had shot the President. It was Leon Czolgosz. He was the son of Polish-Russian immigrants born in Detroit, Michigan in 1873. He was a rebellious person. One report stated that he had a mental breakdown a few years prior to the shooting. During his time recovering from the breakdown he rejected his family's Roman Catholic beliefs and became intensely interested in reading anarchist newspapers. In May he traveled to Cleveland to hear the noted Emma Goldman make a speech about anarchism. After her speech Leon spoke with her about her beliefs. He became one of her followers and went to Chicago and studied her writings. One of Emma's close associates became convinced Czolgosz was a spy and issued a warning about him in his journal entitled "Free Society". Leon was not affected by the reputation that he was receiving. During his time in Chicago he did not contact his family or former friends. He shut that part of his life out. Leon read in a newspaper that President McKinley was planning a visit to the Pan-American Exposition in Buffalo. On September 3 Leon bought a pistol and went to Buffalo. He wanted the shooting to be noticed and make an impact on many people in a festive place. What a better spot to do it in, than a world's fair!

After the shooting secret service agents surrounded Czolgosz. There was so much anger at that moment that they beat him with fists and pistol butts. President McKinley was still seated in a chair when that was happening. He was quoted as saying, "Be easy on him boys." Leon was handcuffed and dragged out of the Temple. He made his statement at he the Buffalo Police Headquarters. Wallace read in another paper that Leon told the police that he was induced to kill by his attention to Emma Goldman's lectures and writings. He decided that the present form of government in the United States was all wrong. Therefore, the best way to end it was by killing the President. He was proud to be an Anarchist and felt no remorse for shooting the President. As Wallace was reading about the details of the event he kept thinking he had heard about Emma Goldman around Rochester. He was not sure why but knew there was some connection to her in town. He made a note to look into Goldman's reputation in Rochester. Wallace had enough information to write his version of what he saw in Buffalo. He wanted to have the supplement printed and ready to go to the customers by tomorrow. He told Alice, Gregg, and Winston that they would all have to work very quickly to get this paper ready. They agreed to work as long as they needed to. The only thing that Wallace was still questioning was Emma Goldman's connection to Rochester. He had a feeling this piece of information could give his story a big boost. He went to the library to find out more about her life. The best way he could find out about her was to look in the old newspapers and magazines. He found some articles she had written. He found nothing referring her to Rochester. The librarian suggested he go back a few years before she became known for her political views. He read everything that made any reference to her but with no luck. It was a tiring job to read newspaper after newspaper with no success. He felt frustrated and defeated but knew this information was going to be important. On his way out of the library a man had been watching him go through all the papers and magazines. He approached Wallace and explained that he had overheard him discussing Emma Goldman. He knew about her political views and suggested he look in the city directories. Wallace had completely forgotten about that possibility. He went to the local history department where those books were stored. They were like a dictionary of people that lived in Rochester. The books were organized in one-year segments. He began with 1900 and looked at books going back in time from that year. He had seen pictures of her in other reports so he knew she was older than him. The 1890 book had been handwritten with many styles of writing. Some were easy to read and others were almost illegible. At last he found a Goldman name that seemed to match some of the things he had heard about her. She had lived in Rochester as a young person. He found out that her name and a man's name appeared at the same address. The directory listed occupations for each name if you were employed. Emma Goldman was listed as having worked in a sweatshop in Rochester. Wallace's interests were rekindled. He looked at the next year finding the man's name gone. How could he find more information about her? He went back to the print shop and began his article about his experiences at the Temple of Music. When he arrived at the shop everyone was busy organizing the Sunday edition. It usually went out on

Monday so all the standard articles and advertisements had to be finished and set on type a day early. Wallace's feature article would be printed last but he had to write it first. He described the wonderful music and palatial environment of the Temple of Music. The headline of the article was Elegance and Inventions Interrupted by Gun Shots and Panic. He included the events that led to the final panic when the President was shot. He used some of the facts he had gathered from the other reports. The part he included about himself being within feet of the assassin was sure to make it more interesting. No reporter that he knew had been as close to the event as he. He wrote how Czolgosz had his hand wrapped with a handkerchief to cover the gun making it look like he had cut himself. He mentioned the graciousness of the President and the grand reaction people had to the entire event. He described the panic and fear of the stampede as terrifying. The Exposition feature article took the front of a whole page and ironically the back of that page had the advertisement for the Seneca Powers Hotel's Exposition Package. Spend your days at the Seneca Powers and travel in style to the Pan-American Exposition where excitement awaits you. When everyone in the print shop realized how one side was exactly opposite from the other Alice asked if that should happen. As they were looking at this situation Miss Holleran came into the shop. She heard about all the things that had been going on and came to see if Wallace and Winston were okay. After they told her about the things they saw and did and the fact they witnessed the President being shot they asked her what she thought of the two sides of the paper. Since she helped Wallace edit the paper and she was a teacher they were relying on her to make the final decision. As she read the report about the shooting and the events after it she was puzzled about Emma Goldman's name. She kept going back to it as if she was trying to remember something. All of a sudden she said, "I think I know that person!" As it turned out Miss Holleran was Emma's teacher in school. She explained that she was a difficult student. She had a defensive attitude toward any type of rules and regulations. When she got out of school she worked in a sweatshop and married a man who proved to be a poor choice. She spent a few years in an unhappy marriage. Miss Holleran lost track of her shortly after leaving school but was told by other people who worked in the sweatshop about Emma's attitude toward authority and government. That story gave Wallace the last bit of real information he needed to make his article better than the rest. He informed Miss Holleran that she had made his day and finished his version of the day at the Temple. Alice told Winston she was very proud of both of them and that she was glad to be a part of such important stuff.

Wallace printed extra copies of this week's paper. They worked through most of the night getting the print set and then the final printing. Wallace realized he had to get that new machine he saw at the Exposition that could print things at a faster rate than doing one copy at a time with a hand press. Miss Holleran complimented him on his expertise in constructing and writing such a good newspaper article. He was impressed with her air of certainty whenever she went into her teacher mode. He felt tired from such a long trip and all the excitement of it but had a sense of pride and satisfaction in what he had accomplished.

The paper was finished and ready to be delivered at 6AM Sunday morning. There were three buggies ready to deliver this special edition. He and Miss Holleran stayed at the shop to provide extra copies for the newsstands in town. While they sat in the shop Miss Holleran asked Wallace about the other parts of the trip to Buffalo. He told her about all the new inventions he saw. He told her about the plans he had made for his home someday. He told her about Winston and how much he loved the amusement rides. She asked if he went on the rides with Winston. He told her that he did but was glad when it was over. She laughed and said, "You two make a great team." She thought Winston was good for him because he brought out things in Wallace that no one else could. She felt that Wallace was good for Winston too because he would help make him successful. He looked at her and wondered how she seemed to know so much and what might happen in the future. He had enough courage to ask her that very question. Her response was quick and to the point. She said, "Take time to do what you like to do and don't be afraid of anything or anyone."

Chapter 19

Miss Holleran went home after all the papers had been distributed. Sunday was a special day for her because it was the day she went to a social hour at the woman's club. She gave Wallace her best and told him she would see him during the week. He sat in the shop all alone thinking about the last few days and all that had happened. He felt like this was the beginning of something new but was not sure what that would be. He thought about a new campaign for the Seneca Powers Hotel. The Exposition Package was nearing its end. The Pan-American would be closing on November 1 and he knew that a new advertising campaign should be planned for. As he sat at the desk in the shop he kept thinking about what Miss Holleran said about doing what you want and not be afraid of anything or anyone. Then he began to think about Winston. He could not stop thinking about how he affected him when they were in Buffalo. He knew that Winston was fun to be with but did not always like his behavior. He wondered why he felt so connected to him. While sitting in the quiet of the shop he decided that he would make Winston his associate in whatever business dealings he created. That way he could have him involved in his life while developing his own financial future. He wondered what he could offer Winston to keep him as his partner.

Alice, Gregg, and Winston returned to the shop in time for lunch. While they ate lunch they told Wallace about the deliveries and comments they had heard. People were waiting for the paper. Some people thought that knowing Wallace he would have some news in print earlier than usual and they were right. One of Alice's friends on her route told her that she was certain Wallace would have more information than other newspapers. Alice made new friends on her delivery route. She was happier now than ever especially when she heard people compliment her son. Frank on the other hand did not find it to be so wonderful. He felt as if Alice had abandoned him. He was struggling to keep the horse and buggy shop profitable. There was more and more talk of this new thing called a motor buggy. He tried avoiding the notion that it was going to be the end of the era of fancy buggies for people to ride in. He told Alice that he wanted her to make lots of money doing her outside work. She knew he was feeling defeated and worried and did not dare to tell him that she was not being paid for her work. She felt her compensation was making new acquaintances and helping her son.

The newspaper supplement was a huge success. Just as Wallace had hoped, a few of the newsstands in town requested copies of the Weekly Page to be sold at their stands. This meant that more copies would have to be printed. It also meant Wallace could now suggest that Mr. Helfer put an ad for the hotel in his paper, since people in town would see it and travelers might pick up a copy. He had a two-fold plan to present to Mr. Helfer and was anxious to make an appointment with him. As he was walking into the lobby he began to smile and think about the secretary. She was famous for that face she would give Wallace whenever he came to the office. He thought of it as the face with the smile upside down and the wrinkles matched the direction of the frown. He looked forward to seeing her because it was a challenge to make her respond. Just as expected he went in and got "the face" and made the appointment. She wrote the appointment in the book and asked if he was done yet. He politely smiled and said, "Yes, with the appointment but not with you." At that she gave him a withering look and showed him to the door. When Wallace was walking down Main Street he felt good about his plan and knew that the secretary would be a lot of fun.

Wallace went home and started to draw some sketches and write jingles for his new advertising campaign for the hotel. His instructors at Mechanics Institute were interested in his work and ideas. He was one of the first students to have been successful with advertising long before graduating from college. He stayed up late into the night making sure that the advertising sketches were just the way he wanted them to be. It was the first full week of school in September and he still had a feeling something was going to happen. He had been home from Buffalo for almost a week. It seemed like a long time ago that he and Winston had been there. He told Winston that he would meet him after his appointment with Mr. Helfer. His appointment was at 3PM and he suggested that they meet at the soda shop. Winston liked the root beer floats there. Wallace thought that would be fun too.

Mondays were the hardest for Wallace. He was exhausted from his work on the newspaper and working on advertising ideas. He went to school and used his free time checking the proposal for Mr. Helfer. He asked his art instructor if his ideas were good enough. His teacher told him that they were great and that he should be the teacher. Wallace needed that boost. He was feeling like it was not good enough this time. The teacher told him that those drawings were the best yet and not to worry. When he finished his classes he walked to the hotel. As he approached the hotel he regained his sense of confidence.

Wallace walked through the lobby of the hotel and took a deep breath. He knew the first person he would see in the office was the "face woman." He opened the door and walked in and sat down. She stared at him over the top of her glasses. She told him Mr. Helfer would be ready soon. Wallace studied her a bit more. He never realized how big she was. He was so taken back by her sagging smile that the rest of her body never stuck out. He studied her breasts that hung to her waist and wondered why she could not do something better with them. He began to have a good time thinking about how she put herself together every morning. Her hair definitely was not done at a beauty salon. She had a hair net holding it all in place. She wore a dress with a belt that disappeared under the sag of her breasts. They looked like watermelons. She was wearing a black dress with little white dots. Wallace focused on her large lips and claw-like nails. He thought that maybe she worked in one of the brothels downtown at night. He began to laugh out loud when she glared at him and asked, "Is there something wrong with you?" He looked at her and said, "No, I was just admiring your outfit." She glared at him as Mr. Helfer came out of his office. He asked if everything was all right. Wallace said, "Things could not be better today." He smiled at her as they walked into the office. Mr. Helfer asked how his trip to Buffalo was and what he had learned. Wallace explained about all the new inventions and ideas he saw. Mr. Helfer asked if any of those ideas could be used for the hotel. He said that some could be. His first idea was to have an entertainment and recreation section in his paper. He explained that the Weekly Page was now being sold in town at newsstands. Mr. Helfer said that he had heard about that and was proud of such good advancements. Wallace thought a section of his paper for the hotel would be a good idea. It could list the upcoming events in the hotel with any special deals or entertainment that may be coming to the hotel. He suggested that they feature the chandelier rooms as part of the new ad. There were Waterford chandeliers in the dining rooms and Wallace thought an ad like that might attract a higher class of people. He wanted Mr. Helfer to think about hiring consistent entertainment for the lounge. He thought that a piano player, a dance floor and a theater would be a great asset. Many of the hotels only had one area for entertainment. A grand hotel should have a variety of places for relaxation. Mr. Helfer sat in his chair and shook his head. Wallace thought he was saying no. In fact Mr. Helfer was so amazed he was speechless. He approved of the entire package of ideas. He said he would have Hilda begin working on contracts for renovating the main floor and lobby. Wallace wondered who Hilda was. He figured it must be someone from the business office. The door opened and in walked the "face woman." Wallace never thought she had a name! Mr. Helfer explained what had been discussed and gave her instructions on what needed to be done. The work would begin within a week. He felt the upcoming fall foliage season and the holidays would be a perfect time for a new hotel atmosphere. Hilda took notes while Wallace stared at her standing next to him. He was almost afraid of her now, since he had never seen her standing up. He knew she could flatten him in one move. When she finished she turned to him and said, "Good job, boy." Wallace hated to be called boy but chose to ignore her. He knew he could win her over eventually.

After Hilda left the office Mr. Helfer discussed the finances of his work. He told Wallace that the last Exposition-Package and poster advertisements at the train station had increased business. Wallace was to be paid 2% of the profits. He asked what that meant in terms of dollars. Mr. Helfer said that it was enough to buy 10 shares of stock in the car company. In their agreement the hotel would match that and add 10 more in his name. His hotel earning amounted to 20 shares of stock. Mr. Helfer told him that he was well on his way to being a wealthy man. They finished the meeting and agreed to meet again when it was time to decide on the types of entertainment and advertising. Wallace left the office and Hilda was back on her chair. He smiled and tipped his head to her. Instead of the usual face she tilted her head a little. Wallace did not know what that meant but it seemed better than the frown.

He left the hotel and went to the soda shop. He could not wait to see Winston. When he arrived Winston had already ordered the sodas. Wallace came into the shop and nearly jumped on him. He gave him a big pat on the back and a nudge. He was so excited that Mr. Helfer agreed with his ideas. Winston thought it was great. They talked about the ideas for the hotel. Wallace told Winston that he was definitely going to have to be more in charge of the print shop. Winston yelled out a big hurrah and Wallace told him to behave. Winston told him to be happy about all these things and stop being so careful. They finished their sodas and walked home. Winston usually had dinner at Wallace's house. Winston's mother was dead and his father was an alcoholic so Alice filled the spot as his mother.

Wallace liked this too. He wished Winston could stay with them. During dinner the main conversation was the hotel along with Winston taking over the print shop. Alice was happy for both of them. She held both of them together and squeezed and kissed them. Frank was surprised that the hotel was doing so well. His contribution to the dinner conversation gave everyone the feeling that all the businesses in town were doing poorly. Wallace knew his father was feeling defeated. He also knew his father would have a very difficult time getting used to the new ways of life.

News of the recent events in Buffalo spread throughout Rochester. Newspapers were featuring the shooting of the President. They included information about the inventions that were part of the Exposition. Everyday there was a new invention described in the papers. Wallace had seen these inventions first hand and realized he needed to include them in his paper. While he was at school he would plan his next edition of the paper. He had a few days to get it ready. He began to sketch new logos and slogans for the hotel. One slogan was, "Come to the Seneca Powers," a hotel with an arcade of lavish activities. While he was planning his advertisements for his paper he picked up other papers at the newsstand. He read about the current events and about President McKinley's condition. He was resting comfortably and was expected to recover. Below the article was a description about the newly developed machine that could take pictures of the inside of the body. Wallace remembered seeing that machine. The article explained that the doctors were not sure if they should use it on the President. They did not know if there would be any side effects. If they had used it they may have been able to see the bullet. The last part of the article told about the hospital room at the Exposition where the President was taken. The hospital had no electricity! With all the lights for the buildings and grounds at the Pam-Am there were no electric lights in the hospital. The doctors had to use a pan to reflect sunlight onto the table where they were treating President Mc Kinley. He could not believe that with all those lights and the pride in the electricity coming into the fair that there was no power to the hospital. He decided to focus his story on the aspect of the planner not having electricity at the hospital. He knew that would attract attention. He understood the tactics of news reporting. He realized that you had to take the offense and write with questions rather than all factual statements. Let the reader get into the issues and formulate their own ideas and opinions. This will create the editorial section of a paper. People will love to write their ideas and opinions about issues presented in the newspaper. Wallace got his plan ready and had Winston and his group begin the next supplement for this week's edition.

The typeset was ready for the printing press to begin printing the weekly paper. Everyone was there helping to make sure the paper would be ready on time again this week. It was Saturday September 14. Frank came running into the shop that was something he had never done before. Looking totally in shock he announced that the President had died today! Sudden shock came over everyone. He said he heard from someone at the saddlery shop who had a friend who just came from Buffalo with the news. Wallace knew he had to change the newspaper. This news was too important to wait for another edition. He would have to revise the article within an hour. He rewrote the article about the new machine that took pictures of the inside of the body. He explained that if they had used it they could have found the bullet that eventually gave the President a gangrenous infection that killed him. Now, Vice-President Theodore Roosevelt was the President of the United States. The country was in a state of shock. The events of the wonderful Pan-American turned to death. Wallace made that the title of this week's paper; "The Pan-American Turns to Death." They set the type and began printing the revised article. They worked all night and at daybreak the papers were ready to go out. His would be one of the first papers to get that news out to the public.

The news spread like fire. The Weekly Page became know for its fast coverage. No one actually knew how this news article had been printed so fast. It was just luck that Frank had heard the news and passed it on to Wallace. The reports of the assassin began surfacing after the President's death. Leon Czolgosz was still imprisoned. His trial was scheduled for October. Every paper was featuring the funeral of the President and upcoming trial. Emma Goldman was imprisoned and questioned but was released and shocked the public with her statements. She said, "Czolgosz had committed the act for no personal reason or gain. He did it for what is his ideal: the good of the people. That is why my sympathies are with him." Wallace used the news and put it into his own words. He convinced people about the issues and used his personal touch making it seem like a living room conversation. When Monday came the owners of the Rochester Post Express came to Wallace's shop. They were looking for him but he was at school. These two men waited all afternoon until someone came along. Winston was the first to show up at the print shop. He asked them what they wanted because he thought they were angry with Wallace. They explained that they needed to see Wallace. As they were talking Wallace came into the shop. They introduced themselves and began a discussion about the merger of the two newspapers.

Chapter 20

PRESIDENT MCKINLEY'S FUNERAL AND the trial of Leon Czolgosz were big news items in the fall of 1901. There were reports about the Vice-President Roosevelt and his trip to Buffalo when McKinley was shot. Theodore Roosevelt came from a mountain climbing trip when he found out about the shooting. It was reported that McKinley would recover and return to his duties as president. Mrs. McKinley was appreciative that everyone was there to support her while they waited for the outcome of the assassination attempt. The shock of his death hit hard when they previously expected a full recovery. Wallace wrote an article about the lack of electricity in the Exposition hospital. He presented the information in forms of questions to the readers. He had been thinking about this form of reporting long before but never actually tried to publish it in this format. He asked the readers what their opinion was about the lack of lighting for such an important place as a hospital. He stated that he realized that the possibility of the President needing medical attention was the last thing that anyone thought would happen. Did they only want lighting in all the most obvious places? Did the planners try to save money on places that may not be used as much? Why was there no foresight about all the aspects of an affair as large as the Pan-Am? Hadn't they learned from the failures of the Chicago World's Fair just a few years prior to the Pan-American or was it cheaply and gaudily done? Some critics did think it was cheaply constructed and gaudy in its appearance. Wallace posed one last question about the shooting as a conspiracy against the President and was it a long-range plan with the anarchists? Who really was involved in the event and how far back was the plan for the shooting? He hoped the readers would respond with opinions and facts that would encourage them to have their voices heard in a newspaper. Winston thought he was asking for lots of criticism and possibly attacks from the public. Wallace told him that it was worth a try. If it was a failure they did not need to try it again.

Leon Czolgosz's trial was scheduled for early October. He was imprisoned and questioned repeatedly about the reasons for his actions. The country was still recovering from the events at the Exposition. The Pan-American had 2 months left before it was to close. The Exposition Company was worried that attendance would drop after the shooting. They kept close records and were surprised that it stayed consistent even though there had been a tragedy. The newspapers were full of articles about anarchy, the trial, and Emma Goldman's affect on the movement. Wallace had hundreds of responses to his questions from the public. There were so many responses that he needed to include a two-page insert of letters to the editor. The readers felt they were able to speak out and let their ideas be heard. The newspaper had grown to six pages. Wallace was thinking about the offer the Rochester Post Express had proposed to him. He was not ready for what they wanted to do. He liked the idea of having a little competition with another paper with the same number of subscribers. He knew that if he did not respond they would want to pursue him even more since his editorial section was growing.

Leon Czolgosz's trial became top news. Jury selection was a long and difficult process. It was surprising to find out that many people secretly sided with the anarchist views and sympathized with Leon. Wallace decided to devote a section to his paper that would give his readers a chance to respond to what anarchy was. He thought he might discuss this idea with Miss Holleran. He knew she was a free thinker and a smart woman. She would give him the right direction with such a sensitive theme. During the meeting the idea of a section devoted to anarchy was discussed. Miss Holleran was very direct in her concern about reporting the facts and not opinions. She warned Wallace that an article such as this could be mistaken as an affirmation of anarchist ways. She found it to be a good way to create debate amongst the readers. When she taught school she was in charge of the debate teams. Wallace was one of her regular debaters so she knew he had good training. They agreed on a format for the article and she agreed to edit it. When they were finished meeting she stood up and shook her head and said, "I am so proud of you and glad to be a part of your future." Wallace now knew what he had to do.

He introduced his news article with the title "Why Anarchy?" He felt a question is a good way to begin a conversation. He wrote that anarchy is the absence of political authority. He remembered that Czolgosz said he committed the crime for the good of the people. He felt that government was not for the people. Anarchism is the theory that all forms of government are unnecessary and should be abolished. He gave the effects of anarchy as being political disorder and confusion. It is the lack of principles and a common purpose. A ruler is not needed. In Wallace's next part of the article he began asking questions. How can anything get done under anarchy? Who sets the purpose for the country? What happens when things go wrong? Is there any plan for future advancement? Who is in charge of the finances? What if the country is invaded? Do we need armed forces? Whose philosophy do we follow in the education of our population? He gave some insight into Goldman's campaign for anarchism and how it affected Leon. He did not include anything about the plot against the President. He wanted to focus only on anarchism. He took the article to Miss Holleran for her to review. She sat in her chair with her half glasses on. She had a habit of peering over them with a smirk on her face. She did that as a technique so you would never know if she liked it or not. Finally after the reading and glancing over the glasses routine was over she gave Wallace her approval. He told himself it was going to be okay but had that slight sweating and jittery feeling until she gave her approval. She thought it was fine and he needed to clean up some of the grammatical errors. She felt he was careful not to implicate himself as an anarchist. She jokingly told him she did not want to visit him in prison. They had two days to write the article, set the type, print the paper and get it ready for delivery. Winston told Wallace they needed a better printing method. He told Wallace to buy the new printing press that they saw at the Exposition. Wallace felt like he was being told what to do. He kind of liked it when Winston took charge.

The trial of Leon Czolgosz began in October. After all the difficulty in jury selection the trial was very short in duration. Newspaper reporters were planning on a major trial with many witnesses called to testify. To everyone's surprise the trial lasted only a few days and Leon Czolgosz was found guilty of killing President William McKinley. He was sentenced to be hanged until dead on October 20th. One of his last remarks was, "I killed the President because he was the enemy of the good working people, I am not sorry for my crime." There was no reference to any one else who participated in the anarchist movement. The trial was over and the execution carried out. Buffalo became known as "The City of the Assassination." The major newspapers carried the news of the trial and the concluding events of what happened in Buffalo. The Weekly Page had overwhelming response to the questions about anarchy. People responded with concerns about how country under anarchism would survive. Some suggested that anarchists could not possibly be thinking about the entire operation of the country. Others thought anarchists should be put on an island to see if they could survive. Most felt they were satisfied with the current form of government. It was clearly a good way for people to share their opinions. The editorial page was a success.

Wallace and Winston felt that the paper had reached a point where they needed to expand the operation. They decided to investigate the new printing machine and find a shop that could handle a larger operation. Miss Holleran informed Alice that she was to become the secretary and bookkeeper. They would need to hire a few more people for the shop and delivery people. Miss Holleran suggested that Wallace include Frank in the plans for expansion. He thought about it and asked his mother what she thought. Maybe Frank could be in charge of the delivery routes, transportation, and the staff of delivery people. He would be good at that because of his experiences at the saddlery and buggy shop. Wallace went to his father's shop and found him working on one of the few buggies that were there. He remembered when he was a little kid how busy the shop was. Wallace discussed the plan for expansion with him. He asked his father if he wanted to be a part of the newspaper operation. He stared at Wallace for the longest time and finally said, "I was hoping you would ask me to be part of your business." It was the first time that Frank seemed happy with Wallace. Wallace returned to the shop and talked to Winston about the plan for moving and hiring new people. Winston was uneasy when the subject of new and more business was discussed. He told Wallace he was not sure he could keep going on like this. Wallace became angry with him when he said that. He looked him and said, "I can't imagine doing this without you. We know each other very well. You are my partner and I care about you." Winston wanted to say more to him about how he was really feeling. He was not sure if what he felt should be talked about.

Chapter 21

WALLACE BEGAN HIS THIRD year at Mechanics Institute in the fall of 1901. He was so involved with the newspaper company and the hotel work that going to school seemed like a burden. His teachers saw the frustration he was experiencing and made an appointment with him to discuss his use of time in school. He had four instructors who were directly involved with his courses of study which were advertising, marketing, architecture and English. He met them at the main office in the faculty lounge.They met on Monday morning, which was Wallace's worst day of the week. He thought they were going to suggest he curtail his sideline activities. His advertising instructor began the meeting by complimenting him on his successes in the newspaper and hotel endeavors. He sat and listened and wondered where this was going. His marketing teacher suggested that he combine his schoolwork into half-day sessions. They were willing to schedule him for independent study assignments and would make appointments to meet with him on a regular basis. They felt that he still needed conference time to discuss his work with regard to the newspaper and the hotel. In order for Wallace to earn the degree they needed to call it independent study under advisement. They told him that he was one of the few people to ever be placed in this type of program. Wallace thanked them and explained how difficult all the work and jobs had been to accomplish. They agreed and felt this would ease the pressure he had placed upon himself. They had documents prepared for him to sign endorsing his plan for graduation. He was to meet with them monthly or if he needed a conference it could be arranged at any time.

Wallace left the lounge and headed for the print shop. Wallace was working with Winston on the plan for expanding and moving the shop. When Winston saw Wallace walk into the shop he asked him why he was so early. Winston did not go to classes on Monday because he was on a work-study program. He was able to use his manager's job at the print shop as credit toward his graduation. Wallace told him about the new plan for graduation. Winston laughed and told him that before long the teachers would be listening to him. Wallace agreed and began looking at brochures for a new printing press. He had a few choices but mainly about machines that could print different sized papers. Winston told him it was best to buy the middle sized one. He thought that would be enough for the size paper they were printing. They would need a larger shop for the equipment and storage of the additional supplies for the larger operation. Wallace asked Winston if he had found any vacant places that would be good for a shop. They needed to choose this next place together. They left to look at the new shop location then to the company where they could order the new printing press. They were both excited about the expansion and walked down the street just about ready for anything.

As they walked by the hotel Wallace told Winston that he needed to present the advertising and entertainment ideas to Mr. Helfer in next few days. Winston asked him what they were going to be. He told him it had to be something a little classier than the rest of the hotels in town but also a bit more fun. Winston was thinking that fun for Wallace was not the same type of fun he would suggest. After seeing how disinterested Wallace was at the Midway in Buffalo he probably thought a rocking chair would be loads of fun for him. Winston thought better of saying that to Wallace.

They arrived at the new shop. Wallace could not believe that it was his father's original saddlery shop. Winston had no idea that Frank occupied that shop some years ago. Wallace thought that it was ironic that he was going to be in his father's original shop but now it would be a printing shop. Winston said, "Frank is going to love this." Wallace laughed and said he remembered being there when he was a little kid. He thought his father would feel good that the space was still being used for a family business. He told Winston that whatever makes him happier would be good for his mother. Since the shop was empty for many years Winston wondered how much Frank would charge for rent. Wallace had not thought about that. They decided that would be good dinner conversation that evening. The shop would be perfect for what they wanted to do. It had large areas for the printing press and storage spaces for paper and inks. Since the saddle and harness shop had doors large enough for buggies and horses they could use it to load the papers inside and not have to contend with the weather. There was even an office that Winston could have for himself and another one for Wallace. They figured out an area for Alice to have a desk for her book keeping. It was perfect in every way. Now they just had to deal with Frank.

Wallace made an appointment with Mr. Helfer to discuss the upcoming promotions. His new advertisements used more stylization in the written script for the hotel giving it more of a flare. The new brochures and posters would be a sketch of a chandelier under the hotel's name. He proposed an all inclusive weekend package. The guests would receive a coupon book when they checked into the hotel. There would be choices for shows, local foliage, lilac or lake tours, beauty treatments, massage, and different levels of dining at the hotel. As a complimentary service there would be shoeshine chairs available in the lobby. When the weather was inclement the hotel would offer a Seneca Powers Hotel umbrella that the guests could keep. There would also be transportation to the train station.

Wallace wanted the hotel's entertainment to have varieties that were not yet widely used. He heard of shows that were considered by some people to be showy and adult oriented. Burlesque was live entertainment that had scantily dressed performers. Sometimes men would dress like women for parts in the show. The shows were colorful, exotic and sexually suggestive. In the proposal, the front of the new theater would have a large area that could accommodate an orchestra, a burlesque show, and dancing. When they were not having shows the hotel could use the area for conventions. His first suggestion for a convention was to have a "20th Century Invention Show." The people showing new ideas and inventions would receive discounts for their room. This sort of show would draw business into the hotel for food and accommodations. He listed other types of conventions in his proposal that would attract a different level of interest. He suggested a weekend devoted to horoscope, palm reading, mediums, crystal ball reading, and supernatural predictions. He thought that a home show might be possible; people were interested in improving their homes and gardens. He made a folder with all the ideas for Mr. Helfer. Wallace wondered how many of his ideas would be used and how receptive he would be to the idea of a burlesque show.

Wallace dressed in his well-groomed manner. He was feeling more comfortable and less tense with his meetings with Mr. Helfer. As he walked into the hotel he looked around at the work being done on the main floor. This will be a grand place with lots of activity he thought. He walked into the office and was greeted by Hilda. This time she was expressionless because she was too busy or so it seemed.

He sat in his usual chair and waited for Mr. Helfer. Hilda was very quiet and withdrawn today; he wondered what happened since the last time he was in the office. He asked her how she was. She peered over her glasses wearing just about the same type outfit as the last time he had seen her. Everything was black except her nails and lips. With a curt tone she asked him why he cared. Wallace smiled and told her that she seemed different today. She stood up and all he could focus on was her bust. She roared, "I don't like the way you have changed Mr. Helfer." At that moment he came out of his office and told Hilda to be quiet. She sat down and Wallace could only stare at her. She glared at him while they were getting ready for the meeting.

The three of them sat in the office. Hilda was ready to take notes. She sat in the chair motionless while the two men conversed about how the renovations were going. Everything was progressing as planned. They decided the project could be completed by mid-November. They would then have a few weeks to get ready for the holiday season. All the last minute details and furnishings were to be completed at that time. Then Mr. Helfer asked Wallace about his new thoughts for the hotel. He glanced at Hilda but she turned her head when he began to speak. He was uneasy because of their previous encounter. He wondered who was really in charge of that office. Mr. Helfer told him to go on and tell him all the good news. With that Wallace began to focus on the reasons he was there. He decided to ignore Hilda. Mr. Helfer liked the advertising ideas and instructed Hilda to get those ideas under way and to notify the company that made their stationery and posters. She seemed upset and sucked her teeth in disapproval when he said that. Mr. Helfer ignored her. Then came the entertainment ideas. Wallace carefully explained the convention ideas first because they were the easiest. The larger stage, tours, coupon book, and complimentary services were all fine. He was beginning to feel more confident as they talked. When Wallace started to explain the burlesque shows he felt a surge of enthusiasm. He decided to really play that part up. He started with, "The city needs adult entertainment." Hilda then started coughing. He continued with the description of what type of shows they might have in the theater. Wallace laughed as he discussed the exotic and colorful costumes. The music and program would be like a huge party with seductive acting and dancing. The patrons could participate in the singing and dancing while the actors maneuvered around the theater. There would be drinks and dinner served. All of a sudden Hilda jumped up and yelled, "And I suppose you will have women of the night waiting in the lobby too. This sounds like a brothel." Wallace laughed when she said that thinking that she might know about that since she looks like she runs one at night. He thought better of actually saying that. Mr. Helfer told her to sit down and told her that if she did not control herself and be co-operative he would find someone who would be. She sat down as if she were stunned. Mr. Helfer continued on as if nothing happened. He asked to see the drafts and proposal for entertainment. Mr. Helfer had a devilish smile on his face when he reread the burlesque and theater ideas. He began twisting the tips of his moustache while be pondered the ideas. He asked how they might find people to perform shows of this type. Hilda blurted out, "In the gutter." Mr. Helfer looked at her and sternly said, "Hi-i-i-ilda you are pushing me!" She went back to her notes. Wallace was beginning to enjoy the show right in front of his face. He suggested that they could have comedy acts as well as burlesque. Mr. Helfer asked if that was because of the comedy show right here in the office. Wallace told him not really but was thinking that is what gave him the idea. If only Hilda knew what she had just created.

Mr. Helfer sat back in his chair and looked at Wallace. He told him that since it was a new idea and he was not sure how it would be received. He decided that it was worth a try. Upon agreement he set the date for the first show to be New Year's Eve. He told them both that it was a New Year and time for some new ideas and fun. Hilda just sat there and stared at both of them. The meeting was finished after an hour. They had even included comedy, which was something Wallace had not considered.

Wallace left the hotel knowing where he would be this New Year's Eve. He thought about putting an advertisement in his paper near to the opening time that would give the hotel some coverage for people who did not usually come into town. He would put it in the paper free of charge to Mr. Helfer. As he walked to the print shop he was chuckling about Hilda. He knew she was in for a real surprise. When he got to the shop Miss Holleran, Winston, Alice, and Frank were there. He wondered what had happened. They acted like they were having a meeting. When he sat down Winston told him that the new print machine was on its way. Miss Holleran told him that Alice recorded a profit for the last quarter. She suggested he use the profits to invest in more stock in Eastman Kodak Company. When that was decided Winston said, "You are probably wondering why Frank is here?" Wallace shook his head. Winston told him that he discussed the details with Frank about the old saddlery and buggy shop for their new location. He continued to say that Frank was not going to charge any rent for the space because he was glad to have it used, especially for a family operation. He was happy to be included as the boss of the delivery staff. Winston told him that they would be moving within the next few weeks. Wallace was surprised at all the decisions that were made. At first he was uneasy about Winston approaching his father about the shop and with him being part of the operation. Then he thought that this is exactly what I have wanted Winston to do was to be more assertive and directive. He looked at everyone and agreed that it all sounded great. Everyone except Winston left. Wallace knew they had to go home for dinner but wanted to have some private time with Winston. He told him about the hotel and all that had happened. He wanted to tell Winston how much he appreciated his work in the shop. Wallace came close to him and told him that everyday he feels closer to him and hugged him. They did not discuss the hug but Winston was on fire. They hurried home to have dinner.

Before anyone knew it they had to get the paper ready for delivery. There was so much excitement about the move and the hotel discussions that time was flying. Everyone worked all night to get it ready. They knew the new printing press was going to make the work go faster. Wallace stayed back at the shop until everyone left for his or her routes. After that he took his in-town deliveries to the newsstands. He told the newsstand operators he would be back on Monday to see how many papers were sold. Monday was going to be a busy day for Wallace. He had to finalize some plans with Mr.Helfer. He decided to go into the Arcade Building for something to drink before he made his rounds to the newsstands. He bought some coffee and was sitting at a table in the main hall of the building. There were people coming and going into different shops and offices. He was enjoying his coffee and thinking about the work that needed to be done for the shop and the hotel. While he was looking out at the crowd a young woman came to his table and asked if she could sit down because there were very few seats available. She acted a little shy but that was expected behavior around young men. She smiled and sat down. She asked him his name and he told her. They did not say much for a few minutes. Wallace noticed how nice she seemed to be. She appeared quite sophisticated for a young woman. He wondered where she was from and decided to ask her a few questions. Wallace asked her name and place of residence. She introduced herself as Eveline Lounsberry and told him that her family just moved to Rochester from Canada. They came from Napanee, Ontario Canada that was about 30 miles west of Kingston. Wallace told her that his mother was born in Canada and that his grandmother came to Rochester after his mother was born. Eveline told Wallace that she had just graduated from a private school for young woman in Canada. She told him that it was scary being here not knowing many people. Wallace was surprised at how mature she acted. She portrayed confidence herself that is what he admired in people. She told him about the music and theater events her family attended in Canada. Wallace had not gone to many musical or theater events yet. He felt a little behind in that area. He told her about his printing business and the hotel work. He made sure she understood that he received a scholarship for his college work at Mechanics Institute. She seemed very impressed with his story. She told him that her family was living on Lafayette Place in Rochester, which Wallace made a mental note of and knew where it was. She told him he was a very nice young man. He knew she must have come from a cultured family because he did not know many people who talked about music and theater. He thought about burlesque and knew that probably was not the type of theater Eveline had ever attended. He noticed the crowd thinning and realized that time was slipping away and he had a lot to do. Wallace stood and told Eveline that he really needed to get back to his shop. She looked up at him and told him she really enjoyed speaking with him. Wallace felt the need to tell her that he hoped he might see her again. She informed him that she was usually at the Arcade on Monday because she was hoping to find some work in Rochester.

Chapter 22

THE WEEKLY PAGE INCREASED its readership to include areas closer to town. People wanted more copies for the newsstands in downtown Rochester. Frank had to hire another person to help with the deliveries of papers. Wallace was beginning to be less involved with the operation. He wrote and organized the format for the paper. The new printing press and type sets made the paper easier to get ready every week. The owners of the Rochester Post Express were still interested in combining their paper with the Weekly Page. Wallace did not want to entertain that idea. He knew the offer was always available. Winston was well organized and had become an effective manager. Wallace was pleased with the work he was doing in the shop.

Mr. Helfer was in constant communication with Wallace regarding the hotel's new image. They decided to have new signs made for the hotel with large advertisements for weekly events. They implemented a standardized dress code for the employees. The uniforms would have the emblem for the hotel on each jacket for the men and dresses for the maids. The menus and hotel information were to be printed in the script style to match the hotel's letterheads. An office would organize the entertainment in the hotel and assist guests for out of hotel activities. Mr. Helfer conducted interviews to fill this newly created position. The furniture and newly decorated lobby and entertainment area was nearly complete. The papers in town began their coverage of the hotel after one of the owners had lunch there. Up on arrival he found the restaurant under renovation. He asked what was happening and learned about the plans. The public did not know what the hotel was being turned into. Wallace told Mr. Helfer that he was going to begin a section in his paper featuring articles about the new hotel. He told Mr. Helfer he was not going to divulge all the entertainment ideas yet. He wanted Mr. Helfer's hotel to be first in burlesque, diverse conventions themes and dancing in the ballroom.

Every Monday Wallace would make his trip to the newsstands collecting the revenue from the sales of the newspapers. He thought about the girl that he met at the Arcade Building. He was not sure if he should go back to the Arcade to see her. He liked her style and found her interesting. After going to all the newsstands he stopped for his cup of coffee. She was not there. He was disappointed and wondered who she really was and how true her life's story had been. He thought she was genuine and hoped they could see more of each other. He finished his coffee and left wondering about Eveline. He walked back to his shop and found Winston working on the next week's paper. For some strange reason Wallace wished Winston was not there. He was feeling dejected about not seeing Eveline and wanted time alone. Winston sensed his mood and asked him what was wrong. Wallace ignored him and walked away. Winston asked again and Wallace barked, "None of your damn business." Winston was thoroughly stunned. This was his closest friend turning on him when he was only showing concern. Wallace never acted like that before. Wallace stormed out of the shop without

Winston. He stared at the door feeling totally rejected and confused. This would be the first time in years that they would not have dinner together and share their thoughts and companionship. Feeling as if he was carrying the weight of the world on his shoulders he trudged home to find an inebriated father and suffocating silence that made him feel as though he was abandoned.

Wallace got home as dinner was being served. Alice wondered where Winston was and asked him. Wallace told her that he did not want to talk about anything. Frank sat at the table and discussed what a good day they all had at the shop. Alice told Wallace about the accounts and that Miss Holleran was pleased with business. Frank mentioned what a good job Winston was doing as manager. Wallace said nothing. He kept wondering where Eveline had been today. He had not mentioned her to anyone. Wallace ate in a hurry and decided to go see if he could find out where she said her family was living. He left their apartment on Park Avenue and began walking toward Lafayette Place. He was almost there when he remembered that she had never actually told him the number of the house. Anger overwhelmed him and he kicked the tree that was nearby. It was getting dark outside and turning into a cold November evening. He walked up and down the street in the icy rain wondering why he was so determined to find out more about this woman that he had just met. He forgot to wear a hat because he was in such a rush to leave the house. He had to find out where she lived. By now it was getting late and there was very little light coming from anywhere. He felt like a bum walking the streets so he decided to go home and try to forget about the whole day. When he got home he was drenched and frozen from the rain. He went into his room and took off his wet clothes. Alice came to the door and asked if he was okay. He growled at her to leave him alone. She too had never seen him behave this way.

The Seneca Powers Hotel was in full swing with the advertisements for the newly remodeled hotel. A major part of the advertising was directed at the upcoming New Year's Eve celebration. It was to be an all-inclusive price. There would be two choices. The first was called the Powers Grand Package. This would include an overnight stay, dinner for two people, an exciting new form of entertainment, complete set of favors, and a bottle of champagne at midnight. The second package was the same except there was no hotel room in that package. There would be four choices of dinner in both packages. The drinks would be the responsibility of each guest. Wallace suggested that posters be placed in locations around the city. Wallace made arrangements for them to be placed in the rail station in Buffalo and Syracuse. He thought maybe people might travel by train for the evening. Mr. Helfer was not so sure about all the advertising but thought it might be worth a try. Wallace had been so busy with all the holiday paper advertising and hotel work that he was not so bothered by Eveline now. He had apologized to Winston and told his mother he was having a bad day when all that happened a few weeks ago. He was on his Monday collection routine and decided to make another stop at the Arcade Building. When he walked in there she was at a table. Wallace was not sure what he should do. Just as he was ready to go to speak with her a young man came to her table and sat down. Wallace was shocked and turned around and walked away. He did not want to see anymore. He left the Arcade feeling more miserable than the last time he had been there and not found her. He walked to the hotel where he had the meeting with Mr. Helfer. He was not in any mood to do anything but knew he had to do his job. His work was still important to him. Time was closing in on the grand re-opening of the hotel. He reminded himself that its success was his future. Then he thought of Hilda. How was he going to deal with her? He had no energy to be part of her behavior. He knew she did not like what he represented. Now he represented a miserable young man. She would love seeing him be down and out. He went into the office and there she was. She looked at him and said, "Nice to see you today." Wallace looked at her and nodded his head. Then she said, "You look terrible." Wallace was really in no mood to hear anything from the face woman who in his eyes always looked terrible. He told her that he was not doing so well. Her response was that he better get used to it because he was not getting any younger. She then proceeded to lecture him on how miserable people become as they get older. It was like an epiphany as he sat there thinking that it could not possibly be true for everyone. His attitude miraculously changed. What a huge favor this detestable woman had bestowed upon him. Wallace was certain that not everyone becomes miserable with age. He looked at her and said, "You can have a bad day and feel miserable but not everyone stays that way. Some people work their way out of misery." Hilda sharply replied, "You always have a quick tongue and have to have the last word." Mr. Helfer walked out into the office and said, "You two getting along better." Hilda just looked at Wallace and scowled. Wallace got up from his chair and went into Mr. Helfer's office. The meeting went very well. Wallace was rather glad he spoke up to Hilda because it made him feel better about how to handle his feelings.

The holiday season was at its peak. There were only a few weeks before Christmas and then the New Year's Eve celebration at the hotel. Mr. Helfer informed Wallace that reservations were coming in at a good rate with almost half purchasing the Powers Grand Package. He told Wallace he could have some complimentary tickets for the evening. He thanked him and left the office. Hilda was on her chair watching Wallace leave just twiddling her thumbs. He was not sure if he should kiss her or kick her. He decided not to do any of those things. He left to go on his collection routine at the newsstands. As he got closer to the Arcade Building he decided to take a positive attitude toward the possibilities of getting to know Eveline. He had to move slowly with an open mind. They would be friends first and work everything out from there. He wondered what the strong attraction was that drew him to her. As he walked in to the coffee area, there was Eveline sitting at a table. She saw Wallace and smiled and waved to him. He did not want to appear overly anxious. He strolled over to her table and sat down. She was as nice now as she had been a few weeks ago. He felt relief for this because of all the negative thoughts that had possessed his mind. She told him she missed seeing him and was really glad to see him now. She had been with her cousin all last week who came from Canada to visit her family. He had returned to Canada and now she was still looking for work. Wallace did not dare share with her his desperate search for her house or his thoughts about her. They discussed what they had been doing and what type of work she was looking for. She wanted to be a secretary. Wallace thought about how much better the hotel would be with her instead of Hilda. They enjoyed the conversation and discussions of likes and dislikes. Wallace decided to invite her to the celebration at the hotel. He did not want to miss the opportunity to get to know her better and spend time with her. She said she would ask her parents. He told her where his shop was located and invited her to stop there sometime. She seemed delighted with the invite and agreed to stop by and tell him if she could go to the party. Since it was time for his appointment to see his instructors for the monthly meeting at Mechanics Institute they said their good byes and parted ways.

Wallace finished his meeting at school and hurried as fast as he could to tell Winston about Eveline. He got to the shop to find Alice and Frank there with Winston. He explained to them all about his actions the past few weeks. He went on to tell them about Eveline and how they had met and how he had hoped to see her again. When that did not happen he went out that night looking for her home. When he saw her with another guy the next day he was really upset but today found out that the man had been her cousin. Alice thought he was lovesick but Frank thought it was childish. Winston just stood there staring at Wallace not understanding his excitement.

Chapter 23

THE FINAL PREPARATIONS WERE underway at the Seneca Powers Hotel. The employees were doing last minute cleaning and organizing for the grand opening to be held on New Year's Eve. Wallace had spent many hours with Mr. Helfer with last minute details for the evening. There had been multiple advertisements in local newspapers about the December 31, 1902 celebration. The night was featuring an evening of fabulous dining, cocktails and exhilarating entertainment. The shows presentations included multiple performers decked in colorful costumes with lush sets and mood-appropriate music. There would be an orchestra for dancing between the shows. People around town were curious about the renovations to the hotel. The hard work of promoting the evening was working. According to Mr. Helfer only a few tickets were not sold which he decided to have available at the door for last minute sales. It was sure to be a full house.

Wallace was looking forward to the evening since Eveline's parents had agreed to allow her to go to the party as long as Frank and Alice would be there. Wallace invited Winston to the party. They would be at the same table with Mr. Helfer and Hilda. The tables were set for eight people. Since there was one seat left Wallace decided to invite Miss Holleran. He got one of the last tickets and took it to her house. She was delighted to be included and told Wallace that she did not usually do anything on the last day of the year. Her philosophy was that you do not have a party at the end of every month so why on December 31st? She said she would break her philosophy just this time and winked at him. He was delighted that she was coming. He thought they would all have a great time. As he was leaving Miss Holleran's house she told him that she read that George Eastman had donated $60,000 to the University of Rochester. She told him that the money was to be used to build laboratories for research. It was the first gift to the university from George Eastman. Wallace thought that was a good sign and that the company must be doing well. He was happy to hear that because he was investing money from the Weekly Page into the Eastman Kodak Company. She assured him, as she had many times, that he was well on his way to being a wealthy man. Wallace left feeling like 1903 was going to be good year. While he was walking home he thought of all the things that were going on in his life. He had a successful newspaper business and had been hired to be the advertising agent at the hotel. He had a friend that he felt a close emotional attachment to but was not sure why. Then he thought of his new friend Eveline and wondered if they would become better friends.

Tomorrow was the grand opening of the hotel. Wallace had to meet with Mr. Helfer before the festivities were to begin. He stopped at the printing shop to make sure the paper was ready for the New Year's issue. Wallace wanted to have a section reserved for the hotel and the party. When he walked into the shop Winston was the only person there. Wallace asked him how he was and if he was excited about going to the party. Winston hesitated and looked away when Wallace asked him about the evening. In a sullen voice he told Wallace that he was glad to be invited. Wallace thought this was a strange response from him. They had spent many New Year's Eves together. Winston was always happy to go to events with him. Wallace did not have the time to dwell on this subject so he started toward the door yelling to Winston that he would see him at the party and then left. He walked out of the shop and Winston never looked at him or said anything.

He felt puzzled that Winston was acting so strangely. He wondered if he had offended him in some way. He knew he was the last person he would want to hurt. He made up his mind to make it a priority to deal with Winston after the New Year. He walked into the office and of course Hilda was in her spot. He found himself doing the same thing with her each time. He looked straight at her chest and not her face. He was fascinated with all that cleavage. Hilda of course stared at him knowing what he was doing and said to him sarcastically, "I'm up here." This startled Wallace into saying, "Sorry, my mind was elsewhere." She just looked at him and rolled her eyes. Wallace sat down and began thinking about tomorrow with her in close proximity all evening. Mr. Helfer walked in and saw the two of them sitting quietly. He looked at Hilda first and then Wallace and said, "I've never seen such serenity in this office." Yes, the lull before the storm with her around, Wallace thought. They all went into the office to discuss the final details of the upcoming evening. The food and drinks were all in order and the wait staff was instructed on how to proceed with the evening. The last item was the entertainment. Wallace explained that he found an orchestra that would be playing Ragtime music during dinner and between the shows. There was enough space now for dancing since the shows would be on the new stage. Mr. Helfer was pleased that it had all worked out.

Mr. Helfer wanted was a better explanation of the live entertainment. He knew from earlier meetings that it was called burlesque but was not sure what that was going to be like. Wallace proceeded to tell him that there were to be shows with a variety of characters doing comedy, dancing, and strip tease. Hilda started to laugh uproariously and finally managed to ask, "Are we all supposed to take our clothes off?" Mr. Helfer looked at her and joined in her laughter. Wallace stared at her and visualized the theater blowing apart if she took off her brassiere and if those big bombs were hitting everything. They would surely damage something. She stopped laughing and became very quiet. Wallace thought that everywhere he had been today everyone turned quiet. He wondered for a second what was going on. Winston had been acting so strangely while he was there and now Hilda. He was beginning to think people were going mad. He continued with his description of the shows. There were to be three shows. He tried to explain that burlesque was comedy making a mockery of the wealthy. Mr. Helfer looked stunned when he mentioned this. Wallace assured him that the audience would end up laughing at themselves. Hilda spoke up and said in a fun little voice, "Everything seems funny after a few good drinks." Mr. Helfer looked at her and then Wallace and said, "There must be a live wire in here." Hilda just smiled and looked at Wallace. This convinced him that everyone was going mad. Wallace rose from his chair saying his good byes. He told them that he would see them tomorrow evening and assured Mr. Helfer not to worry. Both Hilda and Mr. Helfer smiled and said, "Oh, we are not worried." Their tone of voice was a little hesitant.

Everyone was getting ready for the party. Alice and Frank dressed in their church clothes since they did not go out very much and all they had was one outfit. Wallace spent some of his money and bought a new bow tie, leather gloves, and a new hat. He bought comfortable shoes for the evening because he was sure he would be dancing with Eveline. He decided that his suit was fine for the evening. Winston got ready at Wallace's. He felt like he lived there because he was spending less and less time with his father and more time with Wallace's family. They made him feel like he belonged there. They were both in the bedroom getting ready to go to the party and began talking about how things were and what might happen in the future. Wallace asked Winston what he thought of Eveline because he really liked her and thought that they might get to be good friends. Looking in the mirror Winston said he was afraid of Wallace becoming too involved with her. Wallace smiled at him and said, "Who knows we could even get married someday." Winston had held his emotions in check for too long and finally admitted to him that he was jealous of her. Wallace looked up from tying a shoe and laughed telling him that he was crazy. Winston looked at him with a frown turning his back. It was then that Wallace realized that they both had the same feelings for each other. This was one more thing for him to work on. What kinds of feelings were they and how deep did they go? Wallace knew then that Winston was acting on instinct rather than logic. They were finally ready to go and they looked great. Patting Winston on the back Wallace joked with him telling him that he really cleaned up well. He still had his dark beard and lots of hair but he really looked great to him. Wallace had even trimmed his moustache and waxed it to points. They were sure to have a great new year.

Mr. and Mrs. Lounsberry arrived with Eveline at 6PM. Everyone introduced themselves since this was the first time anyone had met. It was clear to Wallace that his parents were not of the same class as Eveline's parents. They were more refined, which explained Eveline's cultured appearance. Even though there was this division everyone was cordial to one another. Alice made sure to make Mrs. Lounsberry comfortable with arrangements for the evening explaining that they would make sure Eveline was home shortly after midnight. After some idle chitchat Wallace announced that he should really be getting to the hotel. He did not want to arrive late since he was the one who had organized and planned the whole affair. They laughed and agreed that it was time to go. Eveline thanked her mother and father for allowing her to go to such a grand event. Wallace had not thought of it that way but felt proud to have been in charge of the origin and completion of the grand evening ahead. Frank had arranged for one of his special broughams to transport them to the hotel. It was the plushest one still available in Rochester. Everyone was happy to go in the brougham because it was very cold outside. Winston climbed in and Wallace assisted Eveline in and followed sitting in the middle of the two. Frank and Alice sat across from them. They made one stop for Miss Holleran who got into the carriage and sat down. "Who have we here?" she asked looking at Eveline. Wallace introduced her to Eveline as a friend. Winston mumbled under his breath, "Isn't that nice." Miss Holleran looked at the three of them across from her and announced, "Everyday I seem to be more and more confused about you two boys." She seemed to have infinite wisdom into the situation and its future outcome. The atmosphere in the carriage was jovial and full of electricity in anticipation of the extraordinary evening ahead and everyone just smiled.

The brougham pulled up to the front of the hotel. As they walked into the lobby people were heard commenting on how lovely the hotel looked and how classy it looked. One woman was overheard saying that it was no longer a commoner's hotel.

Mr. Helfer and Hilda were waiting inside for Wallace's group to arrive. They departed the buggy greeting one another with everyone a buzz about the new look of the hotel. Hilda looked so much different tonight than during the day in the office. She actually was dressed so that her body parts were not the first thing you noticed. Wallace thought that she must have strapped them in somehow. She wore a suit and a blouse with a slight ruffle in the front. She had on a pair of shoes that sure looked like she was ready to dance. She continued to be a fascination to Wallace because of her varied moods and actions. Mr. Helfer was dressed in his usual attire with nothing much different from his daily office outfits. People stood around becoming acquainted with new people and greeting old friends that they had not seen for a while. Wallace started getting anxious because he wanted to get into the real part of the hotel. He felt a sense of excitement thinking about the food and entertainment. He turned to Eveline and asked her how she was doing. She smiled, commenting that she enjoyed places like this and was really excited for the evening to begin. The thought that she probably went to places like this all the time in Canada crossed Wallace's mind. Mr. Helfer approached Wallace and told him that their group was to be the first to enter the theater. He had reserved a front table near to the orchestra and stage. He told him he wanted to get a bird's eye view of the show. Wallace thought to himself, you are going to get more than that. He just smiled at Hilda and Mr. Helfer. They went into the theater and the tables were decorated with large floral arrangements. Mingled in the arrangements were noisemakers and hats to be used at midnight. Hilda was proud to announce that she ordered the arrangements for each table. Wallace looked at her and said, "Looks great Hilda." She looked at him and replied, "You ain't seen nothing yet boy." He hated the word boy, which she loved to call him but he chose to ignore her. On the way to the table Wallace noticed that Miss Holleran was looking pretty good herself. Winston jokingly asked if she dressed up like that to get a man tonight. She laughed in a sarcastic way and told him men were only good for one thing and that was to be worker bees. Winston pulled out her chair and as she sat down she looked at everyone and said that she preferred woman to men. This brought conversation to a halt as everyone looked at her and said nothing. Wallace spoke up to break the shocked silence to say he had always wondered about that when she had been a teacher because she never mentioned men at all. Miss Holleran smiled in her funny little way and told everyone that Wallace was always very perceptive. After a short while the conversation revolved around to how good the drinks were. Hilda reminded everyone that things are funnier after a few good drinks. She had just ordered her second one. Wallace told everyone that they needed to remember the names of the drinks they were having. They looked at one another and asked why. He leaned over and informed them in a whispered voice that one of the shows had names of cocktails in it. Hilda piped up and chimed in that she might have to have more than two. The anticipation was evident to everyone at the table as they sat there wondering what this enchanted evening held in store for each of them.

The cocktails started arriving to the tables in twos. Winston ordered a "dirty man martini", thinking it was hilarious. Glancing around the table at everyone he said that a dirty man was one of his favorite things. Wallace just looked at him and smiled with Miss Holleran catching this look and saying "Really." Wallace ordered a drink called a "top banana"; it was a drink with banana liqueur and rum in it. When he told everyone the name Winston spoke up and said, "He's not lying." Everyone laughed except Eveline. She sat quietly sipping her glass of wine. Since she was only 17, her mother had given her permission to have one drink. Wallace glanced over at her and wondered what she must think about all the revealing conversations at the table.

The dinner was being served in five courses. An onion soup was the first course that everyone enjoyed. An intermezzo was served next which was a rainbow sherbet that was perfect for the occasion. Winston was being either his comical or simple self and asked if they were at a concert when he heard the word intermezzo. Wallace glared at him across the table. He remembered Eveline telling him how her family went to concerts and musical events in Canada. Eveline turned to Winston and told everyone that when she was a little girl she thought that was a part of a concert too. Winston was surprised and relieved that someone else thought the same way. Winston turned his head and Eveline winked at Wallace as if to say she was trying to save him from looking like a fool. The salad arrived after the sherbet with a large piece of green leaves and little bits and pieces of salad fixings. Frank looked at his plate and said he wondered if they were all going on a diet in 1903. Everyone laughed politely but appreciated the style of the presentation. Alice said very little during the meal seeming preoccupied with something. Wallace asked if she was all right and she said she was thinking about her family and how they had lived in Canada. Her mother went back to Canada where she died shortly after being with them in Rochester. Only Frank knew the story of Alice's mother and the behaviors she exhibited while living in Rochester. Alice still had not gotten over her mother's hatred for her and Wallace. She wanted to know more about her father too. Glancing at Eveline reminded her of herself when she was that age and the fact that she was born in Canada and had been a fine young woman also. She wondered if she would ever know the true story about her father.

The dishes were cleared from the table and soon the aroma of the main courses filled the air. The main course was very plentiful with choices of beef, pork, fish, or chicken. All were equally appetizing. Mr. Helfer explained how difficult the process was to find a chef that could cook so many different types of food. While they were eating the main course Frank jokingly said that the diet did not last very long. The quantity was more like he was used to eating. Everyone was enjoying their lavish meal and there was not much said about that remark. The orchestra was beginning to play music. Mr. Helfer raised his glass and made a toast to Wallace for his young progressive ideas for the Seneca Powers Hotel. Everyone joined in and agreed that it was beautifully done. The table was cleared of the main dish as the dessert arrived. It was a pound cake drizzled with a liqueur of your choice. It was very simple but classy. Eveline told everyone that she liked simple and classy. Winston stared at her and wondered if she was referring to him. Wallace was so busy watching all the action and people that he barely knew what was happening at their table. It was at that moment that Wallace sensed the difference between his family and rest of the people at the table. This made him uncomfortable to realize how he was so different from them. He knew he was on a road to much success with many adventures in his future but they had gone as far as they could go. He felt sorry for them but knew they were what they were and he accepted it.

The wait staff was very efficient in the clearing of the tables. Every table was cleared and new glasses and small candies were placed at every table. Hilda was again very certain to let everyone know that was another of her ideas. Wallace kept looking at her trying to figure out why she needed to be so outspoken about what she did for the evening. Everyone agreed that it was a nice idea as she soaked up the attention. Winston kept watching Wallace study the entire atmosphere. It was almost as if he was taking a mental picture of the entire room. Winston could not help but ask him what he was looking at. Wallace explained to him that he wanted to make sure that all the details had been attended to. Winston looked at him impatiently and told him he was too fussy. Wallace told him he could never be fussy enough. Eveline overheard the remarks and asked how long they had known each other. They looked at one another and said at the same time, "Since high school." She chuckled and said loud enough for everyone to hear that they acted like an old married couple. Laughter erupted around the table. Winston smiled and remarked that he would love to be married to someone like that. There was very little conversation after that.

The music began to change to more lively arrangements with syncopated ragtime music using a piano and the orchestra. The first song was one that most people were familiar with. The dance was called the cakewalk. You and your partner would move around the floor in various directions. Almost everyone got up from their seats to try dancing around without bumping into each other. If you bumped into someone you had to sit down. The last couple on the dance floor won a cake. Mr. Helfer walked over to Hilda and asked her to dance the cakewalk. Standing up she agreed and told him in a joking way that it would be a piece of cake. How corny could she get thought Wallace. He turned and asked Eveline if she would like to give the dance a try. She accepted and Wallace escorted her to the dance floor. Winston did not feel like dancing so he stayed at the table and watched everyone attempt this dance. It was not as easy as everyone thought it would be. You had to try to avoid touching other dancers and the floor was quite crowded. To cause a little disruption Wallace deliberately maneuvered Eveline around toward Hilda. She was all over the place with Mr. Helfer that she was an easy target to bump into. Mr. Helfer saw them coming and turned Hilda so she could not see Wallace and Eveline approaching them. Hilda backed into Wallace's backside. She turned and smiled at first but then saw who it was she gave one of her faces to Wallace. He laughed and said, "Fooled you." She and Mr. Helfer had to sit down. Winston had witnessed the whole incident and when they went back to the table Winston was still laughing at how funny it looked. As Hilda sat down he told her that her behind must have still been shaking. She was not nearly as amused as others were while she ordered her third drink. Everyone hoped that maybe this drink would help her have more fun. The dance was finished and everyone sat down. Most people were laughing and enjoying the evening. Miss Holleran sat at the table and finally asked Winston if he liked to dance. He glanced down at the table and told her that he thought he was too clumsy. When she did not reply he looked up at her and told her he might give it a try before the night was over.

It was about 10 o'clock and the new show was scheduled to begin. The curtain opened and there was a sign that read "A Burlesque Show." There were people dressed in gorgeous colored outfits. The woman had on shoes that were higher than anything a woman would dare to wear. They danced around the stage to lively music. They waved ribbons and scarves of different colors. As they wiggled and danced around the stage they drew the scarves through their legs ever so slowly. The men in the audience went wild. The women were not as excited by the display of maneuvers of the scarves and ribbons. One of the burlesquers was called Miss Lemon Drop. She had small yellow candies hanging from her breasts and some hanging around her waist barely covering the necessary areas. Wallace laughed when she came out in nearly nothing for clothing. Alice asked if she might be cold. Miss Holleran was so enthralled by Miss Lemon Drop that she told Alice that she hoped she took it all off. Alice said nothing and Frank agreed with Miss Holleran. Alice suddenly became quiet. As Miss Lemon Drop swung her way around the stage to the music her lemon drops began to go in opposite rotating circles. The men in the audience began to roar and chant. They would clap and yell for more. Miss Lemon Drop was a big hit for the opening number. Mr. Helfer just sat in his chair with a flushed face. Hilda asked him if he wanted more to drink. She told him that the show is only going to get better. After Miss Lemon Drop finished her performance the "Top Banana" appeared on the stage. He was the one who was considered the "ringleader" for the show. When he announced himself as "Top Banana," Winston told everyone that was Wallace's favorite character. He made sure that everyone knew Wallace liked being the top banana. He continued to tell everyone that Wallace really showed that he was top banana when they were in Buffalo at the Exposition. Wallace looked shocked when he said that. Eveline looked at Wallace and asked what that meant. Everyone else sat there waiting for an answer of some sort. Wallace said that Winston must have meant that he had organized the two days and all that they did when in Buffalo. Winston then piped up and added that was true but when they stayed in the guesthouse together he really showed his top banana. A few people cleared their throats but Miss Holleran said, "That's my boy." Wallace was so taken back by all the discussion about Buffalo that he did not even care if she referred to him as boy.

The Top Banana introduced the next part of the show. He explained that burlesque was a type of variety show characterized by comedy, dancing and strip tease. The men in the audience went wild again with the mere mention of strip tease. The women appeared disgusted and angry that their men were behaving so poorly. Winston told everyone at the table that they might not live to see 1903. The drinks were being served as fast as the waiters could bring them to the tables. Mr. Helfer whispered to Hilda that these people were really spending money tonight. She sneered at him and asked how many of these men were going to live to talk about the New Year. When the Top Banana finished introducing the second act, out came the jugglers. They were men dressed in tights that outlined all the necessary parts a woman might like to see. It turned into a comedy when they were juggling money. The Top Banana announced as they juggled money this is what the rich people do. The audience began laughing and the Top Banana said, "I told you that you would laugh at yourselves." The audience laughed harder as the money flew away. Frank spoke up and said, "It may be funny now but it was not funny a few years ago." Alice called him a stick in the mud. Before you knew it everyone did realize how much fun laughing at yourself could be. Eveline just sat in her chair saying very little and smiling politely. After all that had happened tonight, Wallace wondered if she would ever go out with him again.

After the jugglers finished there was a short intermission. People were able to dance and mingle with one another. Comments were heard about how good the show was. Most of the men were having a good time. The women were not as happy with the show as the men. Wallace assured people when he spoke with them that everyone would have a chance to enjoy themselves. Some of the women wanted to know how in the world that was going to happen. Mr. Helfer had a chance to find out if people liked the hotel and the evening as he visited with different tables. The opinions varied at that point in the evening. He was beginning to wonder if it was all worth the effort and money they had invested in it. When he returned to his table he told Hilda what he had learned and she told him that she had told him so. He did not want to hear that from her but he did have to consider that she was on her fourth drink.

The show was about to begin again. There was a rush for another beverage, as people got ready for what may happen next. The men in the tights lined up on the side of the stage. Winston heard a woman at the next table say, "I wish my husband had that much to show." Another woman said, "I want to see more." Winston winked at Wallace and said that he would too. Wallace smiled. From the back of the theater a procession of gaily-dressed people paraded toward the stage. Hilda piped up and said, "We are being overtaken by more scantily clad people." The men were cheering and the women quiet. Miss Lemon Drop introduced them as Boom Boom, Fanny Tastic, Tanguray Twist, Dirty Martini and Trixie Will Do. Wallace was happy to remind everyone that now was the drink performance. Winston told everyone that he liked the dirty man martini better than the lady version. No one responded to him even though he thought it was pretty funny. The Top Banana appeared with a list of drinks that were available in the hotel for this evening's event. He had a hat with all the names of the men in the theater. He was going to pick names out of the hat. If your name was chosen you could go with the drink you really wanted to try. The crowd went crazy. All the men were yelling at the drink they wanted. The women thought that they only wanted the size of the breasts not the drink. He chose a man in the back. The gentleman came up and stood next to Miss Lemon Drop. Winston's name was drawn and he went to Dirty Martini. Mr. Helfer was called and went to Boom Boom. When Hilda told everyone he chose her because she reminds him of her they all laughed. An old man had his name called and he chose Trixie Will Do. Frank wondered out loud if that might be his last chance and Alice glared at him until she realized it was pretty funny. A middle aged man was called next and he chose Tangueray Twist. He told her that he loved a twist. When she told him he would get a good one the audience laughed out of control. Wallace spoke up and told people around him that audience participation was a great way for people to have fun. From the next table a woman answered him saying, "Yes if you are not the one chosen." When the last name was to be chosen everyone was quiet. The final name was Wallace's and he had no choice but to take Fanny Tastic. Eveline burst out laughing when he went up to the front and Fanny Tastic reached out to greet him. Hilda also laughed saying, "That's not all he's got." Alice looked at her and gave her a disgusted stare. Winston yelled out to the audience when Wallace went to Fanny Tastic saying, "He sure does." Everyone cheered and laughed when Wallace raised his hands like a champ in a boxing ring. Miss Holleran sat in her chair and just shook her head. Hilda asked everyone that was left at the table if they thought they were at a circus. Finally, the audience calmed down and the men chosen were to get their drinks served to them by their girl. As they were enjoying the drink the ladies would entertain them. Most of the ladies used their tassel twirling talents to its best advantage. At one point all the tassels were twirling in the men's faces as they were sipping their drinks. It was very close contact. The women in the audience were hysterical and clapping. Many women were heard telling others that some of those men will never get that again. The music was playing to the speed of the swinging and gyrating entertainers. No notice was taken to Miss Holleran when she spoke up saying, "I wish I were one of those men up there." She just shook her head. The drinks went down very slowly for the men on the stage. The ladies finally slowed down and the act was finished. Hilda wondered why they were referred to as ladies. All the women laughed and exclaimed with emphasis, "Some ladies."

It was nearly 11PM and there was another hour before the New Year. There was time again for dancing and conversation. The attitude toward the evening was beginning to change. The women rather liked the men in the tights and the men liked the tasseled ladies. The last part of the show was about to start. They were asking what was going to happen next. This time a new character appeared named Miss Knockers. She admitted that she did not have to justify her name and that all you had to do was look at her. The men in tights surrounded her. She worked her way around them feeling for the right size and what she termed as the right fit. Now the women were cheering and clapping. The men were not so happy seeing the women so aroused by the men in tights. Winston admitted to everyone that this might be the best part of the show. Hilda glanced over to him and told him that he had his chance and now it was her turn. Wallace wondered what she would do to the poor guy she got a hold of. In a flash out came Mr. Big Manhattan with a big hat and wearing a loincloth. The women were screaming. Eveline started clapping and cheering right along with everyone else in the crowd. Hilda started fanning herself exclaiming that it was getting hot in there now. Miss Holleran did not appear interested in what was going on. Frank was staring at the women in amazement and Alice did not dare admit to anything just yet. Next was Mr. Horseman who was wearing a headpiece designed like the mane of a horse. He had on a type of pouch that hung half way to his knees. Winston nearly jumped out of his seat. Wallace was enjoying all the anatomy being shown tonight by both men and women. The last man to come out was Mr. Buns. He walked out on the stage and turned to the audience and displayed how the muscles in his buttocks could work.

The sounds coming from the audience were so loud and boisterous that Mr. Helfer was afraid of being raided by the police. Hilda told him to be quiet and let her enjoy herself for a change. She told him that it was too late to worry about anything now. The women's names would be chosen from a hat and the men would entertain them. Some women did not think it was proper to be seen up on stage doing things like that. Hilda was hoping to get chosen so she could have all the men to herself. Wallace glanced over at a very rowdy Hilda and was surprised with how much fun she was having. He thought this was probably the first time she had seen anything so entertaining. Winston was staring at all the performers saying he wanted to take them all home. Frank seemed astonished by everyone's behavior. Alice finally admitted to everyone at the table that she wanted Mr. Buns because she was impressed with his co-ordination. Frank looked at her shocked and asked her what was wrong with his co-ordination. She quickly told him that he did not hold a candle to the moves that guy was making. Everyone at the table burst into loud laughter at that remark. Across the table Hilda ordered her fifth drink. She had been right about anything after two drinks getting funnier and better. Winston looked at Wallace and said, "She's going to be a mess in the morning."

Top Banana came out wearing a yellow hat and yellow banana style cover for his appendage. Winston yelled out that he knew someone just like that with Miss Holleran saying, "There are no more secrets after tonight." Much to Wallace's surprise Eveline said, "I'm really beginning to like this group." He took this opportunity to ask her if she would ever consider seeing him again. She looked at him surprised that he would even ask and told him that she was certain she wanted to go out again. The first woman called to the stage was an old lady. She slowly made her way to the stage with the assistance of her red-faced companion. When she finally got there she stood eyeing each specimen up and down and finally chose Mr. Manhattan. She admitted that this was her choice because she had always enjoyed that drink. As she told Mr. Manhattan that she wanted a big one from him the crowd cheered. She looked out at the crowd and announced that this may very well be her last and turned to Mr. Manhattan and asked him if she could wipe her mouth on his loincloth when she was finished? Screaming laughter rocked the hall. The second lady chosen was Alice. She stood up and looked at Frank saying, "I may never come home." As she headed toward the stage she could hear the laughter behind her. She climbed the steps and without hesitation went right to Mr. Buns. She made no bones about why she wanted him. She brazenly told him she needed lessons to train her husband to have such co-ordination. Sitting at their table Wallace mentioned to Winston that he was shocked because he had never seen his mother behave this way. Winston glanced over at him and told him he was jealous. He agreed that he was probably right. Miss Holleran just smiled at the two guys and their conversation. Hilda was sitting on the edge of her chair waiting for the next name to be drawn. The third name was a woman who had just been married. She was a little shy about going up to the stage but her husband encouraged her to go. Winston leaned over and whispered to Wallace that he probably wished it were him going up there instead of her. She went up on the stage and chose Mr. Horseman. She looked out at the audience and quietly told them that he reminded her of her new husband. This motivated the women in the audience to start yelling, "Lucky girl." Winston chimed in,

"She is really lucky." By this time Hilda started getting miserable because she figured her chance at any man up there was over. She sat in her chair much like she did at work. Wallace saw the return of the face woman. Just then a voice from the stage called out her name. She jumped up and ran to the stage taking the steps two at a time and throwing herself at him said, "Take me Top Banana, I'm yours." She was so excited she started dancing around Top Banana gyrating herself at him. Wide-eyed Wallace said to Mr. Helfer, "Have you ever seen her like this before?" Just as wide-eyed, he did not answer and only gave a shrug of embarrassment. Each woman was given a drink of her choice. While they drank it their man would dance around them and assist them in any way they could. The old lady with the Manhattan had him serve it to her and she continually wiped her mouth on his loincloth. Every time she wiped her mouth something jumped at her face. The audience went crazy. Hilda was trying to taste the banana. She was on her knees but the banana kept moving. Mr. Helfer was shocked that a woman her age could turn into such a mess in public. Wallace reminded him that she was acting like all the people she criticized most. Mr. Helfer did not say a word. The newly wed woman was the calmest of them all. All she did was to pretend to ride him like a horse. She kept saying, "hee haw ride." Her husband seemed embarrassed but Frank thought that he was one lucky man. The whole scene disgusted Miss Holleran. Alice finally had her chance to let it all out as she worked on the co-ordination part very well. She was able to feel the multiple muscular movements a number of times. He even gave her instructions in various positions. She looked out into the audience yelling out to Frank, "Don't wait up for me tonight." Everyone laughed out of control. Wallace did not know if his mother would ever be the same again. Eveline had a great time and told Wallace that her family would never act this way but she really liked it. Wallace just shook his head in amazement.

Winston was watching all the action on the stage and remarked about how those women were such a mess on the stage and all over a few men. Eveline quickly reminded him that he would be a mess up there too if given the chance. Wallace laughed and agreed with her. The women were finally appeased and appeared very tired as they headed back to their seats. Hilda nearly crawled back with her blouse half open and her hair a total mess. Mr. Helfer stared at her and asked her if she was okay. Looking him up and down she said, "Never better." Alice approached Frank and informed him that she had some new moves for him when they got home. Wallace laughed and asked Winston if they dared go home with them. Miss Holleran piped up and said, "You two have made your own moves." Eveline laughed and asked when the next party was going to be.

The clock struck midnight and it was Thursday, January 1, 1903. The champagne was uncorked and everyone celebrated the New Year. The people who were at the celebration party thought that it was the best they had ever been to. There was no other place in town that had anything quite like the Seneca Powers Hotel. The grand re-opening had been a huge success. Many patrons wondered what the hotel was going to do to top this night. Mr. Helfer looked at Wallace excitedly and said, "When's our next meeting?" They agreed to get together early in January.

Chapter 24

One of Wallace's first projects of the New Year was to begin planning the next event for the hotel. The reviews and coverage of the re-opening of the Seneca Powers Hotel had been overwhelmingly positive. Wallace knew that they had to maintain that momentum for the next event. He stopped by the hotel to make an appointment with Mr. Helfer. When he walked in to the office only Mr. Helfer was there and he asked him where Hilda was. Mr. Helfer told Wallace that she needed a few days off after all the fun she had at the New Year's Eve party. Wallace laughed and told him that she probably was still trying to get in touch with her man from the stage. They both laughed and agreed that Hilda was in very high spirits that night. Mr. Helfer ended that conversation by telling Wallace that she had too many spirits and needed to work on better control of herself. He agreed and they began to discuss the next major undertaking for the hotel.

Wallace explained some of the exhibits he had seen at the Pan-American Exposition. He thought that Rochester might be ready for a convention that would focus on the latest invention for modern living. Mr. Helfer agreed and they discussed what that convention might include and how they would proceed. Wallace gave him some examples of things that were in the Electric Building. He told him about the impact electricity was having on current life.

He explained about the telephone that Buffalo Bell had on display and how they showed it in operation. The automobile was another area that could be part of the convention. Wallace told Mr. Helfer that he was going to write an article for his Weekly Page that would focus on the future of the automobile. Wallace talked about the production of food and new methods for preserving food. Wallace was trying to design the convention as a smaller version of the Exposition. He thought that spring would be a good time for the convention as a rebirth of knowledge and energy for the new season. Mr. Helfer agreed that spring was always a good time of year for things that had to do with the home and outdoor activities. They set the date for mid May. Mr. Helfer explained that his office would take directions from Wallace on how to schedule the various people and companies for the convention. The hotel manager would be in charge of the staff and have the advertisements prepared. Wallace told him that he would have the title and the graphics for the event ready in a week. He suggested that the hotel offer complimentary accommodations for the weekend to those who were bringing displays for the show. He thought a flower show would make the event very welcoming and colorful and add a touch of class to the event. There could be areas for garden designs and techniques for growing a perfect garden. He told Mr. Helfer that he would form a committee with some of his associates for the decorations and flower displays. Wallace suggested that they meet with the restaurants and chefs in the hotel to co-ordinate food displays and menus that would be a part of the weekend. Mr. Helfer made sure his list of responsibilities was complete before Wallace left the meeting. He told Wallace that it was strange not having Hilda around to organize his notes and that he felt like he was Wallace's secretary today. They both laughed and agreed that no one could take Hilda's place.

Wallace went to school to meet with his advisors after his meeting with Mr. Helfer. It was his last year in college and graduation was coming soon. They asked him how his projects were coming and if he needed any help on matters at hand. Wallace told them about his success with the hotel. He talked about his newspaper and how it had relocated to a new location that offered more space. They were delighted with the information about the new printing press. As part of Wallace's final report his advisors told Wallace that they were going to make an appointment to visit the areas that he had been working on. Wallace felt like he was being put on the spot. They told him that they had heard so many positive things about his work around town that they were intrigued and wanted to see for themselves what was really happening. They assured him that his final grade was not in jeopardy. That statement made Wallace less tense. He wanted to finish his four years with the highest grade he could receive. One of his advisors laughed and said, "Don't worry, Louise has kept us very well informed." Wallace looked puzzled and asked, "Who is Louise?" "Oh that would be Louise Holleran, she's my best friend." Wallace was shocked but asked the woman, "How long have you known her?" The woman told him that they had shared an apartment for many years. Wallace looked at her and smiled but in his mind he was trying to figure out Miss Holleran. He wondered why her life was such a secret and why he was not told about her keeping track of him outside of school. The advisory group finished their meeting with Wallace and they thanked him and reminded him that their next meeting was going on a tour of his accomplishments.

While Wallace was walking down Main Street he began to think about the meeting. For the first time he felt like he was reaching the end of many endeavors. He never thought these projects that all started as a class project would turn into so much. He knew that there were many people who had helped and encouraged him along the way. He still wanted to know why Miss Holleran behaved the way she did for so many years. He thought he knew her but now after that meeting he wondered what the secret was. He began to think about the tour with his advisors and how that would be. He was so busy thinking about everything that he did not even see Eveline walk right up to him. She stopped and cleared her throat. Wallace snapped out of his trance and smiled and said hello. He was really glad to see her. He asked how she was and what she had been doing and she told him that she was on her way to an interview for a stenographer at the Seneca Arcade Building. He smiled and said that he would never forget that place because that it was where they met. She told him she was nervous and hoped that she made a good impression so they would hire her. Wallace told her not to worry and that she would do very well. She said that she needed to be there in ten minutes so he wished her luck and went on his way. He had to get the advertisements ready for the hotel. The paper was ready for print except his article about Henry Ford who was trying to raise money for his automobile company.

Winston was working on the final printing details at the shop when Wallace walked in. He told Winston about all the things that happened during the day. Winston told him that all he had done today was to be at the shop getting his work done. Wallace explained about the tours with his advisors, Miss Holleran's part in his college affairs, and the hotel advertisements that needed to be designed. He told Winston about meeting Eveline and Winston said, "I thought you were over her." Wallace glared at him and said, "You are hoping I would stop thinking about her." Winston looked at him and said he was right. He then admitted to Wallace that he had feelings for him and that he did not want to have to share them with her. Wallace looked at him and asked him, "What kind of feelings?" Winston told him to think back to the night they stayed in Buffalo. Wallace looked at him and rolled his eyes upward and went about his business in the shop. Wallace kept trying to convince himself that Winston was just trying to complicate his life. Every time he thought he had it reasoned out he kept remembering how the night in Buffalo had been. Secretly he was trying to figure out how he could make that happen again. He already knew how Winston felt about him. How could he have two people in his life that he felt something for? He shook his head and added that to all the other things he had on his mind. Right now he had to write the article about Henry Ford. He sat down and began to write about the new form of transportation in the country. He explained that Henry Ford had a vision to develop a company that would make a buggy that would have energy from a gas driven motor instead of a horse. There had been some mention of that form of transportation but Ford was trying to raise $28,000.00 to begin the Ford Motor Company. He explained that Ford invented a system that would move the product through a line that would speed up the production of the car. He concluded his article with the idea that this was only the beginning of greater things to come. He asked people to consider being a part of the new company by donating funds. The money would be considered a share or stock as part of the company. In essence they would be a supporter and stockholder to the Ford Motor Company. He put the type together and Winston prepared it for printing. He did not say much to Wallace while they were finishing the paper. When it was being printed they went to their separate offices. The day had been long and tiring.

After dinner Wallace asked his mother if she knew anything about Miss Holleran. She looked at him with a puzzled frown. He told her that Miss Holleran's name was Louise and that she knew a woman on his advisory board. He told her that they had been sharing the same apartment for many years. Alice did not act surprised when he told her all those things. He wanted to know if she knew more about her and why it was such a secret. Alice stopped washing the dinner dishes and looked at Wallace. She told him that both women agreed to stay quiet about their lives. They wanted to give him all the time and space he needed to develop his skills and talents. She told Wallace that Miss Holleran had fond feelings for the professor. Alice told him that if he knew all the information about her and the advisor he might have acted differently. No one wanted to get in the way of his wonderful talents. She explained to Wallace more about how her mother treated her and how she died. Wallace stood there and looked at his mother cry when she finally told him how hurt she had been by not understanding her own mother. She continued to explain that both Miss Holleran and she decided to remain quiet and let him go as far as he could. If he began to fail then they would be there to help him. Wallace watched his mother wring her hands and move around the room while she was talking to him and finally went over and gave her a hug and a kiss. She started crying again and told him that she wished her mother could have been able to do that for her. He quietly asked his mother if any one else knew these things. She told him that even his father did not know about her own mother's behavior. She finally admitted that she still knew nothing about her own father, his grandfather.

Wallace went to bed shortly after their conversation. The next person he wanted to see was Miss Holleran. He put that on his list for tomorrow along with the advertisements for the convention. When he went into the bedroom Winston was there. He had been staying at Wallace's house now. Winston's father had been put out of his home and was living in the poor house. His drinking had taken its toll and he lost his job. Alice was kind enough to take responsibility for Winston. Frank was not happy about that but Alice told him that it was none of his business. She reminded him that it had been a good thing that someone had done that for her mother when she came to the United States. Wallace saw Winston sitting on the bed and went over and sat next to him. Winston was quiet and seemed sad. He told Wallace that his family had been a disappointment to him and that he should be grateful to have such a caring family. He wished his family had been like that. Wallace told him that he did have the same thing but that it was with his family. Winston looked at him and told him he was happy he was there now. Wallace felt Winston's body next to his and began to feel a sense of excitement. He liked how rough Winston looked even though he knew he could never be like that, he felt tantalized by him. He remembered what Winston had said about the night in Buffalo. He remembered the breeze coming through the window and the sun shining on the bed when they woke up. Then he laughed about when Winston was hanging over the edge of the Electric Tower and how much fun he had on those unnerving rides on the Midway. It was getting late and they knew it was time to go to bed. They each had another long day tomorrow.

Everyone was at the shop very early the next day. Miss Holleran showed up to help with the office work. The deliveries were ready to go. Wallace stayed back so he could go to the local newsstands with the papers. It was a perfect time to have a private conversation with Miss Holleran. Before he left he told her that he needed to speak with her. She was concerned by the tone of his voice and sat down and asked what the matter was. He told her about his meeting with his advisors and his discussion with his mother. Miss Holleran's face appeared frozen and lifeless. Wallace got to his question about his female advisor. He asked her about the secrecy. She began slowly explaining why they decided to remain in the background of his development. He believed her since it matched his mother's story. Then she began her explanation of the advisor and the living arrangements. She explained that people had a difficult time with relationships that did not go along with traditional ways. It was not the way she wanted it but it was the easiest way to stay out of the limelight. Wallace stared at her as she spoke. She explained how much she cared for this woman and wished she could have felt more comfortable bringing her to the grand re-opening. She told Wallace that if they had both got on stage Miss Lemon Drop would not have lived to see the New Year. She laughed in her funny way along with Wallace. As far as his projects and need for help she never worried about him. She knew he was okay but wanted to be there for him. He realized at that point that there were many people that cared for him. The people and relationships that he was connected to were all very different. He told her that the last few days had been very interesting. He had learned so much about himself and his friends and family. At that point she asked about how he and Winston were getting along. He looked puzzled and asked what she meant. She told him in her stern teacher way, "I have been honest with you, now it's your turn." He was not sure what the answer was that she was waiting for. She sat staring at him and he hated her staring at him like that. He felt like he was on trial. He admitted that he was not sure what he felt for Winston. They had been friends for a long time and he enjoyed his funny outlook on life. He admired him for who he was and felt bad that he had such a terrible life. He laughed and said he wished he could look as rough as Winston. She smiled and told him he could never pull it off and to this he agreed. She told him maybe that is why you like him because you know you can never be like that. He told her that Winston sees things in him that he cannot figure out for himself. She smiled and waited while Wallace explained that he felt an emotional pull. It was like the floodgates had been open. He went on to admit what happens to him every time he sees Winston. She wondered if he had dealt with those feelings as of yet. He told her he felt like he should not deal with it and she looked at him and said, "Oh you will some day." She assured him that he would be fine and that everything would work out. He was happy to have had the time to talk with her. It was always comforting talking with her. He said that it seemed like you were talking with your grandmother. She quickly replied, "Thanks, now I feel really old." She laughed and told him to get on his way, he had advertising to do.

As Wallace walked to the hotel he had an idea for the advertising campaign for the convention. This time he was going to go into the office and show Mr. Helfer how he designed things for the hotel. Just before he got there he saw Eveline walking up the street. He went up to her and asked how the job interview went. She told him she was on her way to work and that they had liked her and hired her. Today was her first day of work. He admired her outfit and told her she was sure to be successful. He asked her if she could come to his house for dinner sometime. She told him she would ask her parents and let him know. They agreed to meet the next day at the Arcade, which they considered their meeting place. He got to the hotel and decided that the convention would be called "The Modern Home Show". He walked into the office and low and behold there was Hilda. She had returned and was her usual self, which was unpleasantly cool. Wallace decided that his challenge had returned to haunt him. He looked at her and asked, "Did you need time to recover?" She peered over her glasses and told him to forget he ever saw her that night. He looked at her and said, "I'll never let you forget that night." She hoisted herself off the chair and lumbered her way to Mr. Helfer's office and announced that the "boy" was here. When he walked by her he sighed and walked in and closed the door. Wallace presented an example of the main advertisement in script type that looked like a breeze blowing. He wanted to include sketches of flowers and small examples of what was going to be in the convention hall. It would be a collage of things for the modern home of 1903. They completed the work and established a timeline in preparation for the show. Wallace would meet with him after the program was set. They established an office staff with a manager for hotel events. These people were now the ones who organized the shows for the restaurant and would organize which companies and stores were going to be in the convention.

Wallace was in charge of the flower show and garden designs. They would meet in April for final plans. Wallace left the office and wished Hilda all the best. She asked him as he was leaving, "How long before you return?" He smiled and said, "Sooner than you think."

Eveline met Wallace the next day at the Arcade. He finished his collection of papers and money from the newsstands. She was on a break from her job. They talked about her job and if she thought she would like it. She told him that her parents thought it would be a fine idea for her to come to his house for dinner. Wallace told her that now he had to make sure his mother would make dinner for them. They laughed and wondered if anyone else was going to be eating with them. Wallace told her about the convention and she asked if it was going to be as much fun as the New Year's Party. He was not sure anything could match that night. He asked if she and her family could come to the convention. Eveline said she sure would like to attend even if her family did not want to go. Since it was a daytime event it was easier to do things without her parents. He studied her outfit. She was dressed in a sporty outfit yet it was totally appropriate. He liked her way of being fun and honest about things. Some of the girls he knew were stuffy and were too bossy for him. He wondered if that is why he liked her. She only had a half an hour for her lunch break so she needed to go. Wallace knew he had a million things to do also. She waved goodbye and wiggled her nose at him. He waved back but no wiggling of the nose.

The responses the Weekly Page got from the article about the potential Ford Motor Company were more than Wallace expected. He began getting inquiries about where to send money for the stocks. He really did not want to get in touch with the Rochester Post-Express. He was still not interested in a merger but knew they would have more information on how to become part of Henry Ford's campaign. He and Winston would go to their office together. They walked over to the office and found the Vice-President of the company in the office. Wallace thought that might be a good sign. They discussed how business was and the reason for their visit. Wallace explained the need for information about becoming part of the Ford Motor Company. The Vice-President explained that he should not give that information. Wallace thanked him and asked why he was so hesitant about giving out public information. The Vice-President told them that the Weekly Page threatens the President of the Rochester Post-Express but that he would not co-operate with them. He still wanted to buy the paper operation from him. Wallace told him that he was sorry but it was not for sale. He understood but asked them not to tell where the information came from. They parted in agreement. Wallace was certain he would not breathe a word of that meeting and threatened Winston with a paddling if he said anything. Winston told him he would love to have Wallace paddle him. Wallace ignored that remark. Wallace wished Winston was not so suggestive all the time even though he like it.

Wallace notified people of the address and policy for becoming a shareholder in the Ford Motor Company. It was time for him to cash in on what he had earned at the hotel. The agreement was that the hotel would match his earning and put money into this thing they called a car. He went to the hotel and found Hilda out to lunch. He was glad he did not have go by the "face of unhappiness". He went directly into the office to find a startled Mr. Helfer afraid he had missed a meeting. Wallace assured him that this was a different meeting and explained what was going on with Henry Ford. He wanted to be a major contributor to the new venture for the Ford Motor Company. Mr. Helfer told him he had heard about some campaign for money. Wallace asked him what amount of money would be available for him to invest. Mr. Helfer got out the ledger and flipped it around to find Wallace's earnings. The total Wallace had earned was $485. He told him the hotel would match the amount. Then he told Wallace that the hotel had shown a profit since he became involved in the re-organization of the hotel, and he was to share in those profits. Mr. Helfer offered him a 1% profit sharing option. His profit share for that quarter was to be $30. Wallace was delighted and accepted the offer. Wallace wanted to be a major stockholder in the new company. His birthday was in a few weeks and he would be 23 years old. He may very well be the youngest shareholder of the new company. He knew he was taking a gamble but somehow had the feeling it was going to be a good one.

Chapter 25

THE ADVERTISING SECTION OF the Weekly Page was showing information about events in town and things that were happening in nearby cities. One of the largest advertisements in the Weekly Page was for the "Modern Home Show". Wallace encouraged Mr. Helfer to use not only his paper but also all papers for coverage of the event. Advertisements were placed in Buffalo and Syracuse papers. Wallace thought that people would make a vacation of it and come to Rochester for the show and the local places of interest. A special rate was offered if you stayed in the hotel while seeing the show. As a bonus to the special rate your admission was free to the convention hall. The first floor was being transformed into a home of the future complete with the gardens for outside landscaping, new designs and decorating techniques for the interior. Electric lights were featured in the sample rooms. The furnishings were brought from Buffalo and Syracuse with some of the larger stores sending their furnishings from New York City. The railroad could easily transport everything from door to door. The flower show and garden design committee was set up by Wallace and he drew examples of various types of gardens for the convention. He thought it would be impressive to have a large circular fountain that would have water with a purplish hue. He was co-coordinating that with the lilacs that would be in bloom at the same time as the convention. He hoped this would encourage visitors to take a tour of the parks and gardens in town. Scattered throughout the show would be demonstrations of garden designs, gardening techniques, and flower arranging. Spring was a perfect time to show what could be done to make the outside of a home come alive. Mr. Helfer was feeling pretty proud of what the hotel was turning into. He liked the variety and color that was coming into the hotel. Hilda on the other hand kept asking him how much longer he was going to go along with the boy. He told her as long he as wanted to and that she needed to perk up a bit and stop being so unhappy about everything. She told him that she would be happier if the boy left so they could return to a normal way of operation. Mr. Helfer told her that she could leave if she did not like the new operation. She toned down and told him that she did not want to leave him. He told her she had a choice either change or leave. The conversation ended. Wallace had set up the refreshment menus with the kitchen staff. They were to circulate through the crowds offering a cool beverage as people were enjoying the environment. There would be a coffee and cookie stand around the fountain area. He believed that if you fed people they would stay and most likely buy some of the items that were on sale. The budget was very low for the free stuff. Mr. Helfer was more than happy to have the staff follow those orders for the food. A buffet of food would be available in the main restaurant. It would be part of the room rate if you were a guest in the hotel. The visitors from other places would be offered a free dessert if they ordered the buffet. It was to be a weekend event. The notable patrons of Rochester would be invited to an invitation only showing on Friday evening. A dinner would be served around the fountain. Wallace's advisors would be invited to see his accomplishments at that time. When Mr. Helfer told Hilda she was going to dinner for the pre-opening of the show she wondered if it was going to turn into the last party she went to. He told her that he was going to limit how many drinks she could have. She looked at him and said, "You're no fun."

Wallace asked Alice if he could invite Eveline for dinner. Alice was happy to do that for Wallace. She thought she was a nice girl and agreed to cook a great dinner for them. He wanted to have the whole family there too. Alice was concerned about the size of their apartment and hoped it would be large enough. Wallace told her it would be fine because the food would make up for the lack of space. She laughed and told him to invite all of them. He told her that he already had. She laughed and said, "That's my boy, always a step ahead." Wallace met Eveline and she said her parents thought dinner would be fine. Wallace informed her that her parents were invited too. The dinner would be next Saturday evening. Wallace went on to the shop to finish the newspaper for the week. He wanted to make sure that everything was in order for his advisors when they visited the convention. They would be having dinner together on Friday evening. He designed a special program for the invited guests. This was his final examination before graduation. He had to make it good!

The weekend was going to be a busy one. Wallace invited Eveline to the dinner at the convention on Friday evening as well as the family dinner on Saturday evening. Winston was included in the Saturday dinner but Wallace did not put his name on the list for Friday evening. Winston was upset about this and asked why he was not included because he had helped on the flower committee. Wallace told him that he could not do everything with him because people might wonder what was going on. Winston told him he was a coward and was afraid of himself, which Wallace denied. When he was on his way to the hotel he thought about Winston's remark. He was angry with him but knew he was right about why he was afraid to show how he really felt about Winston. He kept remembering what Miss Holleran said about how people viewed things that were not done in conventional ways. He wanted to let it all out and try not to worry about what people would say but something told him not to. He walked into the office and there was Hilda. She told him that she heard they were having dinner together. Wallace thought she was talking about the family dinner and told her that she was not invited to his home. She huffed and got up and went into Mr. Helfer's office and asked him about the dinner. Wallace was behind her and was making a face at Mr. Helfer when she twirled around and saw his face and she went wild. She screamed, "Why is this boy getting away with so much." Mr. Helfer told her to calm down and explained the dinner confusion. Wallace realized it was the Friday dinner she was referring to and felt like a fool as Hilda glared at him with her hands on her big hips. Wallace thought he should probably apologize to her and said, "Oops, sorry." She stormed out of the office saying, "That's all I get is an 'oops, sorry!'" Mr. Helfer watched her leave and just shook his head. They discussed the details for the weekend and decided it was as ready as it could be.

There were a total of 50 guests for dinner on Friday evening. Wallace's advisors were present. He was a nervous because they had never seen any of his accomplishments. The mayor and his wife were invited and Mr. Helfer and Hilda were seated next to them. Hilda seemed to be very proud of herself to be so close to the mayor. Wallace and Eveline were a few places away from the center. She told Wallace she felt like she was still in Canada. He asked her why. She told him that her parents were on the board of trustees for a college. They often were invited to special events like this. Wallace knew then he had met someone who had been exposed to a higher-class of living. The advisors were seated together and were discussing the overall presentation of the show. They were impressed with the attention to detail that Wallace had shown throughout the entirety of the convention. The program he designed had each person's name hand written in a fancy script on the front cover. Inside was the menu, credits for the show, the presenters, and acknowledgments of companies, stores, and people who contributed to the event. Dinner was served after they took a tour of the convention. They were each given a glass of champagne as a celebration to the modern home. While they sipped their drinks they listened to the sounds of water cascading in the fountain and saw how the lights had been arranged to accent the different displays. Everyone had only the best to say about the show. Mr. Helfer made a toast to Wallace saying, "Wallace had made the hotel into a gold mine and that he would someday be a millionaire." Everyone raised his or her glass for the toast but Hilda could barely lift hers up. Wallace saw that and wondered what was her problem. The evening was a success. His advisors without hesitation gave him the highest grade possible for all academic areas. He would graduate with honors and could not wait to get home to tell Winston and his mother. Lately Frank had not been in a very good mood and seemed like he was drifting away from Wallace. Wallace still thought his father was jealous of his success. The evening came to a close and

Wallace escorted Eveline home. As Wallace walked home he thought about what his future would hold. He felt like he had so many ideas and could they all happen.

On Saturday Alice was rushing around the house trying to make the place look as good as possible. She was making her favorite recipe of roast prime rib of beef. She planned to serve it with mashed potatoes, Yorkshire pudding with hard sauce and fancy green beans almandine. She had Frank buy bottles of red wine. He sarcastically told her whatever he would buy would not be good enough for Wallace and his friends. Alice was disgusted with his remark and told him so but he did not seem to care what she told him. Wallace was not there to hear that but Winston was and he told Wallace about the conversation. Wallace shook his head and said he thought things had changed between Frank and him. Eveline's family arrived promptly and brought flowers. Wallace thought that was impressive. He asked Eveline if she got them from the convention. Everyone laughed and thought that might have been a good idea. There were enough flowers for the whole city there. The dinner was scrumptious with the Yorkshire pudding as the highlight. Eveline's parents, Mr. and Mrs. Lounsberry, explained that it was one of their traditional favorites. Alice was happy to have made such a hit with the dinner. For dessert she made a double chocolate cake with fudge frosting. She even took the time to make little tips with the frosting on the top of the cake. It looked artificial. Everyone knew when he or she tasted it that it was authentic. Winston sat on Wallace's right side and Eveline on his left. During dinner Winston kept touching Wallace's leg. Wallace did not react to any of the gestures. Occasionally Winston would laugh out loud and everyone would look at him. Wallace kept asking if anything was wrong. Winston kept telling everyone "Life is really funny." When he said that everyone had a puzzled look on his or her face and wondered what he meant. Wallace knew Winston was referring to his liking him and Eveline at the same time. He decided to put Winston on the spot. He said, "Hey Winston at least this time you got invited to dinner." Suddenly the touching stopped and Winston responded, "So, you're trying to be with both of us at the same time tonight?" Wallace told everyone that Winston was upset that he was not at dinner last night at the convention. Then in order to calm the atmosphere Mr. Lounsberry said, "Don't feel bad neither were we." Everyone laughed and coffee was served.

In July Wallace received a letter in the mail. It was addressed to Wallace Paine, Stockholder. He opened the letter and it was from the newly incorporated Ford Motor Company. It was a thank you and an announcement to the shareholders that the corporation was official. It explained that the first Model A was to appear on the market in Detroit, Michigan. Wallace knew that had to be headlines for his paper. He told Winston that he wanted to get one of those cars soon. Winston told him he was crazy and that he would never be able afford it or know how to use it. Winston thought the idea was hilarious. Wallace told him that he would have the last laugh when he drove up in the Model A. The letter listed the Model A at $750.00 for the basic model. There were options such as a rear tonneau with two seats and rear door for $100.00 extra. There were two choices for tops. One could be a rubber roof for $30 and a leather roof for $50. Wallace told Winston he wanted the best one they could make. Winston told him that he already had the best one made. Wallace asked him what that meant. Winston said that he was the best one that could be made. Wallace told him that he was too corny. The last part of the letter explained Ford's description of the Model A. It was the most reliable machine in the world. The Model A was to be painted red or black. He could not wait to have a red one.

Wallace printed the information about the Ford Motor Company on the front page of the paper. It was a hit. The Rochester Post-Express owners came to the shop to discuss a merger again. This time Wallace was in a different frame of mind. He was thinking of moving out of the small weekly paper into a larger more widespread newspaper. Winston was there when they arrived. He told them Wallace would be back in a little while so they decided to wait. Winston tried to convince them that they were wasting their time. He did not realize that Wallace had a different idea altogether because he thought Wallace told him everything. He was about to find out differently. Wallace returned to the shop and appeared delighted to see the men. They went into his office. Winston was not included. The conversation was about a merger of the two paper companies. Wallace was in favor of the idea with a few important conditions. He was to be paid for the shop and the equipment. His employees would continue their employment. Their pay would be increased by 2%. His employees could not be fired and the only way they could leave is if they quit. He wanted to be an owner of the Rochester Post Express. Frank would be the circulation manager and Winston would be the assistant for the company. The re-organization would take place in one month. The men were agreeable to all of his conditions. His final demand was that a portion of the earnings for his employees would be a stock option. They could choose either the Rochester Post Express or Eastman Kodak

Company. He would continue contributing his money into Eastman Kodak Company. The money he was to receive for the sale of the Weekly Page would be placed in an account for his own discretionary use. He would sell his business to them for $2000.00. Wallace had thought about this plan the night he walked home from Eveline's after the hotel dinner. He knew he was ready to move on. The thing he was certain of was that he wanted to protect and care for those people who had worked very hard for him and with him. They agreed to have the contracts and the money transfers ready in a week. The merger was scheduled for late November. Winston had been pacing around the office. He asked Wallace what that was all about. He told him he could not tell him. Winston knew something had just happened.

The fall of 1903 was to be the first time for a World Series. It was to be a baseball game between two top teams in the country. The event was to be held in October. This year it was going to be between the Boston American League and the Pittsburgh Pirates. Newspapers were printing articles about the number of games and the rules for winning. Wallace knew that would be one of the last things he would be writing about in his paper. He felt a little sad about dissolving his company because it had been his first job and he remembered as a little kid thinking about the idea of owning a business. He knew he had to keep moving because too long in one place does not help you to succeed. He had seen this in his family and knew he did not want to be like them. The World Series game time came. All eyes were on this new idea for competition. The newspapers were covering the games daily. Winston was like a little kid running around with a cap on his head and pretending to be a ball player. The rules for winning the series were that you had to win the best of nine games. Finally at the end the Boston American League won. There were those that were happy and then those that were not happy. The newspapers would have questions to their readers about whom they thought might win. Readers sent their comments and opinions about the game to the Weekly Page. It became quite an editorial section for sporting events. Wallace was happy to have been able to use that as one of his last big news items.

November was the month for the merger. Wallace called a meeting with his group at the shop. He explained that at the end of the month the Weekly Page would no longer be operating. Alice looked like she was going to cry and Frank's face was like stone. Winston stared at Wallace like he was leaving forever and Gregg and the other employees did nothing. Wallace explained that he had provided for all of them in their employment and salary. They would be moving to the larger paper printing plant. He explained the stock options for them. Alice and Frank said they did not want that because they knew nothing about that sort of stuff. Wallace explained that would be to their benefit in later years. They all agreed to have Wallace help with their financial decisions because he had the brains for the job. After the meeting and some sadness, especially with Alice, she explained how this was her first job outside of the home and she had met good people and made friends. She remembered how sad she was when she left the Rochester Women's Club. She hoped that there would be more new friends coming along. Winston hung back to talk with Wallace because he wanted to know why he was not told about this before the others. Wallace explained that he had to be treated like the rest of the employees and this made Winston angry. He told Wallace he thought they had a different relationship than that. Wallace explained to him that business was business and friendship cannot interfere with that. Winston explained that he would just walk away from him if someone better came along. Wallace tried to explain that would not happen and that he had special feelings for him. Winston asked him when he was going to start to show those feelings. He wondered if Wallace had forgotten about the night in Buffalo. Wallace told he would never forget about that. Winston told him that he was not sure anymore because he was tired of waiting for a closer relationship. After he got that feeling out he asked Wallace where Eveline fit into the picture. Wallace explained that he had different feelings for her. Winston just shook his head and walked away.

Chapter 26

The Rochester Post Express was a profitable move. After Wallace's employees adjusted to the new environment they realized that moving was a better opportunity for making new friends. They liked the pay increase and were involved in more aspects of the operation. Winston and Frank organized the circulation department the same way they had for the Weekly Page. There were more delivery routes and they were more complicated with the number of people subscribing to the paper. They created a schedule so each area was serviced at the same time of day. The rotating method saved the company money. Wallace and the two other owners noticed a savings in the payroll and an increase in profits. Wallace reminded his business partners that he had trained his people well. They did not want to admit it but could not argue about the facts and figures.

Wallace and Eveline had been spending more time together. They would meet for lunch during the week. Sometimes Wallace was invited to Eveline's house for dinner. Winston was never included and stopped talking to Wallace about his time with her. When Wallace would return home from dinner or a date with her Winston acted as if Wallace had just arrived home from work.

Wallace and Eveline's family were members of Christ's Episcopal Church on East Avenue. They never talked about church until one time both families were at the same Sunday service. Now Wallace and Eveline started attending church together because the families did not count that as a date. Wallace and Eveline's parents thought it was a wonderful idea that they were all of the same religious background. Eveline was telling Wallace about the church they used to attend in Canada. She spoke about her experiences in the choir and how much she enjoyed singing. She thought she might like to be a member of the choir again. Wallace laughed and told her he could not carry anything much less a tune. She thought he was funny and witty. After Eveline joined the choir Alice joined too. Every Wednesday evening they would go to choir practice together. Wallace was waiting when the rehearsals were finished so he could walk Eveline home. This went on for a few weeks until one night in a snowstorm Wallace asked Eveline if he could put his arm around her. He winked at her and said he was cold and maybe they could keep each other warm. Eveline smiled and told him she would like that. Wallace knew he was falling for her.

Wallace decided that Winston needed to be more a part of his new relationship with Eveline. He invited Winston to meet them for lunch at the hotel. While they were having lunch Hilda and Mr. Helfer walked in. They stopped and spoke to one another. Hilda was her usual unpleasant self. Mr. Helfer reminded Wallace of their meeting the next day. He remembered and told him he would see him them. At that, Hilda sucked her teeth and told everyone that the boy never forgets. They walked away and Wallace was angry at those remarks. Eveline noticed how his temperament had changed and told him not to let that old lady bother him. Winston piped up and said, "I've told him that before but he doesn't listen to anything

I tell him." Wallace frowned at both of them. Mr. Helfer and Hilda sat across the room. Hilda was positioned so she could watch the young folks.

The next day Wallace went into Mr. Helfer's office and had to go through the "face woman" screening. Hilda's glass chain was twisted around her neck and she was struggling to act like everything was okay. Wallace noticed that the chain was so long that even though it was tangled up her glasses were still resting on her cleavage. He thought it was pretty amusing to watch her try to be so proper with such a tangled mess. As he walked by she asked how his lunch was with his boyfriend and girlfriend. Wallace was stunned and tried not to react to that question. He told her fine and went into see Mr. Helfer. As they were discussing plans for some of the next events for the hotel, Wallace asked if he could reserve the dining room sometime in the near future. Wallace explained that he was thinking about asking Eveline to marry him. He wanted to have a party in the hotel. Mr. Helfer said he could have any date he wanted. A strange look came across his face when he said that. Wallace wondered what that was all about. Mr. Helfer admitted that he had heard that Winston was closer to Wallace than most friends would be. There had been gossip about their friendship and people were wondering how Wallace's girlfriend would fit into all of this. When he heard this he knew exactly where that came from. He asked who was saying those things. Mr. Helfer would not repeat any names. Wallace did not need a name because he knew it had to be Hilda. She was out to get him because of all the things that had changed at the hotel. It was clear to him that she felt she was in second place with Mr. Helfer. Before Wallace she had made the suggestions and now it was him. Mr. Helfer would not say one way or the other about the rumors and possibilities that Hilda was part of the issue. Their meeting ended and a dinner date in April was set. Wallace walked passed Hilda and not a word was spoken by either one of them. Mr. Helfer stood in the door and knew he had two problems to deal with.

Wallace tried not to let the rumors about his relationship with Winston bother him. He knew he liked Winston and Eveline both very much. He made plans to ask Eveline's father if he could marry her. They were a proper family and he knew manners were important. He invited Eveline's father out to lunch at the hotel. He thought that was an appropriate atmosphere to have a conversation about the possibility of marrying his daughter. Wallace made sure he was dressed and groomed perfectly. He wore a tailored jacket and trousers. He had his gold watch in his pocket because his motto was: time was worth keeping. Eveline's father met him in the front of the hotel and commented on how carefully put together and handsome he was. Wallace knew he had made the right impression. While they enjoyed their lunch Wallace explained how much he cared for Eveline. He told him that she was a very interesting and intelligent young woman. After a short while Mr. Lounsberry asked if Wallace was working up to something. Wallace blushed and admitted that he wanted to ask if he could marry his daughter. Wallace waited for the answer for what seemed like hours and finally received Mr. Lounsberry's approval. Wallace thanked him and assured him he would take good care of her. The lunch ended and to his surprise Mr. Helfer had paid the bill in advance. Wallace thought this was pretty impressive.

When Wallace arrived home Alice told him that she saw Miss Holleran and that she wanted to see him. He wondered what she might want since she was no longer working for the paper company. He walked over to her apartment. When he rang the bell his college advisor answered the door. They were both surprised because they had never seen one another outside of the advisory rooms. He was invited in and Miss Holleran was sitting in the parlor. She explained why she resigned and Wallace understood. She wanted to let him know that if he ever needed anything or anyone to talk to she would always be available. She explained that he had a lot going on and lot of potential. He would meet people along the way that would try to undermine him. While she was talking he thought about Hilda's actions. Miss Holleran referred to her friend and all the remarks that they had to live with. Wallace did not see anything wrong with their style of living. This break from conventional living was an issue for people. He thought about talking to her about Winston and how he felt about him. He began telling her that he was going to ask Eveline to marry him. Miss Holleran did not move a muscle as she stared at him with a concerned face. When he finished she asked where Winston fit into this arrangement. Wallace knew this was what he wanted to talk about and wondered how she could be so smart and know this before he even said anything. He told her about their time in Buffalo and how he thought Winston had stronger emotions for him than he did for Winston. Miss Holleran looked at him and said, "Oh really." She wondered why he was having such a hard time showing Winston how he felt. Wallace admitted he thought it would be easier to avoid all that. Miss Holleran then asked him why he was marrying Eveline. She mentioned that she did think she was a lovely girl. Wallace admitted he liked her and that it was easier openly showing his emotions with her than with Winston. Miss Holleran told him that it was more acceptable to everyone not necessarily easier. Miss Holleran then asked him how he expected to keep Winston happy and still be married. Wallace was not sure about that. She emphasized the importance of letting people know how you feel. Wallace decided that he could care about both of them but in different ways. At that, Miss Holleran cleared her throat and admitted there were sure different ways to show affection. Wallace smiled and agreed and they both laughed. She told Wallace that he was some operator and she truly hoped he could keep both things separated. He told her he hoped so too. Wallace told her that they would be invited to his wedding. They would be sent an invitation as soon as he asked Eveline.

Before he asked Eveline to marry him he told Alice and Frank about his intentions. Alice told Wallace it was a wonderful idea and Frank was indifferent. Wallace thought that was a strange reaction from his father but considered what type of person he was and how he had behaved with him before. Wallace went to Eveline's house and her father knew why he was visiting. They were sitting in the parlor with cookies and coffee served. He began by telling them how fond he was of Eveline. He continued by complimenting her parents on what a good job they had done to make Eveline a fine young woman. Then he asked if they would let Eveline marry him. She sat as still as a statue and Wallace felt like he was frozen in time. Mr. Lounsberry stroked his beard and Mrs. Lounsberry smiled. There was no noise from anywhere or anyone. After a long silence they approved of the marriage. Eveline was happy and Wallace made sure they knew that she was the only one he cared for and loved. While he was saying this he thought of how Winston was going to take the news. They agreed to be married on the first Saturday in April.

Wallace told them that his birthday was on April 1. They could celebrate his birthday and anniversary all in the same month. They smiled and Eveline announced everyone that they could celebrate her birthday and Winston's in September. There was a strange smile on everyone's face when she said that. Wallace asked how she knew when his birthday was. She laughed and said we were both born on September 17. They had discussed that at the New Year's Eve Party. Eveline asked if Winston was going to be his best man and Wallace agreed. She thought he would want to be as close to him as he could that day. Wallace felt like everyone was speaking in riddles lately. He wondered what people saw or knew that he was not aware of or could it be that he was trying to cover too much up?

Wallace went home. When he walked into the bedroom Winston was lying on his bed. He had just finished bathing and had only his shorts on. Wallace sat down on the bed and told him he had something to talk to him about. While he was saying this Winston was drying his hair and rubbing his chest. Wallace could not help but admire Winston's body. The rough look and dark beard appealed to him. He began by mentioning how much he liked Eveline. While he said that Winston stopped rubbing himself and stared at Wallace. Wallace told him that he and Eveline were getting married. He wanted to know if he would be his best man. Winston in a sarcastic tone told Wallace that he was his best man and that he would never have another like it. Wallace told him that was not what he meant. Winston smiled and agreed to be with him on his wedding day. He told Wallace at least he could be right next to him all the way. They discussed the date and what was going to happen for the dinner. Winston wondered who his date was going to be. Wallace jokingly told him that it could be him. Winston thought that would be perfect, two men and a woman.

Eveline's and her mother went to the church to discuss the ceremony. While receiving information from Mrs. Lounsberry about their affiliation with the church in Canada they realized that Eveline had not been baptized. It was suggested that before the wedding it would be proper to have a baptism. Eveline had lunch with Wallace that same day and told him about the mix up. He told her he was not concerned and that he would sponsor her for the baptism. She thought that was wonderful. She explained everything to her parents and they agreed that baptism was a good way to start a marriage. They made an appointment with the priest and scheduled the ceremonial baptism for February 28. The wedding was then planned for Saturday April 3. Eveline's parents would become members of Christ's Episcopal Church on the day of her baptism. There were so many ceremonies being planned because of the wedding. It was sure to be a wonderful time.

Wallace was walking on Main Street when he saw Mr. Helfer. He asked Wallace to join him in his office if he had some time. Wallace was on his way to work but thought he could make time for a short meeting. After his last encounter with Hilda he was glad to walk in with Mr. Helfer. Maybe Hilda would act differently when they came in at the same time. When they approached his office the door was slightly open. They both looked at each other and walked in. They startled Hilda who had her feet on the desk while snoozing. Mr. Helfer snapped at her telling her that was unlady like. She told him she liked to be unlady like. Wallace stood there and could not believe how she behaved toward her boss. They went into the office and he told Wallace that she had never been a lady. Wallace was more and more confused every time he came into that office. Mr. Helfer asked Hilda to come in to take notes. She sauntered into the office and sat down in another of her unlady like positions. She was reminded that they had business to do. Hilda apologized for her mannerisms. She remarked that she did not want to offend the boy. Wallace prided himself in maintaining his composure and did not react to her. Mr. Helfer told Wallace that as a wedding gift and a thank you for all he had done for the hotel he was paying for the wedding reception. It would be complete with flowers, drinks, dinner, and cake. Hilda blurted out, "You are paying for this farce." She asked if he was crazy. There were two men and now a woman involved with the hotel paying for it. Mr. Helfer reminded her that he was the owner and she was the secretary and that he would spend the money the way he wanted to. Wallace finally decided it was time to ask her a question. He asked, "What happened to you to make you so mean and vicious against young people?" She told him to mind his own business. She asked how a boy could walk into a hotel and turn it into such a fiasco. She asked if she could go back to her desk. Mr. Helfer finished his meeting and Wallace left.

When Wallace sold the Weekly Page he negotiated a discretionary fund for his portion of the sale, which was around $2000.00. When he worked on that financial arrangement he preplanned what that money would be used for. He wanted to have money in different accounts with various conditions for its use. He never divulged how and where these funds were or for what purpose they could be used. This particular fund was being saved for his first vehicle. He knew he wanted to be one of the first to have a Ford Model A Runabout. He had been waiting until they were available. He knew from what he read and heard that a Runabout fully equipped would be about $1000.00. That would leave him another $1000.00 for anything he might want to invest in. He liked the red color because it would be perfect and noticed on the streets. He ordered the car and hoped it would be ready for the wedding. He did not tell anyone about his plan for the Ford.

Wallace received notification a few weeks before the wedding that his order for the Model A was changed. The original model had problems with overheating and slipping transmission bands. They were equipping a newer version with a larger more powerful engine and were renaming it the Model AC. It was being built to go faster, about 28 mph but still painted red. Wallace decided that it would be worth waiting for because he wanted the newest and best one they made. Since he had stock in the company he thought he should be one of the first to own a Model AC. It was good that he did not tell anyone about the purchase. Frank mentioned one day that some people were encouraging this Henry Ford guy by buying his stuff and trying to put the buggy business under. Frank did not know that Wallace was one of the first shareholders and would soon be the first owner of a Ford. Frank mentioned that Ford was trying something called an assembly line that he thought was crazy. How could a line pull things along while the product was being made? Frank wanted to know why one person was not good enough to make it himself. Wallace understood his father's anger and Frank was not willing to accept new ideas. The fact was that when the car arrived he could not hide it.

The wedding day was fast approaching. There were 100 people coming to the wedding and reception. Frank had arranged for a brougham to be used for the wedding party. The hotel was hosting out of town guests from Canada.

Alice decided to invite her mother's sister Aunt Catherine to the wedding. She had not heard from her or seen her in years. Catherine accepted the invitation much to Alice's surprise. This made her a little nervous. The last contact she had from her was the letter informing her of her mother's death some 20 years earlier. Alice hoped she would accept the invitation so that maybe she could find out more about her mother and maybe her father. Alice was remembering how strange her mother had behaved and wondered what Catherine really knew. Alice told Wallace that his Aunt Catherine was invited to his wedding and he looked at her like it did not matter to him because he did not know her. He realized his mother wanted to see her again and the wedding was a good reason to invite her. He told her that he was glad she might be seeing her mother's sister.

April 1 was Wallace's birthday. Instead of a birthday party they had a pre-wedding party. There were people invited for the birthday along with the wedding party and the parents. Winston said it was like a three in one party. Wallace asked him privately if that was a joke about the three of them. Winston told him no but that it might be fun. Wallace wondered if he would ever stop making suggestive jokes. There was so much happening; it was more fun to have one party. Someone asked Wallace what they were doing after the wedding. He said that they were going to the Crescent Beach Hotel for the night. He rented a small apartment close to their families when they returned. It was better they have their own place to live. Alice was remembering their small apartment when they were first married. She was reminiscing about her days with the Women's Club of Rochester. She saw a lot of Eveline in herself. She was a young, pretty and a classy woman. She hoped that their life would be better than hers had been. At least Wallace knows his father and mother, she never had. Hopefully when they had children they would know their grandparents. Alice was glad her Aunt Catherine accepted the invitation. She was much older but Alice could still see a resemblance of her mother in her aunt. She was glad to have this time with her. Wallace was polite and thought it was nice she had come. Frank did not know much about her and the only reason Alice knew her was because of her mother. They left Canada when she was an infant. Catherine was very sympathetic about how her mother had passed but did not discuss much more than that. Alice felt like she was not telling her everything and she stopped questioning her. She would have to be happy with finally seeing someone from her past.

The wedding was grand. Everyone enjoyed the ceremony and music. The hotel was a special place for such a grand occasion. When it was time for Wallace and Eveline to leave the reception Winston asked if he could carry their bags. Eveline smiled and told him he could carry them next time. When they arrived at the Crescent Beach Hotel Wallace told Eveline about the time his family went there when he was a little kid. It was still a beautiful hotel on Lake Ontario. The veranda was as inviting as he remembered it the morning they had breakfast many years ago. He told her how he promised himself that he would someday live in a grand way. She seemed happy to hear about how he had such big plans for so many things. She asked him how he managed to do all the things he had accomplished so quickly. He responded that it was easy and that he had challenged himself to see how many things he could accomplish in his life. She thought that was a huge undertaking. She began to wonder for the first time where she fit in to his master plan.

Chapter 27

THE CRESCENT BEACH HOTEL offered a honeymoon suite that overlooked Lake Ontario. Spring was a good time to visit the lake. The trees and flowers were just beginning to grow. The yellow daffodils reflected the sun and the red emperor tulips were a contrast to them. Wallace told Eveline that they reminded him of how red hot the summers seem to be. They took a stroll around the grounds of the hotel as evening approached. They watched the sunset over Lake Ontario. There were a combination of red, orange, and grayish blue hues as the sun disappeared over the horizon. They were uncomfortable about their first night together. Eveline went behind the changing screen to dress into her nightclothes. Wallace stared out the window and thought of Winston and the night they spent in Buffalo where they did not need a changing screen. When Eveline came over to Wallace she hugged him and gave him a kiss. He stood there like he was frozen but hugged her back and went to get his clothes changed. Before they went to sleep they discussed the day and both agreed that they were very tired. The time before sleep was not as fulfilling to Eveline as she had hoped for. Wallace apologized for his lack of energy. She told him that she understood but could not help but to wonder why he seemed afraid of intimacy. She had seen him embrace his mother and Winston. Maybe things would be better when they were rested. Wallace was feeling strange himself and could not stop thinking about the night he and Winston had spent together. There was so much more energy even after a whole day at The Exposition. He rolled over and kissed Eveline good night.

The next morning they had breakfast in the same spot that Wallace's family had sat in years before. They discussed how they had slept and what they were going to do today. After a pleasant breakfast they decided to go back to their new apartment on Park Avenue. They took the trolley back to Rochester. It was a beautiful spring day so they walked from downtown to Park Avenue. While they were on their way Winston walked up to them and asked how the night went. They both agreed that they enjoyed the hotel but were tired last night. Winston looked at Wallace with an eye of wonder. He wanted to ask Wallace what happened but knew that was not the right time. They agreed to meet the next day at the newspaper office. During the rest of the walk home they discussed what they had to do to the apartment. Eveline was going to decorate it and Wallace was going to get some furnishings from the Larkin catalog. He had been saving certificates that could be used for furniture and household items. His mother gave him all her certificates whenever she purchased items. He knew he had enough to at least get a sofa and chair. He was hoping for a Larkin desk lamp. Wallace moved his bed to the new apartment. Now Winston had the bedroom to himself. It seemed like a death when they moved the bed to the new apartment. Eveline was fussing around in the kitchen while they were setting up the bed. Winston told Wallace things were going to change. Wallace did not want to hear this from him. Wallace thought about last night with Eveline. For some reason last night and the Buffalo night made him feel strange. He just wanted it all to go away.

Life began to have a routine. Eveline continued her work as a stenographer and Wallace was busy with the newspaper company. Winston and all the other employees were happy with their work. News from around the state and nation was always arriving for printing as part of the newspaper coverage. Wallace had been following information about a man who was an architect from Chicago. He was commissioned to design buildings in Buffalo. Frank Lloyd Wright was designing the Larkin Building on 680 Seneca Street in Buffalo. Ever since Wallace was a young person he followed the Larkin plan. He admired the Larkin philosophy of buying more quantity and saving more money. They started the first mail order department. Elbert Hubbard was the brother-in-law of John D. Larkin who was the man who created the company and its' famous "combination box". They were the founders of the company. Darwin Martin worked as one of the bookkeepers. He became corporate secretary. Wallace kept track of this man because he admired his ideas. He guided the company to its rise into corporate power. Wallace read that he created a unique ledger system for tracking sales and maintaining accounts. Darwin Martin was friends with Frank Lloyd Wright and commissioned him to come to Buffalo to design his home on 125 Jewett Parkway. Frank Lloyd Wright had an architectural style much different than any former building planners. He believed that the land and the building should blend together and that no one thing should compete with other parts of the environment. Wright believed that no house should ever be on a hill or on anything. It should be part of the hill. Wallace was fascinated with what this man thought and his use of natural surroundings to compliment the building. He decided to do a feature article about Frank Lloyd Wright. He planned to have it as part of the Sunday home section. The theme would be "Homes of tomorrow." He began with the Victorian style. He emphasized the ornate design and the amount of intricacies in its construction. He contrasted it to Wright's designs. He focused on the horizontal lines and use of the natural surroundings to make a complete design. Wallace gave examples of the amount of windows and stained glass Wright used in the plans for his establishments. He included his opinion of Frank Lloyd Wright's affect on him. He explained how his work was far ahead of any other type of architect. His work would look modern in a hundred years. He felt that a person like Wright was considered radical for the times but in his mind radical was good. He concluded the article with a challenge to the readers. He told them he would someday have a house with Wright's designs and wanted to know how many people would want the same type of home. Wallace was excited to see what the responses would be.

There were many responses to his article about Frank Lloyd Wright. Some were not as glowing as he had hoped for. Some individuals felt the man was odd and should not be recognized. Others felt he was only dealing with the wealthy and not the common people. There were some who wanted to know more about this architect. The general opinion was that he was strange and not many people would have a need for such a unique structure. Wallace was amazed at the narrow mindedness of so many people. He thought that his plans were perfect and showed genius and would be valuable. One person wrote that there was no value in such simple construction. The old style would last the longest. He was disgusted with the majority of responses. He realized then that he was not like most people. He discussed the responses with Winston and Eveline and they thought it was funny that he was so upset. They told him that he was not like most people and that is why they cared for him. They admired his ability to be different and be very successful. They felt that his success was a result of his individuality. He knew he was different than most and accepted it.

September arrived and Wallace knew that it was up to him to do something for Eveline and Winston for their birthdays. Since they were both on the same day he thought a party for them would be fun. He went to Mr. Helfer's office for one of their planning meetings. Wallace thought about how many times he had been to that office and how many times he had to encounter Hilda. He thought about his first times with her and how she behaved at the New Year's Eve party a few years ago. He felt sorry for her because he could not imagine being so unhappy and miserable. He thought maybe he would try another approach with her. Maybe she was waiting for someone to like her. He laughed when he thought about how someone could like such a person. Then he thought about how a man who liked big cleavages could live with a face that looked so unhappy. Could it be that someone needed that type of treatment? Hilda was a forceful woman who wanted to be in control. He shook his head and decided to leave it alone. He walked into the office as her head rose slowly and she peered over her glasses. He looked at her and immediately knew no one would ever want whatever she had to offer. He said, "Good day Hilda." She asked him what was good about it. Wallace smiled and responded that everything was good about the day and even her. She laughed and told him he was crazier than she thought. Mr. Helfer opened the door and asked them if the contest was over yet. She told him there never was a contest and she was always the winner. Wallace agreed saying, "You're a winner alright." He realized he was not going to work on her because he had better things to do. The meeting began and the three of them sat in the office discussing the fall promotions and holiday events for the hotel. Business had continued to increase and Wallace's pay and matching hotel pay meant he could buy 10 more shares in Ford Motor Company. Mr. Helfer asked about the status of his car. He explained that they were improving it and that it was to be sold as the Model AC. Hilda piped up and wondered how much flashier things could get around here. Mr. Helfer told her to mind her own business.

The birthday party was discussed. Mr. Helfer thought it was fine idea to celebrate both people's birthday together. Hilda agreed and told them that they were all together anyway. She wanted to know what type of party he was planning and was everyone supposed to come in threes or could there be two women and one man? She went on to question if there could be three men and three women and even named it a triangular party. She hoped to see who would be eliminated first from the triangle. Wallace was appalled at her thoughts. She looked at him and told him she knew who would be gone from his triangle. Mr. Helfer asked whom she would bring to such a gathering and she told them they would both be surprised. Wallace told her that she might not be invited and it was then that she assured him she would behave. Mr. Helfer concluded the meeting and Wallace left the office angry and confused with what Hilda had said. He wondered why Mr. Helfer allowed such behavior. Maybe she has something on him.

She certainly has something on Winston, Eveline, and himself.

Wallace finalized the plans for the birthday party. He invited all the people from the newspaper company. He wanted Eveline's parents to invite the people they wanted. Alice wanted to include some of her old friends from the Woman's Club. It was turning into a big affair. Winston had no one to invite. His father was not mentally well and still living in the poorhouse and wanted nothing to do with him. Alice assured him that they were his family. He knew that but would rather go away with Wallace for his birthday. He told Alice that and she looked at him and told him she knew that too. Wallace informed the restaurant that the final count for the party was 57 people. They would have a cake made with both names. Wallace made sure the names were in a triangle with his name on the bottom. He thought that way neither one of them would feel second in line. Winston was 23 years old, which was the same age as Wallace, and Eveline was going to be 20. The theme was going to be "A New Age" that would be written on top of the cake. He wanted them to understand that it was going to be a new age for many things. He planned on making a birthday speech about them. He wanted to emphasize that a new age brings new things. Wallace knew there was a change in the wind. He knew something was going to happen.

The party was fun. During the dinner Wallace presented his speech. He discussed how important both people were to him. He told how much he tried to find out about Eveline when he first met her. He spoke about his trip to the Exposition with Winston. He talked about how much fun Winston had on all the fast moving amusement rides. The funniest one was when he told the people about him hanging off the Electric Tower trying to attract attention below. There was a lot of laughter during his speech. No one seemed to question the triangular theme of the party. Eveline and Winston were on either side of Wallace when they thanked him for such a good party. They agreed they liked being part of his triangle. Hilda asked Mr. Helfer what was so fascinating about Wallace. She wondered what he offered to the triangle. She smirked when she told him that he probably kept them both happy. Alice thought the party was nice but Frank thought the party was a little more than they were used to. Alice told him to lighten up and have some fun and that she thought some change was good. He was getting boring according to her. At the close of the party Wallace asked for one more minute for an announcement. Eveline shrugged her shoulders and looked at Winston because no one knew what he was going to say. He explained about how change was good and he gave the party a title for a reason. He continued by saying that the new age is bringing a new set of experiences. He announced that he had been offered a job in Buffalo. He was going to be advertising manager for the H.O.Cereal Company. He was to begin his new responsibilities January 1, 1905. There was silence in the restaurant. Eveline had no idea that he had even applied for this job. Winston stared off to the side of the room and Alice and Frank said nothing. Eveline's parents had a quizzical look on their faces. It seemed as though everyone had been left out of the planning of this new adventure that Wallace had decided to endeavor. Mr. Helfer sat and looked at Hilda and for the very first time Wallace received no reaction what so ever from anyone. He concluded with the idea that he still had 3 months left in Rochester. He wished Eveline and Winston a happy birthday and a happy new age. Eveline told everyone that he probably had planned this for a long time. She thought that everyone was just along for his ride. Then she remembered the discussion on their wedding night about challenging himself to accomplish as many things as he could in one lifetime. She knew he had that plan already in place. Winston spoke up and said, "So much for the triangle, he just broke it." Hilda commented to Mr. Helfer that finally they would be rid of the boy. He did not find her too funny. Everyone began to leave the restaurant. Wallace did not have much to say either. He wondered if he had just done the right thing with this announcement. He thought it was a good theme. Was it about him though and not Eveline and Winston?

When Eveline and Wallace got home there was a discussion about the news of going to Buffalo. She said the party was fun and she had a good time. She told him how disappointed she was in the fact he did not talk with her first about his news. She believed the new job was good for him but that he should have at least told her first and that she deserved that before everyone else was told. He apologized for his lack of thought about how he presented the information. Eveline accepted his apology and began to talk about how the next few months were going to be handled. They realized there was a lot to do before they left Rochester. Wallace informed Eveline that they did not need to go to Buffalo before January. She asked Wallace where they were going to live. He told her that the company had an apartment rented for them on 112 Delaware Avenue. When he said that her eyes lit up and she informed Wallace that Delaware Avenue was one of the fanciest streets in Buffalo. She told him her parents knew a wealthy family not far from that address.

She began to think about how much fun this adventure might possibly be. Wallace told Eveline that his new car was being delivered to Rochester at Christmas time. He explained to her that it was the newer one he ordered and that it was still going to be red. It was one of the first to be built. He wanted it when they went to Buffalo to live. He told her about all the new improvements. He ordered the one with two seats in the rear. It will have a leather roof and it could move faster than 28 mph. Since he was one of the first shareholders he thought he should have one of the first Model AC's.

Winston went to Wallace's apartment the next day. He was not very happy with the news about Buffalo. Eveline had already gone to work so they had the place to themselves. Wallace had just finished getting ready for work. Winston wanted to know how Wallace felt about leaving Rochester and their friendship. Wallace told him that he was sorry to leave but knew it was going to be better to move on. Winston asked if he was going to miss their friendship. Wallace was not sure if he was going to miss the friendship. Winston was crushed that he did not say something more positive about how he felt about them. Wallace told him that he probably took their friendship too far and made more of it than it really was. Winston was furious with that remark. He told Wallace that he was just running so that he would not have to admit his true feelings. Wallace denied that remark. Winston told him that they would see when Wallace needed him around for their get-togethers. He asked Wallace if he was afraid of Eveline and finding out about things. Wallace said he was not afraid of Eveline. He told him that there are lots of things she does not know. Winston asked him why he got married then. He told him because it is easier to get ahead when you are married than being single. He said that people like Hilda would not talk as much. Winston told him he was self centered and manipulative. Wallace denied that remark and asked him to leave. Winston felt cast out and rejected. He told Wallace that he was just like his father. He hoped Wallace did not end up crazy and alone because if he uses people they will not stay forever. Winston was getting emotional and turned and stormed out. Wallace stood alone trying to figure out how it all went so wrong. He thought he was helping people but maybe he mistook helping for his own personal advancements.

Chapter 28

THE LAST FEW MONTHS that Wallace and Eveline spent in Rochester went by very quickly. There was much for Wallace to do with his job at the Rochester Post-Express. He was excited about moving but also was sad to leave something he founded many years before. For him it was a bittersweet time. He had created a business, made enough money to invest in Eastman Kodak Company and merged with a larger newspaper firm. He felt a sense of pride and accomplishment in those endeavors. He felt that he helped his friends and family move into jobs that had a future and a means to invest some of their earnings. Eveline came into his life and now they were excited about the move to Buffalo. She was looking forward to living in a fashionable part of the city. Her father had sent word to his friends on Delaware Avenue that his daughter was moving to Buffalo with her husband. He explained that they would be living a few blocks from them. There was a job available for her at a very prestigious law firm in Buffalo. It was a few blocks from where they were going to be residing. The H.O. Oats Company was further away from Delaware Avenue so Wallace would take the trolley to the south end of town to work. Most industries and businesses were located there because of the superior shipping facilities. The railroad lines had their junctions in that part of town too. Wallace's new boss Mr. Harmon lived further down Delaware Avenue nearer to where The Pan—American Exposition was held a few years earlier. He reassured Wallace that they might be riding the same trolley to work everyday.

There were some issues Wallace would have to face before he left Rochester. He needed to deal with Winston. The friendship had taken on a much different tone than before Wallace denied his intensity of friendship with Winston. They would see each other at work and Winston was still living with Alice and Frank. Since Wallace and Eveline were married they did not go to see the family as much. They were invited to dinner that was usually on Sunday. Other times they went to Eveline's parents' home for dinner. There were days when Wallace felt overwhelmed with how much effort was required in a marriage. Things were so different than when they were dating. He liked the idea of going home after a date but now he was always home on a date. He missed Winston's friendship more than he thought he would. How was he going to resolve the problem? He knew that he was going to be the owner of one of Ford's first cars. How was his father going to respond to it? Frank's livelihood was destroyed by the invention of the automobile. The horse and buggy days were nearly over. If it had not been for Wallace organizing the printing shop as he had his father would be out of work. His father was a very proud man and found it hard to accept that his son accomplished more than he ever did. Frank was once the important one and those times were over for him. Wallace decided that no matter what his father would say or do about the automobile that he was happy and knew he had earned the car.

Shortly after Thanksgiving, Wallace and Eveline were walking down Main Street when they saw Winston with another man across the street. Eveline suggested that they should go over to speak to them. Wallace was not sure who Winston was with. He thought he knew all his friends. He was a little hesitant to go but they did. Winston spoke to them both. Eveline asked who his friend was. Wallace had an uncomfortable feeling about who this person might be. He introduced him as a new buddy. Wallace did not say a thing. Eveline asked what his name was and Winston introduced him as Louis. Wallace wanted to know more about Louis but knew that was not a good time. Winston was certain to let everyone know that they just came from lunch and were going home. Wallace thought about them going back to his former home. How could that be? As he was thinking about that he remembered how he felt when he saw Eveline with another guy. He was trying to compare that time with this time. He hoped Louis was a relative. As they walked on further Eveline asked him why he was so quiet and he did not have an answer for her. She finally asked if he was upset about just seeing Winston with someone else instead of him. He denied it to her but was upset because there was so much more that she did not know.

Christmas was getting closer and Wallace had been working with Mr. Helfer on the plans for the last events at the hotel before his move to Buffalo. Hilda was actually being much more civil when he entered the office. He figured it was because he was leaving and she could take over again. The hotel was another bittersweet parting. He felt like he made a difference in the hotel and its operation. On the other hand he had a tough time with Hilda. He knew he probably learned a lot from her behavior. At least he learned how to deal with a personality like hers without a confrontation. During their last meeting Mr. Helfer told him that if he were to ever return to Rochester that he could have his job back. Hilda did not say a word when he said that. Wallace figured she hoped that would never happen. She sat quietly throughout the meeting. Even Mr. Helfer wondered if she was all right and asked but she assured him that she was never better. Just before the meeting was over Hilda asked Wallace who his friend's new buddy was. Wallace froze when she asked that and his first thought was to punch her. He calmly explained that he did not know what she was talking about. All she said was, "Oh really." Mr. Helfer told her that was none of her business. Wallace could not wait to get out of that office. He told Mr. Helfer he would see him again and thanked him as he left. All Hilda said was, "Good luck boy."

Eveline was getting things ready for their move to Buffalo. She was very good at organizing. The families were beginning to act like they were never going to see them again. Both mothers kept asking them over for dinner. It was getting to the point that they were out every night. Eveline enjoyed it because she did not have to make the meals. Wallace liked it too but he did not dare tell Eveline that their mothers were much better cooks than she was. Wallace knew better than to suggest such a thing. Whenever they were invited to dinner at Wallace's family he worried if Louis might be there too but it never happened. Wallace wanted to know in the worst way what was going on with Louis. He even asked Alice about him but she only told him Louis was nice boy and that she liked him. She told him that Winston needed a friend now that he was moving to Buffalo. Wallace felt bad for Winston especially knowing how his life had been. He thought why does everything that is good have to be shaded by something bad?

The week between Christmas and New Year's Day was the time Wallace's new car was scheduled to arrive. He had not made a big deal about it because of his father and what others may think. He received a letter from the Ford Motor Company in the middle of the week. He thought it might be about the shares he had recently purchased from his last salary from the hotel. Instead it was a letter in regard to the delivery of his car. They regretted to inform him that his car could not be delivered to Rochester. The only city for delivery near to Rochester was Buffalo. They explained that it would be easier to ship it to Buffalo from Detroit because of better shipyards and railroads. They offered him rail transportation to Buffalo to receive the car. When Wallace first read the letter he was upset to think he could not drive the car to Buffalo. His next thought was the condition of the roads between Rochester and Buffalo. They were mainly dirt roads and rough surfaces. Then he thought that might be a better plan anyway. Eveline and he could take their stuff on the train and Ford would pay for their tickets. Now he would not have to tell anyone in Rochester about the car especially his father. Someday they could make a trip to Rochester in the new car. Wallace felt like all of this was turning out for the best.

Wallace's new job was to begin on Monday, January 2. He and Eveline were happy that they could spend the end of the year with the people in Rochester. Wallace got the railroad tickets to Buffalo for Sunday. They were to leave Rochester at 10AM. Everything was going according to plan. Wallace and Eveline wanted to have their families and friends go out for a dinner to celebrate the New Year and their new adventure. They all agreed to go to the Seneca Powers Hotel because they always had fun there. Wallace made the arrangements for the dinner with Mr. Helfer.

This time was not going to be the same as other holidays. They wanted a dinner to celebrate the end of one thing and the beginning of something new. Mr. Helfer reserved an area on the side of the dining room for 7PM that was away from the larger party groups.

Everyone met in the lobby just before 7PM. Wallace invited Winston but he would come only if Louis were invited. Wallace did not want him to bring Louis but he knew this might be the last time he would see Winston. He told him that he could bring Louis. Winston thanked him but made sure Wallace understood why Louis was around. This was because Wallace was denying his true feelings for him. When Winston told him that he knew he had made a mistake. Wallace wondered how Winston could be so certain of his feelings for him. The atmosphere was festive. There were holiday decorations on the tables and the usual classy arrangement of napkins and dining accessories. Everyone laughed and reminisced about that first party at the opening in the new hotel and how wonderful it had been. The women still talked about the time on stage with the men. This time Winston made no comments about the entertainment. He only referred to them as gone just like the Top Banana. Wallace knew he said that for his benefit. He knew Winston was hurting inside and finally became aware about what all this meant to Winston. Eveline was having a good time with Louis. She thought he was cute and refreshing. He was her age and did not seem to have any problems with how things were between Wallace and Winston. Frank blurted out that maybe Eveline and Louis would become friends. Alice shook her head and rolled her eyes. Eveline's mother told everyone that her daughter seemed to have all types of new friends with her father chiming in "I can't wait to see who she'll find in Buffalo."

Everyone laughed and she blushed. Eveline told them that she could not wait to get to Buffalo. Winston did not say anything and just sat and looked down at his plate. Eveline sensed that Winston was not too engaged with the conversations. She told him that she wanted him to come to Buffalo to stay with them sometime. He looked at her and a sparkle came into his eye. He told her he would love to come to Buffalo. He wondered if Louis could come too. She told him that he really needed to come by himself. Wallace had no reaction but was thinking to himself how good that would be.

Midnight came and everyone celebrated the New Year with a glass of champagne. As usual the dinner presentation was top-notch. Mr. Helfer came to the table to wish Wallace and Eveline well. Mr. Helfer took Wallace aside and whispered something in his ear while everyone was chitchatting about the past parties and events. Winston caught sight of him doing that and wondered what he said to him. Wallace looked puzzled while Mr. Helfer was speaking with him. Wallace nodded his head as if in agreement. The group was walking out of the restaurant into the lobby when Winston told Wallace that he saw Mr. Helfer telling him something. Wallace was surprised anyone had seen him do that. There was so much confusion at that time. Winston asked what he said and Wallace told him that it was something about Hilda. Wallace told him that he did not have time to talk with him. How was he going to find out what Mr. Helfer had to say? The train was leaving in 9 hours and they might not be back for a long time. After the good-byes everyone went off in different directions. Wallace and Eveline walked to their apartment. Winston and Louis walked with them so they could have some last moments together. Winston wanted to say good-bye to them privately. Surprisingly he would miss both of them and not just Wallace. Louis stood there watching while the three of them hugged each other. Eveline kissed Winston and then Wallace and told them that the two of them were like one. To this they both agreed. Louis wondered what had just happened as they walked down the street. Winston told him that they had been friends for a long time and had many experiences together. He explained about his father and how Alice had been like his mother and Frank like a father. He told Louis that he would probably be close to Wallace for the rest of his life.

Chapter 29

On January 1 the snow began falling and winds began to blow across New York State. As Wallace and Eveline were waiting for the train in the morning the people in the train station were all worried that they may not get to their destination. This was a blizzard that many had not seen in years. The trains had been delayed because the tracks were covered with blowing snow. The temperature was a frigid 5 degrees. The plows that were attached to the front of the engines were not able to clear the snow enough for the trains to go ahead. The train to Buffalo was delayed for three hours. Wallace told Eveline about the delays when he and Winston were trying to return from Buffalo after the Exposition and the assassination of President McKinley. He told her about the fun they had at the Pan-Am and all that happened to them in two days. She told him that she never went to the Exposition but that her parents went with their friends that live on Delaware Avenue. They stayed at their mansion on Delaware Avenue but she was not included. She laughed and told Wallace it was for adults only. He asked her how big her friend's mansion was. She told him they had servants and a driver for their fancy carriages. He thought about that style of living in comparison to the way his family lived. His father was the provider of the carriages and that family actually lived in high style. Eveline told him about the home they left in Canada when they moved to the United States that sounded to Wallace like the mansion on Delaware Avenue. As they finally boarded the train Wallace wondered why Eveline was so attracted to him and not someone of a higher-class. They found a seat on the train and tried to get warm because the doors were open and the wind was blowing snow and cold air inside the train. They watched the workers load their trunks into the baggage car. When the car was loaded they could not close the door because the snow had drifted against it making the runners fall off the track. After they reconnected the baggage car door the train slowly left Rochester. The conductor announced that they were going extra slow because the engineer could not see very far ahead. The plow that they used on the front of the train was not able to clear the snow fast enough because the snow was drifting higher than the train. At one point it looked like the train was going through a tunnel. Even though it was morning the sky was dark grey with heavy clouds and the snow was blowing so hard that it seemed like nighttime was upon them. They sat quietly hugging one another to stay warm. Wallace said, "What a way to begin a new adventure." Eveline looked at him and said nothing. She was thinking about how life was going to be living away from her family. She was hoping that she would not miss everyone too much. She knew the family on Delaware Avenue so at least she could visit them. Probably she would meet new people at her new job at the law office. Wallace could tell she was pensive so he reassured her that things would be fine. He told her that they would have everything they wanted if they just worked at it together. She smiled and appeared more confident. The conductor was very good about calming people down when the train would sway and jerk around. The wind made the train shake and the bumps on the rails from the snow pack made it feel like they were riding on a wagon instead of a train. It was a tedious trip that took an extra two hours. The train arrived in Buffalo mid-afternoon. The trunks were unloaded from the baggage car and there they stood in the frigid air with snow blowing all around. Wallace asked the conductor who could help them transport their possessions to their new home. Just as he was speaking to the conductor a burly snow covered man came up to Wallace and Eveline. He tipped his cap and asked if they were Mr. and Mrs. Paine. Wallace shook his head. The man had a raspy voice and was smoking a short stubby cigar. It shook in his mouth as he spoke with them. Eveline did not dare move a muscle. His hands were dirty with big rough hairy fingers and bulging knuckles. He told them that Mr. Harmon instructed him to stay there until the train from Rochester arrived. He figured they were the only two people getting off the train that looked scared and lost. He assured them as he blew nasty cigar smoke at them that he would take good care of them. Wallace looked at Eveline with an uncertain eye. They stood there as the man hoisted the trunks up on his shoulder and put them in a buggy. Wallace stared at him when he lifted the trunks up in the air like they were made of paper. The burly man took Eveline's hand and helped her into the buggy. Wallace was not sure about what the man was going to do or where they might end up. It was a cold ride because it was an open-air buggy. The winds were bitter cold and pierced their faces like needles and pins. The man offered them his scarf to cover their faces. They accepted but quickly cast it away. It smelled foul like an old cigar or something that had never been washed.

There were very few people on the streets and only a few buggies were around as they approached Delaware Avenue. The man knew exactly where he was taking them. He told them the place was an apartment building that was considered one of the finest ones on the street. It was right in downtown so they could walk to everything. The buggy pulled up to the front of 112 Delaware Avenue. It was a six family block. Their apartment was on the second floor. The hallway was lit with gas lamps that flickered as they walked by. Wallace was telling Eveline that some places had electricity nowadays. As they were shown into the apartment they were greeted with a flickering fire in the fireplace. The driver explained that he had been instructed to have the fire going when they arrived. He told them that he wondered if it would last because he had been waiting at the station much longer than expected. He threw more wood on the fire and it rekindled and burned furiously. He hauled the trunks into the apartment and explained that the furniture was not new but was used by another couple that had just moved from the company. This was an apartment that the HO Company maintained for new management employees. The man was now chewing on the tip of the cigar with saliva running from the sides of his mouth while he told them he was leaving. He stood at the door as if he was waiting for something. Wallace looked at Eveline and she motioned to his pocket. Wallace realized that the man was waiting for some money. Wallace gave him a tip and thanked him for his time. He tipped his cap to Eveline and she smiled. She was thinking how dirty he appeared with his stringy hair hanging below his ears. He reminded her of a hobo. He left and they stood in the living room wondering what to do next. Wallace had to go to work the next day. Eveline was luckier because her job did not start for another week. She would have time to unpack and organize the place for them. They would have to get used to living in a new place and find out about their neighborhood. Eveline told Wallace that she was happy that they had finally arrived and that it had been a long trip and they needed to get some rest.

Wallace was excited about his first day on his new job. He was going to be the advertising manager for the company. The H.O. Company was a large company that dealt with grains and preparation of corn and oats. They had made advancements with drying processes too. The cleaning and drying house was a six-story fireproof building constructed entirely of brick and steel with concrete floors. It was the first of its kind. The company was using steam and motors that would blow the steam across the oats for drying. They were the first to develop rolled-oats for breakfast food. It was the first grain company that was committed to a virtual fireproof operation. Grain elevators were noted for having fires that could ruin a company and put people out of work. The company was interested in having an aggressive advertising campaign. They had been looking for a young and creative person to formulate new ideas for advertising. They had read some of the news articles that Wallace wrote when he had his newspaper in Rochester. They told him they were especially impressed with the section in the paper for responses. Their philosophy at H.O. was to encourage customer involvement. When they met Wallace their first question was how he could make their products look better and sell more. Wallace had thought about that when he applied for the job. He told them that slogans and jingles would help people remember the product. He explained that slogans and jingles were things that people could not get out of their heads. If that approach was successful, when the customer saw the products, they would automatically buy it. He thought that children would be a good audience to appeal to. Children ate breakfast, wanted to be entertained and usually wanted a prize if they ate what their parents gave them. His first goal was to design an advertisement that would say those exact things. Mr. Harmon and his secretary-treasurer Mr. Booth could not believe he had the plan already worked out. They gave him his budget and the people that he would need to help him make the first plan happen. While Wallace was designing the advertisement for the children he thought about something similar to the Larkin Plan. The coupon idea was a real attraction and kept people buying from the Larkin's. Why couldn't he develop something that would be like that idea but have a different twist? While he drew up the logo for the company he knew the circus was a big attraction in Buffalo. The country was in the midst of "The Golden Age of the Circus." The trains would roll into town with many animals, tents, poles, circus entertainers, and the side shows. As much as he hated the Midway at the Exposition he knew most people with children loved the circus, rides, and the sideshows. He decided to include with the rolled oats an H.O. coin. When you collected 20 coins you could turn them in for a free ticket to the circus. The company would purchase hundreds of the tickets from the circus at a reduced rate. They would still make money on the product because people would feel they were getting something for free. They knew people had to eat breakfast so why not rolled oats.

While Wallace was working on the circus promotion he had another idea that was focused on children. In addition to a coin he was trying to think of a prize for eating rolled oats. He decided to incorporate Hengerer's Department store in the promotion with the HO Company. He knew parents would do anything to keep their children happy. Wallace thought about putting a wrapped item in each box of oats. Along with the coin for the circus ticket there would be a sample of a small toy. When the box of oats was finished the prize package could be opened. The key was to make the package hidden in the box so you would have to finish the whole thing before you could get the prize. There would be a special compartment built in each container. Whatever the item was could be redeemed at the department store for free. The items were not very costly so when Wallace presented the idea he would have to reassure Mr. Harmon and Mr. Booth that these would not incur a huge expense. The plan would bring business into Hengerer's Department store. It was a co-operative move on their part and everyone was likely to make it profitable. He needed to create a style for advertising just as he did for the Seneca Powers Hotel. This company was much different than the classy hotel style he created in Rochester. A grain-cereal company was not classy but was something everyone needed. He used a bold block pattern. He created big, wide, and massive lettering for the name of the company. His slogan would be "Eat H.O. Oats and get Big and Strong." Again, he knew that would appeal to the growing population. Parents would want their children to be strong and healthy. These themes would encourage a healthy life style by eating the right food for breakfast. He proposed that the new promotions be placed in magazines, newspapers and all the streetcars. Wallace thought that the more you show the products the more business will be created.

Wallace had finally reached a point in his job that his ideas were being accepted without any criticism from Mr.

Harmon. It was almost like working for Mr. Helfer. The only thing missing was a person like Hilda. He laughed when he thought about her. Wallace was able to spend money on promotions. He convinced the officers that if they spent money they would make money. He suggested that a line of clothing for children with the H.O. logo might encourage more and varied sales. Simple caps, gloves, and suspenders could be featured in the store. Parents could buy them as presents and other sales would happen while shopping in Hengerer's. He referred to it as a marriage between the two companies. An H.O. Oats display was set up and presented to Mr. Harmon, Mr. Booth and the promotions department at Hengerer's. Wallace was sure to have it well organized and appealing if a department store was to consider using it. In order to make it work he needed a gimmick. He thought about it for a while and decided to use a clown. He thought that if a clown were part of the display children would be sure to want to get something from the clown. It was a hit! He recommended a "White Clown" instead of an "Auguste Clown." A white clown was fancier. An Auguste Clown was colored red and was usually the buffoon of the show wearing stripes, checks, and oversized accessories. In a circus the white clown was like the Top Banana who ran the show with the other clowns. Wallace liked the reference to the Top Banana when he remembered the burlesque show in Rochester. The Top Banana was the one! Hengerers contracted with a supplier that would produce the merchandise for the store. They created a cereal bowl with a clown on it and the H.O. logo. A complete line of breakfast utensils was manufactured so that children could have an entire place setting of H.O. oats items. Never before had two completely opposite companies created such a profitable blend of business.

Eveline's new job was much more involved than her former job in Rochester. She was a receptionist for a large law firm. She was in the main office of a firm that occupied the entire floor of a building in Downtown Buffalo. She liked her job because she interacted with many people. She enjoyed buying new clothes for work that were of the latest fashion. Eveline had a sporty yet classy way about her appearance. She would always wear a wide brim hat that she would carefully and deliberately remove and place on the hat rack when she entered the office. She wore her hair in a high bun that would not be noticed under her hat. Jewelry was a necessity for her. She loved the pearl earrings and matching necklace that Wallace had given her. She wore them almost everyday. The dresses she wore were a bit fancier than most women might wear for work. The men in the office took notice when she would arrive in the morning. It was like part of the morning routine to see what Eveline was wearing that day. She loved the attention. Her dresses usually had wide necklines that were edged in lace. Some of them had over sleeves and under sleeves with pleated chiffon or other types of silk or lace. She had a small waist that would compliment the narrow belt and a flared skirt type bottom. She had a liking for shoes. Some of her shoes had buckles across the foot and some had leather buttons that went up the side of the foot. Still others had small fabric sewn in designs for variety. Wallace told her that she should always look good and that she could use her salary any way she wanted to. One day while she was walking on Delaware Avenue she found a dress shop that sold accessories to match the dresses. She was in heaven. She would go to the shop every week when she got paid. She would have some of her clothes handmade and buy others that she liked in the shop. The lady who owned the shop was a friend of her parent's friends who lived further up the avenue. When Eveline told her why she was in Buffalo she was included in a young socialite group. It was fun being recognized by new people who were a step above the rest. When she told Wallace of her adventures and invitation to a socialite group he thought that was a perfect way to spend her time.

Time was moving very fast for Wallace and Eveline. They had met many new people either through the socialite group or being invited to corporate functions. The department store idea with the HO Company proved to be good way to meet people who were involved in the growth of Buffalo. Eveline began to shop in the ladies department at Hengerer's also. They were considered the largest department store between Chicago and New York City. It was compared to shopping at Macy's in New York City. Wallace started to buy his suits and apparel in the men's department at Hengerer's. After a while the salesmen and women knew the Paines when they came into the store. Styles were changing for men. The suits were now tailored with smaller lapels and trousers were tailored with a cuff on the bottom. Shoes were being made with less ankle support. Spats were not used as much either. Dress shoes where tied with shoelaces with a six-hole lacing rather than up the ankle style. Bow ties were still fashionable but now a tie that would hang to the waist was part of the latest style for men. Depending on the occasion the men's hats had changed also. Some were caps and some were still top hats but some were wide brimmed with a short stack for a top. They were useful in the summer. They were made with straw that was loosely woven for air circulation.

Wallace still carried his pocket watch that you could keep inside your jacket now or still wear it on the outside of the coat.

Toward the end of the summer Wallace received news that his car was being delivered to Buffalo. He was thrilled to think that he was finally going to have one of the first cars. When Eveline got home from work Wallace met her in the entrance to the building. She thought that was strange since she always got home first. Many nights he would not arrive home until after dark. She always knew something was up when he changed his schedule. He greeted her and asked how her day was. She told him fine and asked what was wrong. He laughed and said, "There's no problem, my car is coming soon." Eveline then asked him how he paid for it? Wallace hesitated because he did not want her to know about his financial affairs. He told her that it was a present from the newspaper company in Rochester. She looked puzzled but made no response about the particulars of the money. Wallace justified it in his mind that it was a gift. The only little thing he left out was his discretionary fund that he had set up with the newspaper company. He thought to himself, what is a little lie by omission?

It was a typical western New York autumn day. Wallace had to pick up his car at the railroad station. It was the only car being delivered to Buffalo that day. He was sure to be at the station by noon. He took the morning off from work. He thought about driving the car. He really did not know much about it. He read about the steering mechanism and the crank that helped it start. Somewhere he read that he might need a pair of goggles. He thought that was funny but had purchased a pair for what ever the reason might be. He felt like a little kid waiting for the train. He kept reminding himself that he was one of the first people to own a car. He heard the whistle of the train and saw the black smoke from the engine as it pulled into the station. There it was all by itself. His very own Ford and it was red. The men carefully rolled it off the train. Wallace stood there watching this machine come at him. The man in charge handed him an envelope. Wallace opened it and found some papers that explained about the car and how it worked. The first thing was how to start it and make it go. He knew there was fuel in it because the directions said that. The crank thing in the front was interesting as he went over to it and began turning it. Suddenly the car sputtered and shook. The man at the station said that he might want to get in it and see how it moves. Wallace got in the seat and held on to the steering mechanism. He looked scared to death. The car did not move but just shook and sounded like a machine working. He thought that there must be something wrong with it. Maybe he got a bad one. As he was moving his feet around he touched a thing on the floor. All of a sudden the car jerked forward. Wallace screamed and everyone roared with laughter as he started down the path to the road. They yelled, "Good Luck." Finally he realized that the thing on the floor made it move but how could he make it stop? He remembered reading about a thing that you pulled slowly to make it slow down. He found that, and pulled it and the car slowed down. His goggles were hanging around his neck. He laughed when he realized it felt like a necklace. He put them on his face. He moved slowly toward Delaware Avenue avoiding horses and buggies and swerving around to miss people. People were pointing and laughing when he passed by. Wallace did not think it was funny but was to busy learning what the machine could do. He found out about the reason for the goggles. Lots of bugs and dust were flying in his face and before he knew it his goggles were so dirty that he could not see where he was going. By this time he was in front of 112 Delaware Avenue. He was happy he had made it home without any mishaps.

Wallace decided to leave the car in front of the apartment building in back of a horse and buggy. He figured it was as good as any place to keep the car. People passed by and hesitated and wondered what it was and what it was doing there. Wallace stood next to it like it was a prize he had just won. While he was explaining to a lady passing by about the car Eveline walked up the street. She stopped and appeared to be in shock. He waved at her and smiled and pointed to his car. She walked up to the car and stared at it. Wallace laughed and told her that it was not a disease. She shook her head and thought it was beautiful. She did not know what to expect. He asked her if she wanted to go for a ride. She hesitated but got into the passenger side. Wallace did the crank thing and she screamed when it started shaking. He stuck his head up from the front of the car and acted confident. He knew how scared he was at first but would never admit that to her. He got in the drivers side. She was frozen, no motion, no conversation. There was a crowd in the street watching them now. Wallace put on his goggles appearing completely confident. He touched the thing on the floor and the car jerked forward which made Eveline scream again. Down the street they went going about 5 miles an hour. She told him she was afraid that it might kill them. Wallace told her to enjoy the ride and pushed the thing on the floor harder making the car go even faster. They went around the block toward Main Street where there were streetcars, horse and buggies, and people to avoid. Eveline was still screaming when they turned onto Main Street. She covered her eyes and Wallace laughed hysterically. All of a sudden he thought of Winston. He thought of their time at the Exposition when they were on the rides. He now saw Eveline as scared as he was on then. He felt like Winston laughing and being the funny guy now. He saw Eveline scared to death and he realized he did miss his buddy Winston. They arrived back in front of the apartment building. Eveline slowly got out of her seat while Wallace cleaned off his goggles. They looked at the car as if they could not believe it was there. Eveline was not sure she wanted to do that again. Wallace told her they would go further the next time.

Chapter 30

The advertising plans at the H.O.Company were paying off. Both Hengerer's and the H.O.Company were seeing profits. It was a good blend of businesses. Wallace had received a number of pay raises as a result of his advertising expertise. He created a new jingle for the company every few months. His latest one was, "H.O. is more than oatmeal and is health in packages." Every time he created a new slogan or jingle he would have it advertised in all the public places in Buffalo. As part of his branching out of Buffalo he sent the advertisements to other cities. They would have advertisements in the newspapers and magazines throughout the country. The products were being sold everywhere. A new production plant was opened in Cedar Rapids, Iowa. All the national advertising would be sent from the corporate office in Buffalo. Wallace's job in Buffalo had a different salary base. He received an annual salary. There was no negotiation of matching his salary as he had in Rochester. If he chose to invest in a company he was free to do what he wanted. He did invest one-third of his earnings into Larkin Company stocks.

Frank Lloyd Wright had been commissioned to design buildings and homes in Buffalo. He was designing the Darwin Martin House at 125 Jewett Parkway. Martin was a Larkin executive and wanted Wright to design a prairie style home for him and his wife, Isabella. In the same neighborhood, Wright designed a home for Martin's sister and brother-in-law. A gardener's house was designed and built making it a small community of Wrightonian homes. The Larkin Building was completed in 1904 just a year before Wallace started working in Buffalo. He mentioned to Mr. Harmon something about the Larkin Company in a conversation. Co-incidentally there was an annual meeting of company executives the next Monday. Wallace was included in the meeting. It was to be held in the new Larkin Building at 680 Seneca Street. Wallace offered to escort Mr. Harmon and Mr. Booth to the meeting. He told them that they could have a ride in his new car. They thought that would be a fine idea. They were looking forward to having a tour of the new facility that Wright designed. It was the most up to date building and everyone in Buffalo was eager to see it.

The Larkin Building was a showplace. The company had spent four million dollars on the construction of the building. The building was referred to as one of the finest buildings Wright had ever designed. It had a large central atrium rising to the full height of the building. It was constructed of red brick with a pink tinted mortar that made it unique from inside to outside. The central court of light came from windows between brick piers illuminated side galley offices. On the top level there was a kitchen, bakery, dining rooms, classrooms, a conservatory and a branch of the Buffalo Public Library. There was a roof garden paved with red brick. This served as a recreation area for employees, families and guests. The meeting they were attending was being held on the roof top areas. This would enable all the company executives attending the meeting to view their properties from the roof of the Larkin building. It was a very impressive setting that offered a citywide view. As Wallace, Mr. Harmon, and Mr. Booth entered the building they noticed the building had on either side of the entrance two waterfall-like fountains. There were globes on the tops of the building's central exterior piers. It was like a huge monument to architectural grandeur. Wright had incorporated the newest inventions for the building. He designed electrical fixtures that enabled employees to work in plentiful lighting. He designed another first for a major office building, which was an air-conditioning system that would purify and cool the air. The focus for the building was to be clean and appealing to everyone. It could maintain 1800 employees who were secretaries, clerks, and executives of the flourishing mail-order company. The company wanted to attract women employees to an industrial section of the city. Larkin believed in giving women equal employment. Larkin was the first to have benefits for his employees. It was called the Larkin Benefit Association. It was a self help plan to provide financial benefits to employees in cases involving sickness, need, and death of family members. Larkin hired trained nurses for both office and factory employees. There were medical facilities and rest rooms for men and women throughout the company. During the opening remarks Mr. Martin was quite proud of what the company stood for and offered their employees. At the same time the latest endeavor with Frank Lloyd Wright was discussed. Martin gave a description of his home being created on Jewett Parkway. He jokingly boasted that Wright was given virtually an unlimited budget for the design of the Martin House. During the construction fifty men were paid $2 a day and worked 10 hours, six days a week for two years. The brick and wood house had

15,000 square feet with an open floor plan. Almost every room looked out onto gardens and trees on the property. At the close of the speech they were all invited to see the home on Jewett Parkway. He was given a standing ovation. Everyone agreed that the Larkin Company was a multi-million dollar business, which stood for progress and integrity.

It was quite an afternoon.The meeting had been highly motivating and talking with the different executives was interesting.Every company had a slightly different approach to their operations. One of the Larkin executives made a point to speak with Wallace. He was interested in having a meeting with him. He had heard about his successful advertising plans both in Rochester and now in Buffalo. Wallace was delighted to set up an appointment with him for next week. Later Mr. Harmon asked Wallace what the conversation was about. Wallace was a little hesitant to tell him but thought it may be a good negotiating tool for a raise in salary. When he told Mr. Harmon about his appointment there was a brief silence. Mr. Harmon thought that was a good idea. He told Wallace maybe he could get some new ideas. Wallace did not take that the same way. He did not respond to that statement. He thought that maybe a new direction for himself might emerge from his meeting. On the way out of the meeting there was a lot of discussion about seeing the Martin House. Wallace decided that he was not going to see the house with the people from the H.O.Company. He knew it would be a good place to drive on the weekend with Eveline. Wallace drove back to the office with Mr. Harmon and Mr. Booth. They were asking Wallace about owning a car and what the costs were. They were a few years older than he was but they had not thought about a car yet. Wallace thought to himself, as they were discussing how such a young guy could have such a nice car, why was he always about 10 years ahead of men his age? He laughed to himself and thought it is because I have a plan.

The weekend arrived and Wallace and Eveline took a ride to see the Martin house. Wallace made sure that he had an idea of where the street was. He asked a few people in the neighborhood. They all said to stay on Delaware Avenue almost to the end. Jewett Parkway was near that point. There was a park near there too. Wallace remembered the park from the Exposition. Then he remembered this area. The difference was that this time he was going with his wife and not Winston. How things had changed in 5 years. They got into the car, which still made Eveline nervous. Wallace had more experience operating the car now, which made this ride much smoother. They rode down Delaware Avenue and went past the mansion her families friends lived in. Eveline told Wallace that they could stop on the way home to visit them and Wallace told her he thought that was a good idea. He really wanted to show off his flashy red car. They saw many large homes as they drove on Delaware Avenue. The closer they got to the park the more Wallace remembered the whole area. He was explaining to Eveline all about the facts and figures about the building of the Martin House. They found Jewett Parkway and there on the corner was an enormous house. It was not like any of the other houses in the neighborhood. It was long and seemed to extend from one street corner to the next. It had low-pitched rooflines. There were hundreds of windows. Concrete decorations featured the corners of the house. It was difficult to call it a house because it looked like an office building and not like the conventional home. Frank Lloyd Wright believed that the house should be part of the environment and that both the inside and outside should become one. The use of windows and landscaping created a year around feel when inside the house. Wallace knew Wright was committed to entirety. He would design the entire property including furniture that would be bolted into the floors. They got out of the car to take a walk around to see other parts of the property. They could see a veranda and pergolas that connected the gardens. There was an oriental connection with some of the gardens and designs. The floricycle that Wright designed was a semi-circular garden that was set away from the house. It contained a variety of plants that would bloom year-round. They noticed as they walked down the side street that there were formal gardens around the house and some would be used for cutting gardens. They could hear water running from a fountain. Some of the grounds could not be seen from the street. Wallace remembered that Darwin Martin referred to Wright's work as organic architecture. Now he knew what that meant. It was as if you lived inside and outside. He stood on the corner of the street looking at the house. He liked the style of the house especially the stained glass in some of the windows. The roofline and its heaviness seemed masculine to him too. He told Eveline that a house like this needs a certain type of person living in it and asked her if she liked it. All she could manage to do was to stare and say it looked huge to her. He then asked if she would like to live in a house like this and she said, "You probably already have it planned." He laughed and told her that he did not have the plan yet but would soon.

On the way back home Wallace was wondering what he was going to hear at the meeting next week at Larkin's. Eveline was quiet and appeared tired. Wallace's mind was in high gear. Between seeing the Martin house and the meeting he did not know what to think of first. He knew a house like the Martin's had to be for special people. They had to be able to live the part that the house represented. That house represented success in every way. He thought that would be a good goal for him. He knew he could have a house similar to that but maybe not as big. He wondered where he would have it built. He did not think he would stay in Buffalo forever. Between everything he saw at The Pan-American Exposition just a few blocks away 5 years ago and now this house; he made a plan. They pulled up in front of the mansion of Eveline's parent's friends just as the butler was opening the front door. A woman came outside and saw Eveline. She was happy to see her. Eveline introduced Wallace to her while the woman admired Wallace's red car. This made him feel very happy as Eveline and he went into the house. The butler took their hats and stared at Wallace's goggles smiling while asking if he had just come from the undersea world. Everyone thought that was funny. The butler smiled and said, "Sporty chap." The house was very ornate with gold objects everywhere. The rooms were excessively decorated with things from all over the world. Eveline told Wallace that these people traveled all the time. The maid was quick to serve refreshments and pastries. Wallace had never been in such a place but Eveline seemed to be right at home. They had a conversation about their visit to the Martin house. The woman commented on the car again and how much she liked it. She had heard about the Martin house but had a slightly different opinion of it. She thought it was cold and impersonal and laughing said that she liked the gaudy and overdone style of her home better. Wallace wondered again as he often did how he got tangled up with all these people. If they only knew where he came from the story might be different. He learned to be quiet when he was not sure of what to do. There was a much different side of him when he was on his own. He knew he could survive doing anything. He also realized everything would be okay if Eveline had all she needed. That is probably why they got along so well. The visit came to an end but Eveline did not invite the woman to visit them. When they got into the car Wallace asked her why she had not invited her to visit them. She acted reluctant to tell him that she was afraid of what she might go back and tell her parents about their apartment. Wallace was stunned and said nothing. He felt like he was not good enough for her class of people and her way of life. What then did Eveline see in him?

Wallace's meeting at the Larkin Company was the next day. He had a week to think about what it might be all about. In his usual fashion he dressed up in his best business suit. Everything in place and clean was his motto. He made sure his pocket watch was with him because time was worth keeping. Every time he had an important meeting he made sure he had his old watch. It was like a trusty friend and timepiece that meant good luck was on its way. He drove the car to the appointment. He was getting to like driving the car around town. Someone always noticed him in it. Just as he was parking the car, Mr. Jackson, who Wallace was to meet, walked up to the car. He was impressed with the car making a great first impression. The discussion focused on what Wallace knew about shipping and advertising beyond the United States. Wallace was put on the spot with this question. He thought about what it would be like to send goods to other parts of the country but not out of the United States. Since Buffalo had such a good shipping industry and a waterway to the ocean, maybe something could be developed. Mr. Jackson wanted Wallace to think about a plan for an import and export business. He suggested that Wallace think in terms of being founder and owner of the company. Wallace asked why just him? Mr. Jackson explained that it would be a separate operation from the Larkin Company. Wallace sensed a complex set of conditions with the proposal but found it intriguing. They set another time to meet about a business of that sort. They would meet at the Statler Hilton Hotel for lunch next week. He was a little confused and yet excited with the possibilities of doing business in foreign markets. He drove back to work and reviewed his latest set of advertisements for the upcoming season. Business had been booming with the promotions he instituted for the company. Mr. Harmon and Mr. Booth were happy with the financial aspect of what had happened in the last two years. They asked Wallace to sit with them in the office. Wallace thought something was wrong. His head was spinning with the meeting he just had and now another meeting. They thanked him for his loyalty and wanted to know how his meeting had gone at Larkin's. Wallace got the impression that they thought he might leave and go to work for Larkin. He explained that there was some discussion about an import and export business being developed. He told them it was not connected to the H.O.Company. They looked puzzled and asked what he was doing about the import and export business. He told them he had to think about it and get back to Mr. Jackson next week. They asked him to keep them up to date on the progress of that idea. Wallace thanked them and wondered why they were so interested in what Mr. Jackson wanted.

Chapter 31

ECONOMIC GROWTH THROUGHOUT THE United States was on the rise. Industries were booming. The economic news reported large profits due to imports and exports. Wallace kept track of what were the most popular items being traded in the country. He met Mr. Jackson at the Statler Hilton Hotel. It was a newly constructed hotel and a fine example of a modern facility. It was the first hotel to have a bathroom for each guest room. No longer did a guest have to share facilities in the hallway.There were 360 rooms with many large convention rooms and restaurants all within the hotel. It was in the center of downtown Buffalo, near to shopping, theater and restaurants. Mr. Jackson paid for the exquisite lunch that was served on gold plates and stemware that had been engraved by Hawkes Crystal Company; a world famous engraving company in Corning, New York. Many of the glass displays in the hotel were of Steuben Glass.

Wallace listened to Mr. Jackson explain about the reports of the multi-million dollar business in foreign trade markets. He asked Wallace what he had decided about the possibility of developing a trade company. Wallace asked him why he did not want to be the founder. Mr. Jackson explained that it was better that he remain out of the trade company because of his involvement with the Larkin Company. Wallace told him that he had to be concerned about his job with the H.O. Company. It was then that Mr. Jackson explained why Mr. Harmon and Mr. Booth were so interested in this meeting. Mr. Jackson wanted to create a business that would trade Larkin soaps in the Orient. He could arrange for the soaps to be repackaged into a more appropriate container that would appeal to the woman in the Orient and Europe. They would market it as something with a more exotic name other than Crème Oatmeal Soap. Mr. Jackson could arrange to have large quantities sent from the factory to an address in Buffalo then transport them by train to New York City. From that point they would be sent by ship to Europe and Asia. Wallace asked why Mr. Harmon and Mr. Booth were so interested in this idea; Mr. Jackson had already discussed the idea with them. Since the soap was marketed as oatmeal soap it would be easier to pass it off as cheap hand soap. They could send it overseas in a basic container like you might ship oatmeal in. It would keep the shipments dry and then they could sell the oats on the streets in foreign countries. Mr. Jackson carefully included that there could be other items sent along with the soap. Wallace began to see that this was more than a soap sale trade. Wallace's bosses had already agreed to use their grain elevators for storage of items that were ready to go to New York City. Wallace was confused about why he would have to be the founder. Mr. Jackson said they would all be equal but since Wallace was younger and not as well known as the others they felt it would be a good way for him to make big money with them. He would appear to be the main man and the other men would be financing the operation. They would all get an equal percentage of the profits.

Wallace thought about it for a while. He had questions for his bosses at the H.O.Company. When he returned to the office he asked to speak with them in private. Wallace told them what he had learned about the connection with Mr. Jackson and the proposed company. They explained that they thought it was more appropriate for Mr. Jackson to present the possibilities of a trade company to him. The Larkin Company was supplying the soap that was the main seller. The oatmeal was being used as a packing material because it was cheap and a good cover. Wallace questioned the phrase, "a good cover." He wanted to know what they were covering up. They told him that it would make the product look cheaper in transport but then could be converted to a high priced item when it arrived in the other countries. They would have people in other locations repackaging the items sent from the United States. Wallace knew from the reports he had read that there was tremendous importing and exporting going on in the country. He was beginning to think it was worth doing. He asked them what was going to be shipped back to the United States. Mr. Harmon and Mr. Booth became a little uneasy with that question. Wallace knew that there was more to this plan than they had originally mentioned. They explained that they were all going to have a meeting if Wallace agreed to partner with them. The last thing they wanted him to consider was a person who could be the foreman who would head up the operations. Wallace would be his boss and tell him what was happening and he would organize the schedule for shipping to and from Buffalo then from New York. Mr. Harmon asked Wallace if this was something he wanted to be a part of. The potential for profits was tremendous. Wallace asked if he could have the night to think about it. They agreed that would be fine. They would await his decision and see him in the morning.

While Wallace was going home that evening he thought about how his life had become so complicated since he left Rochester. He had made lots of money in Rochester which seemed like child's play compared to all the things that had happened in the two years he and Eveline had been in Buffalo. He knew it was a bigger city with more potential but this last idea was like something from a story. He wanted to agree to do it but who could be the foreman? He did not really know many people that would fill that type of position. There were still some questions he had about the cargo returning to the United States. He thought that knowing the two men from HO would at least be better than being alone with the new company. When Eveline came home Wallace was resting in a chair in the living room that was something he rarely did. She asked if he was sick. He told her that he was thinking about business and what he wanted to do with his future. She left him alone. He mentioned the need for another worker. He did not tell her what the business was going to be. He implied it was at the H.O. Company. He told her he needed a person who was willing to be out in the front as a worker heading up a new operation. She listened and casually said with a smile on her face, "Ask Winston." Wallace asked her if she was kidding? She told him she was not kidding and it would be a good way to get him to Buffalo and then they could all be together again. Wallace thought that was a great idea. He would write a letter to him and ask if he was interested in the job. Wallace thought the idea might work out just fine. He would need to get some of his questions answered tomorrow. He sat down and composed a letter to Winston.

Wallace went to work and completed his advertisements for the next month at H.O. Company. He saw Mr. Booth and

Mr. Harmon and told them he had thought of someone to be a foreman. They were pleased to hear that. Wallace told them he wanted to have a few more questions answered at lunch. They assured him that Mr. Jackson would be able to answer anything he needed to know. They asked Wallace how soon the foreman would be available. He said he was not sure because the letter went to Rochester today. They seemed satisfied with that. They decided to walk to the restaurant since it was warm and sunny for early March. As they were walking Mr. Jackson met up with them and they continued to the restaurant. Mr. Jackson asked what his decision was. Wallace explained about the foreman first and then asked the question about the cargo coming back to the United States. Mr. Jackson sharply told him not to talk about that in public. Wallace thought his response was abrupt and suspicious sounding. The other men said nothing and everyone kept walking. They got to the restaurant and took their seats at a secluded corner table. The atmosphere was not as elegant as the first lunch he had with Mr. Jackson. The tone and attitude of the men seemed more suspicious to Wallace than the first time.

While they were studying the menu Mr. Jackson apologized to Wallace for being so short with him on the street. He explained that there were many people out there that were always trying to undercut one another. It was better to discuss things in private. He looked at all of them and made sure they understood that not everyone was your friend. Wallace thought to himself that he was getting into the real world in a hurry. Lunch was ordered and Wallace asked his questions about what was being imported into the United States. Mr. Jackson explained that the four of them would be co-owners. If there were any unforeseen problems they could easily transfer the name of the business to someone or even something else. It was common practice to transfer ownership of homes and businesses to spouses, children, or anyone who could not be held responsible for the financial indebtedness of the operation. Wallace felt better knowing that he would not lose his investments if the company failed. The question of cargo coming back to the United States finally was addressed. Mr. Harmon began by explaining that there was a reason for the oatmeal going to the other countries. Wallace looked at him with a quizzical expression. There was a huge market in America for opium. Wallace had heard of it but knew nothing of its importance to the economy. Mr. Jackson spoke up and reminded him that this was confidential. He made certain that the foreman should never know what was shipped back to America mixed into the oatmeal. It was as if a hammer hit Wallace on the head. The soap was not expensive. The oatmeal was a good packing method and cheap. Probably no one would suspect the transfers. Mr. Booth explained that there was big money in patent medicines. It came in many forms. There were some in a powder and some in a tar ball or it was used for smoking. Whatever the form there were uses for it. Many women were using it to calm their nerves. Others were addicted to it for its hallucinatory effect. When the shipment would return to New York some of it would be kept there and separated from the oatmeal. There would be people who would sell the product and the monies would be deposited in accounts in a New York bank. The rest of it would be left in Albany, Rochester, and Buffalo. As the business grew Mr. Jackson thought other things could be mingled with the oatmeal shipments. He discussed the possibilities of furniture from China. He knew that textiles from Paris and London were good selling items in America. With the new production of automobiles there was a need for rubber in the United States for tire production. He had investigated the market in India for shipments of rubber. There was a need for tobacco and cotton in foreign countries. Mr. Jackson was good at convincing Wallace that there was more to the trade company than just opium. He kept reinforcing how important it was that everything should be kept quiet. Wallace understood. They worked out the details of the formation and financials of the company. The foreman would be paid a salary with a bonus at the end of the year. The four of them would each have 25% of the profits. Mr. Booth had already arranged for a shipping line out of New York City to Europe and Asia. The trade route to Asia was longer than to Europe. The ship would have to either sail around the tip of South America or Africa to get to the Orient. Mr. Harmon told them that the money coming from the Orient would be worth the wait. The items they were getting from Asia were more valuable to them than the things from Europe. He explained that it was a good cover to have things coming from other continents and not just Asia. The authorities would not get suspicious.

The lunch ended and the next meeting was scheduled for the following week. The three men hoped that the foreman would be in place by that time. The plan was to begin trading in one month. Wallace had heard about unscrupulous businessmen in the United States. He wondered as he went home if he was now one of them. It sounded dishonest to him. He decided that he was not actually pushing the stuff. He was just an owner of a shipping company. He figured that he could justify anything if it meant to make money. Winston was never to find out the full dynamics of the operation. He knew he had to be careful with what he said to Winston and Eveline. He hoped that Winston would agree to move to Buffalo. He figured that everything else in his life had turned out well so why not this time. Wallace began to feel like his job at the H.O.Company was secondary to his new work. He began to see how one thing leads to the next. He liked the idea of a new challenge. The more experiences he had, the better it would be for him. He thought of Winston again. Was it going to be the same as before? They were older now and had not seen one another in a long time. Winston was going to have to understand his role in the company. Wallace wondered if they would see each other as they once did. He had mixed feelings. He hoped he made the right decision by asking him to come to Buffalo. There was a part of Wallace that was getting excited about having Winston as a part of their life in Buffalo. He figured it was okay since it was Eveline's idea in the first place.

Chapter 32

A LETTER ARRIVED AT FRANK and Alice's home addressed to Mr. Winston Spaulding. Alice wondered why Wallace was sending him a letter since he was not good at writing letters to anyone. She sent a letter to Wallace and Eveline regularly and hardly ever got a response. Alice would see Mrs. Lounsberry at church and she would inform her of the news from Buffalo. Both mothers got to the point where they did not expect any news and worried that the only news they might get was "bad news." They figured as long as they did not hear anything that everything was okay. Mrs. Lounsberry suggested that they should all go to Buffalo to visit Eveline and Wallace. She told Alice that they could stay with her friends on Delaware Avenue. Alice told her that she would let her know after she spoke to Frank. She knew that Frank would never want to stay in a place that had servants. Alice on the other hand was excited about the possibility of going to Buffalo and being a guest in such a home. The thought of the trip reminded her of her involvement with the Women's Club.

Winston arrived home from the Rochester Post Express just before dinner. He was always happy to see Alice. He told her that he felt like she was the mother he never had. He was a good replacement for Wallace too. Alice told him that there was a letter in his bedroom from Wallace. He sat on the bed and read about Wallace's offer for a job in Buffalo. He was even more excited to know that Eveline suggested that Wallace should ask him to live with them. At first he thought this was a dream. He reread the letter to better understand the details of what all this meant. Winston knew that this was what he wanted to do. Wallace did not specifically explain the type of job he was going to have. He figured any job Wallace offered him would be fine. He knew he would do anything for Wallace just to be closer to him. Now more than ever Winston missed the friendship. He told Alice about the news from Buffalo. She was excited for him but told him she was loosing another son. He told her she could visit them both in Buffalo. It would be like old times. She nodded and thought about Mrs. Lounsberry's offer to go to Buffalo. Alice still had to discuss the offer to go to Buffalo with Frank. She thought that they could all go together with Winston and have a reunion. Dinner was nearly ready and Frank was waiting at the table. Winston explained to Frank about the job offer in Buffalo. Frank thought it was nice and he was glad Winston was leaving. If it had not been for Alice, Winston would have been gone years ago. After Winston finished his discussion about going to Buffalo Alice began her story. She explained how much she missed Wallace and Eveline. Frank stared at her as she spoke. She told Frank what Mrs. Lounsberry and she had discussed. When she got to the accommodations and the mansion idea he hit the table with his fist and told her they were not staying in a place like that. He would have nothing to do with the rich people. He said, "They are the ones who have put me out of business." He told her that the rich people are buying those cars instead of buggies. He roared at her that was the reason he was working at a newspaper shop. Alice told him she was sorry he felt so angry about everything that had happened. He told her that she should be grateful they were as well off as they were. He screamed at her that they would never go anywhere because they were at the end of the road. Winston was shocked at his outburst and left the dinner table to write his letter to Wallace. Alice quietly cleaned the kitchen and washed the dishes. She was in tears thinking that maybe she was at the end of her road. Frank left the room and went to bed.

Winston thought about what he needed to do to get ready to go to Buffalo. He would tell the newspaper office that he could work until the end of the week but would be leaving for a new job. He would take the early train from Rochester to Buffalo on Saturday. He could be ready for his new job on Monday. Winston wanted to let Wallace know as soon as he could about how excited he was about coming to Buffalo. He went to the telegraph office. He would have the letter delivered to Wallace's apartment. Winston wrote: Excited to come to Buffalo . . . will be on the first train from Rochester on Saturday morning . . . can't wait! He left the office and walked down Main Street. Just as he was turning the corner Mr. Helfer was leaving the hotel. Winston told him about his offer to go to Buffalo. Mr. Helfer was delighted that he would be working with Wallace. He told him how much he missed Wallace and referred to him as a "smart chap." Mr. Helfer wished Winston the best and they walked in opposite directions. Mr. Helfer turned and yelled to Winston. He went up to him and asked him if he could give Wallace a letter. Winston agreed to pick it up tomorrow. Mr. Helfer told him that it was something he needed to tell Wallace that he did not have the time to when Wallace was leaving for Buffalo. Winston remembered the night of the party over a year ago when Mr. Helfer whispered something in

Wallace's ear. He wondered what was going to be in the letter.

Alice thought about the reaction Frank had about the offer to go to Buffalo. She felt trapped because of Frank's attitude and insecurities with other people. She liked meeting new people and did not care what their lives were like. She knew that she had to tell Mrs. Lounsberry that they could not go. What was she going to tell her? She would be embarrassed to tell the truth. She knew she could never go without him. It would be very awkward to go alone and leave him home. She wanted to leave him all together. She was sick of his attitude toward Wallace, Winston and now anyone who may be a bit better than him. Alice decided that she would tell Mrs. Lounsberry at church on Sunday that they were not able to go to Buffalo. She would make up an excuse about some job Frank had to do. When Winston came back from the telegraph office he saw Alice and they talked about his future. She told him that she would love to go with him to Buffalo. He agreed that her life with Frank did not always seem so good. Alice smiled. He told her that Mr. Helfer was going to give him a letter for Wallace. He asked Alice if she might know what the letter was about. She remembered seeing Mr. Helfer say something to Wallace at the last party.

The next day Winston went to the hotel to pick up the letter from. As he walked into the lobby he thought of all the times Wallace walked into the hotel when he worked there. He felt like he was taking his place. When he walked into the office Hilda took one look at him and said, "Oh no they're back." Winston was not sure what that was supposed to mean. He explained that he was there to see Mr. Helfer. She pushed her chair back slowly and lifted herself up and shook her hips as she walked toward the office. Winston thought it was pretty funny. Hilda told him that he was probably used to walking like that. He thought it was funny and told her that he hoped he never looked that bad when walking. She sucked her teeth, went into the office and closed the door. Winston thought she was a very strange woman. Mr. Helfer came out of his office with Hilda ahead of him jiggling as she walked. Winston was fascinated with the show. Mr. Helfer excused Hilda's behavior and gave him the envelope. He thanked Winston for taking it to Wallace. When Hilda heard where the letter was going she said in a nagging tone, "The boys are getting back together. Where's the girl? Did he get rid of her yet?" Mr. Helfer told her to be quiet. Winston left the office thinking he had just left a madhouse. After that encounter he wondered what Wallace had dealt with and if he would tell him what was in the letter.

Winston finished his last week at the Rochester-Post Express. He remembered how it was when he worked at the Weekly Page and now was leaving for yet another type of job. He was glad he had the opportunity to go on with his life. He was looking forward to Buffalo. He had never lived anywhere else other than Rochester. Saturday morning he talked with Alice before he left. She was as sad now as she was when Wallace left. She told him that her two boys were gone and wondered if she would ever get to Buffalo to see where they lived. Winston told her she should come to visit them by herself and leave Frank home. She laughed and told him Frank would never allow that. Winston explained how sorry he was for her and hoped they might come back to Rochester to see her sometime. They hugged each other and Winston left. He was going to Buffalo to begin a new life. He thought to himself it is funny how things happen. He got to the train station a few minutes before the train was to leave. He was nervous about the trip because he had never traveled alone. He reminded himself that he had been alone for a long time since he had no real family. He felt better knowing that his family was Alice, Frank, Eveline, and most important of all Wallace. The conductor called out, "All aboard." Winston gave him the ticket and got on the train. He sat down and took a deep breath saying to himself, "Here I go!!!"

The train ride was pleasant. Winston remembered how many people were on the train when they tried to get back from the Exposition. That was like a nightmare compared to his ride this time. He hoped that Wallace would be at the station when the train arrived. He knew Wallace's address because Alice made sure he had it when he left. He could take the streetcar if he had too but really wanted to see Wallace and Eveline when he arrived. The conductor made sure everyone knew that they were getting closer to Buffalo after each stop. When they were about 10 miles from the station Winston remembered the little kid who spotted the Electric Tower when they were approaching the Pan—American Exposition. The Exposition had been dismantled except the New York State Building. The land was restored to its original state shortly after the fair ended which made it appear as if it had never happened. As the train went by what used to be the station for the Exposition Winston remembered how excited he had been when they arrived at the Pan-Am. Then he remembered how scared and uncertain everyone was when they were trying to leave the Exposition. He thought how strange things turn out. As the train came to a stop he was looking out the window for Wallace. He felt like that little kid looking for the Electric Tower only this time it was him doing the looking. He did not see any sign of them and figured that he would have to find his own way to their apartment. He picked up his bags and got off the train and as he turned the corner of the station, there they were. Wallace and Eveline had just arrived. They were so happy to see each other. They held each other in the same hugging position that they did when they left Rochester. Wallace felt the same sensation he always got when he saw Winston. He had not forgotten that feeling. Eveline told them she was happy they were together again. Winston's old attitude and quick remarks returned like they had never left. He told Wallace that he could not wait to see if Buffalo had changed Wallace. He told him that by the looks of him he was better than ever. Eveline told Winston that was up to him to find out on his own if Wallace had changed. Wallace felt his face turn red and Eveline told him he was getting too excited. As they walked from the station Wallace told Winston he had a surprise for him. Winston in his smart way told him that he hoped he had more than one surprise for him. It was then that Winston saw the car. He asked who it belonged to. Eveline told him that was the surprise. Wallace told him that he ordered it before they left Rochester but it was delivered here. Winston wanted to know who drove it. Wallace told him that he did and that he was to sit in the back. Winston laughed and got in the back seat. It was like going on an amusement park ride. Winston asked if it twirls or bounces. They laughed when the car started. Eveline told him about her first ride in the car. Winston asked if he would fall backward when it went forward. Wallace remembered how much fun the Midway had been for Winston, now he acted like he was on the Midway again. This time, they were in a red rolling machine. Eveline assured him that he would get used to it.

Then, Winston asked Wallace what his father thought of it. Wallace said, "He doesn't know about it."

Wallace drove the car like a professional now. He maneuvered the car much better than when he had first started driving. Eveline sat in the passenger seat like she was being chauffeured around town. Winston was sitting in the back of the car enjoying this new way of travel. He told them that he would be their servant from now on. Eveline told him that he was obviously back to his old habits. Wallace thought he was funny when he wanted to be their servant. He was happy Winston was back with them. When they were turning the corner onto Delaware Avenue, Winston asked if they were taking him on a tour of the city. Wallace told him that they were almost home. Winston thought he was joking. He could not believe they lived on such a fancy street. He thought some of the buildings were hotels. Wallace explained that most of these buildings were homes of wealthy people. Eveline told him about her parent's friends who lived down the street. Then Winston told them about the offer Eveline's mother gave Frank and Alice. Wallace was not surprised that his father would have such an outburst. Eveline mentioned that she felt sorry for Alice because she felt that she would never get out from under Frank's influences. Wallace agreed and told them that he hoped to someday get her out of that house. Their apartment building was just ahead and Eveline explained that their apartment was on the second floor. She told Winston about the fireplace and the electric lights in their apartment but the hallways were lit with gaslights Winston asked them if he had to sleep on the floor. They laughed and Eveline told him that he had his own room. She jokingly told him that if he brings anyone home like Louis that he had to keep it quiet. Wallace looked at her and asked why she would say such a thing. Winston spoke up and told them that there is no more Louis and that he now had what he has been waiting for. Wallace pulled up to the front of the building and stopped the car. They got out and went upstairs to the apartment. Winston thought it was beautiful as he admired the furniture and the electric lights. He was fascinated with how they worked. He liked the fireplace with the marble mantle and asked who brought the wood for the fire. Eveline told him that the custodian brought wood when they told him they needed it. They showed Winston to his bedroom. It was the same bed that had been in Wallace's room in Rochester. Winston thought to himself that it was funny how some things never change. He was smiling as they left him in the room to unpack.

Eveline decided that they should celebrate Winston's new job. It was Saturday evening and it was the perfect time to go to the Statler Hilton for dinner. After Winston was unpacked and had time to rest they got dressed and walked to the hotel. It was a lovely evening to walk to dinner. While they were on the way to the hotel Eveline was telling Winston about her job at the law office. She was proud to announce how she was the highlight of each morning when she arrived at work. She told him that most of the men did not live with a person who looked so good so early in the morning. Then Winston asked how Wallace's job was going. Wallace told him that he was doing work with advertising in a department store and advertising in magazines and newspapers while utilizing other companies' products with the H.O.Company. As they were sitting down for dinner Wallace began telling Winston about his new job. He explained that import and exports were generating huge profits in the United

States. He told Winston that his new job was similar to his position at the newspaper office. Instead of organizing the delivery of newspapers he was going to be in charge of scheduling imports and exports out of Buffalo to New York City and then on to Europe and Asia. Winston looked stunned when the words Europe and Asia were mentioned. He had just arrived in Buffalo and now there was talk of Europe and Asia. Wallace noticed the look on Winston's face and asked him if he was all right? Winston snapped out of his shock and asked if he could do that type of work. Wallace assured him that he would be very successful. The cargo was being transported by train or boat through the Erie Canal to Albany and then on to New York City to be shipped overseas. Wallace explained that there were four men who had formed the company. He then gave Winston a description of the Larkin Company and how Mr. Jackson was the man he would be working with, along with Mr. Booth and Mr. Harmon. Wallace would be involved as the fourth person in charge of the company. On Monday Winston would be meeting these men for instructions and plan the first shipment out of Buffalo. Winston asked about what was being exported from the United States. Wallace explained about the oatmeal crème soaps from the Larkin Company and the oatmeal from the H.O.Company. The oats were the packing material and the soaps would be marketed under a more exotic name when they arrive in the foreign countries. The oats would then be used for sale there or be used as packing material for things being imported to the United States. Winston thought that should not be too difficult. He asked if there was anything else coming and going to and from the United States? Wallace told him about the rubber from India that would be used for the manufacturing of tires. Textiles were discussed too that would be coming from India and some from Europe. Wallace explained the importance of co-coordinating the trade routes so there could be as many stops made as possible in one voyage.

During dinner Winston began thinking about all the different things he would be responsible to do. He admitted to Wallace and Eveline that he was a little uncertain if he could do all that was expected of him. Wallace assured him that he was smart enough and strong enough to do anything he was asked to do. His best advice was to listen and not to question things that may not always make sense. Wallace told him that there was a tremendous business in imports and exports and that there was no time to question policies. The faster you move things; the more money is made. Winston had never heard Wallace be so certain and firm about the way he was to act at work. Wallace told him that he was in the big business now. Sometimes there were questions that should not be asked. Winston agreed to be business-like and follow his orders regardless of his opinion or thoughts. While Wallace was giving Winston the firm orders and the attitude lesson he kept thinking about what was really being included in the shipments to the United States. He was not comfortable directing Winston into a controlled position but knew he must never know what the real purpose of the company was. Their first objective was to get the soaps and oatmeal items moving to and from different countries. When that was running smoothly they would expand on what was being imported into the country. For now Wallace knew that Winston had his job set up and he was sure he would remain quiet.

On the way back to the apartment Winston told Wallace about the letter Mr. Helfer had given him. Winston told them about Hilda and her outrageous behavior. Wallace laughed and told him he rather missed her. He thought she was a real challenge. He laughed when he told about how he missed her outfits and her way of moving around the office. Winston laughed and said, "The whole room moves when she is in motion." Everyone thought her mouth was another thing you were never certain of. They laughed and wondered why Mr. Helfer put up with her. Winston gave the letter to Wallace when they got into the apartment. They sat in the parlor as Wallace read the letter. He read it to himself. Eveline and Winston looked at each other wondering if Wallace would have some type of response as he read. Finally, he said, "Now I know why Hilda gets away with everything." Hilda and Mr. Helfer are related. They are cousins. Mr. Helfer is the owner of the hotel but Hilda was given her position through her father's will. She was to always be the secretary as long as she needed employment. Her father did not want her to be without money after he passed away. He stated in his will that Hilda is unstable but better when given a job. Her father knew she loved the hotel and would be better behaved there than any other place of employment. Mr. Helfer on the other hand was given ownership of the hotel in the will. Hilda's father admired Mr. Helfer as a young boy and watched him grow into a fair businessman. In the will Mr. Helfer would take over the presidency and ownership. He further explained that Hilda attempted to change her father's will but he told her she was lucky she was getting anything. Apparently, her former husband and she had a son. The husband divorced Hilda and she began to hate her son because he reminded her too much of her husband. She thought her husband was a little too fancy and the son was following his father's behaviors. He was a very talented and handsome young chap. As Wallace read the letter he realized why Hilda was so mean to him and outlandish with her behavior. All the pieces were beginning to fit into place. Wallace thought he had read the whole thing until he got to the second page. At that point Wallace knew he would never read the letter out loud to Eveline. He might consider reading it to Winston sometime. Wallace was careful what she knew about the financial affairs he had in Rochester and now in Buffalo. Mr. Helfer explained that he was ill and may not be able to continue in his position. He informed Wallace that he was named in his will. Upon Mr. Helfer's death Wallace is to become the president of the hotel. He will control the money, operation, and Hilda until she can no longer work. At that point he is to have her admitted to the Willard State Hospital on Seneca Lake. She is not to know where she is going when that occurs. Her doctor will attend to her in her transport and the doctor already expects to be contacted by Wallace. Mr. Helfer named the doctor and closed his letter giving Wallace the highest regard and hope for his wealthy future.

When Wallace finished the letter he looked at Eveline and Winston and said he could not believe he had finally found out about Hilda. He had already made sure he was not going to convey the ownership part in the will or the care of Hilda. He decided to tell Eveline and Winston that he was named in Mr. Helfer's will but let them think it was for some small amount of money for his contributions to the hotel. When he explained it that way they seemed satisfied. They had more fun talking about Hilda's behavior than anything else. Wallace knew he must keep that letter hidden.

Chapter 33

Winston was to meet Mr. Jackson, Mr. Harmon, and Mr. Booth on Monday morning. Wallace made sure he was calm and ready for his first day on the new job. Eveline had already left for work, which gave Wallace time to spend with Winston. He went into his room and found that he had not dressed yet. Wallace had a flash back of the time they spent in the guesthouse during their trip to the Exposition. He felt that sensation go through his body again. Winston had his back to Wallace as he walked in and his furry back and buttocks caught Wallace's eye. Winston was hoping that this very thing might happen. As he turned to Wallace he deliberately ran his hands down his chest to the lower extremities of his body. He put his hands on his hips with his fingers pointing to the center of his waist. Wallace had never felt as stimulated by Winston as he did at that moment. He went closer to Winston and time seemed to stop. Winston did nothing but stare at him. After some time in the room Winston told him that they had better get to their meeting. Wallace smiled and thought Winston had certainly improved his attitude and physical abilities.

The meeting was held in Mr. Booth's office. Wallace introduced Winston to the men he would be working for. He informed them that the name of the company had been registered and approved. The main office would be in Buffalo with an office in New York City. It was to be called the Occidental I&E Company. Winston was told that there might be occasions for him to travel to New York City for meetings. He looked at Wallace with fear in his eyes. Wallace told him that they might have to travel there together to set up schedules and disbursement of goods. Winston felt better knowing he did not have to go by himself. The first shipment of soaps was to leave Buffalo the next week. Winston would be in charge of making sure the shipments were ready and properly packaged. The group decided to use the railroad to send the shipment to New York. It would get there faster than by boat. Mr. Jackson had set up the shipping company that would transport the first set of cargo. He gave Winston the name of the company and the person in charge and then explained that he could communicate by telegraph to confirm the arrivals and departures of cargo in New York. Mr. Jackson rented a small office near the shipyards in Buffalo. He made certain there was to be no connection to the Larkin Company and the Occidental I&E Company.

After the meeting was finished Mr. Jackson suggested that they show Winston where he would be working. They took a streetcar from the H.O. offices to the shipyard area. Wallace could not offer to use his car because it could only carry four people. He did not want his car seen in that area anyway because of the type of laborers who worked there and what they might suspect. There was to be no connection between him and the other companies. It was a bustling and dirty place with trains coming and going carrying all types of goods. There were ships docked waiting to be loaded and unloaded. Winston was introduced to the men he would be supervising. They were burly and rough acting men smelling of sweat and stale smoke who did not take care of themselves. Most of them were chewing on cigars and using fowl language. They were perfect for this type of work because it was a dirty job and required heavy lifting. Winston felt like a midget compared to these men. Mr. Jackson told him to take charge and be firm with the workers. He was told that they would try to get out of doing things. Next to almost whipping them he was to show them who was in charge. Wallace wondered if the job might be too hard for Winston but then he thought this might be good for him. He could really take charge of things. Winston's main job was to organize the shipments but not be in total charge of the workers. There was a shipyard manager for that. Winston was happy to hear about the additional help. Before they left Winston to his work Mr. Jackson reminded him that he was to only do what he was told. His orders would be delivered to the office each week. If he needed any help Wallace was his contact person. He would not see any of the other men.

Mr. Harmon and Mr. Booth returned to their office and Wallace and Mr. Jackson went to lunch. Winston looked like a lost person when they left but he knew he had to prove himself to Wallace. During lunch Wallace went over the items that were on the list for export. Mr. Jackson wanted the Occidental I&E Company to remain like that and not use the words import and exports in the title. It was registered that way but in reality the shorter the better. He felt that it would be more difficult to identify what was coming and going into the country. He projected that after the first month of operation any problems would be worked out. When the transfers were running smoothly to New York they would expand their variety of goods coming into the country. He had received confirmation of a name of a contact person in Hong Kong. That person would set up the shipments leaving China. The cargo was to be disguised as a different commodity. Wallace had been thinking of adding furniture from the Orient as one of the shipments to New York. When it arrived in the United States it could be sold in New York or be sent to other places in the country. He thought the style would attract a customer who liked the finer and more unique style for their homes. Mr. Jackson was intrigued with Wallace's thoughts. Wallace explained that females could be brought into the country and used as servants but not slaves. Mr. Jackson was not quite sure what he was suggesting. He explained that women could be convinced that life would be better elsewhere. Women whose lives were uncertain and who were young enough could be easily taken to the United States with the offer of a better life. Mr. Jackson asked how they could manage that without being charged with kidnapping. The females would leave their families for a monetary exchange. When they were taken away they would be given a sedative and then put into compartments in the furniture. They would have enough food, water, and air to survive until they arrived in New York. At that time the furniture would be moved to a place for unpacking. The stowaways would go to a person who would assign them to people who would use these girls and women for their own purposes. Usually, the very rich were the people who wanted subservient women and girls. Mr. Jackson looked surprised at such a possibility. He asked if it was a prostitution business disguised as a servant position. He told Wallace it sounded like sex slaves. Wallace explained that there is huge money to be made in human trade from the Orient.

They agreed that the imports from the Orient would be the big money makers. They could use the European market as a cover for the larger Asian market. Between the opiates that would be made into patent medicines, furniture, and human transfers, the operating costs would be minimal because things were very cheap in the Orient. Mr. Jackson wanted to be sure that Wallace could formulate the plan and then have Winston carry it out without them being implicated in the operation. Wallace assured him that he would have it in place within a few weeks. Mr. Jackson asked who he knew that could make that plan work. Wallace told him about his connection with the newspaper business and the advertising connections he had made in the last few years. While working with the Hengerer Department Store he became friends with some of the people in the buying department who had connections in New York City. They had names of people and companies in Europe and Asia for their merchandise. There was a gentleman in Hong Kong that he was going to contact who would be pleased to be a part of the transfer program. Mr. Jackson asked what the man's name was. Wallace smiled and told him that was not to be discussed. He reminded Mr. Jackson of his attitude toward Winston about asking too many questions. Mr. Jackson was taken back when he heard it put to him like that. It was then he realized that Wallace was the person who knew what was going on and how to make it happen. They finished their conversations because Wallace needed to go back to work at H.O.Company.

When Wallace returned to work Mr. Booth and Mr. Harmon asked how the meeting went. Wallace told them it was fine and all the work was underway. He knew he was not about to explain the entire plan for imports to them. He felt like they were not as interested as Mr. Jackson and was satisfied with his report. There were advertising projects that needed to be finished for the new month. In fact, usually Wallace had all the work done well before the month began. He had a notion that his time was more valuable working on the Occidental Company now. He wondered how Winston was making out with his new crew of rough men. He laughed to himself and wondered what he and Eveline would hear about later that night. Winston was sure to have an interesting account of his day. Wallace began writing a letter to Mr. Ling in Hong Kong. Only Wallace would know right now who the contact person was for the human transfers. He planned to have control of the major portion of the companies' income. In the back of his mind he had a plan to eliminate Mr. Harmon and Mr. Booth from the business He hoped that his connection to the major department stores in New York would help get the program set up with Mr. Ling. Once he had the opportunity to meet Mr. Ling at a meeting at Hengerers. Mr. Ling visited the major department stores in New York State when he was introducing oriental decorating ideas to the stores. When he finished his letter he decided that maybe the store could get the letter to Mr. Ling faster than if he did it himself. He left work early and stopped at Hengerers. Wallace spoke with a few of the women he knew in the buying department and they were happy to help him send the letter. Wallace had a way with women. His charm and good looks made women want to be with him and they never felt threatened by him. He knew he could convince a woman to do almost anything for him. As it turned out there was a shipment of items going to Hong Kong in a few days. The letter was placed on the top and marked "Confidential to Mr. Ling". Wallace hoped that the letter got into Mr. Ling's hands and not someone else's. He tried not to think about those possibilities.

That evening during dinner Eveline asked Winston about his first day on his new job. Wallace looked at Winston and wondered what part of the day he was going to discuss first, before work or during work. He began by telling Eveline that Wallace did a good job calming him down before they went to the meeting. Wallace was a bit uneasy knowing what Winston was referring to. He continued with his description of the people he was involved with. He laughed when he described the men and said they all looked and smelled like hobos. Eveline asked Wallace if he remembered the man that had met then at the train station when they first moved to Buffalo. She laughed and wondered if all the Buffalo men smelled and looked alike. She and Winston agreed that people like that had a special place in society. Wallace asked what place that might be? They laughed and together told him not around the Delaware Avenue people. Wallace shook his head and agreed with them. He did tell them that without those workers we could not be where we are. Wallace asked Winston if he would like to work like those men all day. Eveline looked at both of them and told them they would never stand up to one minute of work like that. Those men would have their way with both of you at once. Both Wallace and Winston blushed and thought that the conversation should move to something different. Wallace told them about the work he was doing at the H.O.Company. He told them that Mr. Harmon and Mr. Booth were seeing large profits in the company. He explained how he was going to encourage them to expand and go into other areas of the country with their products. No one seemed especially interested in the H.O. business. Eveline was trying to tell her story about a new man that started working at the law firm. When she described him as dapper Wallace questioned her description of dapper. She said that he was very well dressed and had a muscular body and his hair and moustache made him look extremely masculine. She admitted to them that whenever she sees him she gets a strange sensation. Wallace paused as he sipped some water. He remembered his strange sensation this morning and she could not possibly have had the same kind of feeling. She explained how he always complimented her up to date fashions. The other men usually stare at her but he walks right up to her and starts the conversation. She told Wallace that he had asked her to go to lunch someday and then asked Wallace if he minded. Winston did not say a word and only watched Wallace. Finally Wallace told her that she could do whatever she wanted because he had full trust in whatever she chose to do. Eveline laughed and confessed that she told the man that was what her husband would probably say. She had already planned to go to lunch the next day. Wallace shook his head and smiled. He was glad that Eveline was the type of woman that could take good care of her self. He intended to do the same for himself. Winston made a remark about how good it was that everyone seemed to know what he or she wanted to do. All three stopped and stared at one another.

Chapter 34

EARLY 1908, WALLACE RECEIVED a response from Mr. Ling. He was delighted to have been asked to assist in the operations of the Occidental Company. He advised Wallace that it was of utmost importance that they have a plan for where the transfers would take place. He suggested that they have a meeting in New York City. He was scheduled to be in the United States for other merchandising meetings. He would make arrangements for them to stay at the Waldorf Astoria Hotel. He hoped that Wallace and his foreman could make the necessary travel arrangements for the meeting. Wallace purchased the train tickets to New York. He and Winston would leave from Buffalo on Friday evening and return on Monday. Mr. Ling had standing reservations at the hotel that enabled him to have two rooms available for the weekend. When Wallace thought about the trip he was satisfied that Winston would have his own room. He reminded himself that this was not like going to the Exposition because they had work to do this time.

Wallace responded to Mr. Ling with the schedule and information about Winston. He included some of his ideas about the drop off plan for the transfers. He suggested that they meet privately before Winston became part of the plan. Winston was only to be informed of the furniture deliveries and where to send them after they were taken off the ships. Wallace thought that a warehouse near the docks would be a perfect place to store the furniture and make the transfers. Mr. Harmon and Mr. Booth took a mild interest in the trip to New York when Wallace discussed it with them. They were more concerned with the financial condition of the H.O.Company.

At the end of 1907, the H.O.Company was showing profits and gains in new markets. Wallace deliberately expanded the company's operation to many locations further than Mr. Booth and Mr. Harmon were aware of. As a result of the rapid expansion they began to spend exorbitant amounts of money on personal items while over investing money on uncertain companies. Wallace encouraged them to spend the money stating that business was booming and what could go wrong. In January Wallace met with the accounting department at the request of Mr. Booth and Mr. Harmon. They wanted Wallace to verify that the advertising was the reason the sales were doing so well. Wallace had intentionally maneuvered the accounting department into spending tremendous amounts of money on advertising that was not always used or even finished. During the meeting a few of Wallace's friends in the department made sure that the bosses were satisfied that all was well and not to worry. Something did not seem right though. Mr. Harmon and Mr. Booth had an uncomfortable feeling about the accounting practices. They dismissed it as something a big company goes through. They decided to gamble and invest all the profits in stocks that were risky investments. Wallace convinced them that they were cheaper and could possibly triple in value if the companies grew. They agreed with the hope for making more money. Greed had taken over.

One evening Wallace asked Eveline about the new man that was working in the law firm. She hesitated and then smiled and said, "Oh you mean Rudolph?" Wallace surprised himself when he realized he had never asked what the man's name was. She told him that he was very well mannered and everyone thought he was good for the office. Wallace asked what that meant. She explained that he was smart, well organized and that he liked her. Winston spoke up and said, "How well does he like you?" She laughed and called him a silly fool then told them, well enough to go to lunch once a week. Wallace asked what they had talked about during these lunches. She explained that he had been telling her about the Women's Rights Movement that was in the news. He thought that it was good for women to have more rights than they presently did. Rudolph was a talented concert pianist. Eveline remarked how wonderful it was to know someone again who was cultured and good-looking. Wallace wondered if she thought he was not cultured. He knew he was good looking. She told them that she once had a friend in Canada that was like Rudolph. She admitted that if her family had remained in Canada that she might have married him and that she wonders how her life might have been different. Wallace was not sure he liked the stories he was hearing. Winston sensed that there was friction in the air and he chose to remain quiet for a change. Wallace thought it was best that he not say any more about Rudolph. He did not want to appear threatened by him.

Winston told them about the work he was doing at the shipyard. Wallace jokingly said, "From one extreme to another with our stories." Eveline smiled and waited patiently to hear Winston's tales. The atmosphere in the parlor was changing from the usual casual conversation to one of disinterest. Winston tried to talk about the gruff men and their behaviors and how well the cargo was coming and going to and from New York but felt like no one was listening to him. When Eveline finished her story everything else seemed unimportant. She acted like she did not want to hear about those dirty workers. The conversation took on a different tone when Wallace told them about the meeting in New York City with Mr. Ling. Eveline's eyes lit up when she heard New York City. She immediately told Wallace she would love to go. Wallace felt like he was in the middle. He knew Eveline assumed she would be going to New York City. Wallace explained the purpose of the meeting and that it had to include Winston. Eveline looked displeased about the trip but knew that the business with the Orient had to go out of New York and Winston was the foreman. Wallace decided it was better that he did not tell them about the Waldorf Astoria. Eveline did not ask any questions from that moment on. Winston casually asked how long they would be gone and what he should bring. Wallace told him they would be gone from Friday evening until Monday. Eveline confirmed the dates with Wallace. Winston was excited about going to New York but did not dare make any smart remarks. The air was getting heavier with tension. Then Eveline said, "Maybe it's good you both will be gone that weekend." Wallace asked why. She told him that if he were not going to New York she would have had to cancel the two evenings with Rudolph. Wallace stared at her and waited for the rest of her explanation. She told them that Rudolph was a guest pianist for a concert at Elmwood Music Hall. He had invited her as his guest for both performances. There was a social gathering of musicians after the Saturday evening performance. She was excited about the invitation and wanted to hear him play. She told them that after the Exposition had closed the organ that was in the Temple of Music was installed on a remodeled stage in the music hall. Ever since then there have been organ recitals on Sunday afternoons. She explained that Rudolph knew the people who donated the organ to the hall. Wallace was impressed with the information about the organ since he and Winston were in the Temple and heard the concert given the day the President was shot. He explained that he was sorry she was not invited to New York City but was happy she had a friend to do something special with that weekend. Eveline smiled and said, "I knew you would understand." She knew they would have a good time too.

The first six months of the Occidental I&E Company showed substantial profits considering it was in its infancy. When Mr. Jackson and Wallace reported the finances to Mr. Booth and Mr. Harmon they were not interested. They had recently been to the accountant's department to review an audit of the H.O.Company. There were discrepancies found in the recording of profits and losses. They were more interested in discussing the results with Wallace. Wallace knew why the findings were not accurate. He instructed the accounting office to move money from different accounts attempting to pay one bill and not pay others. He had it timed so that everything appeared to be paid with money remaining but in reality there was no money. Mr. Booth and Mr. Harmon continued spending money for frivolous items and investments. Little did they know that the money was only figures on paper and was not in the bank. Wallace negotiated the advertising bills so that creditors were not being paid in full. He had them paid as little as possible to keep them happy. That way there would appear to be more money available for investing and spending. Many of the risky investments were in companies that were doing poorly or going out of business; which is what Wallace hoped for. His scheme was working. He was certain that Mr. Booth and Mr. Harmon would become so in debt that they would go bankrupt. If that were to happen they would leave and Mr. Jackson and Wallace could buy them out of Occidental. He knew they would need all the money they could get. While they were expressing concern about their company Wallace was very sympathetic and explained that he and Mr. Jackson would be sure to help them out. Mr. Booth expressed his genuine thanks to Wallace for all he had done. Little did he know that Wallace was moving them into bankruptcy. He had other motives for the demise of the H.O.Company.

Winston was excited about the trip to New York and mentioned that he would not be required to be at all the meetings. He told Winston that he would be free to wander around New York. Winston thought it would be like Buffalo but Wallace informed him that he should probably buy a map in case he got lost. The company was paying their expenses but he should have some extra money of his own too. Wallace told him that one evening Mr. Ling was taking them out for dinner. Winston asked if they would have to go to a Chinese restaurant. Wallace thought he was serious and told him not to be a clown around Mr. Ling. They were going for a serious meeting and he wanted Mr. Ling to respect him. He left out the parts about the type of cargo, the hotel, the sleeping arrangements and why he was not invited to all the meetings. Little by little Winston would have a better understanding of his role as the foreman. Winston was not sure if this trip was going to be as exciting as their trip to the Exposition. After Wallace had been so business-like he did not dare ask about the room arrangements. He decided it would be better to wait and see.

The weekend of the trip to New York arrived. Wallace prepared his luggage in his usual orderly fashion and Winston was in his usual disheveled fashion. Wallace gave him some suggestions about the type of clothing he should bring. For the first time Wallace told him exactly what to wear and how to groom himself. He admitted to Winston that he liked him when he was unshaven and rough looking. Winston perked up when he thought about the possibilities for the weekend. They were dressed in new suits and ties. Wallace bought them topcoats for the trip. They each carried an umbrella and wore leather gloves. According to Eveline they looked like real businessmen and they could convince anyone to do anything. Wallace wondered if Eveline had inkling about the human transfers. She had a way about her that she could sense when something was being disguised as something else. Eveline wished them well and Wallace told her he hoped she had a good time at the concerts. She told them she was going to her favorite shop on the avenue for a special gown for the Saturday evening performance and party. She jokingly said she wanted to look good for Rudolph. Wallace tried not to appear jealous. He had a feeling she was trying to do that to him. Winston remarked about what good conversation they were going to have next week about their adventures.

The trip to New York City was long and tedious. There were stops at every town and city. It seemed like everyone was traveling on the late train. Wallace told Winston about the trip Eveline and he had made when they moved to Buffalo. At least this time there were no snowstorms forecasted. Winston told Wallace that he thought about the train ride after the shooting of President McKinley and the confusion about getting home on the train. Then Wallace asked Winston if he had ever thought about what happened to the old woman they met on that trip. They finally remembered her name was Sybil Rose. Winston laughed about her being an actress and the show she put on to get them on the train as her relatives. They laughed and said that she was probably dead. By this time the train was nearing New York City and the conductor yelled out as he walked through the train that they were 10 miles from the train station. Winston felt a little nervous about being in such a huge city. He watched as the buildings got bigger and closer together. He commented that this was no comparison to Rochester or Buffalo. Wallace was feeling the same way but would never admit to being nervous. He thought that would be an admission of lack of strength and drive. Winston wondered if Wallace feared anything.

The train pulled into the station. Wallace asked someone in the station where the Waldorf Astoria Hotel was. The person responded as if they were speaking to royalty. The attitude was one of surprise that anyone staying there would be walking to such a fancy place instead of hiring a brougham. Wallace laughed and explained that they had been sitting for a long time and wanted to walk. The person smiled as if not really believing the story. They were given directions and off they went. Winston nudged Wallace as they were walking and asked why he had not been told about the hotel. He could not imagine that Wallace would stay in anything less. Wallace said, "I did not want Eveline to know everything about the weekend." Winston smirked and said, "I'll never tell." Wallace reminded him that there would be many things he must never tell. As they walked into the lobby Wallace was impressed with the interior. It was decorated with gold trim because it was built during the Gilded Age. Only the very wealthy could afford to develop such a place. The bellhop came up to them to offer his assistance. Wallace excused himself and went to register for the rooms. He felt like he was in his element. He loved the style, class, and clientele that were mingling in the lobby. Winston was chatting with the bellhop when Wallace came back with the room keys. They decided to accept the bellhop's offer to carry their luggage. Winston told the bellhop it would be fun to be waited on. Wallace informed him that this was not the place to make jokes. Winston rolled his eyes and thought I will take care of you later. They used the elevator to go to the fifth floor to their rooms. Winston reminded Wallace of their ride to the top of the Electric Tower. Wallace smiled and told him that he sure did remember that ride. The bellhop told them he was impressed that they had been to the Electric Tower. Winston spoke up and told him that was not the only ride they had been on. Wallace laughed and told the bellhop it was a wonder they even lived through some of those rides. Winston laughed and told the bellhop that Wallace was afraid he might get messed up. The bellhop commented that they seemed to know one another very well and liked going places together. Winston agreed with him and Wallace blushed. When they got to their rooms the bellhop wished them a pleasant stay. Before Wallace could give the bellhop a tip Winston had already done it. He told the bellhop that this time he was the one in charge. The bellhop smiled and looked at Wallace and told him he hoped he could keep up with this guy.

Mr. Ling left a message for Wallace in the hotel's mail service. It reminded him that they were meeting in the morning for breakfast in the restaurant on the main floor.

They would have their first meeting where he could get to know Winston. Wallace reminded him about the importance of being business-like and serious about the operations he was in charge of. Wallace thought it was better to make Winston feel more important than he really was going to be. He hoped that would make Winston more conscientious. They met Mr. Ling and enjoyed the breakfast. It had been awhile since Wallace had seen Mr. Ling. He was a small thin man with white hair. Winston apparently had never been in contact with an Oriental person because all he did was stare. Wallace kicked him under the table to make him stop staring at Mr. Ling's mannerisms and facial expressions. Mr. Ling took a liking to Winston. He told him he thought he would be easy to work with. Winston thanked him and assured him that he would do everything to make the operation successful. They discussed the Buffalo operation and what Winston had accomplished with the schedules and training the employees. Mr. Ling explained that the same schedules would be adhered to in New York. There was another man in charge of the office in New York. Winston was to co-ordinate schedules with him. They would meet him later. After breakfast Wallace and Mr. Ling went to set up a warehouse site and establish the furniture intake plan. Winston was not a part of that meeting. Mr. Ling informed Wallace that he had hired a man to be in charge of the New York operation. He had discussed the transfer program with him and he had been sworn to secrecy. He was told that if he broke that secrecy he would be disposed of. Wallace had never heard such a threat but understood what could happen if the transfer program was made public. Mr. Ling wanted to know if Winston understood the need to be quiet. Wallace assured him that he knew the rules.

The warehouse was directly across from the loading docks. Mr. Ling rented the entire building so there would be no other cargo in the warehouse. It would be safer that way when transporting people. Mr. Ling thought that Winston should see the warehouse and be told that the furniture was being stored there until it went to other cities. He did not need to know anything else. Bill Foote was the boss of the New York office. Winston and he would spend time getting to know one another.

Winston met Bill Foote that afternoon. They went over their operations and spent time looking at the warehouse and deciding how they would communicate. Wallace was pleased that they were able to make plans and set up the schedules so easily. Bill was good at avoiding questions about the furniture. Winston asked about the furniture and why it needed to go to the warehouse and stay there. Instead of telling him it was none of his concern he explained that it needed to be inspected and treated for any bugs or fungus that might have come in on the shipment. Winston accepted that reason and thought it was good to be careful. Mr. Ling felt confident that Winston would be perfect as Wallace's foreman. He hoped that he would not have to be threatened with disposal as Bill had been. Winston told Wallace later that Bill was not like the men in Buffalo. Wallace asked what he meant. He said that Bill seemed very cautious and private about his work. Wallace knew that Winston saw the differences. He explained that working in New York City was more difficult and was more dangerous than in Buffalo. That surprised Winston, and then Wallace told him how people just disappear if they do not do the work they are expected to do. Winston had no reply.

Dinner was scheduled for Saturday evening in a restaurant across the street from the hotel. Mr. Ling made reservations for 8 PM. Since they had been in meetings and touring the shipyards all day Mr. Ling thought an early meal would be better. He was accustomed to retiring early. Wallace agreed that an early evening might be okay with them. They met in the front of the restaurant promptly at 8 PM. Mr. Ling commented on Wallace's punctuality. Wallace gave him his usual response that time was worth keeping. He wore his pocket watch because it had become his good luck charm. Winston remained quiet because he was trying to understand the attitude of the people he had met today. He thought that they were exceptionally careful about what they said and how much information they admitted to. Being quiet seemed to be the best plan. They entered the restaurant and found that it was as fancy as the hotel. There were plush barrel back club chairs surrounding an open fire pit. There were men seated in groups smoking cigarettes and cigars. It appeared to be a businessman's restaurant. Wallace noticed that there were no women anywhere. He thought it best that he not ask why there were no women. He hoped Winston did not start asking about the clientele. Just as Wallace finished thinking about Winston he nudged Wallace and said, "No women." He turned to Winston and shook his head. They found three chairs in a circle and sat down. The warmth and glow of the fire felt perfect because it had been a cold and blustery afternoon on the docks. A waiter in a proper uniform took orders for cocktails. Mr. Ling ordered a Manhattan. He told them that he only had that drink when in Manhattan. They were not sure if that was a joke or if he was serious. They decided to have the same drink. When the drinks arrived Mr. Ling waved his hand to the waiter to go and he walked away. Winston asked why they did not have to pay for the drinks. Mr. Ling explained that there were some things they did not need to know about. Wallace knew what he meant but Winston nodded his head and thought here is another thing that should not be talking about. He was beginning to think he would be glad to communicate from Buffalo and not have to stay here. Everyone was beginning to appear suspicious to him. He was not sure he could even ask Wallace about some things. After they had two cocktails Mr. Ling gestured to the waiter that they needed to be seated for dinner. The table was elegantly set with the finest china and silver. Wallace casually mentioned the hotel in Rochester and how the restaurant reminded him of that place. Mr. Ling asked what the name of the hotel was. Wallace told him it was the Seneca Powers Hotel. Mr. Ling smiled and told him he had been a guest at that hotel because he attended merchandising meetings at Sibley's Department Store. Wallace explained what his involvement had been with the hotel. Mr. Ling commented on the appearance of the hotel. He thought the restaurant and lobby area was far better than any other hotel he had considered staying at in Rochester. Wallace felt proud hearing that type of compliment from someone who lived so far away.

Since the restaurant's specialty was beef so they ordered it for the main course. There were a variety of side dishes to choose from. Mr. Ling had been there many times so he knew exactly what to have with the meal. He ordered a bottle of red wine to be served with dinner. The waiter was well trained in how to serve properly. He never intruded in the conversation and service was perfect. During dinner Wallace explained what his wife was doing that evening. Mr. Ling was interested in hearing about the music hall and the connection to the Exposition. He too had been in Buffalo to attend the Pan-American Exposition. He thought it was too bad that the Exposition was ruined because of the shooting of their President. Winston informed Mr. Ling that they saw him get shot in the Temple of Music. He continued to discuss the rest of that day at the Exposition and how much panic there had been. The conversations were beginning to move away from the shipping discussions. Winston was glad for that. He did not feel as uncomfortable now that other things were being discussed. Dinner was finished and Mr. Ling thanked them for all their time that day. He explained that he was tired and wanted to go to his room. There was no mention of a bill just another hand gesture to the waiter. They left the restaurant and went across the street to the hotel. Mr. Ling reminded Wallace of their meeting in the morning after breakfast. The four men would have the meeting on Sunday afternoon before their train left for Buffalo. They each retired to their own rooms for the night.

Chapter 35

SATURDAY EVENING AT THE Elmwood Music Hall was a grand event. The concert was wonderful. Rudolph played the piano with an orchestra accompaniment. Eveline's seat was perfect. She could see every move he made on the keyboard. She found out that Saturday evening's performance was for charity for the Women's Rights Movement. She realized why Rudolph was so interested in his role for the evening. She knew people were speaking out for more rights for women. It was a hard thing to do because most men did not want women to have equal rights. They were to be in the home and not allowed to have equal say in how things went. She was one of the lucky ones because she had a job, her husband gave her freedom, and her life was better than most women. Rudolph had discussed her role as an example to other women and how they could gain a higher standing in society. He was one of the few men who supported the movement. He was accused of wanting to be like a woman or he wanted a woman to boss him around. He had many threats to him by men who were afraid this movement might change things. Rudolph knew it was time for change. Eveline told Rudolph that he would probably like Wallace. She thought they were very much alike. Wallace had done many new and unheard of things and made successes of them. Rudolph told Eveline he would like to meet him.

The party was in the music hall immediately following the concert. Most of the women there were much like Eveline. They were women who were not afraid to stand up and be seen and heard. She told Rudolph that she liked being on the front lines of new activities. He told her she was just beginning her front line work. They laughed and began to dance.

Wallace felt restless after dinner and the day's activities. He did not want to go to bed yet so he went to Winston's room to see if he wanted to go out. He knocked on the door and there was no answer. He thought that was strange and wondered why he would not be there. He knocked again and still no answer. Wallace went downstairs to see if Winston was in the lobby. Sure enough he was sitting by the fire. He went over to where Winston was sitting. Winston looked as if he was deep in thought. Wallace asked what he was doing down there. Winston told him he was trying to understand the day. As excited as he was about the job and the connection to New York City he felt uneasy about something but could not pinpoint what it was. Wallace tried to make him look at it from the larger scale of work and how much more responsibility he had. Winston wanted to know why things seemed to be a secret. He told Winston that he would feel better about the whole thing once they got back to Buffalo. That seemed to make Winston happier. Wallace suggested they go upstairs for the night. As they approached their rooms Wallace asked Winston to come into his room. Winston was not sure if he understood what the suggestion meant. He decided to go to his own room saying he was very tired. Wallace stood at the door watching Winston walk down the hall. Wallace thought about Winston most of the night and hoped he would return to his old self soon.

Winston did not sleep much either. He thought about Wallace and how much he wanted to go in the room with him but knew it was not the right time.

Wallace met Mr. Ling after breakfast on Sunday morning. They went to the dock office to meet with Bill. Bill explained that everything was in place at this end of the route. Mr. Ling assured him that when he returned to Hong Kong his men would have a group of transfers ready to come to the United States. He laughed and told Wallace that there would be a lot of furniture to distribute. After the plans were set Mr. Ling asked Wallace if he understood the attitude of the people in the restaurant last night. Wallace told him that he was very comfortable but Winston seemed more inquisitive about the lack of women in the restaurant. Mr. Ling explained that the restaurant was where most of the wealthy investors meet for business. It was there that the transfers would be arranged and paid for prior to releasing them to their superiors. There was an office in the rear of the restaurant that would be used for the monetary exchange and realignment of transfer's identification. A vehicle would be waiting in the alley to deliver the transfer after the transaction was complete. Mr. Ling felt that Winston did not have any need to see or know about that part of the restaurant. Wallace understood and realized the restaurant was being used as a front for the transfer exchange. No one would ever suspect such things were going on in a place like that. Mr. Ling told Wallace and Bill that he was going back to Hong Kong and hoped that all would work smoothly.

When he got back to the hotel he wondered what Winston was doing. He went to his room and knocked on the door. There was no answer. He thought where could he be now? Suddenly the door flew open. Winston had been bathing and he laughed and said, "I bet you thought I was out again?" Wallace said, "Everytime I come to your room you have been bathing." Winston had only a towel around his waist and smiled and invited him in. Wallace got that same tingling feeling as always when he saw Winston. This time Winston's towel fell of as he walked away from the door. Wallace watched as he walked toward the other side of the room. He could not help but admire his firm buttocks and muscular legs. He studied the mass of hair that grew from his calves to his neck. For the first time Wallace saw hair in places on his body that he found exceptionally exciting. He turned around and Wallace's eyes moved from the top to the bottom of Winston's body. Neither one spoke a word. Wallace said that he was glad to see Winston more relaxed. After he said that he realized how stupid that remark was. Wallace was fully clothed and Winston naked. Winston looked at Wallace and told him to look closer. He was not so relaxed. Wallace moved closer. Winston decided that it was time to move in on Wallace. They were alone in a different city. He started to slowly unbutton Wallace's trousers and then his shirt. There was no exchange of words only a constant stare. Wallace had the same feelings as if he were just waking up in the morning. Winston looked down at Wallace and told him he liked how he looked. Winston told Wallace that he loved his bare-chest. He liked the way his chest was shaped and how excited he was when he saw his hairless body. He admitted he always wanted less hair on his own body. He put his hands on Wallace and felt how firm he was. They agreed that this was a great way to end a weekend. Just when they were moving to a more comfortable place there was a knock on the door. Wallace said, "Who could that be?"

Winston put on his trousers and Wallace stayed out of sight. It was the bellhop with a letter for Wallace. He apologized for giving it to Winston but knew they were probably together and smiled when he said that. Winston thanked him and gave him a tip as he left. Wallace took the note and opened it. It was from Mr. Ling. All it said was both of you be at the dock office in one hour. Wallace told Winston what it said and decided that something must be wrong to demand such a thing. They were disappointed that their time had been interrupted. They got ready to go to the office. They had no idea what had happened. When they reached the dock office Mr. Ling was waiting outside. He explained that they needed to see something in the office. It was unexpected but nonetheless needed to be dealt with. They walked into the office and there was nothing to see or at least they did not think so. Mr. Ling began by telling them that Bill had been hired with the full understanding that he be careful of what he said to people. Mr. Ling mentioned the words "disposed of." He continued to tell them that Bill was attempting to blackmail him. In reality he was trying to get money from him by using false information about the business. Winston was in shock as he walked closer to the desk. He noticed something red on the center of the desk. Mr. Ling watched as he studied the desktop. Winston looked at Wallace and a look of terror came over his face. It was a tongue. Wallace was speechless. Mr. Ling told them that Bill's body was nowhere to be found. Mr. Ling went to the desk and took the tongue outside and threw it into the water. He returned to the office where Wallace and Winston were still motionless. Mr. Ling told them not to worry; he had someone else in mind that would not dare to blackmail him. They left the office and began walking away from the docks. Mr. Ling told Winston that the new person would be in contact with him next week, but business was still on schedule. Mr. Ling asked that Winston go back to the hotel because he had a few last things to discuss with Wallace. He left scared to death he would be the next to go. Mr. Ling told Wallace that he wanted Winston to be there to see Bill's tongue. He wanted to make sure that Winston understood the severity of inappropriate conversations. Wallace told him that he thought they all understood that now.

When Wallace returned to the hotel there was not much time to do anything but prepare to go back to Buffalo. Winston did not have anything to say to Wallace. They were both in shock and had never seen such a sight. Finally, Wallace said, "I thought it was scary when we saw the President get shot." Winston did not say a thing. He was scared for his own life now. He finally asked Wallace if he thought anything like that could happen to him in Buffalo? Wallace did not think so and told him to try not to think about it. They went to the lobby and checked out of the hotel. They were both so upset that they carried their own bags out of the hotel. The bellhop saw them and told them he hoped they had a good time. They both looked at him and said nothing. While they were on their way to Buffalo they began to calm down. Winston said, "I feel as upset now as I did when we went back to Rochester from the Exposition." Wallace said, "Maybe we should never go out of town again." They smiled at each other with somber faces. Fortunately the ride back to Buffalo was uneventful and they both had time to rest. As the train neared Buffalo they went by the old station where the Exposition had been. The thrill was not like it was the first time. Wallace remarked how time had changed them and how things were now. It seemed like they had been gone for weeks when they got back to Buffalo. Wallace wondered out loud if Eveline had a good weekend. Winston laughed and said, "I bet she did not see Rudolph's tongue on the piano." Wallace could tell he felt better being home. He told Winston that they should keep the murder and the tongue thing out of conversations. He was not sure who in the group in Buffalo might be disguised as a business partner but really out to kill. Winston asked if this was all a nightmare. There was no response from Wallace.

Eveline was delighted to see the two men come home. She had made special plans for a quiet dinner at home that night. She thought they would all have lots to talk about. Wallace was glad there was a plan for the evening that did not involve going out for dinner. Winston told them he looked forward to being home. Wallace went to the office, Mr. Booth and Mr. Harmon were excited to hear about the trip to New York City. Wallace gave them the highlights of the meetings leaving out the transfer details and the murder. He focused on the office, the contact person and scheduling. He asked how things were here at the office. Neither of them had much to say about that. They did say that Mr. Jackson had come by and wanted to see him when he returned from New York City. Wallace told them he would do that tomorrow. Wallace worked on the advertisements for the new wheat flakes that the company was presenting in the stores. It was sure to be a boost to the finances of the company. Wallace was hoping that they could manage to show some profit and then he and the accounting department would not be questioned. He was very tired after all the weekend excitement so he decided to go home early. He got into his car and was glad he had purchased the better top because it was a cold and snowy night in Buffalo. The car stayed warmer with the leather top. When Wallace arrived home he found a strange man standing in the parlor. Just as Wallace was going to ask who he was Eveline walked into the room and casually introduced them. She was surprised that he had arrived home a few hours earlier than usual. There was an uncomfortable feeling when he first walked in. Wallace was feeling like he might have interrupted something. Rudolph was very handsome and muscular, as Eveline had mentioned. Wallace was quite taken by his good looks. Rudolph had a firm handshake; must be from all the piano playing Wallace thought. He could not help but wonder what else might be firm. Eveline explained that Rudolph had a piano engagement that night and left work early with her. She was happy they had finally met each other. There was a strange feeling Wallace got when he looked at Rudolph. It was like they knew each other from some other time or place. They hit it off immediately. Wallace asked Rudolph about his involvement with the Women's Rights issues. He explained that everyone should have equal rights as long as they work hard and do the right thing. Wallace liked that philosophy. Eveline told them that she knew they would like each other. Just as they were having a drink Winston walked into the room. He left work at the usual time because of his workers and their schedules. When he appeared Rudolph looked at Eveline and then Wallace, then Winston, and stood up and introduced himself. He too found Winston to be interesting. After the introductions Wallace explained why Winston was living with them and all the things they had experienced together but leaving certain things out. Eveline told Rudolph how the two of them were great friends and that all three of them get along famously. Rudolph looked intrigued by the arrangement. Then he said, "Talk about equal rights." He looked at Eveline and told everyone that is why she is the way she is. Everyone agreed it was a good arrangement. Rudolph told them that he had to leave and that he was glad to have met them. He hoped they could be together again. They all agreed that would be fun. Eveline was especially excited when she told them that now she would have three men on her side. She laughed and told them that some women could not find one man but she had three.

Dinner was very relaxing. They had a chance to tell their stories about the weekend. Eveline was happy that they both liked Rudolph. She had thought they probably would. Wallace talked about Mr. Ling and how he took them to a fancy restaurant. Winston told about the city and how big it was. They mentioned the hotel but did not mention the name of it. Eveline asked if Winston had a good feeling about the man he was working with in New York City. He hesitated and thought how the tongue looked on the desk. He was not sure how he felt about the man. He only told her he was okay. They agreed that the weekend had been a busy and interesting time. Wallace wanted to know about the Elmwood Music Hall and the organ. She explained that it was used a little bit the other night. She commented on how grand it must have been in the Temple of Music. She was sorry her parents did not take her to the Exposition. There had been so much conversation about it the other night. She told them about how well done the party was after the performance. She remarked on how refined the people were at the party. She told them about the women she met. Some of them knew her parent's friends on Delaware Avenue. It was an early night because tomorrow was a busy day.

Chapter 36

WALLACE MET MR. JACKSON at a coffee shop. Mr. Jackson was concerned about the meeting in New York City. He was exceptionally inquisitive about the proximity of the warehouse and the unloading of the products. He was careful about how he phrased the types of cargo coming into the port. Wallace explained that the entire operation was within feet of the ships. They had secured a place that would be exclusively for their shipments. Mr. Jackson avoided any discussion regarding who the contact person was in New York. He wanted to know how well Winston had gotten along with Mr. Ling. Wallace explained that Mr. Ling was pleased with Winston. He felt that Winston understood the need to be quiet and follow orders. He asked if Mr. Ling was he friendly or distant? Wallace was not sure what he was asking so he told him that Mr. Ling was a businessman so everything was always businesslike. Wallace felt as if Mr. Jackson knew more than he was willing to talk about. Then he asked about the contact person. He asked what Wallace thought of Bill. Wallace was taken by surprise with that question. He asked Mr. Jackson how he knew about Bill. Mr. Jackson told him that he received a telegram from Mr. Ling regarding Bill. Wallace asked when he received the message. He told him that it came a few days before they went to New York City. Now the question Wallace had was if he knew what had happened to Bill. There was a long pause and finally Mr. Jackson wanted to know if Bill was going to be the type of person they would want in the position of imports of transfers. Wallace wanted to leave because he felt like Mr. Jackson was backing him into a corner with all the questioning. He asked Mr. Jackson if he had any more communication with Mr. Ling. There was more silence. He told Wallace that he wanted to get his version of how the plans were set up. Wallace explained that it all was very well organized and the operation was under way. Mr. Jackson did not pursue questions any further. Wallace was careful to end the meeting on a good note. He told Mr. Jackson that Mr. Ling was going back to Hong Kong to monitor the shipments from the Orient. Then with a piercing stare Mr. Jackson asked Wallace if he had any thoughts of operating the company by themselves. Wallace asked him to explain what he meant. He suggested that Mr. Ling might not be the right person to be in business with them. Wallace saw what was coming next. Mr. Jackson did not know how Wallace had been maneuvering Mr. Booth and Mr. Harmon into bankruptcy but Mr. Jackson had another angle. He wanted to eliminate Mr. Ling. Wallace thought quickly and told him that Mr. Ling was very good at his work and had many connections in the business. Wallace's idea was to eliminate the two men from the H.O.Company through failure and then he and Mr. Jackson would have the control with Mr. Ling. Mr. Jackson did not seem concerned about the two men at H.O.Company. He was more concerned about Mr. Ling. Wallace wondered why but did not think it was a good time to ask. Mr. Jackson told Wallace to think about the idea and they would talk in a few days.

Things seemed to be happening much faster than Wallace had anticipated. He returned to the office to find Mr. Booth and Mr. Harmon waiting for him. They were none too pleasant. They began by showing Wallace more financial findings. There had been some improvements in the company because of the new wheat flakes product but the worst was yet to come when they told Wallace that they were tired of the unpredictable operation they were seeing in the company. Many creditors had submitted demand letters for their payments. They wanted to know if Wallace knew why the company was so far in debt. Wallace reminded them that they had made many financial moves on investments that were not secure. He turned the conversation around and told them that they had been very liberal with their personal spending. He was good at moving problems away from himself and looking innocent of any wrongdoing. They informed Wallace that the company would have to be re-organized and that his position may be in jeopardy. Secretly Wallace was delighted because it was all working out as he had planned. He asked what they were planning to do. They explained that they were requesting two things. The first was that they were to be bought out of their interests in the Occidental Company. Wallace told them that he would have to discuss that with Mr. Jackson and Mr. Ling. They told him that he had 2 weeks to arrange those items and the pay them their interests in the company. The second item was that H.O.Company was declaring bankruptcy. Wallace wanted to cheer but thought it was best that he remain calm. They informed him that they were leaving. He could stay as long as he wanted to or until he found a new job. Wallace agreed to their demands. He told them he would have all the negotiations completed within the next two weeks.

That evening, Wallace, Eveline and Winston were having dinner when Winston told them that he received a letter from the person that was the new contact in the New York office. Wallace asked what it said. Winston explained that the letter was written as if Bill had quit and a new person was hired. There was no mention of anything else except the man's name and that contact would be through telegraph or mail. The man's name was Ho Ling who was a relative of Mr. Ling. Wallace thought that it was odd that Mr. Ling would hire a relative. He wondered why that had happened. Winston did not seem to care as long as they had good communication. Wallace was still confused about things. Why was Mr. Jackson acting so suspicious? What were the reasons for Mr. Booth and Mr. Harmon leaving so suddenly? He did not discuss any of his thoughts that evening. He wanted to find out more about Mr. Jackson's intentions.

The next morning Wallace met with Mr. Jackson. He acted like he knew what Wallace was going to be talking about. Wallace felt like he had been set up. He told him about the developments at H.O.Company. Mr. Jackson thought it was good that Mr. Booth and Mr. Harmon were leaving. He insinuated that they were very poor businessmen. They agreed to pay them each 10% of the company's worth. They were to be paid in cash because that way there could be no way to verify a transfer of money. They were both quite pleased that they were leaving and now they could deal with Mr. Ling on their own. Wallace questioned Mr. Jackson about his attitude toward Mr. Ling. He told Wallace that he knew about Bill Foote. Mr. Ling sent him a message about the incident. He only told him he had been eliminated from the company. Wallace then realized that Mr. Jackson had no idea about his disappearance. Now Wallace understood the line of questioning yesterday. He decided not to divulge any of the details of that incident. Wallace agreed to write a letter to Mr. Ling about the changes in ownership and about who was left in the Occidental Company. He played Mr. Jackson's game of deleting pieces of information. He still wondered if Mr. Jackson was into some underhanded activity. They agreed to meet the next week for the final exchange of money with Mr. Booth and Mr. Harmon.

Wallace sent the letter to Mr. Ling that afternoon. He explained what was happening with Mr. Booth and Mr. Harmon. He listed the cash pay off. He told him about Winston receiving a letter from Ho Ling. He did not ask why or how he got the job. He hoped Mr. Ling would offer that information. He did ask Mr. Ling if there was anything he might need to know about Mr. Jackson. He hoped that Mr. Ling would offer some information about him. He thanked him again for the time in New York. There was no mention of Bill. Wallace had many thoughts about what was causing the sudden changes in the way things were going. Part of him was satisfied that everything was happening as it was at H.O.Company. He had been thinking about changing jobs anyway.

Eveline had been telling Wallace about the Women's Rights Movement everyday. He was tired of hearing about it. He thought it was a good thing but did not think it would ever go very far. She told him that Rudolph was looking into having more involvement in the movement. Wallace asked why he needed to know all these things. She informed him that Rudolph might be moving. Wallace did not say it out loud but was happy for that piece of information. He liked Rudolph but was not sure where he was coming from or what he was really all about. Lately

Rudolph was not high on Wallace's list of important people to be concerned about. However, Eveline was certain that even if he moved she would still see him. Wallace wanted to know what she meant by that. She told him that Rudolph was looking into moving closer to central New York. She was not sure exactly where but heard it was a place called Seneca Falls. Winston overheard their conversation and told them that he knew it was the place where women were having conventions to organize themselves for their campaign for equal rights. Wallace looked at him and asked him when he had become so intelligent. Winston laughed and told him that he still had not taken the time to really get to know him. He went on to say that Rudolph and he had spent some time together and they had talked about the movement. Wallace asked how much time they had been spending together. Winston told him that it was none of his business. Eveline laughed and remarked how childish they were acting. They did not appreciate that remark.

Wallace went to work the next day intending to tell Mr. Booth and Mr. Harmon about the details of their termination in the Occidental Company. When he arrived the secretary was sitting in her chair looking as if she was terrified by something. He asked her if she was all right. She said, "No, look in the office." Wallace had a sick feeling when he heard that tone. He looked at her and then toward the door to Mr. Booth's and Mr. Harmon's office. It was slightly ajar. He walked to the door but there was no one in the room. She told him to go in farther. As he did he had the queasy feeling that he would find something he did not expect. He approached their desks and in the center of each blotter were red things with blood under them. Wallace took a deep breath and realized they were tongues. He was not sure what to do next. He went out to the secretary and told her to try to be calm even though he was not too calm himself. She asked him what they should do. At first he thought this was the same thing that happened in New York. Only Winston and Mr. Ling knew about that murder. So, how could this be connected? Were these two men suspected of something? Where were their bodies? It was the same as New York. Since it happened near the water they were probably thrown in Lake Erie and washed down the Niagara River over Niagara Falls. Wallace told the secretary that before they called the authorities he needed to see Mr. Jackson. She agreed not to tell anyone. He left and went directly to Mr. Jackson's office. Mr. Jackson had just returned to his office just as Wallace arrived. He seemed uneasy that Wallace showed up so unexpectedly with such a sense of urgency. He composed himself saying he was tired from what he had just been doing. Wallace asked what that might have been. He told him he was outside working on some soap cargo for the next shipment to New York. Wallace thought that was strange but he was more concerned about what happened in his own office. He asked Mr. Jackson if he had seen Mr. Booth and Mr. Harmon. He told him that he had not seen them in a few days. Wallace thought that was strange because he had not seen them either. He told Mr. Jackson what he found in the office. His response was almost like he did not care or did not want to be bothered. All he told Wallace was, "I guess we don't have to pay them their money now." Wallace told him that was a terrible way to think. Mr. Jackson told him that those two men were involved with many strange and suspicious people in Buffalo. He figured someone wanted to rub them out. Wallace asked what he should do. Mr. Jackson told him to notify the police and not say anything about them. Wallace returned to the office and the police arrived shortly afterward. There was not much for them to take except for the tongues. After the police took some information from the secretary Wallace decided to close the office for the day. He went home to figure out what he needed to do next.

A few days later Wallace received the letter he had been waiting for from Mr. Ling. He explained that the reason he hired his relative for the New York office was that he could have better communication with him. He agreed that it was okay to release Mr. Booth and Mr. Harmon from their interest in the Occidental Company. He thought that the remaining men in the business could more easily operate things because they did not need so many owners. Wallace thought that was a strange way to phrase it but did not worry about how he said it. Mr. Ling told him that Singapore was the next city that the company would be conducting business in. There was news in the papers about the construction of a canal in Central America that would shorten travel time from the Pacific to the Atlantic Ocean. Wallace had read about the Panama Canal. They were not sure when it would be in operation because there had been some attempts to build it but with many complications. President Roosevelt was investing money in its construction but the tropical climate in Central America made construction difficult because of diseases connected to such a hot climate. Mr. Ling explained that having more than one city in the Orient would help improve trade and income. He told Wallace that he was in the United States and he wanted to meet with him again but without Winston. Wallace had a strange thought that maybe his tongue would be next!

It was not long before the bankrupt H.O.Company was in a reorganization phase. Wallace decided it was time to leave and work in a new company. He had been watching the newspapers for employment opportunities. There was a company being developed by Kirstein and Sons. They were the advertising agents for a newly developing company. They were looking for a person who would design and promote the "Shur-On" Company. Since it was in its infancy it would be an opportunity for a person to do all the initial advertising. When Wallace saw the notice he knew it was for him. He liked being first because there was nothing to be compared to. When he got to the section for the application information he laughed when he saw that the position was in Rochester. He decided not to tell Eveline or Winston. He wanted to make sure he was hired and then they could make their plans. This would mean moving back to Rochester and Eveline would have to quit her job and leave Rudolph. He was beginning to like the idea more and more. Then he thought about Winston and what he would do. He decided that it was more important for him to get his life in order and everyone would probably just follow along. He sent the application with his experiences and references to the Kirstein Advertising Agency. He had an inkling that this was going to be a good time to move.

The work at the shipyard in Buffalo was keeping Winston busy. He would come home and tell Eveline and Wallace how the shipments were always heavier when they left than when they arrived. Wallace told him that it was because the soap and oatmeal were packed in heavier containers for added protection. He told Wallace that whenever a shipment came into Buffalo the same men came to take some boxes and not others. Wallace explained that some of the boxes were prepaid and the couriers would be there to get the boxes faster. Winston seemed satisfied with that idea. Wallace knew that there was a factory nearby that was using the contents to manufacture patent medicines. The sales from the opium based medicines made profits soar. As he was telling them about the cargo and the differences in weight he thought about Mr. Jackson's strange behavior when he walked in on him last week. Mr. Jackson does not usually pack soapboxes for shipment. Wallace figured that so much had been happening that it was getting harder to figure everything out. He assured Winston that as long as he had good laborers he did not need to worry about the weight of things. Winston told him that he was being treated like a puppet. Eveline spoke up and started talking about Rudolph again. Wallace could feel himself getting irritated. She told them that Rudolph had found a new job and a place to live and he was moving. She decided to play the Wallace game and not tell all. Wallace's attitude began to improve when he heard Rudolph was moving away. Winston asked what she was going to do without her Rudolph. She looked at him and explained that she would visit him once he was settled. She knew her evasive conversation would cause more questions. Wallace decided to take the chance and ask where he was going. She smiled and excitedly told him he was moving to Rochester. She could stay with her parents and visit Rudolph as often as she wanted to. Wallace was shocked by her attitude and realized that he may never get rid of Rudolph. He asked when this was happening. She told him within the next few weeks. Rudolph decided that Rochester was a better place to live than Seneca Falls. There was more happening in Rochester and Seneca Falls was only a short train trip away. Since Rudolph was such an accomplished pianist he would have better opportunities for a musical life in Rochester. Wallace pretended to be happy but wondered what all this might turn into. Winston told them that he would miss Rudolph because they had struck up a great friendship. Wallace started to think he was being left out. He thought it was time he got a better understanding of Rudolph's effect on the two of them.

Wallace received two letters. One came from the Kirstein Agency and the other from Mr. Ling. He opened the Kirstein letter first. They wanted him to interview for the advertising position at the end of the week and the position would begin in January. He laughed and thought about all his jobs started in January. Happy New Year! He opened Mr. Ling's letter and their meeting was scheduled for the next week. The schedule could work out if he could do both things in one trip. He organized it so he would have his interview first and then go to New York City. He chose not to tell Eveline and Winston about the Rochester meeting. He was only telling them about his meeting in New York and that Winston did not need to attend. He had no uneasiness about the job in Rochester but was a bit concerned about what Mr. Ling wanted. Whatever it was he was planning on being very careful of what he said and what he admitted to. At least they owned a business together. He wondered why Mr. Jackson was not included.

Chapter 37

WALLACE TOLD EVELINE AND Winston about his meeting in New York. He was preparing to leave the next day. Eveline told him that she was spending some time with Rudolph anyway. He was leaving in two days for Rochester. Wallace thought all he would need is to run into Rudolph when he was in Rochester. How would he explain that one? Winston acted like he was left out until Eveline told him that he and Rudolph would have time together too. Little did they know how their lives were going to change. Wallace got to the train station on time and found a seat by himself. He needed some time to think about what he was going to say during the interview. Then he realized that no one was to know he was in Rochester. He could not go to his parent's to stay or go to the Seneca Powers Hotel. If he did that everyone would want explanations including Eveline. As the train approached Rochester the conductor yelled out where they were and how much longer it would be to the station. The train arrived and he got off and walked to the agency office. Since it was very near the Sagamore Hotel he thought that might be a good place to stay. He entered the office and introduced himself. He was told to have a seat and they would be right with him. As he was looking around he remembered how many times he waited in Mr. Helfer's office. How things have changed in his life since that time. Then he laughed and thought about Hilda. Was she still at the hotel or had she been taken away? He had not heard from Mr. Helfer in almost a year. He shook his head and thought that this would all come back to him soon. The door opened and a man who must have weighed 300 pounds came forward. Wallace looked like a kid next to him. They shook hands and went into the office. There were three other men seated around the table. Wallace sat at the end of the table. They asked him to discuss some of the things he had been involved in and his accomplishments. He decided to leave out the Occidental Company. He spoke for a few minutes and they seemed pleased with his discussion of the Weekly Page, the Seneca Powers Hotel, and the H.O.Company. One of the gentlemen spoke up and told Wallace that they had decided they were hiring him. He told Wallace that the minute they received the application from Wallace Paine that he was their man. They agreed that his reputation in Rochester and Buffalo preceded him. They talked to people at the Rochester Post Express and with Mr. Helfer to discuss Wallace's abilities. One of the men laughed when Mr. Helfer's name came up. He asked Wallace if he knew the woman who worked in his office. Wallace said, "Oh you mean Hilda." They laughed and agreed she was really something. Wallace's question was answered. Hilda and Mr. Helfer were still there. They told Wallace what their expectations were for advertising the Shur-On Company. He assured them that he would have unique ideas. He explained what he had done with the Hengerer Department Store and the H.O.Company. They asked him what his salary was at the H.O.Company. He told them and they said he would be receiving 10% more than that with increases and commissions. He would begin working the first week in January 1908.

Wallace thanked the men and left the office. He went out on the street and took a deep breath. He gave himself credit for another step in his move to become a millionaire. He looked around and hoped no one would recognize him. He felt like an escapee. He walked to the Sagamore Hotel and checked into a room. He took a nap before going to dinner. He was happy he did not have anyone with him this time. He wanted to make this move on his own. He went to the restaurant and ordered a martini. He remembered Miss Martini in the other hotel a few years ago. He smiled at the memories of that good time. He enjoyed the drink so well that he ordered a second before dinner. He had to be on the train early the next day to get to New York in time for the afternoon meeting with Mr. Ling. He hoped that would go as well as today's meeting.

The rail line from Rochester to New York City traveled across the state to Albany and then along the Hudson River to New York City. After the train arrived Wallace walked to the hotel. He wondered if the same bellhop was still working at the Waldorf Astoria. As he walked into the lobby he was still there. He remembered Wallace and inquired where his friend was. Wallace told him that he had left him home. The bellhop smiled and asked if he was planning on having a better time without him. Wallace smiled and the bellhop showed him to the same room he had before. He was hungry so he bought some food on the street from a vendor who was selling sausages. It was fun eating while walking along the streets and feeling the crisp autumn air. As he approached the dock office Mr. Ling was waiting for him. Wallace asked him how the voyage was from Hong Kong. Mr. Ling told him that it was fine but he had arrived a few days ago. They went into the office and met Ho Ling. Mr. Ling was very proper with him. Ho was a tiny man who was dressed all in black. He had a long thin moustache that came to a point on either side of his chin. They discussed how communication with Winston was going. All of it seemed fine. Ho politely excused himself and then Mr. Ling and Wallace sat down at the desk. There did not seem to be much to talk about and Wallace began to wonder why he had to come to New York. Mr. Ling began with a question about Mr. Jackson. He hoped that Wallace could explain to him why Mr. Jackson seemed nervous whenever his name was mentioned. He added that the other men had remarked in letters to him that Mr. Jackson did not behave like other businessmen. Wallace listened and thought that it was the same thing that Mr. Jackson said about Mr. Harmon and Mr. Booth. Mr. Ling talked about the need for so many people in the company. Wallace thought that Mr. Ling must not know about Mr. Booth and Mr. Harmon. It was beginning to seem like no one knew about anything except him. Maybe he was referring to Mr. Jackson not being needed. Wallace wanted to start asking questions but something told him not to. Then Mr. Ling asked if he was satisfied with the operation and the profits from the imports and exports. Wallace told him he was satisfied that so much money was coming into their company. Mr. Ling emphasized the importance of having Singapore as another market. He continued to discuss the canal in Central America. He felt that would increase the trade routes and make the voyages much faster. Wallace suggested including European countries. Mr. Ling agreed that then there would be no questions about the contents of the cargo. Wallace mentioned that exotic fabrics, leather, and tobacco could be included in all the markets. Mr. Ling agreed with that idea. Ho returned and Mr. Ling told Wallace to meet him for dinner at 8 PM.

While Wallace was walking back to the hotel he thought about how brief the meeting had been. He came all the way from Buffalo to have a one-hour meeting with Mr. Ling that did not seem to merit an entire trip. He did feel that he and Mr. Ling were working things out very well. Why was he so certain about how things should be when everyone else was attempting to undercut the operation? Wallace decided as long as he was not implicated in anything but business he would not worry. He arrived at the hotel and the bellhop greeted him. Wallace thought the guy had an eye for him. He offered to help him with anything he might need. Wallace thanked him but thought the guy was not his type. He is not rough enough. He got a copy of the New York Times. He planned to relax and read the paper before dinner. As he was going into his room Wallace felt like something was not right. He shook his head and went into the room and took his shoes off and went to lie down on the bed. Wallace stopped cold when he looked at the center of the bed. There was a black scarf wound into the shape of a snake. At the end of the scarf was a tongue! Wallace thought it looked like the devil's tongue or a dragon's tongue. He could not believe it had happened again. Whose tongue was this and what should he do with it? He knew he should not say anything to Mr. Ling. He might be the one committing the murders. Wallace always found the remains of a vicious murder but could not report it or talk about it. He was nervous about the whole thing. He did not know what to do or who to tell. Then he wondered how someone had gotten into his room. The hotel staff would never allow anyone unknown into the room.

After a few minutes he decided to roll the tongue into the scarf and dispose of it on his way to the restaurant. It would be easy enough to put it into a garbage container. He thought it would be better if he did not discuss this with Mr. Ling. If Mr. Ling was trying to see who would break confidence he was certain he did not want to be the next victim. He never did get to read the paper, which did not seem important now. Wallace got ready and picked up the scarf which had a rancid odor and left the room. When he got to the lobby the bellhop mentioned the black package he was carrying. Wallace just smiled and left the lobby. He wondered about the bellhop's remark and if he had done such a thing? He dropped the scarf into the first can he found. As he walked into the restaurant he reminded himself to be calm and pleasant. Mr. Ling was seated awaiting Wallace's arrival. Things were beginning to be very predictable with Mr. Ling. He had the same drink, which was a Manhattan. He had the same dinner and treated the help the same as the last time. There was a difference now a few businessmen came over to Mr. Ling. They were people in New York who owned large stores and trade companies. Mr. Ling introduced them to Wallace. He informed Wallace that he would soon be working with them and he would have less involvement with him. Wallace thought that might be a blessing after all the unsolved murders. At one point there were nine men introducing themselves to Wallace and exchanging information on how to contact them. Now he began to understand the reason for the meeting here by himself. He still wondered who was involved in the murders and how it involved his Occidental Company?

Dinner became quite a party. Wallace realized he was having a great time. These men were friendly and seemed honest. Mr. Ling acted like their leader and they had a very high regard for him. Wallace thought he would not mind being friends with men like this. They were not like the men he had met in Buffalo. He began to see the differences in the two groups. The men in Buffalo were unsure of their behavior in business. The men in New York knew exactly what they wanted to accomplish and how to go about doing it. It was good for him to realize the differences. It occurred to him that with his new job in Rochester he should eliminate the Buffalo office from Occidental. He would discuss that with Mr. Ling before he went back to Buffalo tomorrow. The evening was about over when the waiter informed them that the restaurant was closing. It was 2 AM and Wallace could not believe six hours had passed. Even Mr. Ling did not appear tired. Everyone went outside and said their goodbyes. They were all certain they would see Wallace again. Mr. Ling asked him if he enjoyed himself. Wallace thanked him and told him what a great group of men they were. Mr. Ling offered to meet him in the lobby for breakfast before he went back to Buffalo. Wallace agreed and mentioned that he wanted to discuss the closing of the Buffalo office anyway.

When Wallace returned to his room he wondered if there was going to be anything else to surprise him. There was nothing. He slept very well. It was like the earlier incident never happened. In the morning he packed and went for breakfast. He went to the lobby and met a cheerful Mr. Ling. During their breakfast Wallace decided to tell Mr. Ling about his new job in Rochester and that he and his wife would be moving in January. He was very pleased for Wallace. Then he suggested that the Occidental office in Buffalo be closed. Mr. Ling thought for a moment. He told Wallace that might be a good idea since most of the operation was out of New York now. He told Wallace that when he returned to Buffalo everything would be explained to him. He told Wallace not to ask now but remember why being quiet was so important. They agreed to close the office at the end of the year. Mr. Ling was not sure what Winston would do. Wallace told him he would move back to Rochester. Mr. Ling smiled and told Wallace that soon Buffalo would be only a memory.

They finished breakfast and Wallace thanked Mr. Ling for everything. They shook hands and Wallace walked to the train station. During his ride back to Buffalo he thought about all that had happened. His life had been a series of adventures and mysteries. He hoped that some of the mysteries would soon be solved.

He returned to Buffalo late in the day. When he got home no one was there. He liked the place quiet so he could unpack and relax. There were some newspapers in the parlor that he had not read. Wallace thought it would be a good time to catch up on the news. He sat down and picked up the Buffalo Evening News. On the front page was an article about one of Larkin's top executives who had been murdered. Wallace was shocked when he read that Mr. Jackson's body was found in the alley next to the shipping area. According to the report he had been dead for a few days. They described it as a gruesome murder. His tongue had been cut out of his mouth. He was cut from his throat to his groin and left to bleed to death. The tongue was nowhere to be found. Wallace could not believe that another man was killed and the tongue cut out. The only difference was this body was found and the others were not. If the tongue in New York was Mr. Jackson's then how did it get there? No wonder it had a fowl smell if it was days old. Was this what Mr. Ling had meant about everything being understood when he got back. Just as he was trying to figure all these things out Eveline walked in. She was happy to see him. She explained that she helped Rudolph get ready to move. Then, Wallace told her to sit down, that he had something to tell her. She had the look of gloom and doom on her face. He told her about the meeting in New York and about the new friends he made and how much better things were going to be there. Then, he told her about his job offer at Kirstein's in Rochester. She sounded like a squealing animal when he told her they were moving back to Rochester. He asked her to calm down and behave like a lady. She made a face at him and then started squealing again. He explained what the job was and when it would begin. They laughed at the timing, the New Year. He admitted he did not tell her that he was going to Rochester before the meeting in New York. He did not want to get her hopes up if he was not offered the job. Eveline asked about Winston. He told her that they were closing the Buffalo office and he would probably want to go back to Rochester. She started squealing again and screamed, "All of us will be in Rochester even Rudolph." Wallace hoped that he would not have to contend with Rudolph but that was not going to happen. Winston walked in just as Eveline was having her outburst of joy. He asked what her problem was. She hugged him and told him their news. He looked at them and wondered if that included him. Wallace explained the plans for the closing of the Buffalo office. Winston was happy when he heard the news. He admitted that there were too many things that could be trouble there. He heard of murders and workers who kill each other. He was glad that he had to leave. Wallace thought that he only knows one part of that story. He told Winston that he needed to start the process of letting people go. He would need to finalize the office operations in two weeks. He told him that when they move back to Rochester, he would have to find his own place to live. He understood and thought he might want a place of his own anyway. They celebrated the news with a bottle of champagne and dinner.

Wallace got up early the next day to get to work. He had many things to wrap up at the faltering H.O.Company. The office was nearly empty of employees. The secretary was still working until the final days of the company. She was happy to see Wallace and told him that there was a letter in his office. It had arrived yesterday when he was gone. He walked into his office and found the letter with Mr. Ling's handwriting on it. Wallace sat down and wondered what now. He opened it and began reading it slowly. Mr. Ling began with his highest regard for Wallace's ability to form and develop such a wonderful company named Occidental I&E Company. He was proud to be a part of its operation. He explained why some of the people who were originally involved had to be eliminated. In order for Mr. Ling to find out who was most trustworthy and loyal he tested their character. The first one was Bill Foote, he attempted blackmail, not good for trustworthiness. Mr. Booth and Mr. Harmon threatened to go to the authorities when they found out about the possibilities of human transfers. A tactic such as that would put everyone in prison. The last person to be tested and who failed was Mr. Jackson because he wanted to get rid of me. Instead I had him disposed of! Mr. Ling explained that he and Winston were never suspects to dishonesty or undercutting the company. He admitted to Wallace that they must have been scared, but they never spoke a word of what they found out or knew. Mr. Ling admitted that they were being tested too.

As far as where the bodies went, or who committed the crimes, it was Ho. He would do whatever he was told to do. Ho took the scarf to your room at the hotel. As you know, he is a small man and can go into places most cannot. He crawled through the transom window to leave the scarf on your bed. That is where he went after you met him. Ho was in Buffalo to dispose of Mr. Jackson the day you approached him about what happened to Mr. Booth and Mr. Harmon. Ho put their bodies in the shipping boxes that Mr. Jackson thought were soap and oatmeal for shipment. Their bodies were shipped to Singapore, their tongues placed on their desks at the H.O. Company. As for Mr. Jackson, Ho decided to leave him for the newspapers to report on but to bring his tongue to New York so we could make sure you held strict quiet. Mr. Ling realized that all these crimes would be very difficult to prove given the methods and places in which they occurred. Even if anyone tried to report the murders, there is not enough evidence to pinpoint any one person. Ho is not registered in New York or anywhere. He is a transfer and not a relative. He owned Ho. He ended his letter explaining that after all that Wallace was welcomed into the New York circle of businessmen. He, Mr. Ling would now remain in Hong Kong. He will do business from there, and Ho will do his work in New York. He hoped that Wallace could relax now and enjoy his new career and business in New York.

When he finished the letter, he was amazed at such a complex plan to test trustworthiness and to execute unworthy people. He put the letter in his file of things that people should never see. He laughed to himself and wondered how many more items like this would he put in that file in his lifetime. After all that, he told the secretary that he was going to be leaving. He wished her good luck and suggested she work in a store where there was not so much drama. She laughed and told him she always wanted to work at Hengerer's Department Store. He gave her the name of the woman in charge of hiring. He wished her well and walked out of the office, only carrying his file.

Chapter 38

WALLACE DECIDED TO DRIVE his car to Rochester instead of going by train. The trip would take the entire day because of the dirt roads and weather conditions at Thanksgiving. He told Eveline and Winston as they were leaving Buffalo that this was the beginning of another adventure. Eveline laughed and admitted that the car would definitely be better than the buggies that were on the road. Wallace drove slowly so that nothing would damage the car. It became windy and sleet began to fall when they were half way to Rochester. Buggies would approach them coming from the opposite direction. In order to avoid hitting oncoming vehicles everyone moved off the road into the underbrush and trees. The road was muddy that was making it slippery. The trees would sweep the people as they passed by making them wet from the rain and sleet. They passed a group of people in a buggy that had slid into a rut. The horse could not pull them out of the mud. The men were pushing the buggy and the woman and children were trying to steer it. Wallace went by slowly and stopped the car. He and Winston helped get the buggy back onto the road. They arrived in Rochester at 5PM. They were staying with Eveline's parents and dinner was being served at Frank and Alice's home. Alice began the dinner with a blessing for the food, family, and the return of their kids to Rochester.

Frank had not seen Wallace's car yet. It was dark when they arrived and the question never came up about how they traveled to Rochester. Wallace deliberately left the car at Eveline's. He knew what his father would say when he saw the machine that put him out of business. He told Mr. and Mrs. Lounsberry about it and was happy to show them the car when they got home from dinner. They thought it was grand and wanted to go for a ride before they went back to Buffalo. Wallace decided he would show his father the car when they returned to Rochester. Wallace told his mother about it and she was excited and wanted to come over to the Lounsberry's to go for a ride. She began to tell Wallace that his father was more and more disagreeable. He had some debt that was coming due and he did not have any money to pay it. Alice explained how tired she was of his attitude and that he rarely spoke with her. He would go out to a bar and not return until late in the evening. If she asked him to go somewhere he refused and told her they could not spend any money. Wallace had experienced his father's temper and felt sorry for Alice. He told her that he would give them some financial help when he returned to Rochester. She thanked him for that but was afraid of what Frank would think of such a gesture.

Eveline and Wallace found an apartment that would be available in the middle of December. It was at 72 Scio Street. It was not a company apartment like the one in Buffalo. They had to furnish it. After they settled the rental issues they went to order new furniture. They set the delivery date for the middle of December. Alice offered to be available for the delivery if they were not in town yet. She was excited they were returning and would help them in any way she could. Wallace took Eveline to see where he would be working. The Kirstein office was on

204 Court Street. After that Eveline wanted some lunch. Wallace wanted to stop in to see Mr. Helfer so he thought going to the hotel for lunch might be a good idea. He parked the car in front of the hotel. The people on the street watched him maneuver the car next to the sidewalk. Since the car was red it was like a colorful ornament decorating the front of the hotel. They went into the restaurant and it seemed like no time had passed. As they were being seated Wallace spotted Mr. Helfer. He went to his table and shook his hand. Mr. Helfer was delighted to see them. Wallace inquired about the hotel, Hilda, and Mr. Helfer's health. The hotel was showing continued profits and being occupied by people from everywhere. Wallace was happy things were going so well. Mr. Helfer explained that his health was failing and it was only a matter of time before he would be not able to work. He reminded Wallace of the letter he had sent to him. Wallace assured him that he would follow his orders. Mr. Helfer thought it was terrific they were moving back to Rochester and that Wallace would be nearby to continue the operation of the hotel. Eveline waited at the table until Wallace returned from speaking with Mr. Helfer. Wallace was glad that she was not at Mr. Helfer's table to hear about him taking over the hotel. Wallace had not told her what exactly would happen after Mr. Helfer's death. They enjoyed their lunch and returned to finish shopping.

Thanksgiving weekend ended and Wallace and Eveline left early on Sunday morning to return to Buffalo. The weather had gotten worse than it was when they had arrived. It had been snowing and instead of sleet there was freezing rain. Alice and Eveline's mother Catherine were nervous as they could be about their trip to Buffalo. They told them they hoped this would be the last time they would be so far away. Wallace got the feeling from his father that he was not looking forward to his return to Rochester. Frank was nowhere to be found when Wallace and Eveline walked to their apartment to say goodbye. Wallace asked Eveline if she thought his father had found out about the car and was angry that he was not told about it. Eveline did not say much about his question only reminded him that his father was having a difficult time. While Wallace drove the car the wind blew directly at the car making it shake and swerve. Eveline was nervous and Wallace told her not to start screaming. She did not appreciate his remark and did not say one more word. It was midnight when they arrived in front of their Delaware Avenue apartment. They were happy to be back home.

The last two weeks in Buffalo were spent packing and finishing business. They were given no information on what to do with their apartment now that the H.O.Company was bankrupt. Wallace decided to return the keys to the office. Eveline went to see her parent's friends on Delaware Avenue. Rudolph had already moved to Rochester. The move would be easy because they had no furniture except their belongings. He laughed when he remembered the train ride to Buffalo four years ago. He was excited when he thought about the move and his new job. He had a feeling things were going to be very good for him in Rochester.

Moving into the Scio Street apartment was exciting. The furniture arrived and Eveline decorated the apartment with the newest accessories she could find. Wallace gave her control of the household operation. Since he was in charge of advertising for a new company he had to develop new ideas. Wallace liked the challenge of being the originator of a company's advertising future. The range of production would include any item that had lenses. New York State had just passed an optometry law. This law set the standards for the optical professions. It included regulations for who could practice optometry, the manufacture of eyeglass lenses, and any other lens related products. It had been passed in other states but New York had just ratified it in early 1908. The law regulated how business was conducted and set equal competition standards among optical companies. Since Shuron was so new Wallace instituted an advertising campaign that included people qualified to conduct business. There were people selling optics who were not qualified and conducting underhanded business. He laughed when he began writing the information. He thought about all the people taking patent medicines made from the opium he was importing. He shook his head and tried not to think about Occidental because someone else was doing that type of work for him. In his advertisement there would be three categories for eyewear needs. The first category was for the more fashion conscious customer. The second category was for people who needed glasses but did not care what they looked like, and the third was for protective eyewear on a job. He researched where protective eyewear would be required. He found out that factories, military, miners, goggles for automobile drivers, and steel mills needed these products. His first promotion would be with the Ford Motor Company. He contacted the Ford office and suggested they offer a free set of driving goggles when new cars were delivered to the owner. The Ford Company would pay Shuron for the product and Shuron's name would be on the goggles. Another gimmick he thought of was to offer opera glasses to patrons of the arts. As part of a season pass to the orchestra and opera you would receive a pair of opera glasses from the Musical Council of Rochester. Wallace thought it would be a good time to have a promotion of this sort because it was the 10th season of the Hermann Dossenbach Orchestra. He made an appointment with the Musical Council of Rochester to discuss the promotion. Those in charge loved the idea that a gift would be included with a season pass to the arts. While he was meeting with the music lovers of Rochester one of the men in the group mentioned the 1000th Owner Automobile Club. Wallace had never heard about this club and asked them what it was. The club was for people who owned an automobile. It had originally started for the first 1000 owners of an automobile. Wallace was invited to become a member since he was one of the first to have an automobile. The man he was talking with suggested that Shuron supply the club with binoculars for their members. The club would buy them from Shuron and offer them as a gift with the membership.

Wallace presented his ideas to his bosses at the Kirstein Agency. They approved all the ideas and were surprised with the variety of options he had offered them. During his meeting he inquired if there were any stock options for Shuron. They told him that there were some wealthy individuals that were supporting the formation of the company. Wallace told them that another way to get the company on firm footing was to offer stock options to the public. He challenged them to establish the stock option plan and he would invest half of his salary into the Shuron Company. They told Wallace that he was coming up with more ideas than they could handle. However, with his smooth way, he convinced them to go for all of his ideas. They were a bit hesitant but agreed. He signed the paper for his investment into the company. When he left the meeting and went back to his office he thought about what had just happened. There was a pattern in his behavior. Whatever job he had he always comes out being an owner. He thought about his investments in Ford when he worked for the hotel. As he was thinking about his investment in Eastman Kodak he thought about the lenses in cameras. Kodak had been working on the moving picture. He decided to go to the Kodak office to find out who supplied them with the lenses for their products. He still had his first camera in his office as a reminder to himself about his beginnings with the Eastman Kodak Company. He laughed to himself about how fearful people were when he took pictures with his first camera.

There had been daily newspaper coverage of a murder in the Adirondack Mountains in 1906. The Union and Advertiser newspaper had reported about the trial and now the execution of Chester E. Gillette. Everyone was buying the paper and talking about the guy who killed a girl on Big Moose Lake. Wallace wondered why everyone was so interested in that story. It had happened two years ago and the trial had been very long and drawn out. The murderer's mother tried to change the story and someone else came along with some personality clues about the killer. The new information changed the trial and how it was conducted. It had been an attempt to stall the proceedings. The story was that Chester fell in love with a factory girl sweetheart. Her name was Grace Brown. He had always wanted to live in a higher style but she became pregnant and Chester realized he was trapped and would never improve his life with her. He took her on a trip to Big Moose Lake in the Adirondack Mountains. It was there that he took her out in a boat and drowned her. He thought she would never be found and he would be free to go on with his life. Her body was recovered and he was on trial for murder. There was so much interest in the event because he was convicted of murder and was sentenced to electrocution. The public wanted to know the details of the final day of Chester Gillette's life. Most people did not care about the trial but wanted to know about the electric chair. It was March 30 at 6:14AM that E.F. Davis, the electrician, threw the switch that started the electrocution of Gillette. It took a few electrical shocks to complete the death. The electric chair was in the Auburn Prison and was a relatively new process. At 6:20AM Gillette was pronounced dead. The clergyman attending the electrocution received no admission of guilt and no sign of emotion. As Wallace read the article he thought of Leon Czolgosz's attitude when he was convicted of killing President McKinley at the Buffalo Exposition. When Wallace saw Winston he told him about the story. They agreed that people who murder have no remorse. Winston reminded Wallace of the tongue on the desk in New York. He shrugged that off and knew that Winston did not know the whole story. It seemed true that people who kill others are never sorry.

Chapter 39

THE SHURON COMPANY WAS well on its way to becoming a known optical company. Wallace secured the account for the lenses that Eastman Kodak used for the camera-manufacturing department. He acquired the contract for the lenses that were being used in the cameras for moving pictures. Eastman Kodak Company wanted a small company to work with them on lenses that could be modified quickly. They were pleased when Wallace assured them that Shuron would make lens faster than any other company. He rearranged his stock options to include money to be invested in moving pictures. Some of his associates thought he was taking a huge risk. He explained that his philosophy was to take all the risks you can because one is sure to turn out big. His boss told him that he had a young person's attitude and not one that an older person would ever dare to have. While Wallace was at the Eastman Kodak office building on State Street he had the pleasure of meeting George Eastman. He happened to be in the lobby when Wallace was leaving from his meetings. Wallace smiled and acknowledged him by tipping his hat. Mr. Eastman stopped him and asked what his business was in the building. Wallace explained that he was representing the Shuron Company. Mr. Eastman had heard about the new company and explained how good it was to have new companies in town. He told Wallace that he had given $60,000.00 to the University of Rochester for laboratories in 1904. Wallace wondered why he needed to know that information. Mr. Eastman told him that he wanted to donate high-powered microscopes to the medical school for disease research. He asked Wallace to think about the possibilities of the Shuron Company working on the development of these instruments. Wallace accepted the challenge and told him he would discuss it with his superiors and get back to him the next day. Mr. Eastman liked his confidence and invited him and a guest to a musical event at his home. Wallace told him he would be honored and looked forward to it.

Wallace went back to the office to discuss the newest opportunities for business with the Eastman Kodak Company. It did not take him very long to convince the men of what Eastman had proposed to the Shuron Company. They were amazed at what talent they had hired. He had been working there for almost a year and the business had nearly doubled. He told them he had an appointment the next day to verify the company's acceptance of the work with Eastman Kodak. Wallace could not wait to tell Eveline that they were invited to George Eastman's home especially when there was music involved. He finished his work for the day making sure he had all the paperwork complete for his meeting at 10AM the next day.

Instead of driving to work everyday Wallace rode on the streetcar. On his way home he decided to drive his car the next day when he went to the Eastman Kodak building. He noticed that there were places to park in the front of the building. He hoped to be seen getting out of his car which might make a good impression on people. From the streetcar Wallace saw Winston walking toward their apartment building. He knocked on the window but the streetcar went by so fast that Winston never saw who it was. When he got off the streetcar he watched Winston as he walked up the street. He felt that same sensation again which he had not felt in a long time. He liked how good he felt when that happened. Now that Winston was staying at Alice and Frank's place they did not have any time together. As Winston got closer Wallace studied his dark beard and messed up hair. He had a slow gaited walk that looked intriguingly suggestive. Wallace stood with a smile on his face. Winston came up to him and gave him a bump on the shoulder and asked, "What are you looking at?" Wallace stared straight into his eyes and said, "You know." Winston asked what he was planning to do about it. They went into the apartment where Eveline was organizing some of her needlework. She was glad to see Winston. Wallace started to tell them about his day and his meeting with George Eastman. They were impressed he had met such an influential person. He told them about the work Shuron would be doing with Eastman Kodak Company. Then he told them about the invitation to an evening event at Mr. Eastman's home. Eveline made one of her squeals. Wallace hated that sound. She could not imagine being invited to his home. Her first remarks were, what shall I wear, and wait until I tell Rudolph. Wallace thought that she probably would rather go with him because he would fit into the musical atmosphere. After meeting Winston outside, Wallace wished she would go with Rudolph to George Eastman's home. Then he and Winston could go out somewhere or just stay home and have some fun.

After the excitement of the invitation wore off Eveline told Wallace that his father came to visit today.

Wallace thought that was very strange. He never goes visiting especially during the day because he was supposed to be working. She explained that he wanted to see him and that there was something that he wanted to discuss with him. He told her that he would return this evening. She had no idea what he wanted other than he appeared upset. Wallace remembered that his car was in front of the apartment building today. Maybe he figured out that was his car. Eveline had dinner nearly ready and invited Winston to stay. He reminded them of all the dinners they had in Buffalo. They agreed that seemed like a long time ago. Wallace asked Winston about his job. He had taken a job working for the French's Mustard Company. They were producing different types of mustard. He laughed when he told them about all the yellow mustard seeds he works with. He told them that he might turn yellow if he worked there too long. They laughed and agreed the taste was so much different than anything they had ever tasted.

Dinner was served and while they were eating there was a knock at the door. It was Frank. Wallace invited him to sit with them and have dessert and coffee. Frank began the conversation by explaining that Alice had been keeping things from him. He was very angry with her for that. It was not a woman's place to defy her husband. Eveline thought how lucky she was to have Wallace as her husband and not Frank. He told them that she had somehow paid a large debt and he wanted to know how she had managed it as he stared at Wallace. He asked what involvement she had with them since they have been back in Rochester. Then he wanted to know whose car that was in the front of the building. Wallace knew he had to tell the truth and protect his mother. He hoped Frank had not done something terrible to her. He explained that she came to him for a loan to pay the debt. He emphasized that it was a loan and not a gift. Frank was angry that she would dare to do such a thing. Frank said, "Eveline's attitude has started to rub off on Alice." Eveline sucked her teeth and rolled her eyes when he said that. Then Frank asked about the car again. Wallace admitted it was his. The next question was, "How long have you had it?" He admitted for a few years. Frank slammed his fist on the table and dishes fell to the floor. Wallace told him that was enough. Then he said, "If you can't accept the idea that the car is here to stay and that things are changing then you are in for a very disappointing life." Frank looked at Wallace with fire in his eyes and said, "It's people like you that put me out of business and now I owe you money for that." Then he proceeded to tell them that he had been fired from the newspaper company. Winston asked what happened. Frank asked him, "Why would you care?" Frank turned to Winston and yelled, "All you want to do is play with Wallace in the bedroom and be friends with Eveline." In Frank's opinion men did not do those types things. There was not a sound in the room. Shock took over. Wallace convinced Frank to tell them why he was fired. He shamefully admitted that he was drunk most of the time and he nearly killed someone in the circulation department. Frank looked at Winston and then Wallace and explained that the guy was acting like Winston acts toward you. He looked straight at Wallace. He ended his visit by telling them that he had instructed Alice to stay away from their apartment. If he found out she disobeys him he may have to put a stop to her misbehavior. At that, he got up and walked out leaving the door wide open. It was like a policeman had just interrogated them as they sat quietly. All the excitement of the day was ruined by Frank's angry outburst.

Wallace got ready for work early the next morning. He wanted to be prepared for his meeting with George Eastman. As he was parking the car one of the men who worked in the office where the meeting was being held walked up. He waited for Wallace to get out of the car. He complimented Wallace about the car as they walked into the building. They were the first ones there for the meeting. They discussed the moving picture and how it was constructed. He told Wallace that they were experimenting with different lenses and angles for making the moving pictures seem as real as possible. As they sat talking George Eastman walked in. Wallace presented him with diagrams that reviewed the microscopes and experimental lenses for moving pictures. Mr. Eastman was pleased that it all worked out so well. Then he gave Wallace the details of the party at his home. It was to be held on Saturday evening. There would be a harpist playing in the conservatory beginning at 8PM. Refreshments and food would be served during the intermission. There would be time for socializing and mingling with other music admirers. While Mr. Eastman was excusing himself he asked, "Whose smart car is outside in the front of the building?" Wallace raised his hand and said, "It's mine." Mr. Eastman said, "I thought it might have been yours because I heard about that car at the automobile club meeting." Wallace beamed when he heard that his car was the topic of conversation in such a high-class club.

When Wallace returned from his meeting his boss wanted to know how the meeting with George Eastman went. His boss mentioned that not everyone gets to meet Mr. Eastman. He has a reputation for being very certain of what he wants and can be difficult at times. He is a huge contributor to the music and arts in the city. He is the type of person you want on your side. Wallace's boss changed the subject and asked if he had any knowledge of the mail-order business. Wallace asked him why he was interested in that. He told him he knew he had something to do with the Larkin Company in Buffalo. Wallace wondered what he knew about that involvement. Did he find out about the Occidental Company and Mr. Jackson's death? Wallace explained that the Larkin's were the first to have a mail order business. It was started in the late 1800's. It was profitable because it eliminated the middleman. Both the customer and the company benefited from a lower cost for handling. His boss then asked if they could develop a line of products that could be sold through a catalog. Wallace agreed with him that it was a good idea; especially for people who were looking for exceptional eyewear or merchandise that was used for entertainment purposes. He was asked to work on that idea and see if it could begin in early 1909. Wallace was certain it was possible but he did not want to appear too eager about it. He found it was better to come up with a new plan than to pull out an old idea. His bosses did not know that he studied the development of the mail order process from its beginning. It would be a snap to get it ready. He would have a new format in printing style with a cameo style layout of each product in the catalog. There were many consumers who liked shopping from home and he needed to focus on a higher-level customer. He asked if he could present it in a week. This week was Eastman Kodak's project and that was enough for one week. He learned to spread out his ideas making it look like he had a ton of ideas.

Eveline had been preparing for the evening at Mr. Eastman's home. She purchased a new outfit that would be fit for a soirée. She told Wallace that her parents were familiar with attending such events. When they lived in Canada they attended a different soirée every month. Eveline told Wallace that she felt like she was returning to Canada with the type of event that they were attending. Wallace thought she was getting too excited about it because he viewed it as a business event. He planned to wear a formal suit with tails and wear a top hat. He would definitely drive the car to the party. A valet would park the car as the butler greeted the guests. When Eveline and Wallace were ready to go they looked at themselves in the mirror and agreed that they looked like royalty. Eveline laughingly said, "If Rudolph could see me now." Wallace told her that he would not recognize her looking so perfect. She thought as they were going down East Avenue that she had not seen much of Rudolph. She hoped he was okay. As they approached East Avenue there were more cars on the street than usual for that time of night. East Avenue had been paved so it was smooth and clean of dirt. They had the flutters as they approached Mr. Eastman's estate. Wallace laughed to himself and thought he was so young to be going to something so important. The valet took the car as the butler greeted them and they entered the grand foyer. It was breath taking to see so many people dressed in such finery. The women were strolling around speaking politely to everyone they met. Mr. Eastman was charming and a perfect host. Some wondered why he was not married. Gossip circled around that he had no need for a wife. Mr. Eastman had a reputation of getting what he needed without any continuous involvement. It was rumored that there were men coming and going in the mansion. No one seemed to have the real story. The only fact known was that his mother lived with him and they had a close relationship. There were huge floral arrangements throughout the main floor. Flowers wound around the railings of the grand marble staircase. It was an eye catcher. The wait staff maneuvered around offering champagne. At 8 PM chimes were heard and the guests entered the conservatory for the concert. Whispers of, "Imagine having an organ in your home." could be heard as the guests found their seats. Each morning Mr. Eastman had an organ concert while he was having his breakfast in the conservatory. A stylish woman said, "Such opulence for a gentleman." Mr. Eastman thanked everyone for coming to his soirée. He hoped that everyone would enjoy the program and that there was something new to the program after the intermission.

Chapter 40

THE CONSERVATORY WAS TRANSFORMED into a musical wonderland as the harpist played for an entire hour. There was a gentle breeze that made the palm trees sway. One woman compared the evening to a setting in the tropics. As the hour came to a close Mr. Eastman reminded the guests of the second part of the evening. It was to be held in the music room after the intermission. Everyone was invited in to the billiard room and dining room for food and refreshments. Wallace and Eveline strolled around observing the fine art and furnishings in the home. Wallace was looking at the stained glass windows in the billiard room. Each window had an invention or a means of transportation embedded in the center pane of glass. One of the windows had a red car in the leaded glass window. It was exactly like the car he owned. He showed Eveline the window and while they were looking at it Mr. Eastman came up to them. He asked Wallace if the car looked familiar. Wallace said, "Indeed, it looks like mine." Mr. Eastman agreed and told Wallace that when he saw the red car at the office building he knew the owner must like having the latest inventions. Wallace thanked him for the compliment. He told them the reason he wanted the red car in the window was because that was Henry Ford's first Model A, which was later remanufactured into the Model AC. Wallace explained to Mr. Eastman that he had to wait for his car to be finished because they were making improvements in the Model A. They laughed and commented on the color being red. It was such an eye catcher from the usual black automobiles. Mr. Eastman said, "A red car needs to be driven by someone like you, Wallace, who is way ahead of his time."

The chimes began to sound reminding everyone that the program was to continue in the grand music room. As the guests found a place to stand they commented on the ceiling. It had in each corner a large medallion in the plaster depicting the four seasons. There was a huge picture window overlooking the gardens. In the center of the ceiling hung a large crystal chandelier that was fully lit. There was a young man standing at attention near the grand piano. Eveline overheard someone say he was the page-turner for the pianist. Wallace looked around the room to see if he knew anyone. Off in the distance he caught sight of Rudolph. He could not believe his eyes when he realized that Rudolph might very well be the pianist for the evening. He was speaking to Mr. Eastman and they both began to move into the room toward the piano. Eveline was busy looking the other way and did not see them come into the room. Mr. Eastman began by explaining that he came in contact with this gentleman who had recently moved from Buffalo. When Eveline heard the word Buffalo her ears perked up. Then she saw Rudolph and nearly fainted. Never did she expect to see him as Mr. Eastman's guest pianist. Wallace took a hold of her and told her not to make a sound. For the first time she appeared speechless. Wallace was glad for that. All she said was, "I can't believe he is here." Rudolph took a bow, sat down and began to play. The sound was magnificent. He played softly and moved to a crescendo.

When he finished his first piece the guests applauded. During this applause he saw Eveline. His eyes were as big as saucers when he realized his closest friends were there. His performance was enhanced with the combined sound of the harp and violin that lasted for nearly an hour. When he finished Mr. Eastman thanked him and Rudolph took another bow. Rudolph walked over to Eveline and Wallace and shook hands and discussed how surprised they were about the evening. Eveline asked Rudolph why he had not contacted them. He explained that he was working in Seneca Falls for the Women's Rights Movement and that Mr. Eastman had heard about him from the orchestra in town. Rudolph explained that he had been hired to play the piano for private parties. As he was telling Eveline and Wallace about his work Mr. Eastman came up to them and asked them if they knew one another. Rudolph told him how they had met and that he and Eveline had been friends when they lived in Buffalo. Eveline told him about the weekend at the Elmwood Music Hall where Rudolph performed. Mr. Eastman smiled and said, "I'm glad to see you are all in good company." He made a point of telling them he was happy to see such young people doing good things. Wallace smiled and thanked Mr. Eastman for the invitation. Mr. Eastman told him that they would definitely being seeing more of each other.

The party ended at 10:30 PM. The guests were escorted to their automobiles by the butler. Wallace, Eveline, and Rudolph left together. Wallace offered Rudolph a ride and he accepted. As they were driving down East Avenue, Rudolph asked if they wanted to go somewhere else so they could continue to visit. Wallace said he was tired but if he and Eveline wanted to go somewhere he would take them before he went home. Eveline thought that was a great idea. She wanted to spend more time with Rudolph. Wallace suggested the Seneca-Powers Hotel. They thought that would be fine. He dropped them off at the hotel and Eveline told him she would be home in a few hours. Wallace told them to have a good time. He had other ideas and wanted to find Winston. Wallace drove to his parent's place in hopes that Winston would be there. As he drove down Park Avenue he saw Winston coming out of the apartment building. He stopped and asked him if he would like to go somewhere. Winston was glad it was Wallace. He told him that he had to get out of the apartment because Alice and Frank were fighting. Wallace asked if his father was intoxicated and Winston nodded in agreement. Wallace asked him if he should go in to help his mother out but Winston told him to let them go. He looked at Wallace and told him that they had better things to do. Wallace smiled and agreed. He pulled away from the curb and headed for home. As they were going to Scio Street Wallace told Winston about the party at Mr. Eastman's home and that Rudolph was the pianist. Winston thought that was great because it would give Eveline someone to do things with. Winston looked at Wallace and said; "Now we can enjoy our own activities." Wallace felt that sensation again when he heard Winston's deep voice. They got out of the car and went into the apartment. Wallace told Winston not to turn on any lights. Winston started feeling excited. There was a nudge on Winston's back when Wallace closed the door. Winston did not move because he wanted to enjoy what was happening. Wallace moved his hands from Winston's neck slowly down his back. He stopped mid way and began to slowly massage his back. Winston's hairy back emanated a musky odor that excited Wallace. His hands moved lower to his waist.

Winston's breathing became louder and Wallace's heart pounded. Winston had his hands on parts of Wallace's body that made him feel like screaming with pleasure. The darkness made the moment even more exciting. Winston told him that he had waited a long time for this to happen. As Wallace turned his back to Winston he could feel a strong force against his body. Winston maneuvered Wallace into a position that he had never been in before. He could feel Winston's strong legs against his legs and enjoyed the sensual feelings. He whispered to Wallace that they should have been this close a long time ago. Wallace moaned, as the sensations grew stronger. Perspiration dripped from their heads to their toes. The wetness from their bodies added to their movement and pleasure. Winston wanted to know when they could do this again and Wallace said nothing. Wallace began to act nervous about what just happened. Winston assured him that no one would ever find out. Wallace got them something to drink, as Winston got ready to go home. They talked about how long they had known each other and that they must keep their friendship alive. Wallace mentioned Eveline and Winston reminded him that she was having fun with her other boyfriend, Rudolph. Wallace was not sure he liked the sound of the words "other boyfriend".

Eveline arrived home at midnight. Rudolph escorted her to the door and spoke to Wallace before he left. He told him they had a good conversation and they had caught up on all types of things. Eveline told Wallace that she had invited Rudolph for dinner this week. She mentioned that they could invite Winston too. Wallace smiled and said he might be seeing him and would invite him. After Rudolph left Eveline asked what he had done after the party. Wallace told her he went to his parent's place and that they were fighting. She felt bad for Alice. Wallace told her that he saw Winston. He left out the part about coming to their apartment. Then Eveline told Wallace that when they were at the hotel she heard that Mr. Helfer had been taken to the hospital a few days ago. The doorman recognized her as she and Rudolph went into the lobby. He told her that Mr. Helfer looked very sick and worn out. No one seemed to know much more than that. Wallace decided to find out more the next day. He knew he could not ask Hilda but maybe someone in the business office would know which hospital he was in.

It was April 1, 1909, Wallace's 28th birthday. He was on his way to the hotel to find out about Mr. Helfer's condition. He saw Winston on his way to work and they spoke about the previous night. Wallace smiled and told him he was not sure if there would be a next time. Winston laughed and told him that was his early birthday present but that there should be a next time. Wallace blushed. Wallace went to the business office and one of the accountants told him where Mr. Helfer was. He was told that Hilda had become more impossible to have in the office. Wallace knew he would soon have to deal with her. He thanked the accountant for the information and assured everyone in the office that he would take care of things. Wallace went to the hospital and found Mr. Helfer. He was very subdued and had trouble breathing and could barely talk. He was glad that Wallace had arrived. He hoped someone would get word to him. He reminded Wallace of his commitment to the hotel and to Hilda. Wallace told him that he should not worry and that everything would be taken care of as he wished. He reminded Wallace of how to get to the important papers. He had put them in a separate safe under the floor in his office. The door to the compartment was under the rug in front of his desk. He smiled a weak smile when he said that if Hilda only knew she was standing on her future. Mr. Helfer explained that Hilda would have made his life even more difficult if she knew the whole story. Wallace assured him that he would take good care of all his affairs. He told Mr. Helfer that he would be back tomorrow to see how he was doing.

Eveline had arranged a party for Wallace's birthday. She made no mention of it to him until that evening. She and Rudolph had planned a party for him the other night when they were at the hotel. Wallace was happy to have something fun to think about. He asked who was attending the dinner. She told him that her parents, his parents, Winston, Rudolph, and Miss Holleran. She thought that all the people who helped him become successful should be invited. She was sorry that Mr. Helfer was not able to be there and laughed when Hilda's name came up. She asked him if he really thought she had been involved in his success. Wallace told her that she taught him how to deal with the impossible and then they laughed.

The birthday party was held in a private room in the restaurant. This party was much smaller than some of the grand parties that they had attended in the past. As Wallace and Eveline walked in they were greeted with the news that Mr. Helfer had passed away a few hours before. Wallace knew that this birthday was sure to be much different than other birthdays. He looked at Eveline and said, "I wonder who else will die because usually these things come in threes." She tried to console him and said, "That is not always true." Wallace just shook his head. The rest of the guests arrived and there was an air of discomfort between everyone. Wallace looked at the somber faces and felt like he was at his funeral rather than his birthday party. When he told Eveline that, she told him he was too young to die. Rudolph offered to play the piano while people were having drinks and conversation. Wallace saw Miss Holleran come into the room. He was glad to see one of his old and treasured friends. She too seemed troubled. She asked about his work and all he had been doing in the past few years. He was glad to talk about the good things and people he had been involved with. She asked him how many businesses he was now part of or owned. He laughed when he told her about his experiences in Buffalo and New York City. Winston came into the conversation at the moment as Wallace was talking about New York. Winston wondered what he was going to tell her about the Occidental Company if anything. He only told her about the export and imports of soaps, leathers and fabrics from the Orient. She was impressed with his worldly experiences. After they discussed the hotel and Mr. Helfer's death Miss Holleran told Wallace that her friend who had been his advisor died yesterday. Even though she had passed she wanted to come to see Wallace on his 28th birthday. She explained that her friend was ill with pneumonia and never recovered. The funeral was to be tomorrow at Christ's Church on East Avenue. She asked Wallace if he could attend as her escort. He told her he would be honored to be there with her since they had been by his side for many years and that was the least he could do for her. Winston and Eveline overheard the conversation and offered to be there also. She thought that would be wonderful because her friend had no family and there would only be people attending from the college. Miss Holleran never discussed her private life when she was in school. She had retired so long ago that there were very few people around from her school. It was time for dinner so everyone took his or her place at the large table.

During the dinner Wallace was talking about the new contracts that the Shuron Company had with Eastman Kodak. Eveline was excited to tell everyone about the party they attended at Mr. Eastman's home. Rudolph explained how happy he was when he saw Wallace and Eveline at the party. The group was impressed that Rudolph was hired to be the pianist for that party. He went on to explain what his role had been in the Women's Rights Campaign in Seneca Falls. He was one of the few men that supported giving women the right to vote. At that remark Frank spoke up and said, "Women don't need any more rights, they have taken over enough." Alice turned and glared at him when he said that. Miss Holleran asked why he was so against the idea. He told everyone about how Alice went behind his back on financial matters. He felt that if women were to get too much freedom men would not be in control. Eveline spoke up and told him that men should learn to do more for themselves. She looked him straight in the eye and said, "Slavery is over." He looked at Alice and said, "Not in my house!" There was not another sound in the room for a moment. Finally dinner was served and the conversation moved to other topics that were not so difficult to discuss. The funeral was discussed and Alice offered to go to the funeral with the rest of the group. She thought that everyone at the table should be there. Frank spoke up and said; "You won't see me there. People might think I'm like all of you." There was another long moment of silence. Wallace thought he better find out what his father was really up to with his mother. When dinner was finished and they were waiting for dessert Wallace asked Alice if he could talk with her alone. They went into the lobby and he asked her what was going on. Alice with teary eyes and a shaky voice explained that Frank had threatened to kill her if she was to ever go against him again. He did not want her to be involved with them unless he was there to make sure she obeyed him. Wallace was furious with this news. He asked her why she did not leave. She explained that she threatened to and Frank told her he would find her and kill her. At that instant Wallace thought that this could be the third death in the triangle. He told her to be careful with him and if she needed to get out he would help her do so. They went back into the room to be met by Frank glaring at both of them as if he were ready to attack them. His face looked as hot as fire. It was getting late and there was tension in the air so everyone started excusing themselves to go home. As Wallace left he told Miss Holleran that they would meet her at the funeral in the morning.

After the funeral Miss Holleran invited everyone to her apartment for lunch. All the time they worked together she rarely allowed anyone to visit her at her home. During lunch she explained about her life and her friend and how it was easier to keep a low profile. After lunch Wallace went to the hotel to begin his work with Mr. Helfer's affairs. Eveline, Winston, Alice, and Rudolph walked home. Spring had arrived and the trees were budding and the spring flowers were in bloom. They thought a walk would be just what they needed after all the things that had happened. Wallace parked his car in front of the hotel. When he went past the front desk the receptionist told him that it seemed like old times again. Wallace nodded and knew things would be changing soon. As he went into the office he thought about how some things never changed. There was Hilda slouched in her chair with her breasts resting on the desk. When she saw him she said, "Not you again." He gave her his familiar smile but this time he walked directly into Mr. Helfer's office. He closed the door and locked it. Hilda knocked and asked him why he needed to lock the door. He told her he needed some privacy because he was very upset about Mr. Helfer. She made a face as she stood on the other side of the door and whispered, "I'll bet your upset." He found all the papers in order just where he was told they would be. As he lifted the box out of the compartment from under the carpet he laughed when he remembered Mr. Helfer's remark about Hilda standing on her future. He sorted out the papers for Hilda's affairs and Mr. Helfer's affairs. While he was looking at the different papers he came upon the will. He decided that he might as well read it. Most of what was in the will Wallace knew about. He was the executor and he knew what to do with Hilda. The second part of the will discussed what was to be done with Mr. Helfer's assets. Everything had been left to Wallace. Mr. Helfer wrote that Wallace made the hotel what it was today. He created an environment that would suit any customer. He was to become the president and owner of the Seneca-Powers Hotel. All the assets associated with Mr. Helfer's estate were to be transferred to Wallace Paine. Wallace fell into the chair in amazement when he realized what he had just read. He was just named owner and president of the classiest hotel in town! While he was thinking about what all this meant he thought about the deaths this week and the threats of death on his mother. What a new direction his life would be taking with this new inheritance! Then he thought for every negative there is a positive.

Wallace gathered the paperwork and left the office. He told Hilda that she would see him again soon. She sneered at him when he told her that and he wished her a good day as he walked out. He went to the lawyer's office to discuss the will and the funeral arrangements. It was very simple because Mr. Helfer was to be cremated with a brief memorial at the funeral parlor. There were very few people involved since the only family he had was Hilda. Wallace's family would probably attend to support him. Hilda was his next job. He wanted her to be there for the memorial but needed to have some assistance with her emotional status. The lawyer knew the doctor that was named in the will to be the caregiver for her move to Willard State Hospital. Wallace thought the doctor might help Hilda with some type of sedative during the funeral. The lawyer told Wallace that all the details were set before Mr. Helfer died and he would not have to worry about it. The doctor would come to the hotel when Wallace chose the date. He would administer a relaxing drug by putting it in her water. She would be calmer and then would go peacefully to the memorial service, then on to Willard State Hospital. Wallace wondered why they had not thought of this many years ago. Maybe she would have been easier to be around. When they finished Wallace wanted to go home to tell Eveline about what had happened. He thought better of mentioning the part about the relaxing methods for Hilda. He had a feeling he needed that information to stay quiet. He might need it for his father.

When Wallace came into the apartment Rudolph was there. Eveline told him that they were planning another event for the suffrage movement. Wallace asked Rudolph what else he did for income. He told Wallace that Mr. Eastman paid him nicely for the things he does. The private parties he played for pay very well too. Wallace thought that Rudolph might work out to his advantage if he needed to have help in the hotel. He waited until Rudolph left and then told Eveline about Mr. Helfer's estate. She told him that it was wonderful that he was the sole heir of the hotel. She asked him when he was going to find them a better place to live because he was becoming quite wealthy, so why not live in a better place. He reminded her that was his decision and that she lives very well. She still told him they should live like her parents. Wallace reminded her that her father was much older and that when they were his age they may live in a better place. He was more interested in what he was going to do with the hotel.

The next day Wallace went to work and his boss asked him to have a meeting about an expansion plan for the company. He asked where that might be and when it might be happening. The company was off to a profitable start. They were looking for a new area to start another production plant. The planners thought that next year was the date for the new location. Wallace asked if he would be expected to move. They told him that moving would not be necessary. He could travel to the other location part of the time. They may have to rent an apartment for him when he needed to stay longer than a day. There was a city located on the shore of Seneca Lake. Many large companies were located there. It was central to transportation lines. The railroads came from all directions. There was a canal system that connected to the Erie Canal. Shipping was used to move cargo from one part of the region to another. They told him that the city was named Geneva and was forty-five miles east of Rochester. They wanted to separate the production lines to be better able to expand on all their products. The Rochester plant was not large enough anymore. Geneva was in a different county and operating costs were lower. Wallace agreed to be part of the plan.

He was glad he could have a few months to organize himself for the traveling involved. He remembered how he and Eveline felt when they were given the apartment in Buffalo for his job with the H.O.Company. Now they would have two places. He wondered how Eveline was going to like this news since so much had happened just this past week.

Chapter 41

Mr. Helfer's memorial service was held the following Monday. Everything had been arranged with the doctor and transporting of Hilda to Willard State Hospital. Wallace, Eveline, Winston, Alice and Rudolph attended the service. When Hilda was escorted into the funeral parlor she walked very slowly and needed help to sit down. It was an eerie feeling watching her be so calm. Wallace had never seen her or anyone else in such a state. She was told that a friend of Mr. Helfer had died and she was there to represent him. She knew Mr. Helfer was ill and probably could not attend. During the service Mr. Helfer's name was rarely mentioned. Hilda sat staring at Wallace most of the time. There was no expression on her face until the time came when she was escorted out of the service. When she walked by Wallace she looked at him and pointed her finger at him and said, "I know what you are up to and I'll probably see you again." No one knew what to do or say. The doctor told Wallace earlier that they were taking the train from Rochester to Geneva and then putting Hilda on a steam ship that would go directly to a dock near the State Hospital. At that point hospital attendants would meet her and get her settled into her room. Wallace had her placed in a ward that was designed for higher income people so she could rest more peacefully. After Hilda was taken away Wallace asked if he could have some time with Rudolph at the hotel. When he said that, Winston asked Wallace what he was planning to do with Rudolph. Wallace told him that was none of his business. Winston was worried that Wallace might have an interest in Rudolph. One time Wallace told Winston he thought Rudolph was very attractive and took good care of himself. He compared himself to Rudolph and told Winston that was probably why Eveline liked him. So, Winston being self-conscious was worried about the intention of the meeting. He thought of their time in the Waldorf Astoria. Wallace took him aside and told him to take care of himself and not to worry.

Rudolph and Wallace agreed to meet in the hotel lobby at 3PM. Wallace went to his office at the Shuron Company. His boss was concerned that something might have happened with his decision to go between Rochester and Geneva. Wallace told him about the funeral for his uncle and that his aunt was not doing well and had to be cared for. They continued the discussion of the move to Geneva and that Wallace was still in charge of advertising. He was told that he would be receiving more income when they moved him between two cities. The company was dividing its production into two groups. The Rochester operation would be involved with all the local manufacturing for Eastman Kodak, the University of Rochester laboratory equipment, and the recreational products involved. The Geneva location would be used for the catalog shopping. Wallace was to design a catalog that would illustrate a variety of products using all types of optics. The majority of the catalog would be devoted to eyewear with different levels of pricing from very reasonable to very expensive. The Geneva plant would manufacture the products and package and ship them to the customers. Wallace would use the ideas of the Larkin Company focusing on "shopping from the comforts of home." He continued to use jingles and slogans for the advertising campaigns always remembering those phrases stay in your mind. The one he created for the newly expanded company was "Shop Shuron and be Sure." When he presented the ideas to his bosses they applauded him for such a good plan. They had the theme printed on letterheads, magazines and newspaper advertisements. The theme was on banners on the front of all their factories. During their meeting Wallace explained that he needed to leave early from work. He had a meeting to attend at 3PM about his uncle's estate. They agreed to let him go early wondering how this man can get so much done in such a short time.

Rudolph was waiting in the lobby promptly at 3PM. Wallace commented on his being so punctual. They shook hands and Wallace could not help but look at how handsome and masculine Rudolph appeared. He knew why Eveline took a liking to him. They walked into the office and Wallace found it strange not to be greeted by the "face." By now Hilda was well on her way to Willard State Hospital. As they went into the office Wallace was explaining how he first started with the hotel when he was in college as part of his work in advertising. The job and how well he did was part of his degree in advertising. He told Rudolph about the agreement he made with Mr. Helfer regarding the salary and matching it so he could buy stocks in the Ford Motor Company. Wallace sat in Mr. Helfer's chair and Rudolph across the desk in the chair he used to sit in. He thought how strange things had turned around. Wallace explained that he needed someone who he could rely on for the operation of the hotel. He offered the same plan to Rudolph that he had when he was working there. Wallace explained that he would give Rudolph a bonus in addition to his salary if the profits of the hotel were increased. He wanted Rudolph to improve on the music aspect in the hotel. Wallace asked if a pianist in the lobby would add to the atmosphere. Rudolph was surprised that Wallace offered him the job. Wallace asked why he felt that way. Rudolph explained that he thought Wallace did not like him because he and Eveline were so close. Wallace admitted that in the beginning he was not sure he liked the arrangement. As time went on he got used to it and found it good for Eveline to have another person to do things with. They laughed and agreed that she was not like most women today. She was a rebel on the loose. They mentioned how she talks up to Frank and how he hated that. Wallace told him that he worried for his mother but thought she could take care of Frank. After all the conversation along with coming to a better understanding of their relationships, Rudolph accepted the job. Wallace thought he would have accepted the offer for the job. He wondered how he would find out what was so intriguing about Rudolph.

Eveline invited Winston and Rudolph for dinner that evening. After their meeting Wallace drove them both to the apartment. Rudolph loved Wallace's car. He referred to it as the car only a certain type of man would drive. Wallace asked, "What type might that be?" Rudolph said, "You know, a man who can enjoy everything and everyone and do as he pleases." Wallace was not sure he knew what that meant but had a feeling that Rudolph was more like him than he realized. They went into the apartment and Eveline looked at them and said, "I see two handsome men and they are mine." They looked at each other and laughed and blushed. While they were discussing the Shuron move and the offer Wallace made to Rudolph, Winston arrived. He was coming from work. He wore a uniform that the French's Mustard Company required the employees to wear. He did not have time to change and thought he could do that when he arrived for dinner. He looked very rough and had just enough work dirt on his body to make him appealing to Wallace. Winston winked at him when he walked in and knew exactly what Wallace was thinking. He was unshaven and his hair was wavy and going in every direction. When he walked by Wallace that same musky odor reminded him of the last time Winston smelled that way. As he passed by on his way to wash up Rudolph said, "I don't think I've ever smelled like that, it is very interesting." Winston replied, "You might get to like it." The conversation continued with Rudolph's new position in the hotel. Eveline was ready to do one of her squeals and Rudolph even told her not to make such a sound. Wallace thanked him for saving them all from such sounds. She made a face at them and smiled. She was happy that things were working out for them. As she finished the sentence Winston came back from washing up and wanted to know why everyone was so happy. Wallace began to explain about his job and how he would be in two places and that he was now owner of the hotel. Winston told him that he deserved it for working so hard for Mr. Helfer. Then Wallace told him that Rudolph was the new hotel manager and operator. He was going to improve the entertainment phase of the hotel operation. The look on Winston's face was one of complete rejection. He looked like a little boy ready to cry. All he said was, "Oh." Eveline looked at Wallace and then at Winston. He asked if there was any room for him in all of this. Wallace paused and admitted that he had not thought about it. In his mind he knew that Winston did not have the same qualifications that Rudolph had. How was he going to justify all that? He did not want to be mean to him and he still wanted him for his closest friend. While he was figuring out what to say Eveline announced that dinner was ready. They sat down and had a favorite pot roast that Eveline's mother taught her how to make. Wallace remarked that was her only cooking masterpiece. Everyone laughed including Eveline.

Rudolph was the first to go home. He had a lot to do to get ready for his new job. He had to schedule his piano appointments around his new responsibilities. Winston was getting ready to leave and asked if Wallace could come outside with him. Wallace knew why he wanted him outside. All three men left together. Rudolph went down the street and Winston looked at Wallace and asked, "When are you going to include me in anything?" Wallace explained that the job required certain things. Winston told him that this made him feel he was not good enough. Wallace explained it was not about being good enough. He reminded Winston that he had dropped out of school and had a different attitude toward work. At that remark Winston shouted, "I'm good enough to make you feel good inside!" Wallace shook his head and reminded him that did not have anything to do with the conversation. Winston was hurt and angry and said, "I suppose you are waiting for Rudolph to make you feel good inside?" Wallace said nothing. The conversation ended when Winston walked away telling Wallace that he had never been totally included in Wallace's life. Wallace told him that was not true and that soon things might get better. As Winston walked down the street he yelled,

"You use people to get ahead but I know the truth about you." When Wallace went back into the apartment Eveline asked what all the yelling had been about. Wallace told her that Winston was upset and angry that he was not offered the hotel job. She laughed and told him that he made the right choice. She agreed that Rudolph was more suited for the position and looked the part and would be perfect in that capacity. Wallace agreed with her and they went to bed.

The next day while Wallace was at work his boss was telling him that he had been invited to a party last night. Wallace wondered to himself why he needed to know that. The party was held in the home of Edward T. Boynton who had just moved into his new home on East Boulevard. When he mentioned East Boulevard Wallace knew exactly what house he was speaking about. It was the one designed by Frank Lloyd Wright. Wallace had been by the house as it was being built. Mr. Boynton was a successful salesman for the CT Ham Manufacturing Company. In 1908 he commissioned Frank Lloyd Wright to design and build the house. It was the prairie house design that Wright was so popular for designing. The furniture was included as one of Wright's requirements when designing a home. Wallace was especially interested in it because of his being in Buffalo when the Martin House was built. Wallace used to tell Eveline every time they went by the house during the construction of it, that it was more reasonable in size. The Martin House was too big. He thought he could handle living in a house like the East Boulevard home. Eveline would ask the same question every time they went by, "When will you have one for me?" Wallace would tell her when he was a millionaire. She never really knew if he was serious about that remark. She continued to hope he was serious. Wallace always commented on the design of Wright's homes. Wright used massive amounts of windows throughout the home to make the outside seem part of the inside. Even on a dreary day the daylight would stream into all the spaces. Wright strategically planted landscape that would compliment the interior as well as the exterior. Wallace made mental notes every time he went by the house to hopefully use in his own home someday. His boss explained how beautiful the interior was at dusk. The party was deliberately scheduled so guests could appreciate the transformation of the home from day to evening. He told Wallace that the house was so up to date that it even had push button light switches. The massive hearth was a focal point when lit and reflected light on the many stained glass windows. He compared it to something out of this world.

Plans for the expansion of the Shuron Company to Geneva were happening faster than expected. Wallace and his bosses went by train to Geneva to find sites for the factory. They found a site at 160 Lyceum Street. They nicknamed it Optical Street. It was out of town but near enough that employees could walk to work. The men toured Geneva and found many industries at the lakefront. There were foundries, cereal companies, small businesses, and large businesses. It was a smaller city but very vibrant. It looked like a small Buffalo to Wallace when he first saw the land and how businesses were on the lakefront. While they were walking in the downtown section they came upon small coffee shops, general merchandise stores, and specialty shops. Wallace thought that this might be a good place to live. While he was in one of the stores he overheard people speaking about Willard State Hospital. He asked the woman where that was. She explained that it was about 20 miles on the east side of Seneca Lake. It was easy to get to by train or if you had a car you could drive but the roads were not very good. She asked Wallace if he knew someone there. He said a friend of his had a sister there for rest and recuperation. She smiled politely as if not really believing his story and walked on. He laughed to himself and wondered if she thought he needed to go there.

Before they went back to Rochester Wallace looked at apartments to rent for the times he would be staying in Geneva. He thought it would be good to be near downtown and the train station. Sometimes he might drive his car but was not sure of the roads. He looked at a few places and settled on an apartment at 114 Washington Street that was near Pulteney Park that was the original market place when Geneva was first settled. There was a town square surrounded by row houses and Washington Street began at that point. He liked the sound of the park and the name of the street. Wallace decided that it was perfect for what he needed it for. It would give him time to learn about the city and decide where he might build a home if he were to stay here. His bosses thought it was reasonably priced and they would give him money to furnish it. The agreement was that it was for company use. Wallace asked what that meant. They said if they needed to use it they were all entitled to stay overnight. They would hire a maid to clean and have it ready all the time. The idea seemed logical to him, however they informed him that he would be the one there most of the time. After they rented the apartment they told Wallace he could bring his wife back and have her decorate it. Wallace told them that she would love that.

Chapter 42

DURING THE RIDE BACK to Rochester Wallace's bosses reviewed the timeline for the expansion of the company. They told him that he would eventually move to Geneva. They felt he was the type of person that would do well in a newly formed department. Wallace told them he liked being the first to set up new operations. He explained his philosophy of being in on the ground floor of new companies. They laughed at that philosophy but realized he made good sense. January 1910 was the target date for him to move to Geneva. That would give him about six months to get the plant running efficiently and finish his duties in the Rochester office. While they were working out the details of his responsibilities Wallace inquired about his salary. They admitted they were waiting to see how long it would take for that discussion to occur. They told him that he would receive a 10% increase in his salary and an annual bonus based on the profits of the company. Wallace thought that was a good plan. He then requested to have a contract drawn up with an option for further investment in stocks. He wanted to explore the idea of offering the employees a choice of either a portion of their earnings going toward ownership of a home built by the company for them or contributing a portion of earnings to invest in company stocks. Wallace convinced them that it would be a good experiment for the Geneva plant. If it was successful then they could expand to other areas of the company. Just as the train arrived in Rochester they gave their approval to his ideas. They would meet tomorrow at the office to draw up the paperwork for the proposals.

When Wallace got home, Eveline had just finished writing a letter she had been working on for the Women's Rights Movement. Rudolph asked her to help him with it for the newspaper. Wallace told her he was not sure he wanted her to be publicly known as a radical woman. Eveline was furious when he suggested she stay in the background. She accused him of being like Frank. Wallace did not want to be compared to his father or his attitude. After she accused him of being like all the rest of the men, Wallace realized he did not want his wife to be treated like a slave to a man. He settled down and asked what the title of the article was. She smiled a sweet smile and said, "Women's Rights versus A Male Dominated Society." Wallace was surprised by the title because he had always known women who were independent and able to function without a man's influence. Eveline reminded him that women were not allowed to vote. After she told him all the reasons why women should be upset with men, he knew she was not going to back down. When Wallace thought about the conversation he laughed and said, "Why should I try to stop you now, you have always been a radical woman." They laughed and Eveline asked how his day was in Geneva. He explained about the plant and some of his financial proposals for the employees. He never found it necessary to discuss his personal business with her. He wanted that to be his secret. She never inquired either. Wallace thought it was strange that Eveline was not interested in his financial affairs. He figured as long as she was happy that was good enough for him. The apartment rental came up during the conversation. He told Eveline that his new position would require him to stay in Geneva a few days each week. Wallace told her about the specialty shops and the companies that he saw while he was there. She wanted to know more about the apartment. He told her where it was and that there was a park nearby. Eveline had a quizzical look on her face when she asked if she was ever going to see the place. Wallace knew she was working up to something when she presented the idea that way. He told her that the company was going to pay for the furnishing of the apartment. He asked her if she would like to help him. When Eveline heard that a loud squeal came from her mouth. Wallace shook his head and covered her mouth. He told her she should not be doing that because people might think she was crazy. He asked her, "Do you want to live with Hilda?" After that outburst they decided to go to Geneva on Saturday to furnish the apartment. Wallace told her that he would use the car if the weather was good. He wanted to see what the roads were like between Rochester and Geneva. Eveline thought that would be fun. She liked the idea that they would now have two places in which to live. As she said that, she thought about being able to spend more time with Rudolph when Wallace was in Geneva. Wallace had an idea that he could have Winston come to Geneva for a visit too. Just as they finished their discussion about Geneva and Women's Rights issues, Eveline said, "With all the news I forgot that a letter came for you from someone in New York City."

Wallace wondered who sent him the letter. He had not heard much from the Occidental Company associates in New York for quite sometime. All he had been receiving was large sums of money from the profits of the imports and exports. He told Eveline that he needed to have some time to read the letter and that she could tell him when dinner was ready. She sensed a strange attitude from Wallace when he told her he wanted to be alone. She wondered what the letter was about to have created such a noticeable change in him. She left the parlor and went to the kitchen. As soon as she left he opened the letter. Mr. Burbank who was in charge of the human transport department had sent it. He began the letter by explaining that the programs were operating as planned. He mentioned how business had doubled on goods coming from France and England. The textiles and furs were selling for record amounts of money in New York City. Wallace was feeling quit good about the letter until he came to the second page. Mr. Burbank informed him that there had been an investigation conducted by the police in connection to the murders in New York and Buffalo. A few detectives came to the office inquiring about Mr. Ling. They wanted to know what connection he had to the company and to Wallace Paine. Mr. Burbank told the men that Mr. Ling had been an associate when the company was formed, but was now in Hong Kong. He told them that he had not heard from him in many months. The detectives wanted to know how to reach Wallace Paine. He was mentioned as the person who knew the whereabouts of Mr. Ling and had the most knowledge of the people who were murdered. They wanted to know the whereabouts of a man who worked for the Occidental Company when it had an office in Buffalo. Winston Spaulding was being sought after as one of the accomplices to the murders. When Wallace read that he panicked. His first thought was Winston only knew about the first murder. He never knew about the other incidents. Mr. Burbank concluded the letter by warning Wallace that his presence was being requested in New York by the authorities.

During dinner, Wallace said nothing to Eveline. She asked him what the letter was about. He told her it was none of her business. She gave him an offended look and finished dinner with out any further conversation. Wallace knew that this could be serious for him and Winston. He wondered if Winston was receiving a letter also. What was he going to tell Winston? How could he explain to Eveline about the past and the Occidental Companies' secret imports? He folded the letter and placed it in his case. Eveline was even more suspicious when she saw him lock the case. He told her that he needed to go out for a while. She stood in the doorway staring at him as he left. Wallace went to the telegraph office to send Mr. Burbank a note with instructions for the authorities where to send the letter. He decided to have the letter sent to Winston at his mother's house. After he sent the telegraph he had to get to Winston and explain what might be happening. After the way Winston left the other night he hoped he could convince him to understand the urgency of this. He got to his parent's apartment and Winston had just arrived home from work. Alice and Frank were having dinner and Winston was in his room. After Wallace spoke with them he went to Winston's room and knocked on the door. When Winston opened the door and saw Wallace he told him he was not interested in anything he had to say. Wallace asked him to please let him come inside. Winston slowly opened the door and Wallace stepped inside. Before Wallace could say a word, Winston handed him a letter from a detective agency in New York City. He wanted to know if he had received one too. Wallace admitted he got a letter but that it was not from a detective. He explained that his letter came from Mr. Burbank at the Occidental office in New York. Winston was being summoned to New York City to be questioned regarding a series of murders that happened in New York City and Buffalo. Wallace explained that he was told the same information but that Mr. Ling was mentioned in his letter. He was not told to be in New York. Winston looked at Wallace and asked, "Is there more about this than I know?" Wallace admitted that there was more but it did not have anything to do with him. He thought that because Winston worked in Buffalo for awhile that they probably thought he knew more about what happened after they closed the Buffalo office. Winston wanted to know how many murders there were. Wallace made a general response of, "I don't know, maybe four."

After they talked about the possibilities of what all this meant Winston asked him why he got so many people involved in underhanded schemes. Wallace denied that it was underhanded. Winston accused him of getting people to do things but somehow he steps away and never looks like a bad guy. He told Wallace that he might be in for more trouble than he expected. Wallace asked him what he meant. Winston told him that he lies by omission. Wallace denied being like that. At that remark Winston reminded him of how many times he left out information about his whereabouts or his money. He told him about his avoiding the truth about their friendship. He finished when he reminded Wallace of their trip to New York when he first met Mr. Ling. He told Wallace that he was a lot like Mr. Ling, a guy who steps back before the trouble begins and never looks guilty. Winston told Wallace, "I hope they don't put me on the stand and question me about you." Wallace told him that they needed to be smart and stand by each other. Winston smirked and said, "So you can walk away innocent?" Wallace told him that was not true. He wanted Winston to be careful of what he divulged in the questioning. Then Wallace asked if the letter could be sent to him in care of Winston Spaulding. Winston asked him why. Wallace said he did not want Eveline to worry unnecessarily. Winston told him he would do it, but that Wallace's reason was a lie. He told Wallace that there was so much more about this situation than she would ever want to know.

While Wallace was at work the next day all he could think about was the trouble he might be in with the Occidental Company. His boss would ask him questions and he would not answer them. Finally, his boss asked if he had cold feet about his move to Geneva. Wallace told him that he was looking forward to his new responsibilities. He explained that he had been at his mother's house last night regarding some business, which was very troubling. His boss was concerned and asked if the family was okay. Wallace thanked him for being understanding and that everything had worked out. He told him that he and his wife were going to Geneva this weekend to furnish the apartment. He asked what she thought of the new job. Wallace explained that his wife was very happy for his advancements and that she had many things she liked to do that did not involve him. They laughed and his boss remarked what a progressive woman she must be. Wallace agreed that she was progressive. He left work early and went directly to his mother's home to check for the letter from New York City. When he arrived Alice handed him the envelope and wanted to know what was so secret that he was having mail sent to Winston. Wallace explained that it was something Eveline should not know about. Alice looked at him and reminded him of the trouble she got into for not being honest with Frank. She told him that Eveline was a nice woman and he should not deny her the truth. Wallace did tell a lie when he suggested the letter was regarding something for Eveline. Alice stared at Wallace with a skeptical look in her eye. She said no more but Wallace knew she could tell he was lying.

He left and began walking home. He opened the letter by the streetlamp and read it quickly to get an idea of what to expect. He got to the part where they wanted him to appear in a New York Court and he knew he was in trouble. The court hearing was on Monday afternoon. He needed to make plans quickly. What was he going to tell everyone? He decided to tell Eveline he had an appointment about the import and export company in New York. He would request a few days off from work telling his boss he needed time to get ready for his move to Geneva. He stopped by the railroad station to purchase tickets for Winston and himself. He wanted to help Winston since he helped him with the delivery of the letter. Wallace got tickets for the earliest train to New York. It would arrive by noon; they could take the last train of the day and be back to Rochester late that night. This time he did not want to stay in a hotel. He wanted to get it over with and go back home. As he was walking from the train station, Winston was on his way home from work. This time, neither of them had good feelings for one another. Wallace told Winston he had been to his mother's to pick up the letter. He told him that he purchased him a ticket for New York. Winston just shook his head and did not thank him. After the conversation Wallace handed Winston the ticket and explained his reason for such a quick trip. Winston's remark was, "I figured as much, you don't want to spend too much time with me either." Wallace told him that there were more important things to worry about. Wallace asked him if he wanted them to spend time in prison. Winston said, "At least you couldn't get away from me." They walked off in opposite directions. Eveline asked how things were and what his plans were for the next week. He looked at her and asked why. She told him that on Monday there was a meeting in Seneca Falls for anyone interested in helping with the Women's Rights Movement. Rudolph asked her if she wanted to attend with him. She told Wallace that she accepted his offer. Wallace's first thought was that they might be on the train together. Eveline told him that they would be leaving on a 10AM train. After he heard that, he told her about his appointment in New York. He did not mention that it was a court hearing. He explained that Winston had to go too because they wanted to discuss what his responsibilities had been in Buffalo. Eveline seemed to believe the story. She was more excited about going to Seneca Falls. He reminded her that they were going to Geneva in a few days to furnish the new apartment. Eveline seemed to have forgotten about that. She apologized for not remembering but thought it would great fun.

Every Thursday Wallace met with Rudolph to discuss how things were going at the hotel. They would have lunch in the restaurant just as he and Mr. Helfer had done. It was different in the hotel now that Wallace had taken Mr. Helfer's place. Rudolph was very enthusiastic and was trying new ideas for entertainment and working with the restaurant to improve the culinary aspect of the operation. Wallace continued to help him with the advertising and special events promotions. The relationship between the two of them had a different tone than the one Wallace had with Winston. Rudolph was a confident and classy man. Wallace felt that was exactly what he wanted his hotel to reflect. Rudolph had changed the bellhop uniforms. He had them wearing top hats and tuxedos. The chambermaids were dressed in black dresses with white aprons and a white cap. Since more people owned automobiles now the Seneca-Powers Hotel was the first to have valet parking. Rudolph thought that was a good idea because that was how they were treated at George Eastman's home. They agreed they wanted the hotel to have the reputation of being the classiest hotel in town. As part of the announcement of the new management and owner Wallace wanted a portrait painted of Rudolph and him. It would be hung in the lobby so that the guests would know who was in charge of such an elegant place. In order to improve the ambiance of the lobby Rudolph hired a pianist to play during lunchtime, afternoons and the evening. Wallace was careful when he met with Rudolph not to discuss Eveline. He felt that their business was not connected to Eveline. Wallace wanted the man's work to be left to the men and the women's affairs left out. Rudolph was not sure he felt the same as Wallace did. He wanted to include women in the same activities that men were involved in. Wallace tried to avoid the conversation about the Seneca Falls issues. Whatever Rudolph did on his own time was his business. Eveline liked to be out in the front line with him, so Wallace did not interfere with their friendship. All he knew was that Rudolph was what he wanted and was willing to get to know him better. There was a strange feeling he had about how Rudolph behaved when he was not around Eveline. He could not put his finger on it. He thought there was more to Rudolph than he knew.

Wallace was ready to go to Geneva early Saturday morning. Eveline was not ready because she was more interested in her newspaper article. She had to finish it before they could leave. Wallace disliked the idea that she put that before their trip to Geneva. After what seemed like days she announced that she was ready to go. It was an early autumn day that was sunny and warm. He thought the best route would be to use Route 5 from Rochester to Geneva. As they made their way to Geneva they saw more cars than a few years ago. Wallace told Eveline that when they were settled in Geneva he wanted to get a new car. He had this car for over five years. He had been looking at the new models and planned to buy a 1910 Ford. He was not sure what Ford's newest car would look like, but it had a better roof and was built to carry more passengers and luggage. She told him that this car was too open. It was a nuisance in the rain and snow. They arrived in Geneva at lunchtime. They went to the Nester Hotel in downtown Geneva for lunch. As they walked into the restaurant Wallace realized how much the hotel reminded him of the Seneca-Powers Hotel. The interior of the lobby was elegantly decorated and the restaurant served a plentiful lunch. After lunch they went to the apartment. Eveline liked how it faced Washington Street and was near the park. She liked the statue that stood in the pond that overlooked Seneca Lake. She said it reminded her of Buffalo and some of the parks there. After they decided on what they needed for the apartment they went downtown and chose living room, dining room, and bedroom furniture. They went to small shops for household items. They carried the small items in the back of the car. They laughed and were glad it was a sunny day so nothing would get wet. Wallace said, "All the more reason to get a better car."

Eveline responded with, "We will need a bigger car when we have a family." Wallace nearly went off the road when she mentioned a family. He had never thought of being a father. He asked her if she was kidding. She smiled and shrugged her shoulders. It did not seem like something he planned to do. All she said was, "We'll see." They took the packages into the apartment. The furniture was to be delivered on Monday. Eveline offered to be there for the afternoon delivery. The meeting she and Rudolph were attending would be finished by 2PM. She set the delivery time for 3PM. She and Rudolph could be at the apartment on their way back from Seneca Falls. Eveline was excited about showing Rudolph the new apartment. She asked Wallace if Rudolph might ever move to Geneva. Wallace did not think that was a good idea and asked her who would run his hotel. She told him by that time there would be another person available to do the work. It was beginning to get dark and Wallace wanted to get on the road. He was not sure how long it would take them to return to Rochester. As he was driving up Washington Street he commented on how beautiful the land was just a mile from town. Eveline thought a home around there would be wonderful. As they drove up the brick paved street, they came to a street named Nursery Avenue. It was a dirt road that was the access to a nursery. Wallace jokingly said, "I should build a house on that corner."

Eveline was talking about her trip on Monday with Rudolph on the way back to Rochester. Wallace was not interested in what she was talking about because he was worried about his trip to New York. He was trying to be objective and hoped that it was only an investigation to help find out who really committed the crimes. Since Eveline did not know what the trip was about he had to be careful what they talked about. She asked him if he was telling her the truth. He snapped at her and said they needed to change the subject. Fortunately, they were almost in Rochester and the conversation ended. Eveline was tired and Wallace agreed that it had been a long day and they needed to get some rest.

Wallace met Winston at the train station Monday morning. The train was scheduled to leave a 5AM. It seemed like the middle of the night when the train left the station. They fell asleep for part of the trip. They were not as excited about the trip this time as they had been before when they traveled together. Winston told Wallace he felt like he was riding to his fate. Wallace tried to explain that they might only want information to help them find the murderer. That reasoning was not helping Winston to relax. Wallace told him to quit being so afraid of everything even though he felt scared to death. He knew he could not act the same way or the authorities would surely think something was wrong. After Winston settled down he asked Wallace if they were ever going to be like they used to be. Wallace asked what he meant. Winston told him about how they traveled together and experienced so many things. He explained that he hoped their friendship could get closer. As the train was passing the Geneva area Wallace told him about the new apartment and that he and Eveline would be moving there on January 1. Wallace asked him if he would like to come to stay with him sometime. He told Winston that he needed to stay there during the week until they moved there permanently. Winston could take a few days off and come to Geneva. Winston admitted that he was hoping that would happen. Wallace felt that sensation go through his body again as he spoke to Winston. Now he wished he had arranged for a hotel.

The train arrived shortly before noon. They got off the train and went to Mr. Burbank's office. He was expecting them and offered to go for a quick lunch. The atmosphere was cold and business-like. The last time Wallace had seen Mr. Burbank was the night in the restaurant when they had such a good time. He was remembering how strained conversations were until they knew Wallace was not going to cause trouble with the transports. Wallace wondered if Mr. Ling was involved in the meeting. Mr. Burbank took them to a sandwich shop around the corner where the court investigation was to take place. He asked if they were ready for the questioning. They explained that they were a little nervous. Mr. Burbank laughed and said, "Better you than me." Wallace thought that was a strange remark. He found Mr. Burbank much different than the night when they agreed to be partners. It was made quite clear that all Wallace had to do was be the owner of the business and they would do the rest. Mr. Burbank now had the same attitude as the men at the H.O.Company. They started out okay and then became very distant and cautious. Wallace began to think that he was not seeing things correctly. Why did he always meet people who eventually turned corrupt? They were on their way out of the restaurant when Mr. Burbank informed them that he was not going to be at the hearing. Wallace asked why. He told them that he had nothing to do with any of those issues. He would rather not even be seen there. It was as if they were being set up. As soon as they walked into the hearing Mr. Burbank disappeared. They were greeted by a group of detectives and a few lawyers. One of the lawyers came over to them and introduced himself as the company's attorney who would be their legal counsel. They felt better knowing they had a legal representative. The attorney discussed what was going to happen and what types of questions they might be asked. He informed them that Wallace was required to be there because he was the owner of the Occidental Company. Winston was there because he was a suspect in the murders. Winston nearly fainted when he heard this. The attorney explained that they had evidence that he was in New York at the same time Mr. Ling was murdered. Wallace was shocked to hear that Mr. Ling was dead. While they were gathering the information the hearing was called to order.

Wallace sat in the chair in total confusion. The attorney sat next to him and Winston on the other side. The first person to speak was the chief investigator of crimes committed in New York City. He gave a short review of the names of the people who were killed and explained that the only evidence left behind was the tongue. No one moved as he continued to explain that there had been two murders in New York and three in Buffalo which were all related to the Occidental Company. The most recent murder was of Mr. Ling in New York. A tongue was found on the bed in his hotel room and his whereabouts were a mystery. Wallace was the first to be questioned. They wanted to know if he could prove his whereabouts on certain dates. All the dates were confirmed to be accurate. One of the dates was the day of Mr. Helfer's memorial service. The other dates were verified as accurate because Wallace was working at Shuron. They inquired about the reputation of the people who were killed. He explained that all the people mentioned were honest in the beginning but became suspicious of each other as time went on. Wallace explained that he felt it was greed and the desire to be in charge. Winston began to squirm when he heard the description of the men. One of the investigators asked Winston if he was feeling uncomfortable. Winston turned red and shook his head. They thanked Wallace for describing the personalities of the men. Winston was called to the stand for the next questions. They asked him how long he was employed at Occidental and why his job was eliminated. He explained that he worked for the company when it was in Buffalo for a few years and when that office closed he moved back to Rochester. They accepted that reasoning. Then one of the detectives showed Winston a hotel register that showed him in New York at the same time Mr. Ling was there. They wanted to know the details of his trip. Wallace was amazed to hear that Winston was in New York City. Winston denied the accusation of his being in New York. The attorney reminded him that he needed to be honest about this situation. Before he could answer the question they showed him the receipt for the hotel registration with his signature clearly written. They asked him if he had ever witnessed seeing a tongue after a murder. He admitted he had. He explained it was the man that Mr. Ling first hired to work on the docks in New York. He told them that he had been in contact with him when they first were coordinating the shipping schedules between cities. The investigators looked suspicious when Winston admitted to seeing a tongue. They figured that he had a good idea about how these murders were carried out. Winston denied all the accusations. The attorney explained that they were trying to set a pattern for the serial murders. Winston asked them why they had singled him out. They explained that he was the first solid evidence they found in their investigations. When Winston saw his signature, all he said was, "I didn't do it." They waited and told him that he could not deny that was his handwriting. Their attorney asked that Mr. Winston Spaulding be put in the custody of Mr. Wallace Paine. There would need to be further evidence and a trial by jury before any conclusions could be reached. The interrogation was concluded and the attorney explained that he would begin looking for more evidence that would show Winston's guilt in the murder. The attorney wanted to meet privately with Winston and Wallace before they went back to Rochester. He requested that Winston verify where he was on the date that was written in the hotel register. He advised Winston to be very careful of what he said and to whom. The attorney had a feeling that more than one person was involved in a conspiracy against the founders of the Occidental Company. Wallace knew who killed everyone except Mr. Ling. He could never let anyone know about the letter Mr. Ling sent to him about why and who committed the murders.

The train ride back to Rochester was long and tiring. Winston did not say much. Wallace was upset about what happened in New York. He felt like he was responsible. Winston finally told him that it was not his fault. Wallace asked him why. Winston explained that he did receive a letter asking him to come to New York. The letter was not very clear about the intention and was signed by someone he did not recognize. He received it around the same time he and Wallace had a fight about their friendship. Winston never mentioned it to him. He secretly hoped Wallace would get in trouble and not him. It was all very strange so he threw it away. Wallace wanted to know what the man needed from him in New York. All he could remember was that it was about meeting someone from the past. Winston figured it was a hoax but now he realized that he received the letter around the same time Mr. Ling was murdered. Wallace told him not to worry but the attorney should know about the letter.

When Wallace arrived at home Eveline was there and wanted to know what happened in New York. Wallace explained that Winston was asked some questions by some detectives about his employment for the import and export company when it was in Buffalo. He mentioned that someone was missing and that they were trying to get information for the investigation. She asked why he also had to go to New York. He told her that since he was the owner of the company they wanted his opinion of the other business partners. Wallace did not mention that Winston was being charged with the possible murder of Mr. Ling. She asked if they had to return to New York. He told her that he was not sure. Eveline went into her detailed explanation of her day in Seneca Falls with Rudolph. She made it sound like it was a festive occasion. She told him about speeches about why women needed the same rights as men, especially the right to vote. She explained how some men were there to cause trouble. They accused Rudolph of being less than a man when he was asked what he thought of the movement. One man yelled, "You need to go home and stay in the kitchen with the women. That's where you all belong." Another man yelled, "I'm sure they could find a dress that would fit you." Eveline explained how manly and strong Rudolph was during those moments. After the confusion, another man came along and told Rudolph that he wished he could be as brave. He told Rudolph how he had been beaten up for being in favor of the movement. He lost his job after the beating. That information made Rudolph even more determined to be out there with the women.

Wallace was surprised that there had been so much tension but secretly was happy to hear it. After that, she told him about the furniture delivery. She said that Rudolph liked the apartment and their choices in furniture. It had been a tough day. Wallace went to bed early. Eveline knew there was more happening in New York than he told her.

Chapter 43

WALLACE WAS SPENDING AS much time in Geneva as in Rochester. He enjoyed the challenges of developing the new plant for the Shuron Company. While he was in Geneva he began to make new friends and find his way around town. He found Buckley's City Market for food items. He was not familiar with food prices because Eveline shopped for food in Rochester. The first time he went there he bought some beef for $.10 per pound. He loved sauerkraut so he bought a pound of that for $.03. He realized he was not a cook when he got home with only a few things and did not know what to do with them. He told himself that when Eveline got there she would have to teach him how to buy and cook food. From then on he found places to eat his dinner before he went home. One thing he found that he liked was a new product for breakfast. They were called Post Toasties. When he saw Eveline the next weekend he told her about food shopping. She thought it was hilarious that he did not know how to judge what he needed. They agreed that she would take him to the food store for a lesson. He told her about the Geneva Clothing Company on Exchange Street and how it had new competition in town. McCurdy and Norwell Company had a branch store in Geneva. Its main store was in Rochester. Wallace shopped for his suits there but found the Geneva Clothing Company to be equally as good.

Winston continued working for the French's Mustard Company and was anxiously waiting for information about the investigation of the murders. He was not able to have Alice verify that he was in Rochester on the date of the hotel registration. By chance that was the same weekend that Frank took her for an overnight visit to see some friends. Winston had given up trying to find evidence to show that he was not in New York City at the time of Mr. Ling's murder. Wallace kept telling him that he could not avoid these accusations. All Winston said was, "Something will happen to help me." Wallace decided that it was time to have Winston come to Geneva for a visit. He told him that he needed to take some time off from work to relax and visit him. He explained that he needed to be at work during the day but they could spend the evenings together. Winston was delighted to hear that. When Wallace and Rudolph met about hotel business he mentioned that Winston was coming to Geneva. Rudolph seemed uneasy when he heard about the visit. Rudolph asked if Eveline knew. Wallace told him no but she would not mind anyway. Rudolph did say that he remembered when they shared the apartment in Buffalo. Wallace sensed that he might be a bit jealous of such an arrangement. He knew Rudolph had no idea of what they had done in the past and where they had been. He told Rudolph that Eveline did not need to know about everything. Rudolph smiled and asked if he could come for a visit sometime. Wallace thought that was an intriguing idea. He did find Rudolph to be an interesting man. He wondered to himself what all these friendships would turn into.

Winston made arrangements to come to Geneva. He would leave Rochester after work and spend two days with Wallace. He was excited about getting out of Rochester and was eager to see where Wallace and Eveline would be living. He planned to arrive on Tuesday evening and return to Rochester on Thursday. Winston had no idea what he would do while Wallace was at work but knew it was a new city to explore. He told Winston that Eveline did not know about his visit. It did not seem to matter to him, they had done so many things together that it was not an issue. When Winston arrived Wallace was waiting at the train station. The first thing Wallace noticed was the way Winston walked toward him. He still had that easy side-to-side gait. The closer he got the better he looked. He wore a wide brimmed hat with his bushy hair hanging down from the sides of the hat. Wallace noticed that he had not shaved and a dark rough beard shadowed his face. When he came up to him he said in a deep voice, "Hey." Wallace felt a tingling sensation. They walked to his car and drove through town toward Washington Street. Wallace showed him the Nester Hotel and told him they would go there for dinner. They drove around Pulteney Park to Washington Street. He parked the car in front of the house. Winston thought it was going to be like the place in Buffalo. Wallace informed him that it was not Delaware Avenue. The apartment was not nearly as grand as the one in Buffalo. Wallace apologized for its size. Winston told him that it did not matter because the company was more important. He told Wallace he missed their times in Buffalo. When Wallace did not respond, Winston asked him what was the matter. Wallace blamed it on the upcoming court hearings. He was really thinking about Rudolph and wondered how this visit would be with him instead of Winston. They got ready to go to dinner. They decided to walk through town so Winston could see Main Street. There were a series of row houses that surrounded the park. Wallace explained that the park used to be the market center in the 1700s. Winston thought it was a great neighborhood. They walked past the Smith Opera House on Seneca Street. Winston looked at the entertainment schedule and thought it might be fun to go there. Wallace told him that he was surprised he would like to go to a theater. Winston informed him that there was a lot he did not know about him. They went into the Nester Hotel's restaurant and found a table. Winston remarked on how the atmosphere reminded him of the hotel in Rochester. After Wallace paid for dinner they walked back to the apartment.

When they walked into the apartment Winston asked where he was supposed to sleep. Wallace looked at him and said, "Did you forget about the guesthouse we stayed in during the Exposition?" Winston laughed in his gruff way and admitted he hoped that they would never forget that place. While Winston was getting unpacked Wallace was lying in bed starring at the ceiling. He was thinking about all the different things he and Winston had done in the past. It seemed like they had been friends forever. Winston came into the room completely unclothed. By now, Wallace was in bed with the covers over himself. He wanted to surprise Winston but Winston beat him to it. Wallace could barely contain himself. Winston turned out the lamp and got under the covers. All Winston said was, "No matter what happens in New York, we'll always be a team." Wallace had two things going on in his mind. He could not believe how aroused he was and what it would be like if Rudolph was here too.

The next morning they were trying to convince one another that they did not sleep well because the bed was too small. They laughed when they realized how funny that sounded. At one point Winston found Wallace on top of him. Wallace denied that such a thing happened. Winston told him that he would always deny the truth. Wallace was proud to announce that he could make them breakfast. Winston found this hard to believe. While the coffee was perking, Wallace showed him the Post Toasties. Winston laughed and told him that was not cooking. Wallace agreed but never said he was going to cook breakfast. During breakfast, the day's schedule was discussed. Winston wanted to walk around town and look at the row houses and architecture. He told Wallace to get home as soon as he could. Wallace asked what he meant. Winston gave him a stupid grin as if to say what do you think? Wallace agreed to try to leave work early. He explained how to find the Shuron plant. Winston said he might walk by later. Wallace left and Winston went back to bed. He was lying on his back staring at the ceiling and enjoyed himself as he thought about last night.

Winston investigated the town during the day. He looked in all the shops, had coffee in a café, and lunch in a diner. While he was walking on Seneca Street he stopped at the Smith Opera House where there was an orchestra playing in the evening. The tickets were $.25 to $1.50. Winston bought 2 tickets. He knew how Wallace liked to be treated so he purchased the best seats they had in the house. When he looked at the tickets he was reminiscing about the times they went to the Seneca-Powers Hotel where they had an orchestra playing. He laughed when he thought about the New Year's Eve party and the burlesque shows. He still liked the Top Banana and wondered what ever became of Hilda. He could not wait to go back tonight to see the inside of the theatre. He caught a glimpse of it as he stood at the ticket booth and knew it had to be beautiful. After he left the theatre he walked toward the lake. It was a cold, damp November day. The wind was blowing and there were white caps on the lake. There were factories and warehouses along the lake. He saw a grain elevator with the name Patent Cereal Company written on its side. He wondered if it had any connection to the H.O. Company in Buffalo. As he got nearer to the building he saw a sign by the main doors, which read "Help Wanted." He laughed and thought about what Wallace would say if he got a job in Geneva. He was surprised at how much was going on in such a small city. There were boats on the lake coming from places south of Geneva. They were docking while some were moving east toward a canal that connected Seneca and Cayuga Lakes to the Erie Canal. As he walked toward town again he saw a poster that had written in bold letters, "Women's Suffrage a Concern to All Men." Winston saw the date of the meeting and thought of Eveline and Rudolph. He hoped they never saw that poster on the streets. There was a meeting that night for men who were planning to stop the spread of such things. Winston told himself he would tell Wallace that he wanted to go just to see what kind of reaction he would get. By the time he got back to 114 Washington Street, Wallace was already home. He asked what he saw during the day. Winston started with the men's meeting. Wallace thought he was serious. He told Winston that he would go if he really wanted to. He reminded Winston about how Eveline and Rudolph felt about the issue. After some discussion Winston admitted that he was joking and that he had tickets for the Smith Opera House. Winston told Wallace that he was taking him out for dinner tonight at a restaurant near the theatre. Wallace was surprised at Winston's insistence on going to a theatre. He thought that the men's meeting would be more his style. Winston informed him that he would keep the men's stuff where it had the best effect. Then Winston told Wallace that he found a job today. Wallace told him that he was full of surprises. Winston told him about the cereal company. Wallace did think that maybe someday Winston could consider moving to Geneva. They laughed about what they would do with Eveline. Winston decided that Rudolph could take care of her. While he said that Wallace knew better. Eveline might need to find someone else because Rudolph might want to be with the men.

Dinner was very good again at the Nester Hotel. They both of had a five-course dinner featuring Beef Wellington. They enjoyed a glass of wine that complimented the dinner. The service was very well paced but they had to watch their time because the show began at 8PM. Winston was so impressed with the ceiling that he nearly fell getting to his seat. Wallace was impressed that the seats were the best in the house. The theater was ornately decorated with gold trim that accented the features in the theater. The brochure included a section about William Smith who was the man who financed the building of the theater. He founded Smith College for women and owned many acres of nursery land. William Smith was intrigued with astronomy so he built an observatory near his home on Castle Street. He had varieties of flowering and fruit trees planted throughout Geneva. Wallace found the information helpful since he was new to the area. He thought that Eveline would like to hear about the college for women. He told Winston that might calm her down with her activities with Rudolph. Winston did not think anything like that would stop the two of them from their campaigning. During the show Winston thought about how good he felt about being able to show Wallace a good time. When he told Wallace that, Wallace remarked, "You have shown me many good times." Winston was happy to hear that. After the show they walked home. When they were in front of the house Wallace pointed to the house on the opposite corner of Pulteney Street. He told Winston there was evening entertainment at Miss Clara's house. Wallace asked him if he wanted to go there tonight for some fun. Winston stared at him and in his deep voice said, "No, I have a better idea." He told Wallace that he was the boss tonight because it was his last night in Geneva. He decided that tonight they would reverse what they did last night. The night was chilly so they wore bedclothes. Wallace thought it was a joke but Winston was not kidding. When it was time for bed the lamp went out. The next morning neither of them had on bedclothes. When they awoke they were face to face. Wallace could feel Winston's hair from his feet to his face. Neither of them said a thing. Finally, Winston asked what happened during the night. They decided to repeat what they thought happened by spending another hour in bed. Winston nearly missed his train and Wallace was late for work.

The next day Winston received a letter from the attorney in New York. The trial was set for the next week. There was a letter for Wallace there also. Winston kept it until the weekend when Wallace would be back in Rochester. Alice was getting even more suspicious of these deliveries. Winston told her not worry and that he was testifying in connection to an embezzlement in the early years of the Occidental Company. She wanted to know why Wallace was hiding this from Eveline. He told her the same thing that Wallace told her; so she would not worry. Alice treated Winston the same way she treated Wallace. She knew he was lying to her when she gave him that suspicious lowering of her left eyelid.

Saturday morning Winston went to Wallace's apartment. When he arrived Eveline was on her way to the market. She did not seem to be surprised that Winston arrived so early. She did think to herself that he seemed bothered about something. After she left Wallace asked him if he enjoyed himself while he was in Geneva. He said that he had and that they might be enjoying more time together as he handed him the letter. Wallace looked confused. Wallace looked at him and then the letter. He opened it slowly watching Winston's expression. Wallace read the letter summoning him to the trial too. Since he was the person in charge of Winston's custody he was required to bring him to the trial. Wallace was not being charged with anything connected to the murders. Wallace told him not to worry that his philosophy would work and that something good would happen. Just as he put his hands on Winston's shoulder Eveline came back and stopped short telling them she forgot her bag. She asked what they were discussing. Then she saw the envelope with the address from New York on it. She said, "Oh, Rudolph received an envelope just like that from New York." Wallace wanted to know how she found out. She explained that she was at his apartment when it was delivered. Wallace was not sure why she was there but thought now was not the time to ask for many details. She found the bag she forgot and turned and said, "I hope that whatever these letters are about that you are not in trouble." They watched her smile as she closed the door. Winston asked what Rudolph had to do with all this. Wallace said, "I don't think we know him as well as we need to. I have a meeting with him at the hotel the day before we go to the trial. I wonder if he will mention anything about New York. Something is very suspicious."

Chapter 44

WALLACE MET RUDOLPH THE next day. When he arrived at the hotel Rudolph was not in the office. He asked the secretary if there was any message from Mr. Williams. She was not aware that there was even a meeting planned and said, "Mr. Williams was not going to be in the office for a few days." Wallace knew why but thought it was strange that he would not have been notified about the absence. As he left the hotel he began to wonder if Eveline knew more than she did about the involvement Rudolph had with the issues in New York. He went back to Shuron to finish his work so he could be free to go to New York the next morning. He had a difficult time concentrating because he had so many unanswered questions about everyone's position in the events in New York. As he was in the midst of a new advertising campaign layout his boss came into the office. He asked Wallace if he had time to discuss some new matters about the Geneva operation. Wallace did not want to refuse his boss so he told him he had lots of time to talk. There had been some changes in the name of the company; it was to be The Standard Optical Company. The founders of the company negotiated the name change recently. Wallace was not sure why that was so important for him to know today. He was given the title of Advertising Manager, which seemed to be less than what the job was originally set up for. His boss assured him that his responsibilities would remain the same. While his boss was explaining all the details, Wallace was thinking that it was just like the situation at the H.O.Company. At this point, he had enough to deal with the Occidental Company and tomorrow's trial.

Wallace met Winston at the train station at 6AM. It was November and daylight did not arrive until nearly 7AM. As they sat in the dimly lit passenger car Winston asked Wallace if he had heard from Rudolph. He told him that he was not at work yesterday and had taken a few days off. Winston asked if Eveline had mentioned anything. Wallace told him that she only said he was going to New York for questioning about his life in Buffalo. They both shook their heads at the same time and then Wallace said, "I want this over with and I need to find out where everyone stands on their involvement with the murders." Winston stared out the window and pointed to the Auburn State Prison as the train passed by. He told Wallace that he hoped they did not end up there. Wallace shook his head and told him to stop worrying. Winston reminded him that he was not the one being questioned for a murder. After that there was nothing more to say.

Wallace had arranged for hotel accommodations for that evening just in case the hearing was not finished in time to get back to Rochester. He had explained that to Eveline and she smirked reminding him that they might see Rudolph there too. Wallace did not inquire about Rudolph's plan for the trip. Since he did not discuss it with anyone he probably wanted to be on his own. Wallace had a wild idea that Rudolph was going to have a good time. Winston asked about the room arrangements at the hotel. Wallace told him that they would each have their own room because this was not a pleasure trip. Winston agreed but really was not happy about the whole thing. The train arrived at noon just in time for a quick lunch. It was raining and cold. Neither of them had an umbrella, so they ran to the nearest diner for a sandwich before going to the attorney's office. He requested that they come to his office for a briefing about the trial. The trial was beginning at 1PM. They ate and ran to the office and were on time at 12:30 PM. Wallace laughed when the lawyer commented on their punctuality. Wallace told him about his philosophy that time was worth keeping. He responded, "Smart man." The attorney explained that Winston was being accused of Mr. Ling's murder. He mentioned that four other people had been murdered and tongues were the only evidence found. Every time Winston heard the story he saw the tongue in the office on the shipping docks not far from this office. Wallace on the other hand could remember more than that and knew who killed everyone except Mr. Ling. The tongue he remembered most vividly was the one on his bed in the hotel that was arranged like a snake with the scarf twisted as a body. Wallace hoped that the human transfers and opium trade would not become part of the questioning. The attorney told them that there were other people sequestered to the trial. He warned them that they would be fingerprinted. There were fingerprints found in a few places that would help determine if Winston was actually in the hotel at the time of the murder. He finished his briefing with the news of Rudolph. He told them that he was part of the group that had an origin in Buffalo. When they heard that they looked at each other and asked, "How?" The attorney said, "You'll see."

As they entered the courtroom there sat Rudolph. Wallace looked at him like they hardly knew one another. It was an unusual stare off. Wallace was glad the attorney sat between them so they could not see one another. The judge came in and the jury took their places. He began with the request for fingerprints. While they were being fingerprinted the purpose of the trial was discussed. The prosecutor explained that he would show evidence that Winston Spaulding was in New York City in the same hotel at the time of Mr. Ling's murder. He would also prove that he was the serial murderer for the other victims. At that moment it sank in that Winston could be convicted of murder. Winston looked like he was in a trance. The judge told the court that this trial could be over very quickly if the truth was told. He explained that there was a new device in Europe that could detect if you were telling the truth when questioned. He called it a polygraph test where wires are hooked to the body that could sense tension during questioning. However, it was not available in the United States yet. As the questioning began each person was sworn to tell the truth under oath. Wallace wondered if the oath was worth anything. The first person called was Winston Spaulding. They asked about his whereabouts on the day of the murder. He admitted that he could not prove where he was. He explained that he was in Rochester but no one saw him for a variety of reasons. The prosecutor wanted to know those reasons. Winston continued telling the court that his landlady was out of town and Wallace Paine did not see him either. The prosecutor asked if he knew Mr. Ling. He admitted he did meet him once. He was asked why he ended his employment with the Occidental Company. He explained that the office in Buffalo was closing so he returned to Rochester. He was asked if he knew anyone else in the courtroom other than Mr. Paine. He pointed to Rudolph. Rudolph appeared uneasy. The prosecutor wanted to know how well he knew this man. He explained that he was a friend of Mr. Paine's wife. They had all met in Buffalo. The prosecutor wanted to know if he continued to see him. Winston admitted he saw him occasionally because they all live in Rochester. Winston was asked if there was anything unusual about Mr. Williams or his behavior. Winston thought for a moment and said, "He always appears wherever we go and somehow becomes our friend." The jury made a rustling and clearing of the throats. Winston was asked to step down.

Wallace Paine was asked to take the stand. He thought he was not going to be questioned. Was there something about to happen that he was not aware of? Did he get set up? His heart started to beat faster. He sat down and the company's attorney began the questioning. He wanted Wallace to explain the operation of the import and export company from its infancy to the present. Thinking quickly and hoping not to divulge the wrong information he began with the soap products and oatmeal being exported from Buffalo. He explained that the oatmeal had a two-fold purpose. The oatmeal was good for packing the products and could be sold in foreign markets. He was asked about the types of things being imported into the United States. That was when Wallace had to be very careful about what he said. He explained that the Orient had become a very popular foreign market. He was asked why. He explained that the uniqueness of the furniture, the fabrics and oriental accessories sold very well in the United States. He continued to explain about the perfumes and fabrics that were coming from Europe, especially Paris. There was a strong market for those exceptional items for the wealthy of the United States. The prosecutor then asked him to give his opinion of Winston, Rudolph, and Mr. Ling. He explained that Winston and he had been friends since high school and that his parents had been his guardians because he had no family. He told the court that Winston and he had been very close and had traveled together. Then he was asked about Rudolph. Wallace hesitated while gathering his thoughts. The prosecutor said, "Well." He began with their meeting in Buffalo and that he and his wife became Mr. William's friends. At that point the prosecutor asked why his wife had so much freedom because women did not do things like that. Wallace saw Rudolph's face turn red. He continued to tell about Rudolph's time in Buffalo and his work in the music field. He explained that Mrs. Paine came from a family that appreciated high levels of musical talent and that was why they were friends. He continued about how Mr. Williams arrived in Rochester unbeknown to them and was working for George Eastman. A shuffling was heard in the courtroom when they heard Eastman's name. The prosecutor wanted to know if he had any more information about Mr. Williams. Wallace said there was more. He decided to let it all out. He told them that Rudolph was the manager of his hotel in Rochester. He was very involved in the Women's Right's Movement and that was another reason his wife liked him so well. The men in the room grumbled and made faces with the mere thought of women having more rights. Then he was asked how he felt about that movement. Wallace responded by saying, "That is a fiery issue and will someday be resolved but until then I am letting my wife be free to do what she wants." Rudolph smiled when he heard that. That was the first time he had heard Wallace discuss the issue and not be against it. Lastly, he commented on Mr. Ling. He explained that he was a very difficult person to get to know. He described him as a mysterious person that would not trust you until he was confident you were not going to cause trouble or talk too much. He was not easy to deal with and highly relentless. He described how Mr. Ling had changed his attitude toward him when he realized that he was an honest businessman. The last question was concerning Mr. Ling's involvement with Occidental. Wallace knew this had to be told carefully. He explained that Mr. Ling had various contacts in Hong Kong for the products being shipped to the United States. He was the company's Far Eastern contact. When he finished he was asked to step down.

Rudolph was next to take the stand. Wallace kept wondering what Rudolph's involvement was in this trial as he was being sworn in. The company's attorney began the questioning. It seemed that he had found out information about Rudolph Williams that had not been known by many people. He started by explaining that he contacted the Larkin Company in Buffalo. He wanted to find out about any one who had any connection to the company who had moved from Buffalo. He found out that Mr. Jackson had given his resignation. He was the man murdered on the shipping dock at the Larkin Company. In his resignation he claimed he was beginning a position in New York City for a larger shipping company. There was another person summoned to the trial that was in Buffalo at that time, but now was in New York. The attorney told the court that this was the man who was currently being sought after. The Larkin Company recorded Rudolph Williams as being terminated because of consistent absences, often days at a time. When Rudolph heard this, his face became very flushed. The attorney requested an explanation regarding his termination. Rudolph was reminded that he was under oath. He admitted he had been fired from his duties at Larkin Company not only because of his extended absences but he had some affiliation with Mr. Jackson. He continued to explain that Mr. Jackson was planning to eliminate as many people as he could from the Occidental Company. Mr. Jackson wanted to be next in line to Mr. Paine. His goal was to do away with any one connected to the Occidental operation. During one of their meetings, Rudolph was introduced to a man who knew he was a friend with Mr. Paine's wife. When Wallace heard that, he knew then that Eveline's life could have been in jeopardy. Rudolph admitted he never found out that man's name but he knew about Winston and his employment with the Occidental Company.The unknown man wanted anything that he could find that belonged to Winston. Since Rudolph knew that Wallace, Eveline, and Winston were living in the Delaware Avenue apartment together, it would be easy to find something. Rudolph admitted that the man wanted something that could be used to prove Winston's identity.The attorney deliberately did not ask if Rudolph ever got anything from Winston. He was asked to step down. The court went for a brief recess awaiting the next witness.

The attorney explained why Rudolph was not completely finished with his questioning. They hoped to find the other witness who had something to do with Buffalo and Rudolph. Winston told Wallace that he felt like he was being framed for murder and that if they could not prove other wise he would be found guilty. Wallace finally admitted that everyone seemed to be involved. Now, he wondered if Eveline had any knowledge of this or his life being in jeopardy. The attorney did tell them that the next witness was either going to make or break this trial. Rudolph was not allowed to speak to Wallace and

Winston. Wallace already had plans for what he was going to say to Rudolph when this was over. He was afraid he had misjudged Rudolph. He felt like there was something that he was not sure of. Now he was beginning to get a clearer picture of what his suspicions might be.

The court reconvened an hour later. The judge was informed that the witness they were attempting to locate could not be found. The trial was at a stand still. The judge gave the attorney until the next morning to produce more evidence. Court was adjourned until tomorrow at 9AM. If the next witness could not be located, he would call it a mistrial. Winston looked at Wallace and said, "That means I could be off the hook." Wallace said, "I think we are going to find out a lot more tomorrow." Before they were allowed to leave the attorney gave them special orders for the evening. He emphasized the importance of not talking about the trial to any one. He wanted Winston to sign the hotel register and not Wallace. He asked if they were staying at the same hotel Mr. Ling had stayed in. Wallace explained that the company had standing rooms available. The attorney reminded them again about how important it was for Winston to sign for the rooms. When they were leaving the courtroom, Winston asked Wallace, "Why does he want me to sign for the room?" Wallace smiled and said, "Rooms, remember not room, we are not on a pleasure trip." Winston made a face and asked, "So, why the signature?" Wallace told him that they were working on proving that someone forged your name. So, who could that be? Was it Rudolph? If so why is he still friends and in Rochester? He has no apparent interest in the Occidental Company. He's too much of a "ladies man." As they were walking into the hotel Wallace told him to stop talking about today. He saw that someone had been following them. When he turned around a man took off from the lobby and went down the street.

Winston did as he was instructed and signed for the rooms. Wallace felt strange not being the one to take charge. Winston told him that might be more fun if they were here for something other than a trial. It was an eerie feeling when they were taken to the same floor where Mr. Ling had been murdered. At least it was not the same room. Winston wanted to ask in the worst way if the bellhop knew about the murder. He looked at Wallace and knew that was not a good idea. They went to their rooms and unpacked what little they had brought. Then they went downstairs to the restaurant for dinner. They did not feel like going out of the hotel because somehow it did not seem safe tonight. They were seated in a booth near the windows that looked out to the street. Their conversation was limited because neither one of them dared to speak about anything, especially the trial. They ordered a martini and had a full course dinner with Chicken French as the main entrée. While they were dining Wallace spotted the same man that had been following them. He was standing across the street smoking a cigar. He stood very still and was not bothered by the rainy wind driven weather. Wallace motioned to Winston to look at the man across the street. He saw them look at him. All he did was blow a huge puff of smoke toward them and tip his hat. They felt like they might be the next to be eliminated. After dinner, they went back to their rooms. The doors were bolted and the transom window locked. Morning could not come soon enough.

During breakfast Winston talked about how restless he was during the night. He hardly slept because he kept thinking about all the things he heard yesterday. Wallace admitted that he would be glad when this was over. Winston reminded him again that he might be going to prison and Wallace would be going home. As they were waiting for their food Wallace caught sight of the same man who was in the street last night. He was still standing across the street. It looked like the man had not moved for the entire night. They thought this was creepy since the stranger looked completely drenched. Feeling uneasy about the intent of the man they decided to leave the hotel from another doorway. After they finished eating they packed their belongings and left. The minute they left this same man appeared across the street. They tried not to act surprised so they walked quickly down the street. The man was quicker than they thought; he was only a few feet from them. There was no time for anything but to get to the courthouse. He was now so close to them that they could smell the cigar smoke. He never said a word but kept one hand in his pocket. Wallace thought it might be a gun. That was all they needed was to be killed in New York on the way to the trial. Wallace thought the man was a hit man. Was Rudolph a part of the original scheme with the unknown man? Maybe Eveline did know about all this and she and Rudolph would end up with everything. Wallace told Winston in a half joking way that maybe he should have a will drawn up. Winston did not find any of this amusing. The minute they went into the court building the man disappeared.

Everyone arrived at court on time. The judge began by asking if the witness had been found. The attorney informed him that they had located him. Before the new witness was called into the court Rudolph was called back to testify. Winston asked Wallace, "What could be new since yesterday?" He reminded Winston that the attorney told them there was a reason he would be recalled to testify. Winston admitted he forgot. During the questioning Rudolph still made no visual acknowledgement that they even knew one another. Wallace thought this very strange. The attorney finally got to the question that would help to make or break the trial. He wanted to know what Mr. Williams acquired from Winston Spaulding that could prove his identity. Rudolph hesitated and then explained that the best way to do that was to get a signature and any other handwriting sample from the person. He admitted he did that when they were having dinner in Buffalo at the Paine's home on Delaware Avenue. He continued to give the details as to how he did it. Mr. and Mrs. Paine, Winston, and he were playing a game after dinner. It was a game that everyone had to sign his or her name and write a description of someone at the table. Rudolph smiled and explained that he wrote about Mrs. Paine since they were friends and she wrote about me. The judge looked at Wallace and Winston and made a gesture like it was obvious who they wrote about. The attorney wanted to know how he managed to get all the signatures and descriptions without anyone wondering why he wanted them. Rudolph laughed and the judge made a face when he heard how excitable Mrs. Paine got whenever something amused her. Rudolph mentioned her high-pitched squeals. Wallace was embarrassed to think that his wife was the topic of a court hearing. Rudolph continued to explain that Mr. Paine and Winston went into another room while Mrs. Paine and he cleaned up the dishes and the paper from the game. He offered to take the garbage out while she cleaned the kitchen. Instead of throwing the papers away he put them in his coat pocket. Rudolph had a sassy smile on his face when he finished his discussion.

The attorney looked at him and said, "What did Winston Spaulding write on his paper?" Rudolph quickly replied, "His name." The judge asked, "What else?" Rudolph looked at Wallace and Winston and said, "Mr. Spaulding wrote that he and Wallace are attracted to each other and I really like it." The attorney was speechless and shuffling was heard throughout the courtroom.

After the courtroom settled down the attorney wanted to know what was done with the signature and statement from Winston. Rudolph told him he delivered it to the man who paid him to get the paper. The attorney asked Rudolph if he had any further involvement with this man or the Occidental Company. Rudolph told the court that he decided that what he had done was dishonest. He wished now he never did it but needed money to pay his bills. Since that time he became very close friends with Mr. and Mrs. Paine. He hoped they could forgive him for his actions. He was told to step down from the stand. At first Wallace was angry to think that he was taken in by all of Rudolph's charm and talents. He wondered what Eveline was going to think about all these developments. Now he wondered if the reason Rudolph had been so mysterious about being here in New York was that he was afraid for what the truth might do to his reputation. Wallace was sure he and Rudolph would need to have a serious discussion. A brief recess was taken and court was to take a 30-minute break. During that time, Wallace spoke to Winston about his statement about the two of them. Winston told him how much he liked writing and he had written other things about their friendship. Wallace asked if anyone had read those things. Winston told him that no one even knew where they were. When Winston said that he knew he had lied. Alice found them when she was cleaning his room. She and Winston had a long talk about what was in the book. The recess was over and court was called to order. The next witness was now being called to the stand. Winston felt like he was nearing the end of a bad dream. Wallace wondered how much more he would find out about people he thought he knew.

The door in the back of the courtroom opened and Mr. Burbank was led to the stand. Wallace's mouth nearly fell open. Rudolph acted like he had never seen the man before. Mr. Burbank had been a close associate from the beginning of Occidental in New York. He was the man that welcomed Wallace into the circle of New York businessmen. These were the men who were involved in the collection of money and placement of individuals for the human transfer program. He was Mr. Ling's friend! After he was sworn in the attorneys began their questioning. Mr. Burbank was asked if he knew any of the people in the courtroom. He pointed to Wallace and Rudolph. He was asked to describe them. He stated that Wallace Paine was the owner of Occidental and he and Wallace were associates. He told the court that he knew Rudolph Williams only briefly in Buffalo. The attorney wanted to know why it was only a brief time. Winston was leaving the company and he wanted to have some further information on him. There was a suspicious look on the judges' face. He was asked if he got what he wanted? He told them he did get a signature and a statement about his personal involvement with Mr. Paine. The attorney said that it sounded like blackmail to him. Mr. Burbank replied, "Call it what you will." Then he was asked what he thought of Mr. Ling. He told the court that Mr. Ling was a strange man. He could never be trusted. He claimed it was because he was an Oriental and that they could not be trusted. The judge coughed and shook his head. After those disturbing comments, the judge requested to have his fingerprints taken. Mr. Burbank thought this was unnecessary. The judge reminded him that he was in charge and if he refused he would be in contempt of court. Mr. Burbank had a strange aura about him. Wallace thought he was very angry when he saw him the last time they were in New York. Today he was even more disturbed looking. He was asked to discuss who he thought might have killed Mr. Ling. Without blinking an eye he pointed to Winston. The attorney wanted to know why he thought that way. He admitted that he saw Winston at the hotel the time of Mr. Ling's murder. Winston's face turned beet red. The prosecutor wanted to know if he had proof of those accusations. He told them that was probably why they wanted fingerprints. That proves you were at the scene of the crime. During the questioning Mr. Burbank began to shake and move around in his chair. The judge told him to calm down or he would be removed. As they were getting ready for more questions the policeman at the door came to the judge and whispered something to him. The judge called the attorneys to the bench. He discussed something that seemed to change their attitude. Mr. Burbank was asked to leave the stand. The judge told the court that some additional evidence had just been brought forward and there was another person willing to testify.

There was lots of talking and confusion while they were waiting to see what might happen next. The judge was banging the gavel for order in the courtroom. It took him three times before the courtroom quieted down. Heads turned as the new witness was brought forward. Wallace nudged Winston and said, "That's the man who was watching us last night and this morning." He took his place on the stand and was sworn in. He was asked to identify himself. He stated his name as Jack Cooley. The attorney wanted to know why he was so interested in this case. He began by telling the court that he had known Mr. Burbank for many years. He described him as a devious man. The attorney wanted to know why. He continued to admit that he was supposed to eliminate the two men who were seated in this court. He pointed to Wallace and Winston. He decided not to do it this morning when he was following them to the court. Mr. Burbank stood up and yelled that he was crazy and a liar. The judge told him to contain himself or he would be held in contempt of court. The reason he did not follow through with his orders was Mr. Burbank had been involved in many corrupt dealings with the Occidental Company. Wallace wondered what all that meant. He continued to tell about Mr. Burbank confiding in him that they would become the owners of the business when all the original founders were eliminated. The reason Mr. Ling was murdered was to stop him from going to the police. He was going to report about the series of murders that were all related to the people in charge of the company. When Mr. Burbank heard about his plan to expose him, Mr. Ling was no longer around. The only remains was a tongue. When the courtroom heard this there was a sense of panic in the room. Everyone was talking and moving around to speak to people farther away. The judge was banging the gavel continually until a policeman shot his gun toward the ceiling. A sudden silence came over the room. The judge hit the gavel one last time. He told the court that if that happened again everyone would be held in contempt. Mr. Cooley was asked to step down.

Mr. Burbank was called back to the stand. He was reminded he was under oath. He stared at the court with fire in his eyes. The attorney asked him if what they had just heard was true. He told them that it was true. He hated all the original people who founded Occidental. He was the only person who had brains enough to manage the company. He proceeded to bang his head on the rail in front of the stand. The judge demanded that he stop. By this time a police officer was standing by the witness stand. He was then asked if he knew about Rudolph getting signatures and information about Winston Spaulding. He admitted that he knew Rudolph and did pay him for his work. He mentioned that Rudolph refused to go any further with his plans for him. The judge wanted to know what he was planning to do with the signature. He calmly told everyone that he had all the signatures of all the people who had anything to do with Occidental. By this time, Mr. Burbank was drooling and his eyes were glassy. He explained that he used Winston's signature in the hotel register. The judge wanted to know how he used it. He told the court that he practiced these signatures until they were perfect. Then he could write them down wherever he wants to. The attorney asked if he wrote Winston Spaulding in the register at the hotel. Mr. Burbank said, "Of course I did, I didn't want to be accused of killing Ling." All eyes went to the judge. The judge asked if he was the one who murdered Mr. Ling. He shook his head wildly and said, "I told you he was evil and needed to be eliminated." Winston felt an immediate sense of relief. Then, Mr. Burbank continued with his story. He wanted everyone to hear about how he eliminated all the others. The courtroom was silent. He wanted to set the record straight. He told the court that he was still going to be the sole owner of Occidental Company. He had carefully planned for the elimination of everyone. He was either going to do it by killing or making the murder look like someone else did it. Mr. Burbank was yelling by this time and wanted to tell about how much pleasure he had with Mr. Ling. First he told about his fun with Booth and Harmon; the two men who ran the H.O.Company in Buffalo. He admitted that the only thing left were their tongues after he finished grinding them up. By this time people were nearly nauseous from his descriptions. Then Mr. Jackson continued on telling about the first man who worked the docks in New York. He cut him in half and placed each half in different parts of the river. The judge told him that they had heard enough. The only question that needed to be answered was about Mr. Ling's knowledge of the murders. Mr. Burbank admitted again that Ling knew what was happening. He went along with it until he realized he was part of the elimination plan. The judge ordered him handcuffed and a date for his sentencing would be set later. The judge demanded that Mr. Burbank be put in a highly secure cell. When he was being taken out of the court, he screamed, "I've got all your signatures and I will get your tongues too."

The judge took a deep breath and then thanked everyone for their time. He admitted that this trial was a rare one in all its proceedings. He told them it was one of the most unusual set of events he had seen. He told Wallace, Winston, Rudolph and Mr. Cooley that they should be thankful they either smartened up or they were very lucky. He wished them all good luck and told them they were free to go. When they were in the hallway they all agreed they felt like they had been through a nightmare. Wallace looked at Rudolph and said, "How did you manage to fool us?" He said, "I realized what I was doing was wrong but I needed the money. I am very sorry. Can we try to forget the whole thing?" Wallace nodded his head. Winston was still in shock about the whole thing. Rudolph looked at both of them and said, "You two really like each other don't you?" They both agreed at the same time. Rudolph wanted to know if he could join them going back to Rochester. Wallace could not help but think about Mr. Ling's letter to him. Ho never committed the murders. The letter was a series of lies and Wallace believed him. Now he was angry with himself for being too easy when dealing with people and business.

Chapter 45

January 1910, Eveline and Wallace moved to Geneva. Eveline was excited about being closer to Seneca Falls. She was trying to convince Rudolph to move to Geneva. He did not want to leave his work at the hotel in Rochester yet. He and Wallace had become closer friends since the trial and Rudolph's past actions had been resolved. Winston was not as excited about the addition to their friendship. Wallace suggested that after another year he would consider hiring someone to take Rudolph's position as manager of the hotel. At that point Rudolph could relocate to Geneva. Wallace found that the new job required more time than his previous jobs. He felt like his whole life was working late and not having any fun. He had not heard from Winston in some time, which made him restless. Wallace had the Geneva Daily News delivered so they could keep up with what was happening in the world. The big news was Governor Hughes calling a special meeting of the state legislature to publicly oppose an income tax proposition. This was a heated topic because if it were to become a law, people would be receiving less income because they would be taxed on what was earned. Wallace thought this was not a good idea either; he had his sights set on making his fortune and did not want his money taken away. Eveline saw an article in the evening paper that advertised a new way to acquire merchandise.

It started in Rochester at Duffy-McInnerney Company; Rochester's greatest retail store. It was a system that was developed to help shoppers accumulate stamps that could be redeemed for gifts. When she read it to Wallace he said that sounded like the same thing that the Larkin Company did. These were called S&H Green Stamps. The article mentioned that there were plans for a store like that in Geneva. Eveline told Wallace she was glad that there was so much to do in Geneva. She felt like she was in a small Rochester. He was happy she was satisfied with the move. He wanted her to be content and busy so he could do his work without any resistance from her.

Wallace decided to buy a new car. Henry Ford had just produced the Model T Tourabout. He wanted a new car even though he liked his Model A Runabout. He saw an advertisement for the Tourabout. It was manufactured in black and red. He wondered if anyone would even notice his new car if he bought another red one. He decided to order it in red. He liked the color and wanted it to be something different from what most people would order. Sales and production had risen so quickly that he was able to use some of his returns to buy more stocks and still have enough money to pay for the new car. The 1910 model was being built with steel and some wood. Ford felt it would make the car last longer with lower maintenance. The body was red with brass features on the front and red wheels. He ordered it with a black canvas top that could be lowered in the warmer weather. The car was much larger than his first one. It could carry four passengers and still have room for baggage; it had the best of everything. The price tag was $950.00.

The offices that Wallace worked in were located on 116 Lyceum Street. He had an entire office devoted to advertising. The catalog idea he used in Rochester continued to be popular for showing customers what the company offered from the convenience of their own homes. The employees were taking advantage of the housing option that he introduced in Geneva. Workers had part of their pay set aside for a home that the company would build for them. Wallace wanted to institute some of the same benefits that the Larkin Company offered its employees. He suggested separate restrooms for men and women and provided a nurse's office for illness and injuries. They asked if he was trying to be supportive of women because of the activities in Seneca Falls. He told them that was not the reason. He had heard from his wife that William Smith supported women and their rights and even offered his opera house for rallies. After he said that they were silent. He wanted to increase employee benefits too. He suggested they have leave of absence days available for employees when they needed to be out of work for family matters. Until then, workers had no time for personal business and were often fired if they were not at work. Wallace explained his philosophy of giving to your employees and they will support and work harder because they are being cared for. He wanted to feature real people in the catalogs. He thought if employees were used as models for the products that Standard Optical produced it would strengthen loyalty among the workers. They could have some people holding the products or wearing eyewear. He thought that would reduce the cost of hiring outside people. Until now, many ads were sketches but photography was improving and he wanted to utilize his affiliation with Eastman Kodak. He laughed to himself when he thought that they did not know he was a shareholder of Eastman Kodak. Why not support your own interests was his philosophy. His bosses agreed to try his ideas on a preliminary basis to see if they saw profits increase.

So much was happening in and around the country. President Taft gave a special message to the people about the importance of conserving the natural resources in the country. He was predicting massive reductions in the supply of coal, iron ore, wood, and gasoline. He warned that the automobile was going to consume more fuel than the country could supply. President Taft used the eruption of Mt. Etna as an example of how quickly an area could be devastated and how natural disasters could wipe out entire cities. Wallace found it hard to believe that such things might happen because there were very few cars on the roads and he thought that our fuel sources were unlimited. Was President Taft trying to scare people or did he know something most didn't?

Eveline 's social engagements continued to occupy her days. She went to Seneca Falls with a group of women for a luncheon early in April. She met many women from Geneva. During the luncheon she began speaking with a woman she saw in one of the dress shops in Geneva. The woman introduced herself as Rose Haynes. She told Eveline that she was married to a doctor. She explained that he was doing his medical internship at Buffalo General Hospital during the Pan-American Exposition. Eveline told her that her husband and a friend of his went to the Exposition. They were there when President McKinley was assassinated and they saw him being taken away by a group of doctors. Rose told Eveline that her husband was one of those men. Eveline wanted to know what her husband's name was because she and Wallace needed to establish a doctor in Geneva. Rose told her he had an office on Main Street and his name was Dr. Samuel Haynes. They spent the rest of the afternoon speaking with other women about the suffrage movement and how important it was that they should have equal voting rights. Both women commented that they were lucky compared to most women because their husbands let them do as they pleased. They laughed and said, "As long as we don't get in the way." Eveline and Rose walked home and admired the beautiful spring flowers on Main Street. Rose had her parasol opened because the sun's rays were very strong and she did not want to burn her face. Eveline told her, "Woman like us should not have too much color. We want to look like fair maidens." They laughed and Rose went into the apartment building where Dr. Haynes had his office.

When Wallace arrived home from work, Eveline could not wait to tell him about Rose. She explained how she was in Seneca Falls for a meeting and that she met a woman from Geneva. Wallace was only half listening to her until she mentioned the Exposition. Then his ears perked up and he wanted to know what that had to do with this woman named Rose. Eveline explained that her husband was one of the doctor's who was on duty at the time of President McKinley's assassination at the Temple of Music. Wallace began to think of that day and remembered only one doctor that stood out from the rest. He remembered that he looked at the doctor and he looked back at him. He now wondered if that was the same person? She told him that Dr. Haynes had an office on Main Street. When she said Haynes, Wallace remembered his badge had that very name, Dr. Samuel Haynes. Wallace with a gleam in his eye said, "I remember seeing his name on the badge." He told Eveline that he was going to go to his office to arrange their medical care with him and to see if he was the man he remembered. Eveline reminded him of how good it was that she was doing all these social things. She laughed and said, "You do need a woman to get things going." Wallace just shook his head.

The next day Wallace was scheduled to meet with the Business Council in Geneva. It was a meeting of all the business leaders of the companies in and around Geneva. He was asked to represent the Optical Company. During the meeting he met many of the notable men in Geneva and their first goal was to organize themselves into an official council for the betterment of Geneva businesses. Wallace could not understand why he was asked to be a part of this meeting until the president of the First National Bank of Geneva announced that Wallace Paine had been chosen to lead up the Geneva Board of Commerce. He was asked to stand so that everyone could see who he was. While Wallace was standing the president of the bank explained that William Smith was one of the founders of the bank and helped to organize the Standard Optical Company. He was so impressed with Wallace Paine and what he had offered to the optical company that he wanted him to be the leader of the Board of Commerce. There was applause for what seemed to be forever and then he was asked if he could find the time to do this work. Wallace accepted the offer and everyone was invited to have lunch. During the luncheon Wallace met the men he would be associating with. It was decided that when the organization was in full operation a secretary was needed to manage the business. When Wallace heard that he thought that Rudolph would be ideal for that position.

As Wallace was walking out of the meeting a man stepped up to him and introduced himself as Dr. Samuel

Haynes. He explained how their wives had met yesterday in Seneca Falls. The minute Wallace heard the name he remembered him. He was just as handsome now as he was nine years ago. He still could see the smile he gave him at the Temple of Music when McKinley's body was being taken to the hospital. Wallace shook his hand and felt his firm handshake. He told Dr. Haynes that his wife mentioned the meeting yesterday. As they walked toward Main Street Dr. Haynes pointed to the apartment building ahead. He told Wallace that he owned the building so he could have both a place to live and an office for his practice. Wallace asked if he and his wife could be under his medical care. Dr. Haynes said that he would be glad to do that. Wallace went into the office and filled out the necessary information. When he was finished he and Dr. Haynes shook hands. Wallace left the office. When he was walking home he thought about seeing Dr. Haynes again. He thought that it was ironic that people and things come back in different ways. He wondered what their association was going to be.

That evening while Eveline was making dinner, Wallace read the mail and the newspaper. He received a letter from the Ford Motor Company thanking him for supporting and continuing to reinvest his earnings in the company. The letter stated that on May 1 he could pick up his new car in Rochester. He told Eveline about the car but nothing was mentioned about his large reinvestment in the stocks. She suggested that they send their parents a note and invite them to go to dinner the day they get the car. Wallace thought that was a great idea. He thought that Winston and Rudolph might want to join them. Eveline liked that idea and then let out one of her squeals. Wallace had the same reaction every time that happened. He reminded her that people might think she came from Willard. She shook her head and rolled her eyes. While they were having dinner he told Eveline about the meeting and his appointment to lead the Board of Commerce in Geneva. She thought it was nice but asked why she needed to know. He told her that he met Dr. Haynes. She perked up when he said that. He explained that he went to the office to fill out the information so they could both be his patients. Wallace talked about how handsome Dr. Haynes still was and that he had a firm handshake. Eveline stared at him during his description of the doctor wondering why he needed to tell her that. Then she asked if anything was mentioned about her or his wife. He explained how Samuel began the conversation. Eveline said, 'Oh, on a first name basis already?" Wallace looked at her with a questioning eye. After they finished dinner he saw an article in the newspaper about a new housing craze. It told about the newest type of home that architects were designing and contractors were building. It was a one-floor home called a bungalow. They were being built in varying sizes and had many arts and craft features. While Wallace read about the bungalow he saw many of Elbert Hubbard's style using wood and stone. The article explained that bungalows were often built around larger homes. Frank Lloyd Wright was noted for designing small neighborhoods with bungalows surrounding a larger prairie style home making it a craftsman style community. Wallace showed Eveline the article and she thought it sounded like something she would like. He asked what style she was thinking of. She told him the large house surrounded by the smaller ones. He laughed and told her that he was glad that was what she wanted. She asked why and he told her that he was going to build a big house someday, something like the Martin's house in Buffalo.

Alice received Eveline's invitation for dinner. She told Frank about it and he wondered if they needed top hats for the occasion. She ignored the remark and told Winston about the dinner. He was happy to be included. Alice told Winston that Rudolph was invited too. Eveline requested that Winston tell Rudolph about the invitation. Winston thought that was odd that she did not invite him on her own. He agreed to go to his apartment to tell him about the dinner. Alice was excited that they were coming to Rochester because she had not seen them since they moved to Geneva. Frank asked her how often he would have to be a part of the show. Alice told him that it was time he accepted things as they were and to stop being miserable. He made a point of letting her know that he would be any way he wanted to be. She left the room and Winston went to Rudolph's place. As Winston was walking to see Rudolph he began to think of the possibilities of moving to Geneva. He liked what he saw when he was there to visit. He knew he could probably get a job there. It was time to leave Alice and Frank's place. He was tired of their fighting and Frank's bad behavior. Frank was beginning to remind him of his father, drunk and mean. He arrived at Rudolph's apartment and knocked on the door. It took awhile for him to answer the door. When he opened the door he had on only trousers. He was surprised to see Winston. He invited him to come in and take a seat. Rudolph left the room to finish dressing. Winston thought about how Rudolph looked. He was muscular and in perfect shape. Then he thought about what he and Eveline might be doing and that changed his mood. Rudolph came into the room and sat down. Winston told him that he was invited for dinner at the hotel when Wallace and Eveline are in town on May 1. Rudolph smiled and handed Winston his personal invitation from Eveline. Winston read it and thought it would be nice to have a personal invitation since everyone else got one. He decided not to give his opinion of that. Then Rudolph handed him the second page. Winston looked confused but read it. They had both been invited to return with Wallace and Eveline to Geneva in their new car. Winston looked at Rudolph and said, "Are we staying overnight?" Rudolph laughed and said, "We both want to don't we?" Winston looked at him and did not know who wanted to stay with whom and for how long. Eveline must have written it to be deliberately vague about the visit. Winston told Rudolph that he would be ready for anything. He wanted to see Rudolph's reaction when he said, "I don't wear much and so I don't need to pack anything." Rudolph admitted that he did like to wear a lot but was not sure what he should pack.

Chapter 46

WINSTON WAS EXCITED ABOUT seeing Wallace and Eveline when they came to Rochester to pick up the new car. He had been thinking about doing something different since the invitation was vague about the accommodations in Geneva. There were advertisements in the local newspaper for a new body spray for men. It came from Pendleton, Oregon. It was named Leter Buck cologne after the cattle roundup in 1910. The fragrance had a euphoric affect when he smelled it. Winston had the tingles and thought about how the spray would affect Wallace. He laughed to himself about Wallace's sensations whenever they were together. As he was walking out of the store he saw Rudolph. He asked Winston what was in his bag. Winston smiled and explained it was a surprise for the trip to Geneva. Rudolph had a quizzical look on his face. Winston told him he would not understand even if he told him about it. Rudolph told him about what he had planned to wear so he could impress Eveline. Winston asked, "Was it going to match her outfit?" Rudolph gave him a disgusted look as he walked away.

Technology was advancing at a faster pace than people could keep up with. There was an article about an airship that was 485 feet long. People were amazed that human beings could be passengers in something that could fly. It was named the Zeppelin. The first trip made a successful journey of 250 miles. It took 10 hours and the passengers landed with no mishaps. When Wallace read about it he wondered if air travel might be the next thing he should invest in. There was an entire page featuring the newly finished Grand Central Station in New York City. It had the largest passenger traffic on the globe. He could not wait to see it the next time he went to New York. While he was engrossed in the newspaper Eveline read the social page. There were new fashions for women and the fancier stores in Geneva carried all of them. There was a type of garment called the Pantaloon Skirt. It was not a full flowing skirt as most women were used to wearing. Amelia Bloomer had devised a garment called "bloomers". She liked riding a bicycle and skirts got in the way of movement, so she stitched up the center of the skirt and put a tie on the bottom of each leg. In that way, they could be raised up to avoid dragging the ground for easier walking or riding. It was a highly controversial garment but the Women's Rights movement endorsed it as a step toward more freedom. Eveline told Wallace that she was going to purchase a pantaloon skirt to wear to Rochester when they picked up the new car. She thought Rudolph would appreciate an "up to the minute" outfit. Wallace was not sure what kind of reaction she might get from the rest of the group. She informed him that she did not care because Rudolph was the one she was trying to please. Wallace never liked the tone of her remarks about her desire to please Rudolph. He wondered what the visit to Geneva was going to be like.

Wallace had been working on a new advertising campaign for the optical company. All of his suggestions had been implemented, but he needed to bring higher visibility to the products that were manufactured. While he was planning what he wanted the advertising to look like he thought that eyewear was like jewelry. He wrote his ideas down with diagrams and sketches of eyewear around full-page advertisements. The large banners and posters could be in train stations, maybe even in Grand Central Station now that it was open and attracting huge numbers of travelers. He began with a history of the need for eyewear and why it was so important. He wrote that when the optical company entered the Finger Lakes region in 1864 living conditions did not often require eyewear for improving a person's vision. There were no moving pictures, book of the month clubs, bright lights, automobile headlights, or many pages of newspapers to strain one's vision. He wanted to make it a story about today's consumer of eyewear. The article stated, "The adults without at least one pair of glasses are an exception. Life has been broadened and speeded up to such an extent that the strain on one's eyes has become enormous. Due to the latest styles in glasses people no longer hesitate to wear them. Standard Optical eyewear is so stylish that they add to rather than detract from one's appearance. Glasses are jewelry. Standard makes the most complete and most specific line of eye examining instruments known to the optical profession. It has the most complete and widely used line of lens and grinding machines in the world. With every new pair of glasses, a stylish eyeglass case is a gift to you from Standard Optical." After he finished his work, he looked at the article from the consumer's point of view. He thought the advertisement reinforced the quality of the products and felt that it would be a good addition to the catalog. While he was thinking about the types of people that the advertisement would appeal to another theme came to his mind, "Sunwear." Women would be especially interested in glasses that would keep the sun out of their eyes. He knew that Eveline did not like the sun and would be a perfect customer for such a sporty look. He designed a page that focused on "Sporty Eyewear for Men and Women." He wanted to use real people in this advertisement. He thought of an advertisement showing people playing tennis or on a boat. Since Eastman Kodak was doing business with them he could arrange for a photographer to take pictures using the people who worked in the factory. The costs would be reduced by not hiring models and it would boost the morale of the workers.

Wallace was anxious to introduce his ideas to the owners of the company. He had a meeting with the newly formed Board of Commerce the next day and many of the decision makers would be there. He arranged his writing and ideas much the same way as he always had. He knew visual effects get attention so he used a scroll giving the impression that something important was being announced. When he went home that evening he told Eveline about his idea for summer eyewear. Before he could even finish his discussion she told him that she hoped he would allow Rose and her to be in the pictures. Wallace thought that was preposterous. She asked, "You actually think women in a factory are going to look like sporty women?" He looked at her and agreed that factory women were not the sporty summer type. Then, Eveline asked if he was going to include men in his advertisement. He wanted to know why. She thought that Rudolph could be in a picture for sunglasses or riding goggles. Wallace had not thought about those options. He asked her why she thought Rudolph should be in the pictures and not him. She said, "You are different and not sporty." Wallace was stunned by that remark but did agree that he was more into making money than making trouble. Eveline shrugged her shoulders and left the room. He did not want to give her too much credit for those ideas but he knew he would add them to the advertisement

Saturday was the day they were going to Rochester to pick up the new car. Wallace decided that he was keeping his first car because it was one of the first models made by Ford. He would store it somewhere in the area until he had a garage. He and Eveline planned to take the train to Rochester, pick up the car, and go to dinner with Winston, Rudolph and their parents. They were meeting at the hotel late in the afternoon. It was a sunny day and the trip on the train was relaxing. It was early in May so the countryside was bursting with new foliage that had a greenish yellow hue in the sunlight. Eveline asked Wallace how his meeting went about his advertising ideas. He told her that everything was approved and that they would be working on his ideas very soon. He deliberately avoided the actual date because he wanted to see how long it would take for her to ask about her ideas for Rudolph and her. Without any further discussion on Wallace's part she told him she would tell Rudolph this weekend. Wallace asked her not to but she insisted that there was nothing wrong with such a good plan. Wallace shook his head and decided it was time to hold her back. The Women's Movement had gone to her head and he needed to calm her down. Most men he knew were not pleased with what was happening with women's attitudes. He was happy when the conductor announced that they would be in Rochester shortly. He could not wait to see his new car.

The place where the car was to be delivered was a short walk on East Avenue. So much was changing in

Rochester since he was a kid. Now there was a dealer for new cars. No longer did he have to go to the train yard to pick up the car as he had in Buffalo. They arrived at the showroom where there was a car displayed in the front window. It was black and much larger than what Wallace purchased a few years earlier. When he saw the car in the window he thought about his father who had a buggy shop once not far away. He wondered if he had seen this new place. He was sure his father hated the idea. Wallace and Eveline went into the office and the gentleman greeted them and told them what a smart car he was getting today. Wallace beamed when he heard the word smart. Eveline told the man that all she hoped for was more protection from the weather. The man assured them that this car was much better built than his first car. After the paper work was completed, the man told them to wait in the front of the showroom and he would bring the car out from the back. Wallace was just as excited as he used to get when something new came along. He told Eveline that he felt like a little kid and she told him he acted like one too. He gave her a smirky look.

As the car came around from the back of the building the sunlight reflected on the fenders making them shine like gold. Wallace could not believe how large it appeared to be. The salesman told him that the new vehicles were larger and could hold more baggage and people. Eveline commented on the top and the doors. The salesman told her she would not need to worry about the weather again. It was red just as his other car but had brass on the fenders and a black roof that could be taken down in good weather. The horn was more sophisticated and there was an actual windshield. Wallace laughed and decided he might not need his goggles anymore. They thanked the man and got into the car. While they were leaving Eveline asked when he was paying the man. Wallace told her not to worry that he had already taken care of it. The new car had a much smoother ride. Wallace told her that it was easier to drive and it seemed heavier than his first car. She thought it was more comfortable as she wondered what Winston and Rudolph would think when they rode in the backseat.

They pulled up in front of the hotel a few minutes early. Wallace wanted to see the expressions on everybody's faces. Most of them would think it was wonderful but Frank was a question waiting to be answered. Wallace spotted them walking toward the hotel. Alice was the first to see the car and was pointing at it as they approached. They got out of the car and stood next to it. Winston and Rudolph said it was beautiful and they could not wait to ride to Geneva in it. Mr. And Mrs. Lounsberry were equally impressed and glad their children were doing so well. Alice asked when she was going to get to ride in it. Frank on the other hand stared at the car and then looked at Eveline's outfit. He turned to the group and in a gruff voice said, "I saw that car sitting in that place on East Avenue. I had a feeling it was Wallace's car. No one else would have the nerve to be so wasteful and a woman who looks like that deserves to be in that thing." No one said a word. Wallace wanted to leave without dinner. Alice stood like a statue. Winston made a face, Rudolph nudged Wallace, and Mr. and Mrs. Lounsberry turned and went into the hotel. Wallace and Eveline followed. Frank stayed behind glaring at the shiny red car. Winston whispered to Wallace, "I hope he doesn't do something to it."

Dinner was pleasant enough considering the way things began on the curbside. Wallace figured people were getting used to his father's obnoxious behavior. It was an early dinner so they could have time to drive back to Geneva before it got too dark. Alice and Catherine were typical mothers and worried about the kids getting home safely. Rudolph was proud to tell everyone how much he had done in the hotel. He was satisfied with the wait staff and music was heard in the lobby everyday. Wallace knew that Rudolph's days were numbered while he was talking about the hotel. He was ready to offer him the job as the secretary to the Board of Commerce in Geneva. Alice asked what they were planning to do when they arrived in Geneva. Wallace told her that they would probably stay at their apartment. Winston piped up as he kicked Wallace's foot under the table that Rudolph might want to go to Miss Clara's. Rudolph wanted to know where that was. Winston rolled his eyes and told him it was a place for fun but he might want to work there. Wallace shook his head and Eveline was not sure what Miss Clara's was either. She thought it was a restaurant. Frank spoke up and said, "I know what Winston wants to do." No one acknowledged his remark. Alice spoke up and said she thought it was nice they were spending time together and they deserved to do what they wanted. Frank huffed.

The ride to Geneva was fun. Wallace enjoyed how well the car operated. Eveline was delighted that it did not jump around and that the wind was not blowing in her face. The two guys were happy there were enough seats for them and the bags. Winston commented on how glad he was that he only brought one thing giving more room for Rudolph's steamer trunk. They laughed but Rudolph was not sure he knew what Winston was up to. Wallace jokingly asked what was the one thing he brought. Winston told him that he would find out. There was a bit of grumbling with that comment. As they got closer to Geneva Wallace started thinking about where everyone was going to sleep. The apartment was not as large as the Delaware Avenue apartment. While he was pondering the possibilities, Eveline spoke up and said she had been thinking about the sleeping arrangements. No one made a sound and all that could be heard was the engine. She continued. Since there was only one bedroom it only seemed fair that the guests should have the bedroom. She and Wallace would sleep in the parlor. Still the only sounds were the engine and Eveline's voice. She asked if there was any objection. Rudolph spoke up and thought that the men should stay in the bedroom and she could sleep on the couch. There would be better access for her to the bathroom. The engine still hummed. Eveline looked at Wallace and waited for his response. He thought that would be okay. It was only for 2 nights. Winston said nothing because he was at least glad the men were in the bedroom and not out in the parlor. Winston wondered what he was going to do with Rudolph. The conversation ended when Eveline thought they should try it tonight and change tomorrow night if it was not a good arrangement.

It was 8PM when Wallace pulled up to the front of 114 Washington Street. One of the neighbors was walking by when they got out of the car. He remarked that the car was beautiful and the flashiest one around. Wallace smiled and thanked him and was glad to hear the compliment. Winston stood at the curbside with his hand in his pocket. He kept feeling the bottle of Leter Buck cologne. He wondered what that might do to Rudolph. It might be more fun than he expected. Rudolph was busy pulling his bags from the back of the car. Eveline laughingly asked him how long he was planning on staying. They got into the apartment and sat down for a drink. During the conversation Eveline got her evening things from the bedroom. Wallace kept thinking that she was up to something. Her invitation was vague to both Winston and Rudolph. After all the mysterious behavior in New York with Rudolph and now they were sharing a room and bed together. Was Eveline plotting something with him? Winston was not saying much either. He was more interested in his bottle of cologne that he had such great hopes for. The three men went into the bedroom to get organized after Eveline finished in the bedroom. Winston brought nothing and he was ready. Rudolph was fussing around with his clothes and grooming equipment. Winston in a smart tone asked him if he was thinking about Miss Clara's? Rudolph turned and said, "I'd rather stay here, why don't you go to Miss Clara's." Winston did not know what to say as he looked at Wallace. By this time Wallace was in his nightclothes and in bed. Winston took all his clothes off. Wallace wanted to see what Rudolph's reaction would be when he saw Winston getting into bed next to him. When Rudolph saw Winston's naked body he said, "Just what I thought." Wallace felt that sensation again and liked it. Winston thought he might need to keep his Leter Buck cologne for another time. They watched Rudolph slowly and deliberately remove his clothes. He wore everything that a gentleman would wear. He removed his suspenders, then his trousers that were followed by the socks that were attached at the top with snaps. By the time he got to his undergarments they both said, "No wonder you needed so much baggage." He laughed and said, "I like to be well prepared." He removed the rest of his garments. He stood facing them. They said nothing as they studied his handsome face, muscles and stature. The front of the bed covered him from the waist down. He turned the gaslight down so the room was dimly lit and got under the covers. There was only the sound of breathing. It was a small bed and there was very little room to move. Their skin was warm and moist against one another. Winston was in the middle and Wallace on one side with nightclothes on. He suggested that he should be in the middle to keep their skin from touching. Winston's hand began to investigate the lower half of Rudolph's body. Winston whispered, "There's more than enough for everyone." Before Wallace knew what was happening his clothes had been removed. Rudolph was on one side and Winston on the other side. Wallace liked being trapped and he wanted to explode because this time was more intense than ever before. This was exactly what he wanted.

Eveline had breakfast ready for the men on Sunday morning. When they appeared from the bedroom she asked if they slept well. They made a gesture that it was okay. Wallace told her that the bed was too small for three people. She agreed but thought it was a good way for them to see if they liked each other. Wallace thought that was a strange comment. Winston said that maybe they need to try only two at a time. No one knew what to say after all that had happened the night before. Eveline informed them that the newspaper had some interesting articles that morning. She explained that Elizabeth Blackwell had died recently. They looked at her like she was telling them a fairy tale. She told them that she was the first woman to receive her medical degree. She went to school here in the Old Geneva College. She died in England after being a doctor for many years. Rudolph thought that was great to think that woman had rights that long ago. He thought Geneva would be a great place to live because it seemed so liberal. Then she told him about a convention coming to Seneca Falls in November. The theme was to be "Why Women Should Vote." Now he knew where he belonged and Wallace thought that might be a good idea after what he experienced last night. Winston was not saying much until Eveline mentioned another article in the morning paper about a murder. His ears perked up. "The Twoomey Murder" was the title. The son murdered his father and was caught and arrested in Rochester last December. Dr. Samuel Haynes had conducted the autopsy of the victim. He was a witness at the trial a few months ago and the son was found guilty of alcohol poisoning. He was convicted of first-degree murder and sentenced to 7-14 years in Auburn Prison. Winston wanted to know why he needed to know that news. Eveline said, "Be glad that wasn't you." No one responded much to that article except that Dr. Haynes was the doctor that they saw at the Temple of Music. Eveline asked, "What are we doing today?" Rudolph wanted to see more of Geneva. Eveline offered to take him on a tour of the city. They could see the rowhouses and maybe go to the Smith Opera House for a matinee. She read that there was a singer performing that afternoon. Rudolph asked if the others wanted to go with them. Winston spoke up and told them that he and Wallace had seen the rowhouses and had been to the theatre when he was here before. Wallace said he wanted to take his car for a drive. Winston asked if he could go. Wallace said, "I guess we all know what we are doing." Eveline dressed in a fancy and sporty outfit after breakfast. Rudolph took the longest time to get ready because he wore a perfectly starched white shirt, tie, trousers, and sporty walking shoes. He carried his coat for the theatre as they went off arm in arm. Eveline winked at Wallace as they were leaving. Before Winston could say a word Wallace said, "Get ready I'm taking you for a ride."

They got into the car. Wallace had a determined attitude. Winston had never seen him be so certain about going for a ride. Winston said, "I forgot something I'll be right back." He ran into the apartment and grabbed his Leter Buck cologne. He smiled when he put it in his pocket. Out he came with a smile on his face. Wallace asked him what he forgot. Winston told him that he would find out soon enough. Wallace drove up Washington Street and told Winston that he was going to have a house on that corner as they went by Nursery Avenue. Winston laughed and said, "It's a dirt road." Wallace said, "It won't be for very long." They continued up the street until they came to Pre Emption Road. Wallace turned left to go south to see where it might take them. The road was not as well paved as the ones in town so he stopped where there were trees and some grassy areas and turned the car off. He told Winston to get out. He thought Wallace was upset with him. He got out. Wallace watched him as he left the car. Then, Wallace got out and went over to him. He demanded to know what he had to get in the apartment. Winston stared at him and told him it was in his trousers. Wallace looked at him and thought it was a joke. He told him what the Leter Buck did for him and he wanted Wallace to try some. He pulled it out and Wallace said that it smelled pretty good. Winston explained that it came from Oregon and was named after a rodeo where they tamed bucking broncos. Wallace used some on his neck. He told Winston it had a strange affect on him. Winston smiled and asked, "Like how?" Wallace said, "I feel as tough as one of those cowboys." Winston said, "Me too." The warm sun and seclusion of the tress offered them an opportunity to do things they had to share with Rudolph last night. The only difference was this time Wallace thought it would be more fun if they acted like they were the ones in the rodeo. Just so happened that there was some rope in the back of the car from when it was transported to Rochester. Winston wanted to be lassoed to see if the cologne actually would make him buck. Winston took great pleasure in being tied down and bucked against Wallace.

Later that afternoon, Eveline and Rudolph arrived back at the apartment. Winston was sitting in the living room and Wallace was cleaning his car from the dirt that got on it from their ride to the country. They each told about their adventures. Winston had a coy look on his face when he described the countryside as wild as a rodeo. Wallace walked in and heard rodeo and wondered what Winston was up to. Eveline told them about the singer. Rudolph said he should have been the pianist. Wallace remarked in a pleasant tone that everyone got what they wanted. Rudolph stared at him when he said that and then looked at Winston. Winston gave him a suggestive smile. They decided to go out for dinner. Since it was a pleasant evening they could walk downtown to find a restaurant. Everything was more convenient in Geneva because it was smaller than Rochester so it took no time to find a place for dinner. As they were passing by Dr Haynes' building he saw them and waved. They stopped and Wallace introduced Winston, Rudolph and Eveline. They chatted about the day and how nice Geneva was at this time of year. Winston kept looking at Dr. Haynes during their brief chat. Eveline noticed how obvious he was and asked Winston if he remembered him. Winston blushed and admitted he did from the Temple of Music. He did not mention how good-looking he was until they were further down the street. All Eveline said was, "Is that all you guys think about." Rudolph was quiet because he was not sure what all the connections were.

Eveline started asking what the sleeping arrangements were for that evening after they arrived from dinner. Rudolph began by saying that he did not mind last night and it would be fine for tonight too. Wallace was fine with it. Winston deliberately hesitated to see what the reaction would be if he did not agree. He told them that he wanted to go to Miss Clara's for a while tonight. Wallace stared at him and asked, "Why?" Winston stood up and pulled his cologne out of his pocket and rubbed some on his neck saying, "I want some cowgirls." Eveline squealed and wanted to know why cowgirls. Wallace did not move for fear of what might be said next. Winston told them about the cologne and where it came from and what it could do. He repeated that he wanted some hot cowgirls and probably Miss Clara could get him a few. No one could believe there was such a place nearby. Then Winston told about the time he was here before when Wallace asked him to go to Miss Clara's. It was across the street on the corner. Many men frequented the place for some fun with women of the night. Eveline turned to Wallace and wanted to know if that was his new office. Rudolph did not move while Winston was having a grand time elaborating on his story. Wallace told her that he had only heard about it and was joking about it to Winston. Eveline said, "Do any of you actually know what you like?" There was dead silence. After what seemed like forever she told them that she thinks it is funny that they are still acting like they were at the Burlesque show in Rochester. She did not care what they did as long as she was the center of their attention. They looked at each other, shrugged and smiled. No one went to Miss Clara's because it was late and tomorrow was a workday. When the men were in the bedroom Winston asked if they liked his story. Wallace thought he was working up to a report about the effects of the Leter Buck on him. Rudolph still did not know what they were referring to. Winston still felt the effects from the afternoon and so did Wallace. They looked at each other and offered some to Rudolph. They wanted to see what it might do for him. He liked the aroma. They put some on various areas of their bodies. Winston thought it might be good to inhale it too. They did. Within minutes Winston watched Wallace turn into a tough acting stud. Rudolph watched himself in the mirror as his muscles tightened. Winston moved closer to Rudolph so he could appreciate how things were changing on his body. Wallace told Winston in a demanding tone that they were going to show Rudolph how they spent their afternoon. Wallace lassoed Rudolph and watched him buck. He told him that he needed to be tamed if they were going to be friends. Rudolph was so aroused by what was happening that Wallace and Winston worked on taming him most of the night.

Chapter 47

INDUSTRIES THAT WERE MOVING into Geneva created a need for laborers and leaders. Wallace asked Rudolph if he had thought about moving to Geneva to be a part of the growth in the area. He said he had thought he might want to in a few years after he had the hotel operating to his satisfaction. Wallace respected him for his decision. Geneva had been named "The Gem City" because it stood on the shores of Seneca Lake and sparkled like a gem. Wallace and other businessmen attended the funeral of William Smith who was Geneva's notable and wealthy citizen. He died on February 7 in his mid nineties. Mr. Preston spoke to Wallace after the funeral about a new company that was being organized. He was also the owner of the fancy hotel in town and was planning to give it a new name and image. Wallace asked what name he was thinking about. Mr. Preston heard that he owned a similar business in Rochester. He asked if the name Seneca Hotel would be suitable. Wallace thought for a moment and agreed it was a good name since it overlooked Seneca Lake. Wallace told him his hotel had two names because it merged a few years ago. He avoided the details of how he acquired the property. As they were leaving the funeral Mr. Preston explained that there was a patent ready to be announced. It would be for a company manufacturing safety razors. He referred to it as a novel and efficient safety razor patent.

Mr. H Lynn Henry was granted the patent and the new company would be manufacturing and distributing the razors. He explained that it was going to replace the out dated straight razor and the single edge razor. Mr. Henry claimed the new razor would shave the toughest beard. It would be made from Sheffield steel with no corners for accidental cuts. It would have an easy removable blade and would virtually prevent cuts and infections. The new company needed a secretary and an advertising person. He asked Wallace if he would be interested in the position. Mr. Preston told him to think about it and he would await his response.

Wallace returned to his office at Standard Optical. While he was finishing some work he thought how ironic it was that earlier in the day he attended William Smith's funeral who was one of the founders of Standard Optical. Today, Mr. Preston offered him a job in a newly forming company and he too may be leaving Standard Optical. He was ready for a new challenge. He laughed when he thought about how things change every two years. When he left his office he looked around at all he had implemented at Standard Optical. He thought about the first day he arrived in Geneva to establish the new plant. It was an unknown area and prospects were uncertain. He felt like he was a foundation person and people must see that in him. He had re-organized and improved every job he accepted and made the companies profitable. He hesitated when he thought about the H.O.Company and its unfortunate demise. He justified that with the greed that had taken over Mr. Booth and Mr. Harmon. Since he was successful with the Occidental Company, his hotel, Eastman Kodak, the Weekly Page, and Standard Optical there was no reason not to try for more. As he was leaving the office he remembered that he had an appointment at the YMCA. He became a member to have a place to meet other men and exercise. He wanted to stay in good shape. Since Rudolph was so well endowed with muscles and such he thought it would be a good way to maintain himself. He met many men who were there for the same reason of mixing business with pleasure.

When Wallace arrived home he was greeted with Eveline's long list of social involvements. She and Rose Haynes had become great friends. They had been working on suffrage campaign ideas and had attended many meetings. Rose asked her if they had considered joining the Geneva Country Club. Eveline told her she would ask Wallace. She thought it would be a good way for them to be in the social circuit. Dr. Haynes would be glad to sponsor them. Wallace thought he might need to see him for a check up anyway. They could talk about it then. Wallace reminded Eveline that his birthday was in a few days. She told him that she knew that. He asked if anything was being planned for it. She admitted that she could not top some of his other birthdays. She reminded him that he forgot her birthday last September. The only person other than her mother that remembered was Rudolph. Wallace admitted that he had been preoccupied with work and he apologized. He told her that she did not need to do anything this year. She replied, "Good, I wasn't planning anything." He thought she was rather short with him but he understood. Wallace told her about the new company that was being formed while they had dinner. He told her about the job he was offered and that he was planning on accepting it. Eveline looked at him and said, "I don't care what you do with your work as long as you don't keep moving me around." She made new friends and was part of the suffrage movement and she was satisfied where they lived. She informed him that they would soon need to have a better place in which to live. Wallace agreed and thought it might be time to settle into a real home. She wanted to have a place that could be used for entertaining and be able to have overnight guests. She laughed when she mentioned overnight guest. She wanted to give Rudolph a nicer atmosphere than he received last time in Geneva. Wallace thought to himself that Rudolph seemed very satisfied with his arrangements. Wallace told her that he was interested in the plot of land up the street. She knew the corner he was speaking about.

The next day, Wallace walked to the hotel to discuss the job offer. Mr. Preston was delighted that Wallace made his decision so quickly. He told Wallace he liked fast thinking people. They discussed the timeline for the company to begin operations. Wallace explained that he needed to give Standard Optical his resignation. Mr. Preston looked at him in a strange way. Wallace asked if there was a problem with that. Mr. Preston smiled and said; "I thought that a man like you would take on both jobs at the same time." Wallace was taken back with such a suggestion. He asked if the job required full time. Mr. Preston thought it would consume most of his day. Wallace thought that he probably could do both jobs. He had Standard Optical organized and could do much of that in the evening. He told Mr. Preston that it was possible to do both and he would begin as soon as next Monday. The new company was named The Safe-Edge Company. The factory would be located on the lakefront by the Patent Cereal Company. Wallace would have an office next to Mr. Preston. He decided that since Eveline was so busy with her social engagements and Rudolph's frequent visits he could have time enough to devote to both companies. He had been thinking of ways to accumulate extra income for a building fund for his new home. The type of house he wanted to build would be more expensive than most homes. He wanted a place similar to the Martin House in Buffalo and knew it would be at least four times more than the average home which was $2,750.00. He was not interested in the same size as the Buffalo home. However, something on that line would be perfect on the corner of Washington Street and Nursery Avenue. He told Mr. Preston that his income would be used to build his new home. He was impressed with such long range planning and accounting for various funds to cover all the expenses of such an undertaking. They agreed to meet the next Monday morning to get the advertising underway.

Wallace was thinking how he was going to approach Eveline with his new work schedule as he went home from work. When he came into the apartment she was in the kitchen preparing dinner. She did not say too much to him and Wallace wondered what happened to create such a quiet reception. He asked her if she was all right. She turned to him and said, "She was tired of doing all the housework." She informed him again that they needed to move to a larger place and she wanted a maid. Wallace thought that would be a perfect time to tell her about his new job and schedule. He would let her think that he was working extra jobs to get enough money to build a new house for her. He hoped that might make her be more appreciative of his time and labor. He told her about his new schedule and was glad it all worked out so they could think about moving in another year. Eveline was so excited about the house idea that she did not seem to care what Wallace's working schedule would be. He told her he would be at work from 8AM until at least midnight during the week. Since she did not react to the times he figured it was fine. During dinner she told Wallace that Rose had a maid and that Dr. Haynes did not want her to get herself mussed up. Eveline insisted that she was planning to take the same attitude as of tonight. She informed Wallace that the same maid was hired for their place as of tomorrow. She was not doing any more cleaning for them. Wallace was surprised at her sudden change of attitude. He thought better of discussing the matter and figured it was the Women's Rights thing taking over. As long as he had the money he would do anything to keep her happy. He decided that it was time to set up an allowance for her. Wallace felt that would keep Eveline in better control. He would give her a weekly allowance for food, housekeeping, and her personal items. The annual average income for two people was about $1000. He wanted to see what she would say when he offered her $10 per week. When she heard the amount she let out one of her squeals. Wallace made a face and knew he made a hit with her. She informed him that Rose only got $5 per week. Wallace suggested he go down to that amount. Eveline told him that would not be necessary because she had better taste than Rose. Wallace laughed and said, "You both have the same high price tags." Eveline made a face and left the kitchen with the dishes undone. Wallace sat and thought how easy that was to have bought her off. Now he was free to do as he pleased.

Wallace was reading the mail and the Geneva Daily News after dinner. He received his semi-annual report of the economic conditions of his investments and of the national economy. Ford Motor Company had produced 78,440 cars and had built 22,000 trucks. Ford was still the leader of manufacturing with Willys-Overland cars only at 28,572 manufactured in the year. The average price for a new car was $941.00 and Henry Ford decided to slash the price of a Model T by $80. He felt that by reducing the price that would attract thousands of new buyers. Wallace thought that was a great marketing plan. He was going to implement that idea in the Safe-Edge Company. There was another report that New Mexico and Arizona were the 47th and 48th states added to the union. A funny note was at the bottom of the report that Cracker Jacks were now putting a prize in the bottom of each box. Wallace made a face and laughed when he read that. He did that in Buffalo with the HO cereal box prizes that could be redeemed at Hengerers Department Store. He knew he was ahead of his time. The last piece of news he read about was a proposition in the federal government to implement an income tax. The officials in Washington were debating the idea of taxing incomes of individuals who were making over $3,500.00 per year. If that were to become law people such as himself and Dr. Haynes would have to give up a portion of their income to the government. He was not very happy with that article.

Wallace went to work the next day at Standard Optical. He met with his bosses to discuss his proposition for a change in his work schedule. He explained that Mr. Preston and Mr. H Lynn Henry, who they all knew, were opening a new company in town. Wallace emphasized that there was no competition involved with Standard Optical. He wanted to work early in the morning and later in the afternoon instead of a full day. They asked why he needed two jobs. Wallace played the poor man routine with the needy and neglected wife. He explained that his wife had expensive tastes and wanted to have a maid and a home of their own. She demanded that they move from their apartment as soon as possible. He thought that since he was young and energetic he could accomplish and be successful at two jobs. When he finished his performance they looked at him and said, "Amazing, we all have wives like that and maybe we should all have two jobs." They thought it would be fine as long as their profits and advertising maintained the levels they expected. Wallace assured them he would do his best. He proposed a new idea for advertising while they were meeting. It was directed toward women. After all the times he saw Hilda fussing with her glass chain he thought about a gift with a purchase of eyewear. Women would be given a variety of glass chains with beads and decorations that would compliment the outfit that was being worn. The kit might also include a lotion for cleaning the glasses, a cloth or paper to safely clean the eyewear, and a sample of sun wear. The sample would not be of the highest quality but would give the customer an idea of what sun wear might feel and look like. His bosses laughed and wondered if they were turning into a costume company. Wallace reminded them that people liked gifts especially when they think it is free. That is good marketing. Without any further discussion they approved of this addition to the line of products.

After a long day of finishing the work for Standard Optical, Wallace went home. As he went into the apartment he wondered what he would be greeted with this time. Eveline had been occupied with Rose for the past few days and they had been in Seneca Falls working on newsletters about why women need more rights. Everywhere he went he was bombarded with posters and accusations of how men had exploited women. As he came to the front door of the apartment he heard a familiar voice.

He walked in and there was Rudolph, Eveline and Rose. They were having the best conversation about how upset men were over all the ruckus about women. Rose spoke first to Wallace and was pleasant and reported that she and Eveline were the luckiest women in town. Wallace asked her why. She told him, "We have husbands who let us do what we want and pay for everything." While she was saying that both she and Eveline had their arms around Rudolph. They looked like they were having their portrait painted. Wallace was not sure of what they had planned for Rudolph but knew Rudolph had enough to pleasure two people. Rudolph was happy to see Wallace. It had been awhile since he had been to Geneva. He told Wallace he hoped they would have time to go out for a drink at the tavern. Wallace thought that might be fun but asked what had happened with everyone. They acted like they had been at a party. Rudolph announced that they had been at the convention and had drinks and food. That answered Wallace's question. Then, Rudolph told Wallace that they were posing for a portrait. Wallace shook his head and said, "You do look like you are posing all arm in arm." Eveline piped up in a tipsy voice and said, "My Wallace is very perceptive." Rudolph winked at Wallace when she said that. Wallace wanted to know where this portrait would be hung. Rudolph explained it was part of the convention being held in November and the portraits of those most active in the movement would be honored. Wallace told them that he was happy for them and hoped they had a good time.

Rudolph and Wallace escorted Rose to her apartment on their way to the tavern. She was appreciative of such gentlemen. After she left Rudolph explained that he saw a small tavern by the train station when he arrived earlier in the day. It was a dark and relatively quiet place. It was Wednesday night and not many people were around. Wallace wondered what Rudolph was up to. They ordered their drinks and Rudolph paid. He sipped his whiskey slowly and watched Wallace. After some conversation about what was happening he told Wallace he missed both of them. Wallace thought he meant Eveline and him. He was mistaken because Rudolph meant Winston. Rudolph said that he had seen Winston in Rochester and realized it had been awhile since they were together. He told Wallace that Eveline and Rose were going to a convention that would require them to be out of town for an evening. He wondered if they could set up something. While they were talking, Rudolph's leg kept nudging Wallace's leg. Wallace asked if he liked Winston or was he just going along with things. Rudolph looked at Wallace and told him he would not mind being in Geneva without Winston. He missed Wallace's style and the way he did things. Wallace wanted a little more clarification on the style part. Rudolph flashed one of his handsome smiles and announced that he wanted to be a partner in business and pleasure. He wanted a closer connection in Geneva with Eveline and him. He was not sure if Winston needed to fit in and admitted he did not like to share things. Wallace liked the idea of not so many people involved in too many things. He liked the idea that Eveline was part of the action but there were other issues she did not need to know about. Wallace told him that it would be good for them to spend some time together when the ladies were away. Rudolph was happy for that and hoped Winston would not find out. Wallace did not think there would be any way he would know. A police officer walked by them and tipped his hat as they walked back to the apartment. Rudolph mentioned how much he liked men who wore uniforms. Wallace asked what that was supposed to mean. Rudolph jokingly told him to wear one sometime and he would find out. Wallace chuckled and asked who would be incarcerated. When they got back Eveline asked what they had talked about. Rudolph told her that he mentioned the out of town convention and that he might be coming to Geneva to visit. Eveline thought that was nice for them to have time alone. She asked if Winston was coming too. They shook their heads. She did not say anything. Rudolph took the last train back to Rochester and he told Wallace he was hiring new entertainers at the hotel tomorrow and wanted to be at work early. Wallace thanked him for his good work at the hotel. Rudolph hugged Eveline and shook Wallace's hand and winked at him. Wallace wished tonight was the night for the visit. He left and they got ready for bed.

The Geneva Daily News had a full-page news article on the front page that the Titanic sank in the North Atlantic. It was April 14 and the unsinkable ocean liner was on its maiden voyage when it struck an iceberg. There were over 1500 passengers that had drowned. Among the deceased was John Jacob Astor a wealthy tycoon. How could such a thing happen? The largest ship ever built was guaranteed not to sink. According to the article women and children were the first to use the lifeboats. There were not enough lifeboats for all the passengers. How could a ship line have a new ship without enough lifeboats? People were talking about the mishap all day. There were some people in town who were waiting to hear about relatives who were on the ship. They did not know if they were dead or alive. Wallace was reading the paper in the office before Mr. Preston came to work. He walked into the office and they discussed the Titanic. He asked if he had read that Clara Barton had died. Wallace knew she had founded the American Red Cross. He remembered his mother telling the story that Clara Barton was at the opening of a chapter of the Red Cross in Rochester. He laughed and told Mr. Preston that his mother fainted in front of Clara Barton because she was pregnant with him. They talked about what funny things mothers remember.

Mr. Preston discussed the salary and commissions that Wallace would receive for his work at The Safe-Edge Company. As he was telling Wallace about his annual salary he thought about the income tax issue. He would definitely be taxed. He calculated as Mr. Preston was talking that he would make well over $15,000.00 per year. That did not include income from his investments and commissions. One of his first jobs was to establish a logo for the company. Wallace was happy to announce that he had some ideas for consideration. He thought that each razor should be stamped with the name and with the words Geneva, NY. In that way the city will receive advertising through the distribution of the product both in the United States and abroad. He thought a logo could be a picture of the razor with the printing on it with the words "Safege for Sure" Mr. Preston thought they were off to a great start. Wallace offered to use his import and export company as a means to get the new product to Europe and the Orient. Mr. Preston was amazed that he even had knowledge of such things much less have access to the company. Wallace smiled and thought, "Little does he know about Occidental and that I am the owner."

1912 went on record as the "summer-less year." There were heavy rains with floods everywhere. Any one who owned a car was reluctant to drive very far. If you drove off of the main streets the dirt roads were mostly mud with deep gullies. It was reported that Geneva now had 300 people who owned automobiles. During the summer it was rare to see a car on the streets. People resorted to the horse and buggy. Wallace found a garage that he rented for his cars. After he started the sun wear line of products at Standard Optical the sales for those items was very disappointing. For the first time in Wallace's advertising career he was not successful. He was worried that his luck might be changing. When September arrived the fall and winter fashions were being advertised. Women now liked the idea of having a choice in how they looked when they wore either regular eyewear or sun wear. The chains and jewelry combinations gave many options for high fashion. The newly named Seneca Hotel was having a show called "High Style" for women with the latest fashions including accessories from all the local shoppes. Mr. Preston was happy to tell Wallace that accessories were a major part of the event. The fashion show was an opening event for the newly organized hotel. The Seneca Hotel was advertised as "Geneva's Metropolitan Hotelry that offered the Highest Grade Table Service in Town." It guaranteed prompt limousine service; a driver would come to your home and escort you to the front door of the hotel and return you to your home when you were finished dining. The sign in the front of the hotel read, "Dining, Dancing, and Eating in the Highest Style in Town." When Eveline and Rose saw the advertisement for the hotel in the paper they wanted to know when they were going to go. Eveline told Rose what a grand time they had at the hotel in Rochester and that Wallace had re-organized the place making the entertainment the most fun in Rochester.

The Woman's Rights gathering was coming soon and Rose and Eveline were planning their overnight event.

Wallace asked if she had mentioned it to Rudolph so he could plan his visit to Geneva. She told him that she had done so. Wallace mentioned that he and Rudolph would go to the Seneca to see what the atmosphere was like compared to the Seneca Powers. Eveline told him that would be fun for them to do but hoped they did not find any one better than her. He told her that was not why they would be going. He liked the idea that it was a stylish place and that they would both appreciate the style for different reasons. Eveline smiled as she left the room and said, "You both are very stylish, that's why I like you." Wallace continued to read the newspaper and came across an article about the sale of the Rose Hill Farm. As he read about it he thought about Sybil Rose; the woman he met on the train to the Exposition. He wondered if she was part of the family. He remembered her saying that she lived near Geneva as a child and that her father owned a large farm. The article explained that the 300-acre farm was sold to Edgar Broody of New York City for $40,000.00. The entire operation including servants and equipment was part of the deal. Further down the page was an announcement that on October 15, the Geneva City Hall Bill passed. The vote was 656 for the building of it and 190 votes against it. He thought what a great addition to downtown and it would be adjacent to the YMCA.

Eveline and Rose left Geneva by train for their meeting. They were excited about staying in a hotel. Wallace hoped they had a good time. He knew that Eveline had made certain Rudolph knew when they were leaving and that he was arriving later that day. Wallace made a point of getting home early so he could be ready for Rudolph. They would finally have time together. He hoped they could make plans for many things to come. Wallace wanted to get

Rudolph more involved in the operations of business in Geneva since he had done such a good job at the hotel in Rochester. He saw the relationship to have advantages for both of them in business and definitely pleasure. While he was waiting for him to arrive he glanced at the newspaper. The new income tax law was passed and any idle capital would be assessed a tax. When Wallace read that he looked at the ceiling and thought there goes part of my income. There was great fear about a war in Europe and what that might mean for the United States. There was a knock on the door. As Wallace got up to answer it he said to himself, "I better get that house built soon." He opened the door expecting Rudolph but it was Winston. Wallace looked confused as Winston walked in. He told him that Eveline let him know she and Rose were going away for the night. Wallace thought that Eveline assured him that only Rudolph knew this information. Why was Winston here instead? He wondered if Rudolph was showing up next? Then what was going to happen? He wanted to establish a better relationship with Rudolph not Winston. They sat down and Winston informed him that he saw Rudolph. Wallace waited for more details. Rudolph was angry that Eveline told him the same information that Winston was told. Rudolph told Winston that he could go instead. Winston was very happy to be in Geneva. All he brought was his Leter Buck cologne. Wallace was not very happy with what Eveline had pulled again. She was deliberately vague the last time about the invitation. She told Wallace she informed Rudolph but failed to mention she had also invited Winston. What was she trying to create? He thought she liked Rudolph better than Winston. She referred to Winston as the common boy. Wallace explained how he was feeling about the confusion. Winston assured him that Rudolph was angry and would not be coming to Geneva. Winston was happy for that and said, "Now we can do what we want." Wallace was not pleased with any of it.

Wallace could not wait for Eveline to return the next day. He needed to find out what was going on and why all the dishonesty. Winston behaved like he once did when he felt that Wallace was not being his closest friend. He left early that morning to go back to Rochester. Rudolph never did arrive. Wallace became more disgusted as he waited for Eveline. He stayed home from work that morning. Finally at 11:30, Eveline and Rudolph appeared. They were very happy to report about their "Rally for Rights." Wallace was not sure what was happening. Everything seemed like a dream. Eveline began by saying that he was probably mixed up about last night. Wallace assured her that he was more than mixed up. She admitted that she told both Winston and Rudolph about her trip. She did that so that in case Rudolph decided to go with Rose and her that Winston would not mind keeping him company. Rudolph admitted that he manipulated Winston a little to make him feel he was angry. Wallace told them how disgusted he was with the games that had been played. He told Eveline that if she continues playing one against the other he would get rid of her. She had done enough manipulating and he was sick of it. Rudolph stood there watching Wallace tear into her. He told Rudolph that he had enough of his behavior too. After what they learned about his involvement with them in Buffalo and the trial in New York he was not winning many points in the honesty area. If he wanted to be business partners and companions all this must stop!

Chapter 48

THE MARCH 3, 1913 edition of the Geneva Daily News featured the inauguration of Woodrow Wilson. There was a photograph of the president in the largest inaugural parade ever. Thousands of spectators turned out to see the President and Mrs. Wilson. Part of the front page had an article about the impeachment of Governor William Sulzer of New York and Mayor Martin Glynn of Geneva became acting governor. Dr. Samuel Haynes was featured as part of the political news explaining that he had been elected the chairman of the Republican Committee in Geneva. The news covered another of the many reports of tensions building in Europe with the talk of a major war. Wallace read about a Photoplay Palace called the Regent Theater that was showing moving pictures. He asked Eveline if she would be interested in seeing a moving picture. She thought it might be fun. He wanted to know if she preferred the balcony or the main floor. She thought the balcony would be better because it was up and away from the common people. Wallace laughed and read the bottom of the advertisement that clearly emphasized that the management reserved the right to eject any and all disorderly or objectionable people. It was 15 cents to sit in the balcony and 10 cents on the main floor. Eveline told him that the wealthier people would be in the balcony away from the ordinary crowd. He looked at her and told her she was uppity. She made a face as she left the room.

Wallace had been doing some investigating about the parcel of land on the corner of Washington Street and Nursery Avenue. He found out that Mr. Robert W. Henson owned the land. It was a vast amount of land. Wallace located Mr. Henson and negotiated a deal for the sale of the land. A mortgage was secured for the property for $1,500.00. Eveline and he signed the papers for the mortgage. Eveline was somewhat uneasy about it being so far out of town. There were no other houses in sight. She told Wallace that he was putting her in the deep dark forest. He reminded her that the type of house he was planning would have to be away from other places because it was going to be like nothing any one in Geneva had seen before. He had a feeling that the townspeople would be adamant about such an outlandish structure.

Wallace needed to hire an architect to design the home. He wanted to be certain that this person would accommodate his tastes and style. It was to follow Frank Lloyd Wright's designs of a prairie style home. He investigated the cost and complexities of commissioning Wright to do the work. It was far more expensive than what Wallace wanted to spend and Wright's involvement with customers had changed. A group of people who were formerly allegiant to Frank Lloyd Wright left his studio and created their own group. Wallace remembered reading in the Architectural Record in 1904 that a group of people had formed a school of architects that were called "architectural protestants." Their work was derived from Louis Sullivan and Frank Lloyd Wright. These architects were concerned with residential design and took on the title of "Prairie School." Wallace thought it might be possible to find someone there who could assist in his designs. As Eveline was looking at old issues of Ladies Home Journal she found a plan for a home similar to what Wallace wanted. It was called the "fireproof house." Frank Lloyd Wright had designed it in 1905 and it cost $5000.00 to build. It was constructed mainly of concrete and glass. Wallace thought that he might be able to find someone locally who would work with him to design the house. It may not be a Wright plan or a Prairie School plan but could be a combination of the two that would make it a signature home with all his ideas.

Wallace sketched the house so it would look much like the fireproof house. He wanted his house to be the most modern place possible. He wanted a garage that would have enough room for his two cars. The house and garage would each have electric lights, heating, and a water supply. The kitchen would have modern conveniences; there would be a gas stove instead of the wood-burning stove. The house would have hot water for bathing, cooking, and laundry. The use of electricity was relatively new to homes but Wallace wanted every area of the house supplied with outlets and switches that would turn lights on and off from different areas. He wanted a central vacuum system, washtubs, and a washing machine in the basement. If the house was to be a prairie style home it needed to have many windows. He liked Wright's philosophy that the building should emerge out of its natural surroundings as if it had always been there. The property was on a hill on a corner. He remembered the idea of bringing the inside out and the outside in. He sketched windows everywhere totaling 110 panes of glass with many large openings throughout the house to let in the light. He wanted it to be like the house Frank Lloyd Wright designed on East Boulevard in

Rochester. He visualized a background of tall trees that would give the illusion of grandeur when coming up the street. He remembered the carefully trimmed privet hedges at the Exposition so he sketched those around the perimeter of the property. There would be large gardens with a circular pond and a fountain in the backyard just as he remembered it from the Pan-Am. He included fireplaces in his plan. There would be one in the main living space. A set of French doors would be on either side of the fireplace that would enter into a conservatory. The fireplace would be massive in its appearance and would create ample heat. He wanted the mortar around the bricks to be reddish-pink just like the Larkin Building in Buffalo. He had a philosophy about how a home should feel for guests and owners. He sketched a plaque with the inscription "El hogar dichoso es un cielo mas temprano." The dining room would have starlights built into the wood beamed ceiling with sidelights on either side of the built in cabinets. The conservatory would have the same cabinets on either side of the French doors. He wanted the moldings and woodwork made to look like a mahogany stain. The main floor would have the largest rooms. Frank Lloyd Wright believed that the public rooms should be large, inviting, and airy. The sleeping rooms should be smaller and more intimate. The main bedroom would have access to the bathroom for privacy from the hallway. The center hall and stairway would be huge with a large stained glass window illuminating the area. There would be a room on the second floor with a fireplace and French doors leading to a sleeping porch. He wanted a warm spot in the winter with open air from the porch in the summer. The rear of the building would have a smaller servant quarters that would have a small sitting area, bedroom and a clothing chute to the basement where the clothes would be laundered. He wanted a telephone installed in the house. There were very few homes with electricity, hot water, and telephone service but he would be one of the first. He laughed when he thought of who he might call because there was not that many people that had a telephone. He created a list of every item he thought should be in the house including central heating. There was a radiator and boiler factory in Geneva. He knew that an adequate heating system for the size of the house could be manufactured and installed. Fortunately, the sewer and water system came up to the corner of the street.

He began sketching the exterior of the house. It would be built with a low-hipped roof and cantilevered eaves. He knew that the large eaves had a function other than appearance. They would help temperature fluctuations during the day and throughout the year. It would reduce overheating by shading a portion of the exterior walls during the summer. The innovative part of the design had to do with the roof. The second floor ceilings would be less than a foot from the top of the roof. Vents would feed the resulting small air space from the rooms below to a central chimney that would create constant flow of air. The house needed symmetry and geometric shaped areas to make it an authentic replica of a prairie style home. Wallace wanted various levels of horizontal and vertical layers on the exterior. He wanted both the inside and outside to be primarily geometric spaces, straight edges, rectangles, and squares that would be most noticeable in the windows. The windows would help define all sides of the house as well as the inside. The exterior would be constructed of stucco and wood, with wood frames around the windows. The roofline would incorporate a gutter system not obvious to the house. The corners, rooflines, and vertical, horizontal aspects of the house would be geometric and join at 90-degree angles. He wanted clean order to his home so the house would look modern in one hundred years.

Eveline had been with Rose for lunch and she was excited to tell her about Wallace's recent land purchase. She described the type of home he was planning to build. Rose told Eveline that her father was a contractor. He had built many of the larger buildings in Geneva. Rose gave Eveline her father's address and information. She hoped he could help when Wallace was ready for a contractor. When Eveline got home that evening she gave Wallace the information. He was happy to find out that people they knew might be able to help with the project. She reminded Wallace that she would provide him with all the information he needed. He laughed when she said that and thought whatever keeps her happy. He showed her what he had accomplished and asked if she had any thing to add. Eveline looked at the ideas and the sketches. She thought they were wonderful. She wondered what he was planning to do with the basement. She told him that a room with a fireplace would be perfect for men to use as a social area. She knew that the women would never go into the basement but the men would like that type of stuff. They could smoke cigars, play games, talk business and do whatever men do in places like that. Wallace smirked at the "whatever they do part" but thought it would be a perfect idea. The house would have three fireplaces but who would keep them going in the winter? Eveline told him they could hire help. She suggested that if there was to be a pond and fountain in the yard there should be fish in it during the summer. She thought a concrete fish tank in the basement room would be a perfect place to keep the fish during the winter. It could be in the south side of the room with windows giving light to the fish tank. Wallace agreed that he forgot about fish and storing them in the winter. He did remember to include a filling and drain system for the pond. Eveline smiled and told him that together they would make it a perfect home. Now, who could they find to design the house?

Wallace made an appointment with Rose's father to discuss the building of his home. When he met with Mr. Nigel his first question was did he have an architect? Wallace admitted that he attempted to commission Frank Lloyd Wright but he was not accepting work of this type. He admitted that the fee was more than he wanted to pay. Mr. Nigel looked at the sketches and the extensive list of things to be constructed and included in the home. He was certain he could help Wallace secure a draftsman and that together they could produce a home to his liking. Mr. Nigel did warn Wallace that a building as unusual as his plan was going to be met with criticism. He thought he made a good choice of property considering it was out of town and by itself. He was warned that the townspeople were a very close-knit group and would resist new ideas. Fortunately, Wallace had established a good reputation in town and was not worried about what people might think. Mr. Nigel mentioned a young draftsman he knew from Rochester who was intrigued with the prairie designs. He would notify him and hoped they could get together in a week.

The Safege Company production lines were maintaining the quotas for shipments. The consumer reports were all positive. Wallace was adding catchy phrases to the advertisement. He featured a photograph of a man's freshly shaven face and a hand moving over it with the slogan, "Fresh and smooth as silk." Another marketing idea was to offer a quantity of razors in a package for substantially less money than single purchases. Wallace thought of a way to store old razors. He read reports that people were being cut with old razors when they were disposed of. One woman was reported as nearly dying from an infection she caught when she was cut by an old razor that was in the garbage. Wallace devised a receptacle that old razors could be placed in. It would be a gift when you bought the quantity size package of razors. The additional advertising campaigns were set to be out for the public in one month.

The owners of the razor company decided to expand what they were producing. They asked Wallace if he had any ideas about the other ways they could offer more variety. He thought they might consider a department that would manufacture other blade type instruments. Wallace suggested cutlery, scissors, and army knives. He thought that since a war was on the doorstep of the country they could market a pocketknife with the name "Army Knife." It could have a variety of attachments within the container of the knife. There could be a bottle opener, a screwdriver, knife blade, and a needle. All the suggestions were considered for the next stage of the company and would be ready for production in mid 1914. One of the men at the meeting asked Wallace what he was doing on Washington Street. Wallace asked, "Why?" The man told him that he heard that he had purchased a large plot of land. Wallace explained where it was and why he liked that area. He deliberately made it sound like he was doing something that most people would not understand. The conversation moved into the story that someone in town had rumored that Wallace was odd in the things he liked. Wallace found that to be an interesting comment. He explained that he was not odd just progressive and willing to move into the future. The man who started the conversation was an old time Genevean who resisted change. Mr. Lynn Henry spoke up and supported Wallace and said, "Whatever Wallace comes up with will be a gold mine." The old businessman sneered at them while he puffed on his cigar.

Mr. Nigel made a point of coming to Wallace and Eveline's apartment to tell them that the young man in Rochester was willing to come to Geneva to discuss drafting the house plans. They were delighted that Mr. Nigel was so willing to assist in the planning and contracting of their home. He admitted that his daughter Rose was determined to have him come forward to help. Wallace jokingly said, "These women know how to get their way." Mr. Nigel admitted that women seem to be getting their way more and more these days. Eveline piped up and reminded him that Rose and she were very much a part of the Women's Rights Movement. Mr. Nigel shook his head and said, "I know, I hear about it all the time." A meeting was set for the next day at Mr. Nigel's office on Grove Street. Wallace thanked him and told him he would bring everything. Wallace looked at Eveline and said, "This was a man's meeting." She said nothing.

Wallace arrived just as the man from Rochester was coming up the street with Mr. Nigel. He introduced himself as Thomas Adams as they walked into the office. Thomas had recently graduated from Mechanics Institute and had studied drafting and architecture. He was familiar with the Prairie School and how they had separated from Frank Lloyd Wright. Mr. Nigel suggested that all three of them work together from start to finish so that the house could be completed in six months. Wallace said, "That would be a good present for my wife." They laughed. Mr. Nigel assured them that he had the crew, supplies, and enthusiasm to take on such a project. He wanted to be the first to build a structure like this. Thomas asked for a few weeks to draw up the plans. Mr. Nigel and Wallace thought that was fair and the cost of the building would be determined then. Wallace had a meeting at Standard Optical. He excused himself while Mr. Nigel and Thomas were planning the stages for the construction.

When Wallace got home that evening, Eveline was excited to hear about the plans. He explained what they were doing and that the house might be completed by Christmastime. Eveline was ecstatic to think about a home at Christmas. She could not wait to tell her family. Wallace asked what his father and mother were going to think. Eveline said, "Your mother will love it, your father will hate it." Wallace agreed. Then, she gave Wallace a letter from Rudolph. It had been addressed to him but Eveline had already opened the letter. Wallace was not happy with this intrusion. She informed him that when it comes to Rudolph everything about him was her business. When Wallace heard this he did not say anything but knew that all the mail was now going to be sent to his office. Samuel Haynes mentioned that same tactic about Rose. It had to be the Women's Rights Movement that was making them crazy. Instead of reading the letter he looked at Eveline and told her to tell him what was in the letter. She was happy to announce that Rudolph wanted to move to Geneva now that he had completed his goals for the hotel. Wallace was angry and told her that she was involving herself with his business dealings. He told her that if she continued to manipulate his life that she would not be moving to 380 Washington Street. She could return to her family in Rochester. She asked, "So, who will be moving in Winston and Rudolph?" He told her that was the last warning.

Wallace decided to see how well the telephone system worked from Standard Optical to Rochester. Rudolph had a telephone installed in the office at the Seneca Powers Hotel so people could call for reservations. Using the new telephone system would be quicker than letter writing or telegraph. When Wallace called it took awhile for the operators to connect the line from city to city. This was a new process and usually ended up a dead line. After five minutes he heard a women say, "Seneca-Powers Hotel." At first, he did not know what to say. He asked for Rudolph Williams. He heard the woman say, "This isn't a reservation." Wallace laughed to think they did not know who it was and that he could hear voices so far away. Rudolph came on the line and asked how he could help. Wallace asked, "Do you know who this is?" Rudolph said, "Hey Wallace." Someone in the background could be heard saying it must be a miracle. Wallace explained that he got the letter after Eveline read it first. Rudolph agreed that she needed to be put in her place. He asked if the offer to move to Geneva was still a possibility. Wallace said it would be possible in a few months. A new person would need to be hired in Rochester and the job at the Board of Commerce was opening then. Rudolph explained that he had hired a new person at the hotel who had majored in business at Mechanics Institute. He would train him for the position. Wallace jokingly asked how much training he was planning for the new man. Rudolph laughed and told Wallace that was his job to tame the new guy. He told Rudolph about the construction of the house and all the advertising plans that were going on in Geneva. They ended the call with a plan for him to come to Geneva in a few weeks.

Two weeks later Wallace met with Mr. Nigel and Thomas. The plans were drawn and ready for Wallace's approval. As he was looking at the numerous pages of diagrams and dimensions he realized that the house would be over 3,500 square feet. Thomas reminded him that the Martin house was almost four times larger. After the survey, Mr. Nigel had marked the land for the house. Wallace thought it was time to discuss the financial aspect of this endeavor. Mr. Nigel was used to building structures that were large, unique, and generally not for the ordinary person. The average home construction price was around $2500.00. The cost for Wallace's house would be $6,000.00. Any extra items for above average accessories and highlights would increase the cost. Wallace agreed to begin immediately. He had already been to the Geneva Savings Bank to apply for a mortgage to begin construction. He would finalize the details with the bank later that day. After they were finished with the meeting they walked up the street to make sure the land was surveyed and the position of the house was correct and met Wallace's approval. Luckily, many of the trees did not need to be cut down. The foundation and house could be built with minimal destruction to the landscape. Wallace had already planned to have rows of maple trees on the street side with privet hedges on the perimeter of the lot. He stood on the corner and tried to envision a house such as this sitting by itself. Thomas said, "When it is completed it will sit in a regal and timeless position." Mr. Nigel remarked that, "This is a revolutionary architectural style, I can't wait to see what Geneva will think."

Construction began the next day. Eveline and Rose strolled up Washington Street with their parasols open. It was a sunny and warm April day. When they approached the corner all they could see were men digging, hauling, and stacking blocks for the foundation. Much of the dirt coming from the hole for the foundation was being spread around to build up the land so the house would stand high above street level. It was windy and the dust was blowing everywhere. The women looked out of place in the midst of this dust storm. Mr. Nigel came over to them and told them a place like this was not for ladies. Rose smiled at her father and asked when he was building her a house like this. He smiled and said, "Ask your husband Samuel." Rose said, "Probably never." Mr. Nigel thought sarcastically it was too bad she could not get everything she wanted. They turned and walked back down the street.

Eveline told Wallace about their walk to the construction site. He wanted to know if she was being bossy to all the men. She did not find that too amusing but told him about Rose's hope for a new home. Wallace agreed that was probably not going to happen. He told Eveline that he was only going to go to the construction site when Mr. Nigel called him. The plans were good and he felt they were very capable men. He had enough to do at his own jobs. He and Eveline had an appointment at the bank the next day for a loan. She asked if she was the owner. Wallace told her, "Not yet." She was not sure what that was supposed to mean. He told her maybe later on. They agreed that they would go to the building site on the weekends or when people visited from Rochester. Wallace informed her that Rudolph was coming in a week for a visit. Eveline could not wait to show him her future house.

Wallace thought it was strange that all of a sudden it was hers. It was better to not discuss that remark.

Rudolph made plans to arrive on Friday evening and stay until Sunday. Eveline had made arrangements for Rose, Rudolph and herself to go to a rally for rights on Saturday. Wallace thought it would be polite of her to ask if he wanted to go with them. She informed him that Rudolph already knew about the rally. Wallace knew that he would need to have a serious talk with Rudolph about the amount of involvement he had with the women. The rest of the weekend would be spent enjoying the lake front park and showing Rudolph their new home site. Eveline asked Wallace if he had any plans for the numbers of servants they might be employing. He was under the impression that they might have one since the room in the rear of the house could be servant's quarters. She thought that one might not be adequate. Wallace wanted to know why. She wanted at least two servants. She needed to have one for the shopping and cooking and the other for cleaning, laundry, and waiting the table for meals. Wallace asked if she thought she was living in a millionaire's home. She told him that if he wanted to be a millionaire someday he should start by acting like one. Millionaires have everything done for them. Wallace could not argue about the millionaire part but had not thought about operating such a property. Maybe they would need a groundskeeper. Eveline smiled and said, "You better have Mr. Nigel build a servant house on the property because the back room won't be large enough."

While he spoke to Eveline about extra servants and a possible grounds keeper he knew what he must do. It was a clear to him that he could now get both Winston and Rudolph to Geneva. Rudolph was wealthy enough to have a home of his own. Winston could get a job in a factory and be the groundskeeper. He would discuss the possibilities with Rudolph this weekend. He remembered that Winston threatened to get a job at Patent Cereal Company. He thought that the servant house could be at the end of the property a few hundred feet from the garage. It would not need to be the same design or quality as the main house. He would discuss that with Thomas and Mr. Nigel. He told Eveline that she did have a good idea about the need for additional help. She wanted to know if she would be in charge of hiring the housekeeping staff. Wallace told her that was a good job for her. She could be the queen of the house and oversee their work. Eveline liked that title because it made her feel like she was finally getting to the top.

The next day Wallace met Mr. Nigel to discuss the additional building for the property. When Wallace described the type of structure he was thinking about, Mr. Nigel said, "It should blend into the environment, not look like a dog coop on the edge of the property." Wallace wanted Thomas' opinion. He made reference to the Martin complex in Buffalo. He emphasized that there was a house built specifically for groundskeepers. He thought a small bungalow would be perfect for the area. Frank Lloyd Wright was noted for designing a large home surrounded by small bungalows. When Wallace heard that he agreed to have that type of house built at the rear section of the property. The cost would be much less than expected. There was no need for a basement because a crawl space under the house would be adequate. The house would have small rooms and minimal facilities. A wood-burning stove would be the main heating source. Mr. Nigel estimated that it could be built for less than what he paid for the land. Wallace agreed to have that included in the building plans.

Wallace told Eveline what the new plans were for the property. She thanked him for listening to her. He wondered why she did not make it look like she knew more than him this time. Maybe she realized that men still have the upper hand. Whatever she thought did not matter. Wallace wrote a letter to Winston explaining what he was proposing. He wanted to know if he was serious about a job at the Patent Cereal Company. If he was interested Wallace could line that up for him. All these things would be happening in early 1914. The house for friends and helpers would be ready after the completion of the main house. Wallace decided he would avoid saying a servant's house. He asked if Winston would be interested in being in charge of the property. He signed the letter and added a short phrase, "Looking to a bright future." He took the letter to the post office instead of a mailbox in hopes it would arrive the next day.

Rudolph arrived on the evening train from Rochester. Eveline was hurrying around getting the apartment in order for him. She was making pot roast because that was the only supper she was successful with. She went to the bakery for a pie because she had no idea of how to make one. Wallace arrived home with the news of his position as Director of the YMCA. He enjoyed his time and new friends there so they unanimously elected him to be the director. Eveline only asked if it would require as much time as his other two jobs. Wallace did not think so; it was a monthly meeting of men who were running the operation. Eveline asked how Winston and Rudolph were going to like that. Wallace asked what she meant. She smiled and reminded him that he was in a place with men and they were all interested in the same thing. There was no comment about that remark. Rudolph arrived at 7PM. He was dressed like he was ready to escort a woman to a ballroom. Eveline thought they should skip dinner and go directly to the Seneca Hotel. She heard that they had dancing and wonderful food there. Wallace said that he needed some time to talk with Rudolph and they could go dancing some other time. Eveline became quiet and stayed out of their way. Wallace asked Rudolph what he thought about starting as Secretary to the Board of Commerce early in 1914. Rudolph hesitated for a moment and agreed that was a perfect time line. The new man he had been training would be ready to take over the manager position by that time after Wallace's approval. He told Wallace he would need to find an apartment to rent for January. It occurred to Wallace that Rudolph could take possession of their apartment with all the furnishings. They would be moving to the new house at Christmas and would be purchasing new furniture. He was certain the landlord would be delighted to have it rented before they left. Rudolph agreed with the idea. Eveline went into one of her squealing sessions that disgusted Wallace. For the first time, Rudolph asked her when she was going to stop acting like that and grow up. She looked shocked when he told her that was immature behavior. Later, he told Wallace that was part of his plan to put her in her place. He even thought the Women's Rights issues were getting out of control. Dinner was very quiet. Eveline said nothing only stared at the two men. They talked about the future of the businesses and the new house. Wallace mentioned his idea for Winston. Rudolph thought that was perfect for him. Eveline acted like she was an outsider after Rudolph's remark about her behavior. Maybe there was a bright future ahead after all.

Chapter 49

WALLACE RECEIVED A LETTER from the Occidental Company regarding the additional razor and cutlery merchandise that would be added to the exports. Wallace needed to send a list of countries that would receive the merchandise. Mr. Burbank suggested in the letter that Wallace not consider any of the new items be sent to the Hong Kong markets. He gave no explanation except that they could discuss it at the annual meeting in New York. Wallace responded to the letter and arranged for the meeting to be in January shortly into 1914. As Wallace finished the letter he thought how much he looked forward to seeing the new Grand Central Station. Things had been quiet in New York City after the trial. He wondered what was going to happen next.

While developing advertising for the two companies in Geneva, the owners asked Wallace if he knew of a printing company that could print large quantities of ads for the variety of products being manufactured. They thought that quantity might reduce the cost of printing. Wallace knew of a place in downtown Geneva that might do well as a printing company. He would investigate the cost and requirements to form a printing company. Wallace was looking for ways to move his money around so he could avoid paying income tax. The owners decided to have Wallace set the company up using a portion of his income from both jobs that would be transferred into the printing corporation. If it were a corporation he would not be the sole person responsible for the income tax issues; it would the corporation's responsibility. They thought Wallace was a genius when he proposed the idea. The men at Standard Optical, Mr. Preston with his Seneca Hotel, and the Safege Company all wanted to be part of the corporation. While they were discussing the plan, Wallace thought, "These guys have no idea what I have arranged with the Occidental Company. I make lots of money that no one knows about. They think this is a new idea." Wallace suggested that they have a different name for the printing corporation. He wanted to have a slogan type name. They thought that was corny but they wanted to know what it would be. Wallace called it "The Goodwin Press." He said it would be a "good win" for all of us. The company would be at 217 Genesee Street. It would be a two-fold operation with the first for printing all the advertisements in their companies and the other businesses that would come to them for their printing. Since they were covering up income they could afford to print for less than other agencies. The Goodwin Press would begin operation in January. Wallace offered to arrange the shipment of the presses and organize the factory. It would be easy for him to do that because of his work for the Weekly Page and the Rochester Post. As he was talking about the plans he thought that Winston could be in charge of the operation. He was trained in Rochester for this type of work. He would discourage Winston from working at the Patent Cereal Company and offer the job as foreman of the printing company. He thought that would give Winston the boost he needed to feel equal. Wallace would still want him to be the groundskeeper but have the printing job as his main work. He wanted to keep

Winston as close to the house as possible; he liked the idea of having a place to go to visit him right on the property. Wallace laughed to himself and thought it sounded like he was building a plantation.

Mr. Nigel reported to Wallace twice a week during the primary construction of the house. Thomas spent many days on the site making certain the structure was being built to the specifications. A house of this type with the complexity of construction and weight bearing beams needed to have proper building methods. The cantilever rooflines and all the open areas for windows made it more difficult to maintain balance and strength to the exterior walls. The conservatory was supported on each end with concrete square pillar type structures that supported the massive panes of glass. The exterior weight bearing walls of the main house were reinforced with the same concrete corners from the ground to the top that joined at right angles to the cantilever roof. The front and rear entrances had a large overhanging flat roof. It mimicked the main roof. Mr. Nigel and Thomas had to decide how such a heavy roof would be supported over the entranceways. They arranged for an iron works company to design huge iron rings that would be fastened into the concrete with decorative iron rods extending to the edge of the roof so the roof would remain flat and sturdy. It gave the entrances a grander appearance than if wooden corner supports were used. Mr. Nigel told Wallace that they would be starting the interior of the house in a few weeks. It was early autumn and they wanted to have the house enclosed so that they could have the furnace working and the electricity turned on. He and Eveline would need to select the interior fixtures. They first needed to select the type of glass and where in the house the glass would be placed. Wallace wanted stained glass windows to be used in the main staircase. He would contact a friend of his who was an artisan of glass design at Mechanics Institute. It would be colored leaded glass with a double matching design of a stem with a bud ready to open. He described it as the beginning of new life. There would be two to exemplify the need for two things to work together for a new beginning. He explained it to Mr. Nigel and he wanted to know if it meant humans or plants. Wallace told him it could be two people or things that grow together into the future. Mr. Nigel shook his head and agreed to install it as he wished. The interior would be exactly like the exterior with matching concrete pillar throughout the stairway and hallway to the second floor. There would be structural subtleties in the walls that would be square that would accentuate the pillars that were weight bearing for the second floor. The fireplaces on each floor would be constructed of reddish brown brick with geometric designs to add depth to the fireplace façade. Wallace was emphatic about the mortar being a reddish-pink; just like the Larkin Building in Buffalo. The lights over the mantel in the main reception room were lion's heads holding the light fixture in their teeth. He wanted to create a masculine atmosphere. Mr. Nigel had the pipes installed in the walls for the central vacuum system. When Wallace saw that he said, "We won't need a maid because the house will clean itself." Eveline did not find that amusing. She had been feeling left out of things lately and did not want the hired help idea eliminated. Wallace was glad she was being less demanding and manipulative these days. He wondered when that was going to change.

Alice sent a letter to Eveline and Wallace asking if they could come to Geneva to see how the new house was coming along. Wallace read the letter and was not sure if it would be a good idea. She suggested that both families come together for the day. They could take the early train from Rochester and return in the afternoon. She thought Sunday would be good and then they could have a midday dinner. Wallace thought that would be the best way to avoid his father's long-term visit. How much could he say in an afternoon? Eveline returned a note inviting them next Sunday. They could see the new property and have a picnic by the lake.

The house was ready for the window installation. There were over one hundred openings constructed in different sizes for the variety of windows in the different areas of the house. The glass company had orders for plain glass as well as beveled edge glass for the cabinets, main doors; even the service door window to the garage door would have a beveled edge. The kitchen was fun for Eveline to plan. She was not quite sure what she needed and how big things should be. Everything was electric. She even bought an electric iron to press the clothes. Wallace asked, "Why do we need that. I thought we were having a maid?" Wallace took special interest in the room in the basement. He thought that should be a spot for fun things you might not do upstairs. The fireplace in that room was the largest in the house. The room was heated so the fish tank would stay at a reasonable temperature if there was no fire in the fireplace. Mr. Nigel suggested that in addition to the heat, lights and water supply in the garage that a telephone be hooked up with a bell from the house. It could be used to notify the driver that people were ready in the house to be escorted. Wallace liked that idea because the cars could be kept warm and always washed. He thought that would be one of Winston's jobs.

Eveline received the response for the family visit. They were glad to come on Sunday. Eveline told Wallace that they would be in Geneva at 11AM. She would ask Rose and Dr. Haynes if they would like to join them for the tour and the picnic. Wallace agreed that the more the merrier. Rose had been questioning her father about the house and was hoping to be invited to see it under construction. Samuel had admired the process that was being used to build such a unique home. There was much grumbling in town about the building of such a structure. It looked like it was from outer space. It was rumored that the owner took the Trip To The Moon too seriously when he was at the Pan-American Exposition. He must have lost his mind in space and brought the house plan back to earth. Some people in town were glad it was not in sight of the rest of the city. It was different from what they wanted to see in their gem of a city. Wallace was happy people were uneasy because the house gave them something to talk about. Rose and Dr. Haynes were delighted to be included in the day. Rose offered to help Eveline prepare the food. Eveline was hoping for just such an offer. Wallace laughed and said, "Maids can't come fast enough for you."

Mr. Nigel and Thomas made sure that Wallace was at the construction site after the windows had been installed. It was going to be a big step toward the completion of the house. Many of the windows were permanently affixed to the frame and the windows nearer the floor were casement type windows. Each casement window had two sets of brass fixtures for opening and closing each panel. There were screens for some of the windows that would be able to be taken away in the autumn. They fastened with springs at the top and could swing upward while opening the window. One of the workers reminded Mr. Nigel that eight brass fixtures were needed for each window panel. He asked Mr. Nigel if he had ordered 770 brass fixtures to complete the job. As Mr. Nigel was discussing the hardware quantities with Wallace he reminded him that he and Eveline needed to select hardware and knobs for the doors. Wallace and Eveline were given a few choices and decided to use products from the Penn Fixture Company in Pennsylvania. The company made higher quality items for exceptional homes. They ordered octagonal crystal knobs for the bedroom doors. Eveline was fascinated with the hexagonal knob collection so she selected them in the bathroom. Wallace wanted brass knobs with an etched design around the edge of each knob for the first floor doors. The lighting fixtures came from a similar company that offered unusual but classy lighting features. Electricity was only available in certain areas and to those who could afford to have it installed in their home. Eveline reminded Wallace that he was an exceptional person with an unusual mind so that is why he needed those things. When she told him that he smiled. Wallace loved the way the stained glass windows complimented the grandeur of the main stairway. Mr. Nigel admitted that he thought it was odd when he heard about it. Now, when he saw it in the hallway, it was stunning. Wallace reviewed the molding choices for each room. He wanted a mahogany stained woodwork on the main floor. The main rooms would have a unique style of molding unto itself. The dining room was to be a wood beam cube styled ceiling to maintain the geometric perpendicular angles of the house. The main reception room would have massive crown moldings to compliment the enormous fireplace with statues of lion heads holding the lights over the mantel. He wanted sidelights on the wall at the entrance to the main room. There would be switches installed in various parts of the main floor that could turn lights on and off from different locations. The lighting feature that he chose for the conservatory was a large inverted lantern style fixture that had two functions. The first was to light the room and the second was a focal point that when lit could be seen from the street. It would hang from a chain and would have smaller lights around the main globe as accent lights. It was to be wired so that the globe could be lit separately from the side accent lights. The dining room lights were unusual also. Small lights were installed in the beams that looked like stars when they were lit. The chandelier would hang from a triangular chain fixture. The globe was made of alabaster that looked like a huge bowl fastened to the chains. The worker that did the installation was fascinated that Wallace knew exactly what he wanted and how he wanted them to work. Mr. Nigel counted the number of switches, plugs, and brass plates they would need to order. He laughed when he told Wallace he would order 200 of each item. Wallace approved all of it.

Mr. Nigel told Wallace that he would need to have him return the next week to inspect the progress. The moldings, lights, floors, wall surfaces and doors would be installed. The doors were exceptional for the house too. They were 92-inch doors, some with beveled glass in the entire frame. They had to be specially mounted because of the weight of the frame and glass. The second floor fixtures and moldings were not as elaborate. The woodwork was poplar wood that could be painted. The doors would be a stained mahogany. Smaller brass chandelier lights were in the sleeping rooms. Wallace chose a lantern style light for the top of the stairs to be placed on the mahogany rails that capped the concrete half wall around the stairway. It would have a switch downstairs as well as upstairs. Mr. Nigel asked Wallace what he thought of the bathroom. Wallace remarked that most homes did not have hot water. He knew Eveline would like all the new conveniences in both the kitchen and bathroom. He jokingly told Mr. Nigel, "Eveline will like the bathroom better than the kitchen. She hardly knows what a kitchen is used for." Mr. Nigel laughed and said, "Rose and Eveline must have come from the same shell." They both shook their heads.

It was Sunday and the families were arriving at 11AM. Wallace paced around the apartment while Eveline was trying to organize the things for the lakeside meal. She told him that he should go outside and leave her alone. This time Wallace could not hide things like he had when he purchased the car. How could he minimize on the size of the house and the uniqueness of it. Maybe there would be no sarcastic comments made in front of everyone. This time Samuel and Rose would be there. Maybe Frank would be less caustic with his mouth. All these thoughts made Wallace more anxious. He decided to go outside. It was a pleasant autumn day. The trees were turning brilliant colors. They would be leaving 114 Washington Street in a few weeks and Rudolph would be moving in. They would be at 380 Washington Street. While he was standing on the sidewalk he saw the family coming down the street. Rose and Samuel met them as they were passing by their apartment building. They must have introduced themselves because everyone was laughing as they came closer. Wallace thought that was a good sign. Alice was waving and laughing with Mrs. Lounsberry and Rose. They acted like schoolgirls going to a party. The men were behind them talking but not laughing. Wallace thought that was about right because most men do not like to be happy. He knew that he was happy most of the time so what was their problem?

Alice was excited to be in Geneva to see Wallace. She kissed him all over his face. He blushed as she petted his moustache. The other women laughed and the men shook their heads. Eveline came out of the apartment and ran to her mother like she had never seen her before. Wallace thought about how spoiled she was. She acted like a little girl. He wondered what Rudolph would say about that behavior. After the kissing and laughing settled down Frank piped up and wondered when they were going to see the mansion? Alice glared at him and said, "I thought you said you would be decent?" All he did was raise his upper lip to the right. No one moved. Samuel said, "You know I'm a doctor and was wondering if you have a nervous condition that makes your lip move up and down?" Frank was stunned when he heard that. He shook his head and everyone knew why he asked Frank that question. As they were walking up Washington Street Wallace and Samuel were ahead of the rest. Samuel nudged him and said quietly, "I knew what he was up to and I knew my question would end his attitude." Wallace thanked him and smiled. Everyone was a buzz over what the house was going to look like. Rose and Eveline told them about their trips up the street with their parasols in the dust, dirt, and dirty men working all over the place. The men thought that ladies should be doing other things other than tantalizing construction workers. The women thought that tantalizing men could be quite fun. As they came to the corner of Nursery and Washington, Alice stopped and said, "Oh my God, it is huge. When are they putting on the roof?" Rose spoke first and told her that her father was building the house and the roof was already done. Samuel said, "Rose wants a house too, but I told her not yet. She wants me to build a place like this." Mr. Lounsberry wondered how many people were going to live in such a grand place. Eveline said, "Daddy, only my Wallace and me." Alice wanted to know who was going to care for such a mammoth place. Wallace found a chance to say, "We are having a groundskeeper." Eveline said, "And what else?" Wallace explained that Eveline was not interested in wifely duties and she needed hired help. He told them that she was in charge of hiring a maid to do the cleaning, laundry, and cooking. The other staff person would be her personal assistant for things dealing with social gatherings, serving meals, and helping Eveline care for herself. When Frank heard that he asked, "Are you having a guard posted at the corner too?" Eveline said, "No Frank, we are having Winston be our caretaker." Frank yelled, "I knew it, the boys will play and the girls will be socialites." Samuel asked what was wrong with that? He thought it was a perfect arrangement. Everyone gets what he or she wants. After all that Wallace told them he wanted to show them the inside of the house. They walked through the front door with everyone looking every which way. They were in awe of such an unusual building. Mrs. Lounsberry felt like she was going to her friend's house on Delaware Avenue. Eveline told her that they had visited them and that they did not like the Martin House in Buffalo. So, probably they would not like this house either. Mr. Lounsberry thought it was something from out of this world. Wallace said, "There are some people in town that think I brought it back from outer space when I took the Trip To The Moon ride at the Pan-American Exposition." Everyone laughed, except Frank.

While they were looking around the first floor Alice went to Wallace and hugged him and told him she was very proud of him no matter what his father said. Wallace thanked her as they were looking at the fireplace. Rose and Mrs.Lounsberry wanted to know what the saying meant that was built into the fireplace. Wallace said, "It is Spanish for "A happy home is a temporary heaven." When they heard that they thought that was appropriate for the two of them. Alice frowned and said, "I hope none of you go to heaven too soon." Everyone agreed with her as they walked into the conservatory. They loved all the windows and the hanging chandelier. They all agreed that it was as if you were always outside and inside at the same time. Wallace smiled and said, "That is what Frank Lloyd Wright would want to hear." He was feeling very proud and more relaxed when he heard all the positive comments. While they were looking at the high ceiling on their way upstairs Rose said, "This stairway and upper hallway is more like going up to a balcony with all the openings and walkway around the second floor." Samuel said, "Most people don't even have a parlor this big." As that was being said they were looking at the stained glass windows. At first there were some quizzical looks as it to what it represented. In a hesitant way, Mrs. Lounsberry asked, "What are those two things sticking straight up?" Alice looked at Frank and hoped he would not start criticizing it. Eveline started to speak but Alice interrupted. She thought they looked like phallic symbols. Eveline piped up and explained that they were symbols of two buds ready to burst. Wallace chimed in and explained that Mr. Nigel had a question about it too. He told them the same thing that it takes two things or people to grow and prosper. After Wallace finished everyone liked that philosophy except Frank.

He asked, "Where does Winston and Rudolph fit into that window?" Alice said, "Oh Frank how could you say such things?" Wallace decided it was time to challenge his father's remark. He said, "Yes, maybe it could be Winston and Rudolph. If that is what you see then that is what it is. Art is like that, an individual's interpretation." Samuel and Mr. Lounsberry both said together, "Well put." The women were quiet; they thought it was better to move on. Wallace was happy he could explain that it was designed for that very interpretation. They went to the basement and loved the idea of a man's room. The women were glad they would have a place and the men could do whatever they wanted downstairs and out of sight. Wallace and Samuel laughed and told everyone that they would never tell anyway.

They were fascinated with the fish holding tank in the basement, so they went outside to see the pond and the system for draining and filling it. The men thought Wallace was a genius to have thought of many things. When they got to the garage Wallace demonstrated how the garage doors operated. They went up very smoothly rising from the front in one piece. There were 500-pound weights attached by cables to the doors to keep them in the up position. Alice loved the beveled glass windows in the door. Mr. Lounsberry liked the idea of a heated and an electrified garage. Frank noticed the water and drain. He thought that was really not necessary. Rose thought it was great to have a clean and warm car all the time. She looked at Samuel and said, "If you are lucky enough to own a car." Frank piped up and said, "Only rich people can afford a car. My son owns two. What does that make him?" As they were leaving the garage Mrs. Lounsberry recognized what looked like an earpiece hanging on the wall. Wallace told her it was a telephone to the house so they could call for the driver. He told her that there was a telephone hooked up in the house too. He explained how he called Rudolph the other day in Rochester. No one could believe there was so much in this house. It was like a dream. Wallace showed them where the bungalow would be built in a few months. He called it a guesthouse. Alice wondered if that was where she would be staying when she came to visit. Wallace assured her it was really for the hired help. Mr. Lounsberry wanted to know if Winston was going to reside there. Wallace said, "Yes." Mrs. Lounsberry thought that a plantation was being developed. Alice agreed and was overwhelmed by how large the property was and how big everything seemed. Frank sarcastically said, "Yeah, there is a lot of big stuff going on here." Wallace smiled and thought if you only knew.

Dinner by the lake was relaxing and fun. Everyone settled down under a tree and discussed how lovely Seneca Lake was. Alice wanted to come back again soon. Eveline thanked Rose for helping her with the menu. She admitted she was not good in the kitchen. Wallace raised his glass to that comment. They all laughed and agreed she would need a cook. After they finished eating and relaxing they strolled through downtown toward Pulteney Park. Samuel and Rose said their goodbyes and Wallace and Eveline walked their parents to the train station. Wallace thought that walking was better than using his car. He did not need to hear about that on top of the house comments in the same day. The train arrived and everyone thanked them for such a wonderful day. Even Frank seemed a little mellow when it was time to go. Wallace thought that was strange but better than the usual behavior. Mr. Lounsberry threatened to return the next time in a flashy new car.

Eveline thought that would be grand and they could have a race. No one thought car racing was what he or she needed to do. After the train left they walked back to their apartment. They too seemed mellow. It had been a big day for everyone. Eveline commented on how proud their parents seemed of them. She thought even Frank was proud of them in his own way. Wallace agreed and wondered why his father was so passive.

Chapter 50

Mr. Nigel began construction of the guest bungalow after Thanksgiving so it would be ready for January occupancy. It would have two small bedrooms, a combined kitchen and living area, and a bathroom. He assured Wallace that there would be adequate room for three people. Eveline had already arranged the employment of two women. Sable was a Negro woman who would be in charge of the food shopping, cooking, cleaning, laundry, and serving meals. Eveline met Olitha because she was Rose's housekeeper. Rose had been looking for another woman for the housekeeping duties. Eveline offered Olitha the job. Eveline had seen her at some of the suffrage meetings. She thought that would be good to have her working for her because they had the same philosophy about Women's Rights. She would be starting the day they moved into their new home. Wallace asked what Rose thought of losing Olitha. Eveline told him that she wanted to let her go anyway. Rose had interviewed another colored woman who she would pay much less and would be doing everything. Wallace mentioned that it was interesting that they would employ colored women. Eveline explained that they came very highly recommended from one of the more well to do woman in town. Wallace asked who that might be? Eveline hesitated and admitted it was Mrs. Preston. Wallace wanted to know how they met? When she and Rose were at the fashion fair at the Seneca Hotel earlier in the season they met her. Mrs. Preston had heard of a program in New York City that placed women for employment who had been involved with newcomers to the country. When Wallace heard the word newcomers he thought of the Occidental Company. While he was thinking about the human transfer operation he wondered if that was what the letter was referring to when it mentioned there were some new things happening with the company. Wallace did not respond too much to the reference of New York and newcomers. He knew the annual meeting was coming up in January and he would be sure to find out if there was a connection. Wallace asked more information about Olitha. Eveline told him that she would be perfect for her. She would help her get ready for the day, escort her around town and be available during her socialite gatherings. Eveline referred to her as her personal assistant. When she finished her description of these women and their functions he shook his head saying, "My hard work is going to your head." Eveline made a face as she raised her upper lip, turned and walked away.

Wallace received a letter from Winston and Rudolph on the same day. Winston had submitted his resignation to French's Mustard Company and would be in Geneva for the beginning of the New Year and his job at Goodwin Printing Company. Rudolph's letter was more to the point and very businesslike. The greeting was to Mr. Wallace Paine. He wondered why so formal. Rudolph explained that he was happy to announce that he would be resigning from his managerial position at the Seneca Powers Hotel effective December 31, 1913. He signed it Mr. Rudolph Williams. Underneath that letter was another note. It read, "Hey, can't wait to be in Geneva. Am looking forward to the new job. Am looking more forward to us being closer in business and pleasure." When Wallace read the second note he knew why there were two separate enclosures. He had a tingling sensation when he read the part about closer in pleasure. He put the letter in his personal file box. That box was accumulating all kinds of information that was not for public viewing including his wife. Wallace returned to work on the advertising for both companies. Standard Optical was producing eyewear and lens for many companies now. It was easier to buy the parts from Standard than to manufacture everything in their own factories. Wallace had encouraged Standard to reach out to smaller companies to obtain their business. The Safege Company had just begun shipments to New York City under Wallace's direction to the Occidental Import and Export Company. The more legitimate cargo coming and going would overshadow the opium and transfer programs. Mr. Preston told Wallace that everyone who was involved in the Goodwin Printing Company agreed to avoid any admission of the company's intent. When Wallace heard this he said, "There's nothing to hide, however it is better to treat it as a normal operation. Winston will make certain it goes as planned. He has been briefed many times on these matters. He will have no idea of how the money is handled." Mr. Preston had a strange look on his face when Wallace finished speaking to him. When he saw Mr. Preston's face he thought it was time to discuss the newcomers to Geneva. Mr. Preston acted uncertain when Wallace asked about securing hired help from New York City. Wallace continued telling Mr. Preston that his wife recommended to Eveline some colored women for employment in domestic duties. Mr. Preston's face became red and hot looking. He told Wallace that a man from New

York contacted him because of the hotel. The man did not give his name only initials of a company that arranged women for employment in domestic duties. Since he had the hotel he figured that was why he received the offer. As Wallace heard the story he wondered if Rudolph received the same letter. If he did then why hadn't he been told? Wallace asked what the initials were. Mr. Preston said, "TOE&TIC." Wallace wanted to know what the address was. Mr. Preston told him that it came with a post office box number in New Jersey. Wallace told him that his wife hired two women and Samuel Haynes' wife hired another colored woman. Mr. Preston smiled and said, "I hope my wife doesn't want to get any help." Wallace was more interested in what might be happening in New York and if Rudolph had any knowledge about all of this.

Mr. Nigel told Wallace that the house was finished and ready for occupancy. He wanted to have Wallace inspect the house and garage before they moved in. Mr. Nigel wanted to meet him the next day, December 23. Wallace told Eveline that he was going to see the completed house tomorrow. She wanted to come too. Wallace told her that this was man's business and she was not included. She reminded him that he had said that to her before but always crawled back for her ideas. He did not respond to her accusations. Wallace met Mr. Nigel and Thomas at the corner of Washington and Nursery Avenue. The sun shone between the gray winter clouds. Wallace looked at the house that shimmered like the snow on the ground. Mr. Nigel assured Wallace that the bungalow would be completed in time for the New Year. They inspected the details of the house. As Wallace went to the front door he noticed a funnel like tube extending from the doorframe. Mr. Nigel laughed and told him it was a speaking tube.

It was connected to the kitchen. Anyone who came to the door would speak into the tube. The voice could be heard loud and clear to the servant in the kitchen. Wallace did not remember putting that on the list of things for the house. Mr. Nigel said, "Your wife told me to install it." Wallace asked why. Mr. Nigel told him that Rose suggested Eveline should have one of those. She knew that there would be servants in the kitchen and it would be their job to attend to the people at the door. Mr. Nigel laughed and said, "Samuel is holding his breath that Rose won't want all these things that Eveline is getting." Wallace was embarrassed to think that Eveline was so spoiled and making others look poor but he had himself to blame for that. He thought that giving her everything would keep her quiet. Then, he could do what he wanted, but this was becoming an out of control situation. She is putting her nose into places it should not be. She seemed to think she could do both men's and women's things. Wallace knew it had to do with that Women's Rights Movement; it was making her crazy.

The house was completed exactly as Wallace wished. He remembered the day at the Exposition when he told Winston he would someday have many of the things in his home that they saw at the Pan-American Exposition. The exterior was a concrete color with brown trim and a rose color accentuating the windowsills and roofline. The grounds were frozen and snow covered but he knew that would change in the spring. Mr. Nigel took Wallace to the garage. They felt a warm breeze on their faces as they opened the door. Wallace forgot that the garage was heated just like the house. He told Mr. Nigel that he would bring his cars into the garage today. Mr. Nigel reminded him that he had to go to the bank to sign the papers for the mortgage on the house. Wallace apologized and told him he was doing that later in the day. He mentioned that this was Eveline's Christmas present. Mr. Nigel smiled and thought that was a pretty big present. Wallace told him that he was signing the house over to her as of December 23, 1913. Mr. Nigel asked why. Wallace explained that women have certain rights and they could have a home in their name. In that way, if any financial problems occur in business the house is hers and no liens can be placed on the house or be taken away. Mr. Nigel thought he was very smart for being so cautious. He said, "With all the changes in the country, our money is going to taxes. If we aren't shrewd with our monetary maneuvers, we could lose it all." Wallace said, "I know, I've seen it happen."

The inspection was completed. Wallace thanked Mr. Nigel for all he had done and told him that his payment would be in his hands the next day. Mr. Nigel wished him well and hoped Rose was not going to put Samuel through the same things Eveline had done. They laughed as they walked down the street. Wallace was not happy with the reputation Eveline was creating with people. Something needed to happen to change that. He thought to himself maybe I should get her pregnant. She now has a home for a baby that she has talked about. A baby might keep her mind at home and not in Seneca Falls with the suffragettes. They parted ways and Wallace went to the apartment. When he came into the room he found Eveline frantically packing personal items. They did not have to move most of the furniture because they had purchased new and more appropriate furniture. He told her that they had an appointment at the bank to sign for the loan. Eveline was ready in a flash. It had started snowing and was windy so they bundled up and walked to the bank.

They arrived a few minutes early and they sat in the lobby and waited. While they were waiting Wallace decided to tell Eveline that he was signing the house over to her. Before he could say another word a squeal much louder than ever before came out her mouth. The tellers stopped and the officers came out of their offices asking if she was all right. Eveline said, "You bet I'm alright. My Wallace just gave me my Christmas present. I am probably one of the few women who actually own a house. I can not wait to tell everyone at the next women's rally about this." The bank officer ushered them into his office as he shook his head. He told Wallace that he was encouraging bad habits for women. Wallace smiled but did wonder what he was creating. The paperwork was filled out and signed for a mortgage of $6,500.00. Eveline was at the height of her dramatic performance when she took the pen in hand and slowly and deliberately signed her name. Wallace was afraid that he might be making a mistake by giving her the house. Maybe he should have arranged it differently. He shook his head as he signed his name below hers. The bank officer reminded Wallace that he would see him when the bungalow was completed. There was another mortgage for $1000 that needed to be signed. Wallace looked at Eveline when he heard that and said, "Maybe I should have turned that one over to you instead of the big house." She said, "If you keep that up, you'll be living in the bungalow." Everyone in the bank was listening to their conversation as they left. They were appalled that a woman would dare say such things to her husband especially in public.

Moving into 380 Washington Street was a grand experience. The furniture arrived from Rochester and some from Geneva. Having such a unique home required specific accessories so they wanted the furniture to be a compliment to the environment. Eveline wondered what to do with all the windows. Wallace told her not to worry because there was nothing outside except trees. They installed a few shades in the bedroom and left all the other windows bare. It was like living outside all the time. Eveline told Wallace that this type of camping was pretty good. He agreed. There was very little comment from people in town about the "outer space house". It was a phrase most people understood. They knew exactly where it was and what type of person built such a thing. Wallace still thought it was funny that people were so narrow minded that they could not accept some differences. His business associates and even the men at the YMCA treated him like he still lived at 114 Washington Street. They occasionally asked how living in a fish bowl felt. Wallace would tell them to come up to the top of the hill and find out. The same reaction was embarrassment as to what they might see. Eveline was having a marvelous time organizing the house. She had both maids helping her and they were staying at the apartment to sleep until the bungalow was completed. Sable and Olitha were hard workers and became friends. They had the women's rights issues as a common thread to stimulate the friendship. Rose came with flowers for the house and spent time with Eveline. They discussed the arrangement of things and some plans were made for a tea party later in the winter. Eveline wanted to wait until they were completely settled before having guests. They laughed when they thought about how many women would accept an invitation to the "outer space house."

The last day of 1913 was a quiet one. Sable prepared a special holiday dinner of roast beef, Yorkshire pudding, and vegetables. When she had the dinner ready she left for the evening. It was the first time since they moved into the house that they were alone. Wallace commented on how nice it was not to have people coming and going and asking if everything was okay. Eveline admitted that it had been hectic and she liked a little quiet time with "her Wallace". He hated it when she referred to him as "her Wallace". It sounded like he was her pet. He told her he was going to New York in a few days for the annual meeting of the Occidental Company. She wanted to know if he was going by himself. He told her that he was because Winston was starting his work in Geneva in early January. They discussed Rudolph and when he was arriving in Geneva. Eveline was happy to think that both of them would be here permanently. Wallace asked how much rallying they were planning on doing. Eveline said, "As much as we can." During their conversation they discussed how lucky they were to be in a new home this large. Wallace was 32 years old and Eveline was 28 years old. They agreed that was quite young to have come this far. As they were talking about that Wallace thought that most of the advancement had been because of his hard work and not hers. Eveline took as much credit for the success as Wallace. Could she actually think she contributed as much? He thought it was better to be quiet.

The annual meeting was in two days. Wallace bought a ticket to New York City on the 6AM train. The train would arrive in Grand Central Station before noon. When he arrived at the Geneva station he saw some advertisements for eyewear and Safege razors. The advertisements for the razors had now included pictures of army knives and other useful items that required sharp edges. While on the train he had time to think about all the things that had happened. He thought about the strange co-incidence of TOE&TIC. Maybe it is not a co-incidence. He thought about his other trips to New York with Winston. Some of those trips were fun and some were not. This was the first time he had traveled by himself. There was too much happening in Geneva now to have expected Winston or Rudolph to come with him. While he was thinking about that he wondered why Eveline was not as demanding about going to New York as she once had been. Was she really having more to do with Rudolph than just rallies? Time seemed to go quickly on the way to New York. Before he knew it the conductor was announcing the arrival time into Grand Central Station. The railroads had changed their pattern and approach into the larger station. As the train came closer to a huge building Wallace knew that this had to be Grand Central Station. The train maneuvered its way to a stop. From the window Wallace saw thousands of people coming and going everywhere. As he got off the train he looked around to find which way to go. It was beautiful and brightly lit inside. It reminded him of the Pan American Exposition when all the lights were on. When he got to the street he took a minute to figure out how to get to the Waldorf Astoria. He asked a gentleman bystander for directions to the hotel. Just by chance he was staying at the hotel too and was on his way so they walked together. Wallace explained that his company had standing reservations at the hotel. The man had the same arrangement for his business. He was affiliated with Macy's Department Store and was one of their foreign buyers in the Orient. When Wallace heard that he wondered if he had ever known Mr. Ling. He thought it was better not to compare the two. They entered the lobby and agreed on how luxurious it always was there. They checked in and went their separate ways. Wallace wondered what he might find on his bed when he got to his room. He hoped it would not be a tongue. He hesitated before he opened the door. When he went inside, there was no tongue, there was no Winston, and there was no reason to be worried.

Wallace unpacked and went downstairs for a quick lunch. He was meeting Mr. Wellington and new associates at 3PM. While he was eating he thought about the comment made about slowing the Hong Kong market down and having a similar company in New Jersey conduct transfers of colored people. He decided to let Mr. Wellington talk and maybe all his concerns would be answered. After he finished eating he walked to the Occidental Office. He took a deep breath and walked in. Mr. Wellington was happy to see Wallace and introduced him to two new gentlemen. They had been hired to work at Occidental because a few people had dropped out of the business and moved to the west coast. They did not appear as businesslike as the former men had been. They began their meeting with a financial review of the company. The profits had doubled and the variety of imports and exports had increased. Wallace was aware of that since he directed many products from upstate to New York City for shipping. He felt himself getting edgy with Mr. Wellington's tone. It was as if he had never discussed these things before. Wallace was fully aware of the facts and figures. Mr. Wellington treated him like he did that first night a few years ago. Funny part was that Wallace was the owner then and still was but was being spoken to as if he were a simple worker. He chose to let him talk and watch how he worked his way through the meeting. After awhile Wallace started his line of questioning. He began by asking about the slowing down of the Hong Kong market. Mr. Wellington explained that there had been great pressure on the opiate industry. The government was now investigating a number of items being smuggled into the country. One of them was opium. The other was alcohol. Mr. Wellington talked about articles in the New York Times that reported a narcotics act that was being proposed. It was nearing passage and would curb drug abuse and sales. It would require doctors to register all prescriptions and a tax would be paid on each one that was written. There was smuggling of alcohol too. This would have to be registered and an import tax would be charged. Mr. Harrison was the senator proposing the Harrison Narcotics Act of 1914. The other reason Mr. Wellington suggested a slowing in Hong Kong had to do with the transfer program. When Wallace heard this he waited to hear if the New Jersey Company would be mentioned. Mr. Wellington told the other two men that they could leave the meeting. They shook hands and left. Wallace thought this very abrupt but was more concerned about the transfer program. Mr. Wellington began with an explanation of the numbers of human transfers that were made last year versus prior years. He thought it was because they were not selling the transfers as rapidly as they had been in previous years. He suggested that they change the market. It was not that he wanted to slow the market as much as the type of commodity they were transferring. There was a strong demand for infants and young children now. He wanted to know if Wallace approved of that idea. Wallace's first question was, "Who would care for these transfers while they were coming to the United States?" Mr. Wellington explained that they would have women transfers that would act as surrogate mothers to receive and care for the infants and children. After the children were placed the women would be hired as domestic servants near the drop off point of the children.

Wallace sat very still as he was listening to the changes in the transfers. He felt uneasy about parents selling their children in a foreign country and letting them go to an unknown place. Mr. Wellington sensed his uneasiness and asked how he felt about it. Mr. Wellington explained that these children would likely die in their own country because they had very little care. Starvation and disease was rampant in the Orient. Wallace wanted to know if the new placements for these children would be safe places for babies and youngsters. Mr. Wellington was frank about the safety issue. He told Wallace that some people who buy children are not doing it for the right reason. Some children were put out on the streets as prostitutes or are sexually and physically abused. Wallace shook his head and wanted to say no. Mr. Wellington repeated that if they remained in their own country that worse things could happen to them. He felt that in this country the chance for a better life was a higher possibility. Wallace decided to change the subject. He wanted to address any connection to the TOE&TIC operation to see if there was any connection to Occidental. He asked Mr. Wellington if he knew about that operation. Without any hesitation he told him that was their other office. Wallace wanted to know why another office was necessary. Mr. Wellington explained that the New Jersey office was just across the river. It was easier to bring colored people into New Jersey by boat than the New York harbor. The authorities did not question this route as much as they did in New York. When Wallace heard this he felt better knowing Mr. Wellington was not doing something behind his back. Mr. Wellington was surprised he knew about the office. Wallace was glad he was surprised. He knew that would keep him on his toes. Wallace explained about a person telling his wife about a place that could arrange for domestic servants. The woman lives in Geneva and her husband owns a fancy hotel in town. Wallace did not discuss his hotel just yet. When Mr. Wellington heard this he admitted he sent letters to all the larger hotels offering domestic servants. He told him these were the women who had been purchased to be surrogates to the children in transport. He mentioned that he sent a letter to a Mr. Rudolph Williams at the Seneca Powers Hotel in Rochester. Mr. Wellington remembered him from the trial. Wallace told him they were friends and he was manager of that hotel. It was decided that as long as the children were cared for during their time with Occidental, whatever happened after that could happen anywhere. Wallace agreed to reorganize the system. Mr. Wellington was glad they had time for the meeting since this was a difficult topic to discuss. Wallace walked back to the Waldorf. He had his dinner at the hotel. He wanted to go to bed early because the train left at 6AM.

On the train ride back to Geneva Wallace thought about what was happening to the children and why there were colored women so available for domestic duties. He realized he could not tell anyone about this big money maker for Occidental. He did not want anyone to think he was aiding to the possible torture of children. Maybe he would tell Winston. He needed to talk about it with someone. It could not be Rudolph. If Eveline found out about the infants and children being bought and sold to people in the United States, she would campaign against that treatment with the Women's Rights Movement behind such practices. This time Wallace knew that the program should never be discussed anywhere near Geneva. Then, he wondered about the colored women already in Geneva. They might have been lied to or guaranteed a job and a better life if they helped the little children. Wallace convinced himself that was probably how everything happened. He tried to put the whole thing out of his mind. He would tell Winston though. This had been a very quick trip and the train was only 10 miles from Geneva. He went to the Standard Optical office from the train station.

When Wallace entered the office Winston greeted him. He arrived earlier and was waiting for Wallace to return. He told Winston he was in New York City for a meeting. When Wallace saw him Winston nudged him and asked if he a good time by himself? Wallace blushed a little and felt that familiar sensation. He did tell Winston that he thought about their times in New York and missed him. Winston smiled when he heard this. Winston told Wallace that he walked to Genesee Street to see the new printing factory. He wanted to know about hiring employees and what the company policies were. He wanted to know what his salary would be. Wallace explained that he would have housing in the bungalow and a wage. His first responsibility was to hire as few people as possible to operate the presses. Winston understood the need for secrecy right away and let Wallace know that this place was doing more than just printing. Wallace continued to emphasize the importance of being quiet if anyone asked questions about how the operation was being handled. Winston reminded Wallace that they had been through this hush hush stuff many times before. Wallace told him this is the reason he got offered the job. Winston sarcastically asked him if he was being used again. Wallace told him not in that way. They would have time to be used later. Winston said, "O-O-OKAY!" As long as they were confiding in things Wallace thought he could tell Winston about the children transfer program. As he was telling him about the colored women and how they were getting jobs he realized that Winston had no knowledge of the transfer program. He had already started to tell him about the young people. Before he went on, Winston interrupted and said, "Rudolph already told me about it but said to wait until you brought it up." Wallace was furious when he heard this. He wanted to know how Rudolph found out? Winston told him that Rudolph got a letter from a place in New Jersey that had domestic servants available. When Rudolph responded to the letter he realized it came from an office affiliated with Mr. Wellington at Occidental. Wallace knew from this discussion that Winston and Rudolph only thought it was about servants. He knew that they did not know what these women were doing before they got hired as servants. Wallace decided to change his conversation to make it sound like getting jobs for colored women as domestic servants. After the subject changed back to the printing company Wallace told Winston that he was welcome to stay with them for a few days until the bungalow was finished. The women Eveline hired were staying in their old apartment. Winston accepted but asked if he had to live with two women. Wallace told him that they would have one bedroom and he could use the other. Winston coyly asked Wallace if he was planning on visiting him? Wallace told him that was why he wanted him on the property.

Rudolph arrived a week later. The weather co-operated and the bungalow was completed on schedule. Sable and Olitha moved from the apartment to their room. Winston was not happy moving from the main house. He and Wallace had been spending time in the lower level room. They nicknamed it "the men's quarters for fun". Eveline was glad the men had a place for themselves because she was busy being taken care of by her servants. Rudolph had his belongings sent on the train along with a few pieces of furniture he did not want to part with. Wallace, Eveline, and Winston went to see Rudolph at the apartment. He was surprised when they showed up. He answered the door in his under clothes. Eveline covered her eyes but the men stared at each other. The apartment looked like a dressing room in a clothing store. Winston's first remark was that he was sorry he did not bring his Leter Buck. The men laughed and Eveline made a disinterested face. Rudolph told them they would have lots of time to use Leter Buck. Eveline could not believe that one man could have so many clothes. Wallace thought he had a lot and Winston reminded them that he does not wear too much of anything. Wallace asked him if he was planning on parading in front of Sable and Olitha like that? Eveline told him to leave her girls alone. Wallace said, "They won't have to worry, I'll punish Winston if he tries anything like that." Winston laughed and said, "I can't wait to see what the punishment will be." Rudolph looked confused and asked where he was going to fit into all the relationships. While they were visiting Eveline reminded him they had to attend a rally the next day. Rudolph told her he would be ready bright and early. On the way back home Winston asked what time he was to be at work. Wallace told him that he would come over to inspect the bungalow very early and he would tell him then. Winston knew what that meant and said, "Okay."

Wallace woke up early in the morning to find that Eveline and her "girls" had already left for the women's rally. As he was getting ready to go to the bungalow he thought now there were three women in his house and Rose would make the fourth who were pushing for rights that men were not ready for. He was fearful of big problems arising from all the publicity. It was perfect timing this morning because only Winston and he were on the property. Wallace dressed and went to the bungalow. He smelled freshly brewed coffee as he approached the door. The aroma was as inviting as the thought of what might happen next. He knocked on the door and Winston appeared in his usual attire, nothing. He rushed Wallace inside to where he had a fire in the wood burning stove. Wallace looked at Winston and focused on his hairy chest. It was warm in the room even though it was February. Wallace moved closer to Winston and could smell a hint of his Leter Buck. Winston raised his eyebrows and looked at Wallace's lower half of his body. He asked, "Are you having a problem or have you grown in the last few minutes?" Wallace replied, "I've grown tired of not being with you." Winston offered him some coffee. It seemed like Winston was taking a very long time getting to the matter at hand. Wallace wondered to himself if this was his plan that Winston had to be the one in charge. He was hoping so after he had a longer look at Winston's body. He looked better than ever. Wallace asked if he had gained some weight? Winston told him that he was larger because he had been exercising at the YMCA in Rochester. Wallace told him that he could use the one in Geneva now. Winston gave him an evil eye and told Wallace it would be fun to exercise together. After he said that he took a hold of Wallace and gave him a strong and tight hug. As he was hugging him he moved his body side to side. The bungalow seemed like it was on fire from the friction created by them. Before Wallace knew it Winston did take charge as he hoped he would. His strength was overpowering and exciting. He maneuvered them into a better place. He asked Wallace if he was able to go to work after all that. Wallace sat on the edge of the bed and said, "That's a perfect way to start the day. Of course I am able to go to work." Then he told Winston that he had only 20 minutes to get to the printing office. Winston said, "Now you're the boss."

When Wallace got to work he had time to look at the newspaper. One of the local stores was being renamed and had its main store in Rochester. It was McCurdy& Robinson Company. They were expanding the ownership and size of the store. It would now feature household items, furniture, and a wider variety of clothing. Wallace thought that would be good competition for the other stores in town. There was a more disturbing article about the income tax. People were being reminded that if they earned more than $3,500.00 annually there was a deadline of March 2 to submit their tax return. There was only a few weeks left and Wallace had not done that yet. Mr. Preston walked into the office just as Wallace was finishing the paper and he reminded him of the tax date. Mr. Preston shook his head and said, "That is a joke because they will never be able to get everyone to admit to their income." Wallace smiled and agreed. The Goodwin Company was going to be their savior. Then, Mr. Preston mentioned the expanded store from Rochester. He told Wallace that his wife was going to be the first person to open an account there. They were offering a prize to the first 25 accounts. Wallace hoped Eveline would not see or hear about that. They decided that they had a lot of work to do now that the Safege Company was expanding into cutlery items. Wallace showed Mr. Preston the advertisements he had designed for the variety of knives that were manufactured. There were pictures of table settings with fancy cutlery as part of the table accessories. A kitchen was in another advertisement that featured the servant being surprised with a set of new knives for her use. She no longer had to use one knife for everything because it included a dozen knives. Wallace laughed and said to Mr. Preston, "Eveline doesn't even know how to use one knife, what would she ever do with a dozen?"

Standard Optical was manufacturing more equipment for optometrists. They still produced a huge line of eyewear and were making lenses for motion picture cameras, lenses for science labs, and microscopes. Wallace knew that springtime was coming soon and he wanted to feature the newest line of sun wear. This year he was including advertisements in the Ladies Home Journal, Colliers, and the newspapers. He was going to ask Eveline and Rudolph if they still wanted to be in the pictures as models. When he mentioned it to Eveline she said, "I thought you forgot because you have been so busy with your boyfriends." She told him that she wanted to do the work as long as "her Ruddy" would be included. Wallace questioned the "her Ruddy" part. She told him that is her way of showing her men that she is close to them. Wallace was confused about how close all of them should be. Lately, things had become so tangled up that Wallace was not sure who was close to whom. The other day he told Eveline that Samuel spoke with him and wanted to know when he could come to the "men's quarters for fun." She wanted to know how he knew what the nickname was. Apparently, Winston had an appointment with Dr. Haynes for a new patient checkup. During the examination Winston told him that Wallace had a great private room in his home. Wallace thought he should have a men's party sometime soon. Eveline told him that Sable would only make the food but she was not being exposed to all those men. Wallace agreed and would plan a card game in a few weeks.

March 2, Tax Day, the worst snowstorm in 14 years began during the night. The winds began to blow at 50 mph. By morning there was 6 feet of snow blowing through the streets in Geneva. The city was at a stand still. Most of the state was in the same condition. By midday, tax day was extended until March 4. When Mr. Preston heard this he said, "I told you so. That tax thing will never happen." Wallace was not sure he agreed but was happy to have the extra time. Eveline and Rudolph were scheduled to have their pictures taken in summer outfits and sun wear. It did not make sense to be dressed in such lightweight clothing for such a blustery day. The place where the pictures were to be taken was heated well above normal so they at least looked like they were warm from the hot sun. Wallace watched as they were photographed arm in arm and then hugging one another in the bright sun. He wondered how often they had done that at their rallies. Rudolph had been working at the Board of Commerce for a few weeks now. He took some time off from his lunch to have the pictures taken. He told Wallace that he was enjoying the work and was meeting many men. Wallace asked him what he thought of the businessmen in Geneva. He told him that they were not like the ones in Rochester and definitely not like the men in New York City but they were making big business successful here. Wallace smiled and knew why they were making big money.

Spring arrived in early April. Wallace had been discussing landscaping with Winston. He sketched the plan on a large rectangular board. The perimeter of the property would have privet hedges as they were at the Exposition. When they grew the hedge would serve as a privacy barrier from the street. There would be maple trees planted at the curbside and throughout the property. This had a two-fold purpose. Wallace read that the more trees you have the cooler the house is in the summer because of the shade that is created. The second reason was for privacy. Wallace thought that since there were so many windows that the trees would act as covers for the openness to the house. In the front of the house he wanted pine trees that would eventually grow tall and sleek to contrast the horizontal lines of the house. On the west side of the property, Norwegian Fir trees would be planted that would eventually soar above the house giving it a dramatic appearance from the street. Winston thought the ideas were exactly what the house needed. The only thing he asked for was some men to be hired to assist him with the project. Wallace laughed and said, "You exercise at the YMCA. I thought you were strong enough to do all the work by yourself." Winston smugly responded, "I'm saving my real strength to take care of you." Wallace thought that was a good idea and agreed to find some field workers. He would order the necessary nursery items from the businesses in town that grew plants and trees. There was a large nursery at the end of the street that would have everything he wanted. Wallace wanted the work finished by the end of May.

Times were changing. The Harrison Narcotics Act of 1914 was ratified and required opiate drugs and heroine to be registered and taxed. The illegal smuggling of alcohol was part of the narcotics act too. There was a group of people who felt that alcohol should be illegal in the United States. This became a debate among the Senate and the House of Representatives. There was a vote on a Prohibition Bill in June. Wallace and the men he worked with were not in favor of such controls. It was mainly because women did not feel drinking was appropriate. It was an evil substance that made people crazy. Eveline talked about the same thing and mentioned there were many people who would smuggle it into the country no matter what the bill said. Wallace was surprised she had as much knowledge about smuggling and unlawful deeds as she did. He hoped she never found out about his business in New York. During their conversation she mentioned that Rose and Samuel had invited them to go to a party that was advertised in the newspaper. She had a copy of it and read it to Wallace as they were finishing their dinner. It read, "Don't hesitate but Fox Trot down to the Hotel Seneca and reserve your table for the Sunset Ball." As she was reading it Sable overheard the words Fox Trot and said from the kitchen, "I love to do the fox trot. My Mammy used to run from the foxes, but I like the dances better." Wallace and Eveline laughed but knew her Mammy must have been a slave and she definitely was dancing but not to an orchestra. Wallace was not sure he wanted to learn the fox trot but knew if he did not go she would invite "her Ruddy." He agreed they would go with Rose and Samuel. She was happy and told Olitha later that evening that they would need to start shopping for an outfit that would top any others at the party. Wallace heard her and thought about how spoiled she was.

Rose and Eveline went to the Seneca Hotel for lunch the next day. They reserved one of the best tables near the orchestra. It was a table for 6 people. They thought about who they might include at the table with them. Rose suggested The Preston's since he owned the hotel. Eveline agreed and would have Wallace invite them to sit with them. While they were having lunch Eveline mentioned that she was not feeling as well as she usually did. Rose asked what was wrong. She explained that she just did not have much energy or any appetite. Rose laughed when she said that and then said, "I could understand the appetite thing if you were the cook but Sable's cooking is the best." Eveline made a face but agreed about her ability to cook. Rose thought she should make an appointment to see Samuel for an examination. Eveline hesitated but thought that might be a good idea. When Eveline arrived home Winston was working in the yard bare-chested and every hair was glistening with sweat. She looked at him and made a face and said, "Too bad Wallace wasn't here to see you like that." Winston did not say much to her as she went through the front door. After she was gone he said to himself, "Wrong Eveline. Wallace just left and he saw more than my sweat."

The Goodwin Company was printing orders day and night. Word was getting around about how to buy into the company and divert attention of incomes. Wallace liked the idea of diverting attention from a lot of things. It worked in all of his companies. His motto became, "Keep moving things around, so no one can keep track of them." Winston was enjoying the work because his salary was based on a percent of the profit. He liked living on Wallace's property even better. It had become a daily event for Wallace to go to the bungalow for some morning wake up activity. Fortunately, the weather had co-operated and the plantings were done and the property looked finished. Winston did a perfect job and Wallace was very pleased and rewarded him in many ways. Rudolph had stopped by earlier to see Eveline but spent time at the bungalow too. He wanted to see what Winston's living conditions were like. Eveline asked why it took so long to see such a small place? Rudolph told her that Winston offered him some refreshments. She looked at him and slowly said, "I'll bet." While they were talking about his work and the suffrage movement Wallace came home. Sable answered the door and showed him where they were seated. Wallace felt like he interrupted something. Rudolph told him that he was at the bungalow earlier and saw where Winston was living. Wallace asked what he thought. Rudolph wanted to know what he meant. Was he referring to the place or Winston? At that Eveline said, "Oh really, haven't you seen enough of each other?" They all laughed but Rudolph never answered Wallace's question.

The newspaper was full of reports of unrest in Europe. There was talk of war. Through out the first half of the summer people were speculating if the United States would be a part of such events. On July 28 Austria declared war on Germany. The radio broadcasts had continuous coverage of the situation in Europe. The front page of the Geneva Daily News had a full page on Europe at war. The President assured the Americans that the country would not enter into any affairs in Europe. Most people were content to hear that. The Board of Commerce was having a quarterly meeting the next day. Wallace wondered what the attitude would be concerning a potential wartime effort. Among all the world news was a report about Prohibition. The vote had been taken and the bill was defeated in the House of Representatives. In order for it to pass, a 2/3 votes was required. There were 196 votes for the bill and 189 against the bill. Wallace thought that the vote was too close and wondered when it would be voted on again. The Board of Commerce meeting was well attended. There was not much concern about the war in

Europe. Everyone was satisfied and happy with Rudolph as the secretary of the Board.

While Wallace was at Standard Optical planning for the autumn collection of eyewear he overheard a conversation in the office. Someone had rushed in with an early edition of the newspaper. It was August 5 and Germany had invaded France. The next headline was that England declared war on Germany. Wallace went out to the where the people were reading the paper. Now it seemed inevitable that the United States might be involved whether it wanted to be or not. The President was making a radio broadcast later that evening about the world conditions. Everyone was encouraged to listen to his message. Wherever you went there was a bleak overtone. People were afraid that the country would be invaded and death and destruction might be the same here as in Europe. The President's speech was stern and forthright. He made no attempt to minimize the severity of events in Europe. He reassured the American public that war would be avoided at all costs. Regardless of his speech, people began to turn inward and worry for themselves.

The Sunset Ball was on Saturday, September 5 and the circus was in town on the same day. Winston wanted to go to the circus to see Robinson's Famous Shows. There was a circus museum and a menagerie of people and things to see and do. The Nelson family was the World's Greatest Acrobats. They would be performing a show in the Big Top. The circus was set up at the lakefront because it was near the railroad that brought the circus to town. Wallace was invited to go but he had no interest in a repeat of the Midway at the Exposition. Winston was as excited about the circus as he was when they were at the Pan-American Midway. He wanted to see the sideshows. He was not sure if there really was a fat lady and two headed people. Wallace told him to stay as long as he pleased. They were going to the Seneca Hotel instead. Winston made a face and shook his head when he heard that.

The day of the Sunset Ball was perfect weather for such an occasion. The sunset over Seneca Lake would be ideal for the party. Wallace dressed in his best tails and top hat. Eveline was looking perfectly put together. Olitha had been helping her all day with her hair and all the things women do to get ready. Winston was off to the circus. No one seemed to know where Rudolph was. He drove the car around to the front of the house so Eveline could walk from the house directly to the car. Olitha was helping her all the way. Wallace took it very slow at first and then went faster as they rolled down Washington Street. Eveline did not react to the ride like she usually did. She did not have the sparkle for the party that he thought she would have. He pulled the car to the front of the hotel. The valet took the car to the parking area and the doorman helped them inside. They saw Rose, Samuel, and the Preston's. Eveline was very cool toward Samuel as if she were mad at him. As they were walking into the dining room Eveline spotted Rudolph. Why was he here? Who invited him? He saw them and came over to them. He was handsomely dressed and looking very dapper. He explained that Mrs. Preston hired him to be an escort for women who did not have a dance partner. Eveline was shocked but liked the idea that she might have a better dance partner than Wallace. He showed them a dance card that women could fill out for a time to dance with him. Eveline felt like she had competition. While they were standing there talking Eveline felt faint. She took a hold of one of Wallace's arms and grabbed Rudolph's other arm. Rose gave her some water and she felt a bit better. Then, Samuel said, "Don't you have something to tell your family and friends?" She looked at them and said, "I'm pregnant." No one said a word.

Chapter 51

EVELINE'S NEWS OF HER pregnancy came as a surprise to everyone. After she adjusted to the idea of becoming a mother she decided it was time to tell the rest of the family. She sent her parent's a letter explaining the news and that the baby was due in the springtime. She sent a different type of note to Alice and Frank. She told them that their little boy was going to be a father. She did that deliberately to see what type of response she would receive, especially Frank's reaction to the idea of being a grandfather. Wallace had known that she wanted to have a family but now his concern was his involvement with the baby. He decided to tell Eveline what he was feeling about the new responsibility. Without any hesitation she told him not to worry that Sable and Olitha would be right with her all the time. Wallace did not dare ask who the father might be? Was Rudolph involved with her intimately? As he thought about those possibilities he thought about Winston and his behavior. There was no way he would have been involved with Eveline. Wallace had a stronger idea that it could be Rudolph because of all the time they had been spending together at the Women's Rights rallies. It was most likely his child though but he never was certain of what Rudolph's role in their friendship was. He had been involved with all of them in one-way or another.

When the baby was born, who would it resemble? He thought it was better to leave it alone until then.

Rudolph came to visit Eveline more often than before. Wallace asked him why he was coming to see her so often. His response was, "I want to make sure she is okay. You are so busy with all your jobs someone needs to look after her." She smiled a sweet smile when she heard him say that to Wallace. Rudolph was keeping Eveline up to date on the news about the Women's Rights events and happenings. The newspapers had been printing negative statements about women. Rose was as angry as Eveline was when she read the paper. The headline was "Women's Place Is In The Home." The article went on to say to help women stay in the home there would be classes taught on domestic sciences. The women would have the opportunity to improve their skills because modern household items were now available. Eveline, Rose, and Rudolph all yelled, "Control by Men." Rose said, "We are good enough to be offered classes on domestic duties but are not given the right to vote." There was a rally the next week in Geneva and they were going to be in the front row of the demonstration. Wallace asked where it was being held. Eveline informed him that it was going to be in front of City Hall. He told her that he was not going to be anywhere near the place. Rudolph said, "Are you afraid people might think you are for women's rights?" Wallace turned and went to the privacy of his lower level room.

The next day, Wallace decided it was time to purchase some new clothes. Style for men was becoming less formal. He went to Baker and Stark Clothier on Exchange Street. He liked the advertisement in the window that read, "Our good clothes are a sort of mental tonic that contributes largely to a man's peace of mind." Wallace thought he needed something to help his mental attitude. Lately, things had been tense. He figured it was because of what was going on in the world and at home with Eveline, the women's rights issues and lately Winston was even too busy to have any fun. The salesman introduced himself to Wallace and told him that the prices for suits started at $12.50 and the finer ones sold for up to $24.00. Wallace eyed a suit that was plaid made of fine fabric. He thought Eveline might like to see him in something a little flashier than he usually wore. While he was trying the suit on the salesman told him that such well-made clothes were not seen everyday or everywhere. When Wallace heard that it sold him on buying the suit. As the suit was being wrapped up the salesman directed Wallace to the accessory department. He told him that the hats and haberdashery are as good as the clothes. Wallace bought an ascot, a short brimmed straw hat, and a walking stick. He could not wait to see what Eveline and Rudolph would think of his outfit. The salesman complimented him on his class and style. Wallace told him he appreciated that and thanked him for his help. As he left the shop Wallace thought that the man seemed quite interesting. Maybe he should visit him again. Since all his other friends were so busy it might be time to meet some new people. He turned and asked him if he exercised at the YMCA? His reply was, "Indeed I do." Wallace nodded his head and said, "So do I. I'll look for you." The salesman smiled and studied Wallace more closely as he left the shop.

Eveline had an appointment to see Dr. Haynes for a checkup on the babies' progress. She saw Rose as she went into the office. Rose told her that they would need to get her some clothes that did not show how large she was getting. Eveline made a face of desperation as she went into see Samuel. He asked her how she was feeling? She told him she was fine but did not like the size of her stomach. He smiled and told her it was only temporary. According to what he could estimate the baby was about seven months along. He asked if they had thought about some names for the baby. Eveline wanted a girl but Wallace wanted a boy. Samuel thought that was the usual routine for new parents. He asked her what their families thought about the new addition to 380 Washington Street. Eveline laughed and explained that her mother and father were happy and wanted to be a part of their grandchild's up bringing. She went on to say that Alice was as excited as her parents but Frank wanted nothing to do with being a grandfather. He told them in a note that he was too young for all that. Samuel shook his head and said, "That man needs help." Eveline agreed. As she was leaving the office Rose stopped her and reminded her of the rally downtown the next day. Samuel just shook his head when he heard that.

While Wallace was shopping he saw a sign about a Talking Machine. The poster showed a Playerette that had to be cranked up to make a record turn. If you presented five coupons from the Geneva Daily Times to the newspaper office you were eligible to buy one for $4.98. The promotion was only for the local paper. Wallace knew he had an entire weeks worth of newspapers at home. He would cut out the five coupons and redeem them for a Playerette. He laughed because it reminded him of the Larkin Plan. It was now being done everywhere to stimulate business. He decided not to tell Eveline until he surprised her with it. He studied the recordings and they were only 10 cents. He recognized some of the artists like Mary Garden, John McCormack, Alma Gluck and Harry Lauder. There were dance selections as well as monologues that could be purchased. He hoped Eveline's attitude would improve when she heard music come from the Playerette. While they were all at the rally tomorrow he would redeem the coupons and buy it. Wallace arrived home and showed Eveline his new suit and accessories. She thought it was beautiful and wanted to know if he was going to be in the next eyewear promotion. He said only if she was with him. Eveline jokingly said, "Maybe we could be in the picture with the baby as a family wearing sun wear." Wallace laughed and thought this was a clever idea for an advertisement. He went to the stack of newspapers and flipped through all of the last five days of papers and found out that all the coupons had been clipped out. He wondered who would do such a thing. He did not want to ask Eveline because that would give the surprise away. During dinner, Sable was busy serving the meal and Olitha was bustling around by the rear entryway. Wallace wondered what all the noise was about. Sable acted as if she did not hear a thing. Eveline appeared disinterested in what was going on. Just as dessert was being served, music could be heard coming from the kitchen. Wallace made a strange face and Eveline's ears perked up to sound of the song "Peg of My Heart". All of a sudden the music slowed down almost to a drone. Then, they heard a cranking sound and the music sped up again. Wallace knew what was in the kitchen. Olitha ran out to the dining room and asked if they liked the music. They both smiled and Wallace asked, "Would you like to tell us about what is in the kitchen?" She explained that there was a promotion in the newspaper for a Playerette. She had been saving her money so she could buy it for them. It was a present for being such nice people. She wanted them to have it and maybe the baby would like to listen to music. They were surprised and thanked her. Sable told them she was worried that Wallace might get one first. Wallace laughed and confessed he was going to do just that. When he found the coupons gone he thought something was up.

Rudolph, Eveline and Rose got ready for the rally. It was a sunny but chilly day in March. They wore their heaviest coats to stay warm. Eveline liked her big coat because it covered her stomach that was now huge. The street was crowded with hundreds of people either participating or observing the activity. Rudolph was surprised that there were so many men in the crowd. Rose wondered if they were there to start a riot. The police department had a number of officers patrolling the street. It was not the same as a usual gathering. There was a police banner hanging in front of City Hall. The women in charge of the rally and the speeches were exceptionally jovial. Eveline asked Rudolph if he knew why the atmosphere was different. He did not know anything either. They thought they were going to rally for a less male dominated society. The first woman to speak was the leader of the group from Seneca Falls. She spoke about the need for constant reminders that women were valuable. She referred to the war in Europe and said that if the United States became involved then men would go to war and women would run the factories and do all the things men did. If they were good enough to work because of the war they should have the right to vote and be equal on all counts. There were screams of approval when she finished her speech. The mayor of Geneva gave a short speech about how the city was offering options for women. He referred to the college and mentioned that the attendance was open to women. He spoke of Elizabeth Blackwell who became a doctor at the Geneva College of Medicine. There was some grumbling amongst some groups that could be heard saying, "So What." After the mayor finished the chief of police stood up for a speech. He told the crowd that there was a special event taking place that day. It was the first time that the Geneva City Police Department was hiring and inducting a woman into the police force. The crowd went wild. Cheering and screaming could be heard for blocks away. The woman who was hired stood up and the crowd went crazy again. She raised her hand to calm the crowd. She explained that she worked very hard to convince the department that a woman could do things that a man cannot. The women screamed an approval at that statement. She guaranteed that her position would help in situations where a woman may be beaten by her husband or attacked in the streets. A woman officer had a different attitude toward men. If they committed a crime, they should be treated equal. There had been a case where a woman was not supported by an officer and died because she was neglected. Cheering and clapping went on for at least ten minutes. People were chanting and holding hands to show solidarity in their movement for more rights. It was an impressive scene that received newspaper coverage.

On the way back from the rally Eveline mentioned to Rose that the baby was quite active and she was having sharp pains. Rose thought she might want to stop at the office to have Samuel examine her. Rudolph went back to work because he was working on a project showing how much expansion had occurred in Geneva and the number of companies that were located in the area. He reported to the Department of Labor that there were 91 companies with a total of 2,250 employees. The payroll for these employees ranged between $25,000 and $30,000 a week. While Eveline sat in the waiting room she had a terrible thought. She told Rose that she was worried that there may be something the matter with the baby. Rose told her not to think such things. She told Rose that if anything happened to this baby that she would go crazy. She had wanted a child for a long time and did not want to disappoint Wallace. Samuel came out of the office and invited Eveline in for the examination. She explained how she was feeling and said she hoped nothing was wrong. Samuel examined her and reported to her that everything was normal. The baby was moving around and getting in a better position to be born. When Eveline heard this she let out one of her squeals. Rose knocked on the door because she thought something was wrong. Eveline walked out smiling and announced she was getting closer to the time to go to the Geneva City Hospital. Rose made sure she got home safely. While they were going into the house Eveline thought about how nice it would be if the baby were to be born on Wallace's birthday. Olitha met them at the door and was right on duty making sure Eveline rested and had not a care in the world. Rose left to go home. She reassured Eveline that Rudolph and Winston would be excited to hear the news. Eveline thought that was a strange remark to have not included Wallace in the news. She mentioned it to Olitha and she told Eveline that Dr. Haynes was here earlier today and told Wallace to expect a baby any time.

The next few days were quiet for Eveline. She rested most of the time. She had pains more regularly and they were stronger and harder to deal with. Rose came everyday to make sure she was not upset. Rudolph came to visit one day. He was so occupied with his project about Geneva's expansion that he barely stayed an hour. Winston came home early one day to visit Eveline and explained that his work was so involved he had not come home until late most nights. Eveline laughed and told him that the boys had no playtime lately. Winston smiled and told her that he missed those times. She made a face as another pain shot through her stomach. Winston thought it was time for him to leave. He laughed and said, "I don't know how to deliver a baby." Wallace came home early every night to sit with Eveline. They made up a list of names for the baby and talked about what it would be like with a family. Eveline kept reminding Wallace how lucky she was to have him for a husband. He asked her why. She told him because he was wealthy and could afford to have hired help and take good care of her. He thought that sounded a bit spoiled on her part but did not address her reasoning. He was glad he had time to spend with his friends and that Eveline was happy and taken care of. One night before he came home he saw the salesman from Baker and Stark at the YMCA. He told Eveline about him and his good sales ability. His name was Mike and he was going to exercise with Wallace a few times a week. Eveline looked at him and asked, "What will Rudolph and Winston think about all that exercise?" Wallace acted like he did not find that too funny, although he did have time to find out more about Mike than he talked about.

It was a week later and Eveline was becoming more and more uncomfortable. Dr. Haynes suggested that it might be time to go to the hospital. She had Olitha pack the proper clothing and things she would need while in the hospital. Wallace took time off from work so he could be around for whatever might happen. He drove the car to the front of the house where Olitha and Sable helped her into the car. By this time she was barely able to walk. For the first time Wallace thought she was in trouble. Samuel was there and assured Wallace that she was fine. This was how it was when you are ready to have a baby. Wallace told him he was glad that he would never know that feeling. They laughed and agreed. Wallace drove the car so slowly that he thought it was going to stall most of the way. He tried to avoid any bumps or ruts in the road. When they arrived at the hospital a nurse was there with a wheel chair to take her into the delivery room. Sable, Olitha and Wallace sat in the waiting area. No one said much of anything. Dr. Haynes came out occasionally to talk but nothing was happening yet. By this time Rose found a way to get to the hospital to be there while they waited. While Samuel was talking to Wallace the nurse came out and told him that he needed to come right away because the baby was on its way. Wallace took a deep breath while Sable and Olitha sat like they were in shock from worry. Winston and Rudolph walked in just as Samuel was going into the delivery room. Wallace told them what was about to happen. Samuel had not come out from the room for nearly two hours. At 11PM there was the sound of a baby crying. They looked at one another in relief and then Samuel came out to tell them that it was a baby boy. Eveline had a very difficult time delivering the baby and was sleeping. He explained that she knew it was a baby boy but because she was so sleepy, she had not seen him yet. Samuel wanted Wallace to come in to see his son. They walked down the hall and into the room where Eveline was sleeping. When he walked up to Eveline she was cradling his son in her arms. He did not want to disturb her but needed to see who the baby looked like at last. He reached over and pulled aside the bunting and gasped as he saw his wife holding a baby with brown skin. Wallace was speechless as he looked at Dr. Haynes.

Chapter 52

THE SHOCK OF EVELINE giving birth to a brown skinned baby was difficult to understand. How could such a thing happen? When Eveline awoke she denied that this could possibly be her child. She accused Samuel of tricking her. Rose tried to comfort her while the nurse was dressing the baby. Wallace asked Samuel how such a thing could have happened. Samuel was just as surprised as everyone else. Sable was the least upset of all of them. She told Rudolph and Winston that having a brown baby was common where she came from. She told them about a husband and wife who had a baby just like Eveline did. They did not know how it happened until they asked the family about anyone in their past who might have been involved with a Negro. She told Wallace this just as he heard Eveline wailing in her room. He rushed in and found her out of the bed looking at the baby as if she were in the wrong room. When she saw Wallace she said, "Get me out of here. I'm in the wrong room." Wallace tried to comfort her, but she pushed him away. Samuel came back into the room and suggested a potion to calm her down. Wallace agreed that she needed to rest. After she fell asleep the nurse took the baby and put him in the next room. Samuel thought she would sleep until morning and told them all to go home and get some rest.

The next day Wallace returned with Samuel to see how things were going. During the night Eveline woke up and went to the next room and attempted to strangle the baby. When they saw Eveline the nurse had tied her to the bed so she could not harm herself or the baby again. Wallace hardly recognized Eveline because she was dazed and looked like she had gone crazy. He asked Samuel what they were going to do with her. Wallace told him he had never seen her act this way. She was always sweet and never vicious. Samuel explained that women sometimes have reactions after giving birth. The problem was that Eveline had a Negro baby. He was going to give her another potion to keep her calm. He examined the baby and found his throat had been ruptured when Eveline's fingers dug into his throat. Samuel wanted to know if they had picked a name for the baby? Wallace said, "Yes, Patrick." Wallace also wanted to know why he needed to know his name so soon. Samuel wanted to have the birth certificate written. He told Wallace that the way the baby was breathing he may not be strong enough to survive. Just as he heard the news Winston and Rudolph came into the waiting area. Wallace tried to explain as he sobbed what happened during the night and that the baby may not live. Neither one of the men could believe such a tragedy could happen. Samuel told them that Eveline needed to be kept away from the situation because her mind was very unstable. The nurse would watch the baby and make sure he continued to breath. He hoped the breathing would get better during the day.

Wallace and the rest of the men went back to the house. Olitha was waiting for the report with Rose. Samuel told them what had happened during the night and that Eveline would probably need to go somewhere to rest and recuperate. Sable asked who was going to care for the baby. Rose offered to be available during the day. Sable piped up and said, "I knows about babies they like to see the same color skin." Wallace was not ready to hear about the skin color. He told them that Samuel would decide who was caring for the baby. Rose suggested that all three women could share the responsibility. Samuel wanted to talk with Wallace privately about what he should consider for Eveline's recovery. Sable and Olitha went to the bungalow with Rudolph and Winston. Samuel wanted Rose to stay since she was going to part of the plan. Rose thought that it was better for her to help Eveline anyway since they were closer friends than the hired help. Samuel thought that an asylum would be where Eveline should go. He emphasized it would not be forever. He thought a long period of rest away from anything that might remind her of what happened would be better for her recovery. Wallace wanted to know where that might be. Samuel told him it was Willard State Hospital a few miles away from Geneva on the east side of Seneca Lake. When he heard that he thought of Hilda. Samuel told him there were different areas to live in. He suggested the one that was for temporary residents. It was very nice and similar to being in a hotel. She could have her own room and would be with people of her own type. Wallace was satisfied with the idea. The only thing he wanted to know was how long would she be there? Samuel said it was hard to say. Usually six months for recovery from a shock such as this. The doctors would talk with her about the baby and how she was reacting to the situation. Wallace would be free to see her on the weekends. Her family could be included then too. Wallace wanted to know if she could see the baby before she went? Samuel was not sure if Eveline even remembered giving birth or being pregnant. Samuel wondered if she would even remember trying to strangle the baby or delivering him. Wallace felt like he wanted to cry again. Rose had tears in her eyes too when she heard what really happened that night. After everything had been discussed, Willard State Hospital was best for Eveline. Wallace needed to tell their parents what was happening. Samuel told him that she could stay in the hospital for a few days. She would be given potions to keep her calm until she was moved to Willard.

The next day Wallace decided to go to Rochester to tell the families what had happened. He knew it would be better to tell them in person. Wallace asked Rudolph if he could call the hotel and have the manager get in touch with Alice and Frank and Mr. and Mrs. Lounsberry. Rudolph called and made arrangements for them to meet at the hotel lobby around 11AM. Rudolph offered to go with Wallace. Wallace thought that was a good idea. The weather was very bad for the springtime so Wallace decided to go by train instead of using his car. They took the first train to Rochester. They arrived at 10AM. They had time to settle down at the hotel before the family arrived. Rudolph suggested some breakfast since Wallace had not eaten since yesterday. Breakfast tasted very good and they felt calmer after eating. Wallace and Rudolph sat in the lobby waiting for everyone to arrive. How were they going to take all the news? What were they going to think about a Negro baby? Rudolph told him to stop worrying about how they were going to react. Wallace thanked Rudolph for reminding him of the importance of being level headed at a time like this.

The family arrived at 11AM. Alice hugged Wallace and so did Catherine. Frank and Mr. Lounsberry stood like they were afraid of Wallace. They knew something was wrong because there was no Eveline. Catherine asked," Where's Eveline?" Wallace told them that this was the reason for their meeting. They sat in a quiet corner and Wallace began. He told them of the difficult delivery Eveline had endured. He mentioned her lack of accepting the baby. Alice wanted to know why. Wallace hesitated and finally told them she gave birth to a brown skinned baby boy. All eyebrows went up when the words brown skin were heard. Frank blurted out and said, "I knew it, she was playing around." Alice for the first time in her life stood up and slapped Frank. She said, "I've wanted to do that for years. You finally said the wrong thing at the right time." Wallace told them to stop it that now was not a time to fight. Catherine wanted to know if the baby and Eveline were okay. Wallace said that was another reason he wanted to be with them to discuss the matter. He told them how upset she was when she realized she had a Negro baby and how she attempted to strangle the child. He told them she was restrained and calmed until she could be moved to Willard State Hospital. No one said a word. He went on to tell them that there was some doubt if the baby would live. Alice started crying and Catherine stared at Mr. Lounsberry. Then, Frank asked, "If she wasn't playing around then why did she have a brown baby?" Alice glared at him and Wallace touched her arm so she would not go after him again. Wallace told them the story that Sable told him about a family she worked for that had the same circumstance happen to them. Wallace mentioned that sometimes people had done things in the past that no one ever knows about until something like this happens. When he said that, Alice had a strange thought. What did her own mother do that maybe no one knew about? Did her

Aunt Catherine know more than she told? She was always careful not to tell too much about her sister. All she ever said was that she was unstable and wild. Alice did not say anything about her thoughts. She knew she would need to contact her aunt in Canada. Wallace told them who would be taking care of the baby and that they named him Patrick. Alice started sobbing and so did Catherine. Mr.Lounsberry and Frank were without emotion. Wallace wondered how they could have such little emotion about all of this? Frank was glaring at Alice after what she did to him. Wallace thought that was the first time he ever saw his mother stand up for herself. He was proud to see her spunk. Wallace told them they were going back to Geneva and he would send the news as it happened. He let them know they could all see Eveline after she was settled into her place at Willard. He hoped it would only be temporary.

Alice went right to the telegraph office. They did not have telephone service yet and neither did her aunt in Canada. She did not want to wait for the mail to get there. She wrote to Aunt Catherine to ask if she knew any more about her mother's past. Alice told her that Wallace and Eveline had a baby boy that had brown skin. Did she have any idea why? She had a strange inkling that some information was coming to solve the mystery about her father. Wallace and Rudolph were back in Geneva by late afternoon. Wallace went to work for a brief time to catch up on some work. It was March 31 and there were end of the month duties to be finished for Standard and Safege. Winston left him a note with information about the financials for Goodwin Printing that said money was rolling in. Wallace was glad everything was in order. He did not have the mind to deal with another thing.

Before Wallace went home he went to see Eveline at the hospital. He walked into her room and she was still asleep. The nurse told him she only woke to eat and then went back to sleep. He asked if the baby was all right. The nurse took him to see Patrick. His breathing was more labored than before. The nurse explained that they tried feeding him but he was not able to swallow anything. Wallace shook his head knowing this was not good news. The nurse told him there was nothing he could do tonight and that he needed to go home and rest himself. When Wallace arrived home he found that Sable had prepared a hot meal for him. He ate it as if he had not eaten in a week. He told her about Patrick and his difficulty breathing and swallowing. She shook her head as she walked into the kitchen. He wanted some company after he ate. He was not in the mood to go to bed so he went to the bungalow to see if Winston was home. Olitha came to the door when she saw Wallace coming. He was hoping for Winston but Olitha told him he was exercising. Wallace thought that might be good to do also. He went to the YMCA and found Rudolph and Winston just finishing their routines and going to the showers. Wallace looked at them and realized he was not part of that routine. On his way out of the YMCA he ran into Mike. He was happy to see Wallace and asked if he was coming or going. Wallace told him he was not sure tonight. Mike asked if he wanted to get together. Instead of going into the YMCA they went to a tavern. It seemed as if this was just what he needed was a good drink with someone who was not involved in everything that was happening. Wallace had a good time with Mike. Mike was happy they were together and discussed all kinds of things. Wallace felt that sensation while he was enjoying his time with Mike. He felt he could like him even better than Winston and Rudolph.

It was April 1st and Wallace's birthday. He woke up and knew this one was not going to be a big celebration. When he went to the dining room for breakfast neither Sable nor Olitha knew it was his birthday. He did not tell them either. He ate and was on his way to the hospital to see Eveline and the baby before he went to work. Winston saw him and went with him to the hospital. Wallace asked if they had a good time last night at the YMCA. Winston smiled and told him they did but wondered why he did not stay. Wallace told him he saw a friend of his and they went to a tavern. He did not say much more than that and Winston did not ask questions either. When they arrived at the hospital Samuel was seeing other patients. Wallace asked the nurse how things were overnight? She told him that Dr. Haynes would be speaking with him shortly. Her tone of voice was not good. Wallace knew something had happened. Samuel came out and told Wallace that Patrick had died a few minutes ago. Wallace was motionless. Winston put his hand on Wallace's shoulder. Samuel explained that the baby stopped breathing and there was nothing they could do. Eveline was still unaware of her surroundings and did not know the baby had died. All Wallace could say was, "Great birthday present." Winston realized that no one remembered Wallace's birthday and what a tragedy this day had been. Samuel asked what arrangements Wallace would be making for Patrick? Wallace told him to have the baby cremated. Samuel raised both hands and said, "Okay."

Wallace was in no mood to go to work so he went back home. He told Sable and Olitha about the baby and Eveline's condition. Winston got in touch with Rudolph and Rose and they came to the house. Wallace was glad to have his friends around him. Rose suggested that the ashes of the baby be spread over the lake. She thought that since the baby was not baptized that his ashes should be in the water that never blessed his life. Wallace thought that was a perfect way to deal with Patrick's brief existence. While they were discussing things the telephone rang. Wallace was surprised because very few people had telephones. It was rare for it to ring. Olitha answered it and directed it to Wallace. The operator had a call from the Seneca Powers Hotel. Wallace wondered what else could happen today. He listened to the operator tell the person on the other end that it was okay to talk; it was his mother. She explained that she went to the hotel to use the phone because Rudolph instructed the manager to let her use it if she needed to get in touch with him. Her tone was a mixture of happiness and sadness. Wallace asked her what the matter was. She told him that after he left the other day, she sent a telegram to her Aunt Catherine telling her about Eveline and the brown skin of the baby. She wanted to know if she knew any more about her mother Eva's background. As it turned out there was one more thing she never thought she would need to tell. Eva got pregnant from a Civil War soldier who was a black man who fled to Canada. Alice finally found out about her father and the reason the baby had brown skin. When she finished speaking Wallace told her about Patrick. She started crying and then Wallace did too. Rose tried to comfort him while he sobbed with his mother. He realized what an awful day this was turning out to be. She wished him a happy birthday as they cried. Wallace was able to say he was glad she finally knew about her father. Alice told him that now there is no question why Patrick was a colored baby. She told Wallace she loved him and was sorry this had to happen and hung up.

Samuel met with Wallace about moving Eveline to Willard. She would be sedated to keep her sleepy when they transferred her to the State Hospital. Wallace thought about Hilda and how drugged she looked when she went to Mr. Helfer's memorial service. They would be moving her tomorrow. Samuel suggested the steamboat be used from Geneva because it docked right in front of the hospital. He felt she should have no knowledge of the event or people she knew around at that time. He could visit her a few days later. Wallace thought it was cruel but Samuel explained the separation was easier for the patient if they are not familiar with people. Sometimes the patient gets more upset and hopes the familiar face will take them away to a safer place. Wallace understood. He felt like his whole world had just collapsed around him. Winston, Rudolph, Rose, Sable, and Olitha all sympathized with him. They assured him they would be there to help him. The move would be made in the morning. A steamboat would be leaving from the pier at 9AM. She would be in her room by lunchtime.

Wallace tried to go back to work and have business as usual. He found it difficult to concentrate. Life at work was more trouble than pleasant. He found his creativity in advertising had hit rock bottom. When he arrived home the hired help was sitting around. Wallace began to think that he might need to let one of them go. He did not need full time help for himself. Winston suggested that he could move back to the main house while Eveline was gone. Wallace thought that might be a good idea. The women would have the bungalow and the men would have the house to themselves. When Rudolph heard that he asked when he was moving in. Wallace told him that Winston had lived with them many times before and knew how it worked. All Rudolph remembered was the good times they had in Buffalo at the Delaware Avenue apartment. Wallace thought about Rudolph's conniving way of getting signatures for the devious work in New York to accuse Winston of the murders. Wallace tried to forget those times. Sable and Olitha were happy to have the place to themselves and Winston was happy to be back in the main house.

It was time to go to visit Eveline at the asylum. Wallace drove the car very slowly because some of the road was unpaved. It was a dry day so there were no mud holes and the car did not get dusty. It took an hour to get from Geneva to Willard. He felt like he was going into a prison as he entered the main gatehouse. The guard directed him to the nicest building on the grounds. There was a large veranda for the patients to sit on and enjoy the pleasant breezes off Seneca Lake. There were lovely gardens with flowers everywhere. Wallace understood how a place like this could help a person recuperate from a shock. The closer he got the more nervous he became. He hoped Eveline would recognize him and that she was comfortable. The women at the door invited him into the large reception area. He sat down and waited for them to bring Eveline out to visit. They told him that she was a charming woman and was doing very well. Wallace felt like he was off to a good start. He was looking at all the people in the room when he spotted Hilda at the opposite end of the room. He wondered if he should go over to say hello. He decided that he had enough going on and it was better not to start her up. He turned and saw Eveline coming toward him. She had a smile on her face. He was not sure what to do. She held her hand out to shake his hand. Wallace felt like he was a stranger to his wife. The nurse explained to him residents are taught to act a certain way when visitors arrive. She said, "Hello Wallace. How are you?" He told her fine and asked how she was feeling. She told him fine and wanted to get out of there. The nurse interrupted and reminded her that everyone leaves when they feel better. Eveline made a face and smiled at Wallace. Then she leaned forward and asked if he was there to take her away. When he heard this he realized what Samuel meant by a disturbed person wanting a familiar face to take you away. He told her that he was there to visit. Wallace's back was turned away from the end of the room where Hilda was. While he was talking to Eveline he felt like someone was staring at him. He turned and Hilda had walked over to him and was peering down on him. Eveline said, "Wallace who is that witch looking at you?" Hilda began yelling, "He is the man who made me a crazy witch. He stole my hotel from me." By that time, the staff had hustled Hilda away as she screamed at Wallace for killing her cousin. Eveline appeared unaffected by the whole scene. She had no recollection of who Hilda was. It was then he knew she was in for a long recovery. When he left Eveline did not ask when he was coming back because it was not important. Time did not seem to matter to her. As Wallace left, the nurse told him that she was further ahead than most of the residents. Wallace hated the word resident because it sounded too permanent.

Chapter 53

THE WAR WAS SPREADING throughout Europe. President Wilson continued to tell the American public that the United States would not enter into the affairs of the war. On May 7, the Lusitania sank off the coast of Ireland. It was on a voyage with over 2000 passengers aboard. A torpedo was sent to sink the ship. There were 1457 passenger that were listed dead or missing and only 703 survivors. The country was in shock when people heard about this tragedy. That event marked the beginning of the possibility that the United States may end up in the midst of war whether it wanted to be or not. The newspapers were filled with editorials about the pros and cons of entering the war. President Wilson gave the Germans an ultimatum to cease and desist from all acts of war. The warning was not respected by Germany and the invasions continued. The American public was preparing for the possibility of increased involvement. As time went on the more and more advertisements appeared about the war effort.

President Wilson had private affairs that were consuming his time. He had been courting a woman his daughter introduced him to. The courtship that began on a golf course went on for many months. President Wilson admired Mrs. Norman E. Galt when he was her teacher of the game of golf. She had little knowledge of this Scottish game which was one of the President's favorite pastimes.

After the entire summer of courtship he proposed to her on October 6 and she agreed to marry him on December 18, 1915. They had a small private service in an Episcopal church in Washington. Mrs. Galt had been a close personal friend of Mrs. Margaret Wilson right to the day of her death. The President and Mrs. Galt had been very involved in social matters long before the idea of courtship began. There was gossip about how many years they knew one another and what the real truth of their involvement had been. The newspapers had a heyday in the gossip columns. The newly married couple did not allow any of the public opinion to deter their new life and plans for the White House. The war was taking much more valuable time for the officials to deal with. Small gossip was just that.

1916 arrived with very little fanfare. The issues that were important before were only mildly addressed now. The suffrage movement had toned down. Wallace wondered what was happening to it. He mentioned it to Rudolph and was told that the war was becoming the major emphasis. If the country entered into the war women would become very important as workers in the factories while the men went off to fight the war. Rudolph discussed the change in the commerce affairs that were affected by the possibilities of war. He recorded an increase in female employment during his meeting with the Board of Commerce. The attitude of the companies' owners was not as resistant as before. They realized that women were going to take the place of men. They hoped this would give them the feeling of equality. Wallace reminded the group that he transferred his home to his wife a few years before. He thought it was a good way to calm the restless mind of his wife and protect him from any loss of property if there were financial shortcomings. They laughed when he said shortcomings. One man jokingly spoke up and said, "When you live in an outer space house, that is a good way to send your house and wife to the moon when she acts up." Wallace smiled but did not find that remark too fun especially knowing where Eveline was. Wallace was successful keeping his wife's condition out of the public eye. Most people knew she had a baby but that it had died in childbirth. Samuel made it very clear at the hospital that officials keep the information limited. Whenever Rose was seen in public many people would ask where Eveline was. She got used to responding that she was in Rochester helping her sick mother. The questions slowly ended.

Their family wanted to visit Eveline. Wallace had been seeing Eveline weekly and there were signs of improvement. She was more like she used to be. She was not so strange acting with Wallace. She looked forward to seeing him. Since Wallace was in charge of Hilda's well being, he met with the staff to discuss moving Hilda to another building to avoid any confrontations. When Wallace met with the director of the hospital he told Wallace that Hilda was rapidly declining. After seeing Wallace a few months ago it was as if she had given up. The director was not sure if she would make it to the end of the year. Wallace still had her placed in a different building. He figured it was his turn to make her decisions. Mr. Helfer had confidence in his judgments and would do what he thought best. Wallace mentioned to Eveline that the family wanted to visit her the next week. She asked him why they had not been to visit her in her new home yet. When Wallace heard that he feared that she was thinking she was never returning to Washington Street. He asked the doctor if they should begin reminding her of where she lived and why she was at Willard. The doctor thought that might be a good idea after the family visit. Seeing everyone would be enough and mentioning home might add more confusion and trigger another set back. Wallace agreed to the plan and told Eveline he would be back with their parents next week.

Rudolph had been working in Geneva for nearly a year. He was happy with his work and liked living in the city. He told Wallace he wanted to buy a car. Wallace was delighted and thought a Ford would be a good buy. He was getting large dividends from the Ford Motor Company every quarter and wanted Rudolph to be part of that too. He surprised Wallace when he told him that he was considering an Overland. Wallace told him that his last announcement from Ford was that its car was considered "The Unusual Car" from $325 to a sedan for $645; a much larger version. Rudolph nicely told Wallace that he was going to buy what he wanted and not what the advertisements suggested. Wallace did not like that remark but could not do anything about it. The Overland was called "The World's Most Powerful Low Priced Car." The car could go up to 50 mph and included an electric starter, lights, a magnetic speedometer and could hold 5 passengers. There was more car and equipment for the same price as a Ford. Rudolph asked Wallace to go to the Geneva Auto Dealer on Castle Street to see the model in the showroom. Wallace was not interested in undercutting his investments but he did go out of curiosity. When Rudolph saw the car in the showroom it had a convertible top just like Wallace's Ford and he bought one right on the spot. Wallace told him he should think about making such a move to an Overland. Rudolph said, "Too late." He was to receive his new car in a week.

The family arrived by train on Sunday to visit Eveline. Wallace was able to take everyone in his car but they barely fit. When they were all squeezing into the car he thought about Rudolph's car being able to hold 5 passengers. Maybe Rudolph had a good idea about the Overland but now was not the time to change cars. The ride was pleasant with the weather warm as a July day should be. They arrived at Willard shortly after lunchtime. The staff did not encourage dining with the residents. Too many outbursts occurred when families would be in the dining room. They found a group of rocking chairs that were on the veranda. There was a hint of rose fragrance in the breeze as it blew across the porch. Alice was a bit tense when she saw a woman start screaming at the other end of the veranda. She wondered if that was how her mother might have acted before she killed herself. Mrs. Lounsberry had a fan that she was using in a vigorous way. Finally, Mr. Lounsberry told her to slow it down. She gave him a disgusted look. Frank was his usual disconnected self. Wallace wondered what choice remark he was saving for the group. He could not wait for the whole affair to be over. Since Eveline had been confined to Willard, life was not normal. Eveline appeared from the building with the nurse. She saw everyone and started waving like she used too. Wallace had not seen this much life in her in a long time. The nurse told Eveline that she would be right inside if she needed anything. It was as if nothing had ever happened. She kissed everyone except Frank. Wallace thought that might set his father off but it did not. Eveline told them how nice it was living there. Her mother was happy she was content. Alice told her how nice she looked. Eveline laughed and thanked her. Wallace thought that maybe she was ready to come home when he saw so much happiness in the group. After she told them about her life at Willard she looked at Frank and said, "I have never liked you. You remind me of that guy I knew that wanted to marry me. He tried to make me happy. I pretended to like him but never did. I think he is dead now." Wallace did not know if she was referring to him or someone else. Alice looked at Wallace who had no expression. Mr. Lounsberry asked her if she was confusing him with someone else. Eveline continued, "He took me places to live and was always working. He left me alone with a lot of men. I can't remember who they all were." Then she looked at Wallace and said, "I think you were one of them. You are the only one that comes to see me. All I remember is a man taking me into a room in a hospital and taking something out of me." Wallace was ready to cry. Eveline called for the nurse because she was tired and wanted to rest. They kissed her goodbye except Frank and Wallace. Wallace knew he had to speak with Samuel and the director about her apparent lapse of memory. The ride home was very somber.

The next week, Wallace made an appointment with the director of Willard and Samuel. Wallace needed to know if his wife's lapse of memory was permanent or temporary. He wanted Samuel's opinion of the situation. The director explained that many times people forget the most important or meaningful people in their lives. It could be triggered by a person who is similar to them or a combination of the shock they experienced. Samuel explained to the director what Eveline's past was like and that she had never been told that there was a reason for giving birth to a Negro baby. Samuel suggested that he and the doctor at Willard have a combined appointment with her to talk about the baby. Maybe Eveline would not remember anything or maybe she would think of one thing that would start her remembering the event. Wallace was at the point where he would approve of anything that might help her. They thought it was a good thing she remembered going into the hospital and that a man took something out of her. They would see her tomorrow. Wallace went home and told Winston and Rudolph about Eveline's lack of memory. They were shocked to think that she was so different from what she used to be. Wallace explained how much she interacted with his mother and her parents. His father was the target of her hate. They were surprised she had turned on him. Everyone knew Frank was miserable but she was really telling it like it was. Wallace could not understand why he was treated almost like his father. Rudolph wanted to know if the three of them should go see her next weekend. Wallace would ask Samuel what he thought. Maybe the three of them would trigger something else. At this point no one seemed to have an answer.

Wallace and Samuel drove to Willard the next day. Wallace was to stay out of sight during the session. He would be able to hear what was discussed but it was better she only see the doctors. They met Eveline in a small well-decorated room. She asked where her friends were. The director told her they would be back later. She looked at Samuel and asked if she knew him. He told her he used to be her doctor. It was obvious she recognized him but could not put the pieces together about why she knew him. The director asked her if she remembered anymore about the man who took something from her. She casually looked at Samuel and said, "Yes, I know you. It was you who took something from me." The director wanted to know if she knew what was taken from her. She thought for a moment and said, "Something brown that didn't belong to me. It was a mistake and had to be taken back." Samuel knew then she did recollect the birth. The director wanted to know if she knew why she was here and not home. Eveline told them she missed her home. There was a brown skin woman at her house and that brown thing taken from her should be hers. Wallace and Samuel knew that must be Sable or Olitha she was referring to. Then Eveline wanted to know why they were keeping her friends from her. Samuel wanted to know their names. She told them, Rudolph, Winston, Rose, Sable, and Olitha. The director asked if she had a husband. She hesitated and said, "Yes but he is dead." When Wallace heard that he might as well have been dead. Samuel asked when he died. She told them she was not sure if it had happened or was it going to happen soon? They thought that she was confusing other people from the past and mixing them with the present. The last question was if she could remember her husband's name. She immediately said, "My Wallace." That ended the meeting. Eveline went back to her room. Wallace met Samuel outside and was completely beside himself. Samuel looked on the brighter side. He told Wallace that she does remember everything. It is just in the wrong order.

On the way back to Geneva Samuel suggested that all the friends she spoke about should go visit her. Wallace asked if he should go too. Samuel thought that might not be a good idea. Since Eveline thought he was dead maybe the others could bring more memory back quicker. Samuel would listen to the visit as he did from a place that she could not see him. The next weekend everyone except Wallace went to visit Eveline. They felt like they were going to a prison but soon understood why it was designed like one. As they were going to the veranda a woman was screaming out of a window. She was ready to jump but was held back by a burly attendant. Winston made a smart remark about how big the man was. Rudolph sternly advised him that now was not the time for jokes. When Eveline saw all of them she knew their names and wanted to know why they had not come to see her sooner. The first person she zeroed in on was Rudolph. She wanted to know why he had not taken her to the rally lately. Then she looked at Olitha and wanted to know when they were going shopping for some new clothes. Eveline wanted to know why Sable did not bring her some better food. Then she got to Winston and asked if he knew anything about the guy he used to play with. Winston told her that he sees him all the time. When she heard that she laughed and said, "Nothing has changed." They knew she was alert to everything and everyone. Samuel thought that she now only had a block against Wallace. The question was why and how could she come out of it? Then she wanted to know when they were going to take her away from this place and all go home. Samuel now questioned whether they should take her back to Washington Street. The director met them afterward and thought that a trip there might be okay if she were to return the same day. Rose wanted to know if Wallace should be around. It was decided he should not be present for her first time back.

Christmas was getting closer. Samuel and the director thought a week before the holiday might be a good time to take her home. They explained to Wallace that he could not be seen when she was there. It would be helpful for him to listen to the conversation from a different part of the house. He agreed but was unhappy about what might happen. It was like he was dead. Luckily, Rudolph's car could hold 5 passengers. He reminded Wallace of how his car was bigger than his Ford. That did not seem to be an important part of the discussion. They were sure to have decorations in place and presents for her when she arrived. Samuel told them they should all go to pick her up and take her back to Willard. Consistency was important for this first time out of her environment. They arrived at Willard. She was wearing her nicest dress and coat. She acted as if nothing had ever happened. As they got closer to Geneva she mentioned remembering the lake and the park where they had a picnic a long time ago before she lived in the big unusual house. They laughed and told her that is where we are going. When they parked in front of the house Eveline asked why Olitha was in the car and not outside waiting for her. She was right next to her and squeezed her arm. She laughed and said, "Of course you are." They walked into the entrance way and immediately Eveline threw her coat off just like she used too. Olitha picked it up and hung it in the closet. Sable went to the kitchen and finished the dinner as if she had been there all day. Wallace was in the lower room listening to Eveline's chatter. It sounded so good to hear her voice again. The house was coming alive. Rose asked if she wanted to freshen up? They went upstairs and nothing seemed to change. Eveline went to her dressing table and picked up the brush and makeup like it was yesterday. Before dinner, they exchanged presents. Everything was very normal until there was a present for Eveline from Wallace. When she saw the tag, she asked, "Who is Wallace." She studied it and then said, "Is he the dead man?" Rose spoke up and told her he was a friend that could not be here today. Eveline thought that was too bad and proceeded to open the presents. They all knew she still thought Wallace was dead. He was listening from downstairs and felt crushed to think that he was the one who had to be dead. What did he do to deserve this title of "Dead?"

Chapter 54

THE WOMEN'S RIGHTS MOVEMENT was gaining momentum in early 1917. Alice Paul was an advocate of women's rights who had been lobbying for equality but to no avail. She and her colleagues formed the National Woman's Party in late 1916. It was patterned after methods used in Britain. Tactics included demonstrations, parades, mass meetings, picketing, and hunger strikes. When Rudolph read about the affairs of that group he thought it would be good to attend one of their rallies. President Wilson had avoided committing himself to the suffrage movement during his campaign for presidency. There was to be a political protest in Washington in a few weeks. Alice Paul was one of the leaders of the rally. Rudolph wanted to go to Washington to be part of the protest. He told Wallace about the event and wondered if Eveline was up to going with him. Wallace thought he should ask Samuel what he thought about her going so far from her environment. Rudolph knew that if Eveline were to go, Rose would want to go with them. Wallace agreed to discuss it with Samuel. He told Wallace to make sure Samuel understood it was a non-violent protest to picket the White House. The names of the picketers were the "Silent Sentinels." Rudolph was excited to think they might be going to Washington. They would be branching out from the local demonstrations. Maybe they were ready to be a part of the national movement for women's rights.

The next day, Wallace saw Samuel and discussed Eveline's condition. He reported to Wallace that not much had changed in her mental state. She appeared very normal and was happy in her environment. When asked about her husband she continued to maintain that he was either dead or was going to die. She was not sure where he was. Wallace asked what he thought about her going to Washington with Rudolph for the demonstration at the White House. Samuel found no reason why she should not go. He thought it might be good for her to go further away from Geneva. Since she was going with Rudolph it would be a familiar situation. Wallace asked if Rose would consider going too. Samuel thought that might be even better. Wallace bought the train tickets that day. They would leave on Monday and the protest was on Tuesday. Samuel jokingly hoped they would not get thrown in jail for some wrongful act. Wallace said, "That's all we would need." Then he walked over to the Board of Commerce to tell Rudolph what had been decided. He was happy to think they were going away as they had in the past. Wallace told him he would see Eveline during the weekend and wanted Rudolph to go with him for the visit so he could invite her. Rudolph agreed to go to Willard on Saturday. While he was at the Board of Commerce he saw Mr. Preston. He inquired about Eveline. Wallace was surprised he asked because most people had become use to Eveline's absence in town. He asked Wallace if she was okay. Wallace wanted to know why. Mr. Preston mentioned that his wife heard that Eveline was infirmed at Willard. Wallace denied such a rumor. Rudolph interrupted and told him that he just saw her at their home for Christmas. Mr. Preston had a strange look on his face as if he did not believe the story. When he left Wallace asked Rudolph how that news got out. Rudolph said that maybe someone from Geneva might work at Willard and may have seen him there. Wallace decided to tell Mr. Preston he had someone at Willard that he was in charge of. He was glad for the first time that he could rely on Hilda as a reason for being seen at Willard. Rudolph thought that was perfect thinking before any more rumors were spread.

Wallace picked Rudolph up early Saturday morning. The roads were clear so driving was not a problem. They arrived just before lunchtime. They had about an hour to spend with Eveline. They sat in the large reception room. As she walked into the room she had a familiar presence about her. She was more carefree than she had been recently. She smiled when she saw Rudolph. When she saw Wallace she had the usual confused look about who he was. Wallace decided to act like there was nothing the matter. He was her friend and would tell her things about their past. Samuel thought that might help her to remember that he was her husband. Wallace started by asking her if she liked her Christmas present he gave her since she was wearing it. She looked at him and said, "Oh you gave this to me?" Wallace told her that he knew that pink was her favorite color. She looked at Rudolph and asked how a stranger like him would know what her favorite color was. Rudolph told her that they had been friends since childhood. Eveline laughed and told him that could not be true because she barely knew that man. Wallace was crushed that she still did not realize who he was. Rudolph explained that he wanted her to go to Washington with Rose and him. He explained that they would go on Monday and would be there with the

Silent Sentinels that was a group that was demonstrating in a non-violent way for woman's rights. When she heard that she let out one of her piercing squeals. Everyone in the room turned and stared and even the attendant came over to see if she was okay. She told the attendant, "Never better, I'm going to Washington with my Ruddy." Wallace wanted to crawl away when he heard the "my Ruddy" part. Rudolph made an embarrassing face at Wallace that Eveline did not see. Samuel told Wallace to have Eveline leave from home for the trip to Washington and have them return her to Washington Street after the trip. Sable and Olitha would be on duty as they always were to maintain the routine just as it was before she had the breakdown. Samuel agreed to get Eveline from Willard and bring her home before they left for Washington.

Wallace went to work on Monday morning so Eveline would not see him before they left. While he was at work he thought he wanted to see how she was acting at the train station. He walked to the station and stood at a distance as he saw them waiting for the train. It was a sunny and cold January morning and Eveline was dressed in a sporty outfit with the sweater he had given her. He was happy she was wearing it. She had her arm around Rudolph's waist and Rose had her arm around him too. Wallace thought that was more than they needed to be doing but was glad Eveline appeared to be back to her old self. He kept asking himself why she could not remember him. He was satisfied she was getting away and doing things she liked to do though. As Wallace walked into the office at Safege, Mr. Preston apologized for his reference about Eveline's whereabouts. He told Wallace that he saw Rudolph, Rose, and Eveline near the train station that morning. Wallace thought now was the time to tell him where they were going and why. When he heard about the picketing in Washington he said, "They're back at it again. I thought with all the war stuff the women had calmed down." Wallace shook his head and said, "It's even hotter than before."

Wallace received a letter from the Ford Motor Company listing the stock values and the progress in the company. Wire Wheels were in high demand for the new automobiles. They gave a sporty look to the car and were more reliable. Wallace decided to inquire about the number of factories that were needed to produce the wheels. He thought Geneva might be a good place for a factory of that type. He saw a telephone number on the bottom of the report. He called the operator and gave the number to be called. He waited and heard the different operators connecting his call. A man finally said, "Ford Motor Company." Wallace explained who he was and why he was calling. The man told him that there was a need for factories in a number of areas. Wire wheels would be installed on new automobiles when they arrived for delivery to the customer. Wallace explained his connection to the Ford Motor Company and offered to develop a factory in central New York. The man would mail all the details and requirements for the factory and the production of the wire wheels. Wallace knew exactly where he would build the factory. There was a location on Lewis Street that would be ideal for a factory. The man that Wallace spoke with told him the name had to be the National Wire Wheel Works. Wallace was satisfied that the name had to be consistent with all the rest. When he finished his conversation he thought about the possibilities for yet another company he would own. The specifications for the company would arrive in Geneva in a few days.

That evening Sable and Olitha had prepared dinner for both Winston and Wallace. The women went to the bungalow when Wallace arrived home. They were not as pleasant when Eveline was not there. Wallace was beginning to wonder if he even needed full time help. As they were leaving for the evening, Winston came in. He looked at the women as they left and said, "Oh boy, we have the whole place to ourselves." Wallace began to explain about the possibility of a new company in town. Just as he was telling Winston about it he heard someone's voice coming through the speaking tube. Wallace went to the front door to find it was Samuel. He told Wallace that he came to visit since Rose was in Washington with the others. He wanted to know if they could have some fun in the lower level room. Wallace laughed and invited him for dinner. Winston appeared uncomfortable when he saw Samuel. Wallace continued to tell them about the Wire Wheel Works. Samuel commented that it was a great idea but asked how many companies he wanted to own. Wallace laughed and wondered to himself how much one person could accomplish in a lifetime. Dinner was very good and they remarked about how good it was to have things always done and ready in the house. Wallace told them he was not sure he needed two women servants and maybe Olitha would have to go. Winston said, "Don't let Sable go. Her cooking is the best." They laughed and agreed. After dinner they went to the lower room and entertained themselves. Winston was not happy with the way the evening turned out. He was hoping for more than a cigar and a card game.

Rudolph, Rose and Eveline returned from Washington. Wallace decided he was going to be at home when they arrived. They came into the house like a whirlwind. They were all talking at once about how great the demonstration was at the White House. Eveline was the most impressed with Alice Paul. She referred to her as a very strong and smart woman. When she saw Wallace she was friendlier than recent times. She smiled and told him that the sweater he gave her was perfect to have because it was cold in Washington. Wallace beamed when she acknowledged that it came from him. There was hope for her recovery after all. Rose mentioned how they discussed Eveline's family and Alice. Wallace listened to that and wondered what she said about his father. Wallace told them about the proposed factory. When Eveline heard that she said, "I'm glad I'm not married to you. You would desert me. I like being with "my Ruddy". He is always around." When Wallace heard that he knew she was still confused. Maybe he did leave her alone too much. She never seemed to mind it because she had lots to do. After he heard that remark he thought it was better to discuss the company with Rudolph some other time. Samuel came along and had to hear about all the things that they did in Washington. After a while he thought it was time for Eveline to return to Willard. She was content with the idea but wanted all of them to go with her. She looked at Wallace and said, "I guess you can come along too. You have visited me so you know where I live." It was beginning to seem routine when Eveline referred to Wallace as an acquaintance. He was still very hurt with the circumstances. They went in Rudolph's car because it could hold five passengers. Rudolph reminded Wallace that his car was too small for everyone. Wallace was in no mood to hear that.

The specifications arrived for the Wire Wheel Works. Wallace studied them and went to see Mr. Nigel about the possibilities for building the factory. He looked at the papers and told Wallace that this was not the type of contracting he wanted to do. After building his house he wanted to continue working on unusual properties. Wallace understood. Mr. Nigel knew of a contractor in Rochester who built establishments like this. Wallace contacted the person and was informed that he could be in Geneva during the week. Wallace was sure if Mr. Nigel recommended the contractor it would be a good one. Since this was the first factory to be built from the ground up, Wallace wanted to pattern it after the Larkin Building. The specifications called for a large L shaped building that would have a frontage of 110 feet. The side wing would be 110 feet with a width of 40 feet. All the Wire Wheel Works factories were to be built the same. Wallace thought this might be a good way to maintain consistency throughout the country. Its nickname was the "Daylight Building." There would be a large number of windows throughout the factory. Much like Wallace's house it would let the daylight in and create a brighter atmosphere. As he studied the plans he laughed to himself and thought everyone in town would know who built this place. Since he wanted to pattern the factory after the Larkin Building he wanted to have modern conveniences like separate restrooms for employees. He wanted the new building to have special hospital rooms so all accidents could be treated on the site and have a nurse on duty. There would be a lunchroom and an outdoor picnic area during the warmer weather. The new factory was to have the capacity to produce 300-400 wheels per day. Some of the current factories could only produce 55 wheels per day. There would be a dipping room for applying paint to the wheels. It would dip the wheels four to five times and dry them in a heating area all in one operation. A new clip attachment was designed for quick changing of the entire wheel instead of just the tire part. There would be a need to have a spare tire and wheel with each automobile.

The contractor, Howard P. Sickles, arrived from Rochester. He and Wallace went to the Lewis Street site. Mr. Sickles told him it was a perfect spot to construct a building with those specifications. He said that the foundation could be started immediately. Wallace wanted to know how long it might take to construct the factory. Mr. Sickles said the factory could be up and running by mid July. That was about 5 months to get it built and employees hired. Wallace contracted with him to begin immediately. Mr. Sickles thought he would stay in Geneva during the construction and would need to have a place for some of his workers. Wallace wanted to know how many workers he had. There were four workers. Mr. Sickles' brother lived in Geneva, so he could stay with him. He would need to hire common laborers in Geneva to help with the construction. Wallace offered the bungalow as a place for the four men to live while building the factory. Now Wallace had to let Olitha go and Sable would have to move to the servant's room in the main house. Winston could use the small room off the sleeping porch. At least there was a place for everyone even if Winston was not satisfied; he was still in the main house.

The latest news was that three American ships were attacked by German torpedoes and sank on March 18. President Wilson was calling on Congress to consider war against Germany. Germany had threatened to declare war on the United States first after they were accused of sinking the ships. Time was drawing closer to involvement in a war that the United States tried to stay out of. In addition to the doom and gloom of a war, New York State was proposing a state income tax. The taxes would fund state operations. When Wallace read that, he knew times were changing and he would need to encourage more diversity in accounting for income. He would need to speed up the Goodwin Printing Corporation. Rudolph and he had been jointly investing money in stocks for the companies they were involved in. In that way neither one of them would be singled out as sole owners; that is why a corporation was better. Many of the other businessmen in town were doing the same thing. Another reason to keep the wife happy was to put money in an account for her. Women could not be taxed so they could have large sums of money. The problem with that was; the wife had to remain happy. If there was a divorce she would not have to pay back any of the money. Wallace thought that was a good enough reason for businessmen to give their wives a good life and not divulge any specific information. Those issues and practices would change if women gained the same rights as men so that was another reason to downplay the Women's Rights Movement. He could not wait to hear what Mr. Preston and the rest were going to say about another income tax. The last article that Wallace saw in the bottom corner was the cost of a postage stamp was increasing to 3 cents. He laughed and thought that it was nothing compared to how much he was going to lose with more taxes.

News flashes were everywhere in April. The United States declared war on Germany. Everyone's worst fear had come true. Men were being recruited to go to war in Europe. War bonds became a way to invest in the war effort. Women were replacing men to jobs left vacant. There were many patriotic meetings held at the college gymnasium to unify the citizens for war. The country had to band together to finance and support the troops going off to fight in Europe. The atmosphere had a high tone of hard and fast work. Wallace found himself instructing the people running his businesses to hire as many women it would take to keep things running smoothly. The Occidental Company was increasing their transports to have females of all ages available for placement and work. Many children were forced to work in factories. They were paid nearly nothing and worked long hours on dangerous jobs that men once occupied. Everyone was summoned to help with the war effort even if they remained at home or were enlisted. One of the biggest concerns was that every woman might need to be involved in the war effort. Some of the higher-class women were beginning to hide what they were or what they had to avoid working in factories. Wallace thought it was good Eveline could not be involved because of her state of mind. She could never be expected to work in place of a man.

Winston surprised Wallace when he agreed to move into the small room near the sleeping porch. He liked the idea of being able to use the porch as a place to do as he pleased. Wallace wanted to know what that was supposed to mean. Winston told him he could be free to walk around the way he preferred, clothed or unclothed. He figured as long as they were living in the main house there was no reason to worry about the women. Wallace had not thought of it in that way. Then Winston said, "Now I am in the next room so there will be no more running across the lawn to the bungalow. Sable can use the back stairway and we can have the whole place to ourselves." Wallace smiled but he knew he had to release Olitha from her duties. He hoped that would not upset Eveline when she came home and found Olitha gone. This was a chance he had to take.

He went to speak with Olitha and found her alone in the kitchen. She appeared upset so Wallace inquired about her problem. She told him that she had been given an offer for more money and an extra day off on the weekend. She was sorry to leave but since Eveline was rarely at home her job was not what it used to be. Wallace told her he was upset but he understood. He was delighted he was not the one to let her go. Eveline could not blame him after all. Olitha told Wallace she would see Eveline and explain why she was leaving their employment. Wallace thanked her for all she had done and wished her well. He thought of how lucky he was for that turn of events. Now he would not look like the bad guy.

Mr. Sickles moved his four workers from Rochester into the bungalow during the weekend. Winston watched as they arrived carrying basically knapsacks. He told Wallace they were one step away from being hobos. Wallace did not appreciate the description of Mr. Sickles' workers but he thought the same thing. They were much like Winston, which was the reason Wallace took to him and his unkempt ways. Winston wanted to know when he and Wallace were going to experience the sleeping porch. Wallace thought he was joking but he knew he was not kidding as he watched Winston's backside go out onto the porch. He had a strange feeling there was more to come with the new sleeping arrangements. Wallace reminded Winston that there was mowing and trimming to be done around the property. Winston smirked and asked him what the punishment would be if he neglected his work. Wallace told him he would send him to the bungalow to be disciplined. Winston laughed and thought that might be fun. Wallace knew he could not win when Winston was in one of his moods. He decided to discipline Winston before he got to work on the yard.

Olitha asked Wallace if she could go with him the next time he went to see Eveline. She thought it would be a good way to explain to Eveline why she was leaving. Wallace told her they could go on Sunday. He would pick her up at her new place of work. He asked where she would be working. She hesitated and then told him Mrs. Preston had hired her. She explained that she had always wanted her from the beginning but that her husband was against hired help. Wallace was surprised that Mr. Preston finally agreed to have domestic service. His wife was the one who told Eveline about it and now she hired help. Wallace laughed to himself when he thought that was all because of his company in New York. Samuel wanted to go to Willard with them to check on things and the progress Eveline was making. He told Wallace that maybe she could begin staying at home for an evening. Wallace thought that was great and hoped she would be willing to stay. He told Samuel about Olitha leaving. He wondered if that would upset Eveline staying overnight without her personal assistant. Maybe an arrangement could be made with the Prestons to have Olitha come by when she was staying to help as she used to. Wallace would discuss that with Mr. Preston. It may only be for a few times so it would not inconvenience Mrs. Preston.

Wallace picked up Samuel, Rose and Olitha on Sunday. It was a very warm summer day and there was a refreshing breeze coming off Seneca Lake. When they arrived at Willard, Wallace was asked to speak with the director. He wondered what could have happened. The others sat on the veranda enjoying the pleasant air. The director informed Wallace that his friend Hilda had died during the night. Wallace was shocked to think she was finally out of his life. All he could see was her in Mr. Helfer's office in one of her tirades. He explained that she had no family and she was to be buried in the cemetery at Willard. As he made the arrangements he thought about all the years he was involved with her and how difficult she had been. He did learn something from her though. He learned how to deal with a person who is unhappy, lonely, and depressed. He thought about Mr. Helfer too. He was a good person to take care of her and deal with all her problems and behaviors. The director asked if there was anything he wanted that belonged to her. Wallace smiled and told him no he had everything he needed. He left the office and took a deep breath hoping Eveline's visit would be better. As he was walking to the veranda he thought about all the deaths he had experienced. Was this a premonition? Eveline thinks he is dead or will die soon. He had a queasy feeling as he sat down. Eveline looked at him and said, "I think someone has died." Wallace's face went suddenly pale. Samuel and Rose both asked at the same time if he was okay. Olitha was just about to tell Eveline about the change in her employment. Wallace told them that Hilda passed away during the night. When Eveline heard that she said, "I knew that witch was haunting us." Samuel asked why she thought Hilda was a witch. Eveline said, "She helped kill my husband." Now Wallace really knew she had her facts confused. Samuel asked her how she knew the woman who just died. She told him that when she was dating a nice young man in Rochester her fiancé worked for a man who was related to her. She continued to tell him that the young man asked her to get married. She agreed to it but that witch put a curse on him. As she was telling her version of the story she leaned into the group and whispered to Wallace that he should be careful. Wallace asked her why. She told him, "You look like the man I was engaged to and that witch helped kill him. That is why she screamed at you the first time she saw you here." She sat back and looked at everyone and said, "I'm glad they're all dead." Samuel looked at Wallace who was near tears and Rose sat like a statue. No one had much to say. Samuel decided to have Olitha tell Eveline about her change in employment. Before she could begin, Eveline told her that she knew she was leaving her. Olitha asked her how she knew? Eveline looked at her and said, "I had a feeling you were going to work for someone else." Eveline understood why she would want to leave since she did not live in the unusual house anymore. She went on to say that she did not need to worry about her because she had good help here that gets her ready for the day. Olitha thanked her for being a good boss and told her that she enjoyed all the fun they had shopping. Samuel decided that the discussion of her coming home was not appropriate after all. He told Eveline that they would come back next week to see her again. When she heard that she told them they did not need to do that. Wallace asked why? She explained in a sweet voice that "her Ruddy" was coming for her and they were going away. Samuel asked if she was sure about that. She made no hesitation about the conversation. She told them she was going to New York City. Wallace asked, "Why New York City?" She looked at him and told him, "Because that dead man would never take me there, so "my Ruddy" will take me." Samuel told her that was a nice idea. They would be looking forward to hearing about her trip. They had enough news and it was time to go. Eveline thanked them for coming. She kissed everyone, even Wallace.

On the way back to Geneva Wallace was more confused than ever. He wanted to know from Samuel if all these things they heard today could really be true. Samuel explained that many times thoughts would get jumbled up when a person sat alone and had nothing to do but think. Sometimes they do have thoughts of other people dying or leaving. They often confuse all their closest friends. It is not unusual that friends end up together in their minds. The thing they need to do is to verify the information about going to New York City with Rudolph. Wallace told him he would speak with Rudolph. Every time he heard the "my Ruddy" thing; he could just die. Olitha was happy Eveline was not upset and figured things out in her own mind. It made leaving her easier than she thought it would be. Wallace was going to see Rudolph later that evening and would discuss the information they heard from Eveline. Samuel did decide that Eveline would probably not be staying home with Wallace for quite some time. He was now concerned that she might try some of the things she talked about when she mentioned Hilda. The fact that she tried to strangle their baby in the night was good enough reason to keep her in a place where that was unlikely to happen. Wallace asked Samuel if he needed to tell her family about her current condition. Samuel thought he should wait a week and then invite them to come for a visit at home, not Willard. He hoped some change might trigger a new level of remembering. Lately, there has been more coming out about the past and that concerned Samuel.

Wallace stopped by Rudolph's place to discuss what Eveline told them earlier. Rudolph was just getting ready to go to the YMCA. He asked Wallace if he wanted to come along. He agreed and thought it might be a good way to have time to talk. They walked by the new Wire Wheel Works. It was nearly complete. It would be ready for operation in a few weeks. Wallace was glad that Rudolph had agreed to organize and hire the people needed for the work. They had decided a while ago that they were going to be business partners and cover for each other if one of them was unable to fulfill their responsibilities. Rudolph thought they should do that because of the taxing policies of state and federal governments. Wallace thought that of all the people he was involved with Rudolph had the most knowledge and was good at what he did. Every job Wallace gave him was done very professionally and making big money. While they were walking towards the new factory Wallace told him they went to see Eveline. He told him it was mainly to have Olitha tell Eveline why she was leaving her employment. He explained all the other details that came out. Rudolph was surprised that Hilda's death created so much new information. He even wondered what was going on in Eveline's mind. When Wallace heard that he knew that was a perfect way to ask about the New York trip. Before he mentioned the trip he wanted to find more out about the "my Ruddy" stuff. When Rudolph heard that he laughed and said, "She says the same thing about you. The problem is she thinks you are dead." He went on to say, "Eveline says things like, "My poor Wallace is somewhere maybe dead." Wallace at least realized she meant exactly what she said before; this is how she refers to people she loves. As for the trip to New York City, Rudolph thought it was funny that she thought they were going. He told Wallace that she had a fantasy about going with him to New York. Rudolph told Wallace that he still wanted to go to New York with him. Most of what she was suffering from was overlapping reality with desire.

Wallace was much happier after he had time to talk about that visit. By this time they were in front of the YMCA. As they were walking in they saw Mike who was the salesman from Baker and Stark Clothier. Wallace introduced him to Rudolph. The three men hit it off perfectly. They decided to use the pool instead of exercising. They spent time afterward having a massage. Rudolph thought the best part was when they were in the showers. Wallace felt the best he had in a long time. Even though Eveline was not doing well he at least had friends who understood and he liked their company.

Summer was coming to an end. The new factory was in full operation. Samuel decided that after the last visit from the family; which was not any different than ones before, Eveline would be better off staying at Willard. He was conferring with other doctors in Rochester who had similar patients. They found that attempting to bring the person back to their former environment helped to keep the past alive. They found that a completely new environment was healthier than going back to places that reminded them of the past. That seemed to make sense to Samuel and Wallace. What was he going to do? He could not move to a new city. There was too much happening in Geneva. Eveline liked Geneva and had friends there. Samuel thought that a possibility might be to keep her at Willard where she liked being. After a period of time, a slow transition to a new place might not trigger old thinking. Wallace agreed to keep her where she was and go to her.

After Mr. Sickles finished the factory his workers went back to Rochester. The bungalow was empty. Wallace decided it might be time to subdivide the land. He had a survey done and created a separate lot. He was going to sell it with the stipulation that a bungalow was to be built on that lot. He wanted to maintain the Wrightonian theme of a large prairie style house surrounded by bungalows. He received an offer for the land at the end of October. He thought of all the people and things that came and went in the few short years in that place. Wallace realized how his life was constantly changing even if he did not want it to change. That was one thing he had no control over.

The headlines were full of reports of the battles being waged in Europe. Soldiers were fighting in the battlefields and dying. There was an even bigger push for the country to support and be involved in the war effort. War bonds were being sold everywhere. Another issue that had many people in a rage was the child labor laws. For many years children had been working in jobs that only men were doing. Children were in accidents because of improper working conditions. They were falling asleep at machinery and being killed or losing limbs. The federal government finally up held the Child Labor Law. It was passed on September 6, 1917. There were to be no underage children working in a factory or dangerous environments. They were required to be in school. The Women's Rights groups were in favor of such an act. They thought it was barbaric for children to work in such dangerous places. There would now be more reason for women to work those jobs or become teachers for the larger enrollment of children in schools. Wallace told Rudolph and Winston that under no circumstances were they to ever have children in any of his businesses. He established that rule long before it was an issue. After what the Occidental Company was doing with children he would never be able to have children being hurt or killed in any of his factories. He was not able to give Winston or Rudolph any details about the TOE&TIC operation all he could say was, "No Children."

The November election was a very heated time. New York State was putting Women's Suffrage on the ballot as Amendment No.1. The New York Woman Suffrage Party succeeded in having it part of the elections. There were two factions working against one another. Finally, President Wilson stood up for the women. He had tried to be neutral on the issue during his campaign but now said, "The whole country has admired the spirit and capacity and vision of the women of the United States. Every vote cast for Woman Suffrage is a vote to make New York a stronger, greater force in this war." The opposing group was trying to show that women already had many rights. There was an article in the newspaper that was titled "Special Privileges New York Women Have Secured Under Male Suffrage." It listed many items that referred to monetary issues men supposedly gave women. In reality, it was to protect the money that men were trying to hide. There were demonstrations with many of the people from Seneca Falls and throughout the state. Rose and Rudolph made a point of telling Eveline about the vote and made sure she cast her ballot. Wallace was happy she was so excited about the progress women were making. He was not happy about the possibilities of losing the cover for hiding income under his wife's name. If the vote passed, it would change what women could do with the money that was supposedly theirs. No one asked about how they voted. It was a touchy topic because businessmen were against the idea. Rudolph being a successful businessman and a supporter of women's rights understood the dilemma. He voted for suffrage. He had no wife to use as a cover. He told Wallace how he had voted. Wallace told him he understood why but felt he was stabbing men in the back. Rudolph thought he might be surprised if he knew who actually voted for the amendment. While they were talking about it Winston was happy to report to them that he voted for the amendment. He was explaining how it was very predictable to watch men voting. Some were grumbling about such foolishness but then some were happy to announce their support of it. Winston mentioned seeing Mike at the vote who voted yes. When Wallace heard this he decided to tell them what his vote was. They were certain it was no. When Wallace told them he voted in favor of the amendment they were stunned. Rudolph asked him about the comment of being stabbed in the back. Wallace was slow to admit he was afraid what all the other men in town might think of him. He found it to be a difficult spot to be in because of the business aspect. Winston called him a coward and Rudolph shook his head. They were surprised at his thinking after all the unbelievable things he had accomplished in his life. Much of his success was because of the strong women he was influenced by. They thought now was the time for Wallace to be openly supportive of women

Chapter 55

IT HAD BEEN A year since the United States entered World War 1. There was a stronger push for citizens to buy war bonds. It was the patriotic way for people to be part of the war effort. There were many calls for more military service men to go to Europe. There was some discussion of changing the draft age for the armed services. Secretary of State Baker addressed the need for lowering the draft age required for entering the military. Some men deliberately falsified their age so they could be accepted into the army. The loyalty to the country was at its peak. Everyone worked in one way or another to help the war effort. There were newspaper advertisements about keeping up the pledges people made for war bonds. A familiar advertisement was "Lend Him A Hand." Companies in Geneva would pay for advertisements to encourage the buying of war bonds. Wallace was influential in having the Safege Company submit a full page in the evening paper showing soldiers fighting for victory and depending on the public for monetary support. There was an anniversary meeting at the Armory to show patriotism and help to the government. The public was invited for music and speeches from civic leaders. The theme was "Geneva Must Again Go Over The Top in War Bond Sales." The concern over the military force was a largely debated issue. The newspaper announced "Americans Must Enlist To Win the War." The United States did not plan on needing as much money to finance the war and soldiers it was sending to Europe. Most people thought it would be a short war because America entered long after it began. The European countries were wearing down just as the United States entered with money and forces to assist their war torn countries. It became for America an all out effort to end the invasions in Europe. Families in the United States were receiving word of their loved ones who had been killed in battle. The numbers rose as the war continued. Patriotism was at an all time high. Whenever there was a call for more men, enlistments came in huge numbers. In June, a total of 367,960 men were called to action. The numbers were staggering. There were very few men left to run the businesses. Wallace thought that men his age might be drafted into service. When he mentioned that to Winston, he thought that might be a good way to do something different for the country. Wallace was not as enthusiastic about the idea nor was Rudolph.

The family wanted to visit Eveline. Mr. Lounsberry purchased an automobile and wanted to bring Frank, Alice, Catherine and himself to visit on Sunday. Wallace asked Samuel where they should visit her, at home or Willard. Samuel thought they could try to meet at home. Samuel and Rose offered to get Eveline; Wallace could be at home when they arrived. Samuel suggested Rudolph should not be included in the visit. Wallace wanted to know why? He explained that when both of them were together; it created confusion when she saw two people she has feelings for. If Wallace is the only one there she may respond more favorably to him. Wallace thought that sounded perfect and hoped for the best. He notified Mr. Lounsberry where the visit would be taking place. He discussed with Sable the type of food she would prepare. It was summertime, she thought a picnic in the garden might be less confining than in the house. Wallace liked that idea. Samuel thought that it was okay to have Winston there. He did not have the same effect on Eveline as Rudolph. Wallace was glad to hear that because it might remind her of their times in Rochester and Buffalo. Rudolph had a much different friendship with them at that time.

Sunday was a beautiful August day. Sable set a table near the pond and it was decorated with some of the cut flowers from the garden. Wallace thought about the time at the Seneca Powers when they had tables set near the fountain at the convention. This reminded him of what he had always hoped for in his home. The sad part was that now he had it and Eveline does not recognize him or what home she was living in. Wallace asked Sable what she was preparing that smelled so appetizing? She smiled and told him southern style chicken, potato salad, cole slaw, baked beans and a freshly baked cherry pie. She wanted to know what he requested for refreshments. Wallace thought that because it was so warm, fresh lemonade with pieces of lemon mixed in would be perfect. He really wanted a martini but thought today was not the day for that. Between his father and Eveline, he was not sure anything alcoholic would be helpful. Sable told him she had an old family favorite for fresh-spiced lemonade. As she walked away Wallace watched her lumber her way into the house to finish the preparations. He thought of Hilda when he saw Sable move like she did when she would walk away. He laughed and thought, there goes Hilda's twin only she is a Negro woman. Winston came outside to see if Wallace needed any help. He asked if he was nervous about the visit? Wallace told him not any more. He was through worrying about how things were going. Winston thought that this was a big change in attitude. Wallace only hoped Eveline would come back to him as she used to be. Even though she was spoiled and loud at times, he missed her. Winston admitted that things had not been as much fun. He told Wallace it was more fun working around Eveline. Now she does not even know what we do. While they were looking at the work Winston had been doing in the yard, a large black Ford pulled into the driveway. Wallace thought it strange that Mr. Lounsberry would not park in the front of the house. When he looked, it was Samuel. He deliberately parked in the driveway to change the pattern for Eveline. He just bought the car and had not told Wallace. Rose and Eveline were like two little girls laughing and joking about driving in the driveway and not parking in front and being ushered through the front entrance. Wallace and Winston wanted to see the car because Samuel was very proud of it. Rose said, "I finally convinced him to be like you Wallace and buy a car." They laughed. Eveline wanted to know where Wallace's car was. So, he opened the garage door and there stood both of his red cars. She stared at them like she was remembering something. Samuel asked her what she was thinking about. She calmly told him that she had been in both cars. She thought they belonged to the man she was supposed to have married. Winston whispered in Wallace's ear, "She's getting closer." Wallace had a gleam in his eye. Wallace asked her why she thought they were here. She smiled and told him that the man used to live here but was dead and no one knows what to do with the cars. Wallace's gleam faded. Sable came out to announce the arrival of their families.

Sable directed them to the garden. Alice had on a large brimmed sun hat. Mrs. Lounsberry wore a slight hat but had her parasol opened. Frank never appeared much different, always pants and a pin striped shirt. Mr. Lounsberry was more gentlemanly like and wore a summer suit with a vest. Wallace noticed how it accentuated his rounding stomach. Eveline was delighted to see everyone. She even recognized Frank and had nothing negative to say to him this time. Samuel thought this was a good sign. She kissed her mother and Alice. She did her usual nose wiggling, "Hi Frank." He actually laughed when she made the gesture. Alice hugged and kissed Wallace all over his face. She kissed Winston and pinched his cheeks. She said, "I miss my boys." Sable stood watching all the kissing and hugging and with her hands on her hips said, "Sure does look like a happy family. I ain't seen nothin like this in a long time." Everyone laughed. Winston whispered in Wallace's ear, "Good that Sable does not see what happens with us." Eveline looked around and told Wallace he had done a beautiful job with the house and gardens. He realized that she remembered everything but his name. He wondered what she thought it was. It was better to enjoy what she remembered than to question what she forgot. Sable went into the house to finish the dinner. Catherine asked Eveline what she had been doing lately. She and Rose started up like motors about their trip in January to Washington and the demonstration at the White House. Alice remarked that the trip sounded wonderful and offered to go with them when they went again. Frank piped up and told her she did not need any more ideas. Alice reminded him that she was a new woman and had more rights than before. The men had very little to say about the topic.

During dinner in the garden, Sable received compliments on the food. Winston told everyone that her cooking was the best and Wallace should never let her go.

When Eveline heard that she told everyone, "Maybe it was my cooking that killed the man I was supposed to marry." There was not a motion at the table. Was she joking or was she serious? Did she really think she killed her husband? Wallace sat directly across from her and finally decided to confront her thinking, what did he have to lose? He asked her, "Eveline, who am I?" She stared at him; Samuel did not expect Wallace to go at her so forcefully. He said, "Well?" She looked at Rose then her mother and said, "My Wallace." Alice burst into tears and Mrs. Lounsberry tried to calm her down. Frank looked at her and shook his head. Wallace said, "What the hell does that mean." She told him that was her way of referring to the people she loved. Then he asked, "What am I to you?" She said, "You were supposed to be my husband, but something killed you." Just as she finished, Sable brought out the cherry pie. Fortunately, the incident ended. Samuel told her that she was doing very well remembering things. Eveline smiled and acted like nothing was wrong. Wallace was confused about how he could appear so alive and she sees him like a ghost. According to Rose, the pie was out of this world. When she said that Eveline said, "Just like our house." Wallace looked at Samuel and thought; she has it all but in the wrong order. It was getting toward evening and the dinner was about finished. Mr. Lounsberry suggested they start back to Rochester. Rose and Eveline were walking around the property admiring the gardens. Samuel knew they had to get Eveline back to Willard because there was a curfew. As everyone was leaving Eveline asked Wallace, "When are you going to let me come home?" Wallace looked at Samuel. Samuel spoke up and told her they needed to talk more about that when they return to where she is staying. Wallace was surprised so much more information was coming out. Maybe it was better Rudolph not be in the picture. Maybe a whole new environment was the answer.

Wallace decided that it might be time to have a will drawn up. There had been so many people dying in the war and there was an illness spreading that was killing people as fast as the war. There were reports of an influenza epidemic. He spoke to Samuel about it. He was aware of it and had heard that it attacked young people. It was a quick moving disease and people were dying within days of being infected. There was nothing to help fight the illness. It was like pneumonia. Wallace discussed his idea of a will with Rudolph since they were closely involved with stock investments and company operations. Wallace told Rudolph he would be the trustee and assist Eveline as she would be the executrix. They went to the attorney, Mr. Keyes, and a will was written and signed on September 4, 1918. Wallace's will had a number of stipulations. The first was that all indebtedness his family had with him would be forgiven. His brothers, sisters and parents would each receive $500.00. Eveline, his wife inherited all stocks, bonds, and property except shares of stocks in companies he owned with Rudolph Williams. Wallace wanted Eveline to have everything because he could never repay her for her self-sacrifice and co-operation. The will was to be read on the day of his death and all stocks would be held for five years until all settlements were made. At that time, everything was turned over to his wife. Rudolph was impressed to think that Wallace had so much confidence in him to allow him to be involved with his estate. Wallace reminded him that he was not dead yet and that they had many years of financial and personal involvement ahead. The will was signed and the attorney explained where it would be located and hoped they did not need it right away.

Samuel and Wallace had many conversations about what the next steps should be for Eveline. After the visit in late August, Samuel still maintained that she might do better in a new environment. He was surprised when she openly admitted knowing Wallace and saying that was their home. Wallace offered to move, suggesting that might help eliminate her confusion. Samuel thought it might, but there would be no guarantee. He warned Wallace not to be so quick to let that beautiful home go up for sale. He told him that if he did, Rose and he wanted first right of refusal. Wallace thanked him for his counsel and friendship. As he was leaving the doctor's office, Wallace thought about looking around town to see if there was any property available that might have the same atmosphere as Willard. He thought of a home that overlooked the lake, possibly in the city. If he decided to sell the Washington Street property, he would want a home that was unique and would have the same impact as their home had now. As Wallace was turning the corner onto Nursery Avenue he saw a sign posted at the corner. He stopped to read what it said. It was a notice to the mothers of Geneva. In an effort to assess the physical condition of children, mothers were urged to bring every child under the age of 7 to the high school to be weighed and measured. There would be "Baby Jitneys" available to take mothers and their children from that corner. Samuel mentioned that the Child Welfare Committee of Ontario County sponsored it. The hope was to get a better understanding of the physical condition of under school age children. Wallace smiled while he read it and wondered how many women would be standing out there. It was turning into a busy corner.

World War I was ravaging Europe as the months went on. More and more money was needed to finance the war effort. Quotas were placed on cities to maintain war bond sales. The Geneva Daily News reported that the quota for the city was $1,192,700.00. As of October 12, $516,750.00 had been given.The paper encouraged people to step up and help reach the goal. The article reported that the soldiers in Europe were willing to fight without pay. Victory was more important than the money. Mr. Preston read that to Wallace and they decided to make a large contribution to war bonds.They thought this might be a good way to diversify the money. Things were very tense in the world. It seemed like the war was never going to end and Germany might be the victors. On October 24, President Wilson demanded that Germany surrender. He did not mince words when he made the demand that the United States did not trust any of the German rules or attitudes. If they did not comply then the United States would annihilate Germany.The German forces continued to invade France and surrounding countries. President Wilson pushed the military to go as far as they needed to destroy Germany. On November 11, Germany yielded and the fighting stopped. Large headlines read, "VICTORY OVER GERMANY". People were parading and cheering in the streets.The country felt as if their support at home and abroad helped to bring about an end to a devastating war. Under the headlines in smaller print was the warning of an epidemic that could kill as many people as the war had.When Wallace read this he wondered what else could go wrong.

Chapter 56

JANUARY 1919 BEGAN WITH news of the influenza that had been spreading throughout the country. It began in 1918 and was considered more deadly than the war. Returning American troops brought the virus back and thousands of people were lining up at infirmaries and hospitals for help. The virus spread at an alarming speed. The surgeon General of the Army was stunned by what he saw in Boston. He said, "Every bed was full with men coughing up blood sputum." The disease spread to the general population and killed individuals almost over night. It was an influenza unlike any other. People could be healthy in the morning and become deathly ill in the evening and die by the next day. There were reports that others died a slower death from suffocation from the buildup of blood in their lungs. It was feared that if it did not slow down, it could wipe out the population. Wallace read these articles in the newspaper and asked Samuel if he thought it would subside. He had seen a slowing of the illness and thought it was less of a threat to people. He did think that precautions should still be taken to avoid contact with people who were coughing and had flu type symptoms. Samuel told him some people tried folk remedies like tar balls, kerosene on sugar, boneset tea but with no success. Being careful and being clean was the best defense Samuel could tell anyone.

The Wire Wheel Works was having huge success. Rudolph reported that the demand for the wire wheel production had risen to1000 per day. They were mainly manufactured for the Ford Maxwell. It was the newest model Ford Motor Company had designed. The main offices for the Wire Wheel Company were moving to Hagerstown, Maryland. That location would begin manufacturing wire wheels for all makes of cars. Ford was no longer the exclusive car with wire wheels. When Wallace spoke with Rudolph about the company and how well it was doing, he thought it might be time to order a Maxwell. He definitely needed a larger car. Rudolph reminded him of that every time they went in his car. The Maxwell was the largest automobile Ford made. It could have up to 6 passengers. He wanted to keep his first car as a souvenir. He liked souvenirs just like his first camera. He still had that on his desk to remind him of his first involvement with Eastman Kodak. Every time he received stock statements from Eastman Kodak, he looked at his first camera and thought of his first beginnings with Kodak. Rudolph thought it was funny that Wallace realized he needed a larger car. He told Wallace that he could now take everyone to see Eveline without using his car. Wallace made a face and told him he was right. He would order it at the beginning of February, after he received his dividends for the Ford Motor Company. It would be like a free gift for being a shareholder. This motorcar would be dark green which was the newest color produced. He saw a picture of one with a greenish gray canvas top. The plush seats were the same color as the top. Rudolph said, "That's my Wallace, always one step ahead in everything." When he said that, Wallace looked at him and thought of Eveline and her references for both of them.

Wallace had a meeting with Samuel and the director of Willard to discuss what should be done with Eveline's living arrangements. Samuel continued to maintain that she was very healthy and alert. She was not a menace to herself or anyone. The director had given her more freedom to be independent. She started classes to assist people with literature and conversation groups. She was one of the best residents they had. She qualified to be released from Willard upon Wallace's request. Samuel thought the idea of a new environment away from her past would make the best situation for her coming back to her family and friends. The only aspect that no one had an answer for was her inability to recognize Wallace as her living husband. Wallace asked if it was possible to have her return to live with him in a new environment with her current mental block. Samuel and the director both thought it was possible if certain things were present. First, until she regained her complete memory, she and Wallace should have separate sleeping accommodations. Sable should be present as a full time assistant to the house. If possible, Olitha would be a good person to have return. Maybe Mrs. Preston could make some adjustments so Olitha could be on duty part of the time. The most important aspect was to have a different home to come back to. Wallace asked if he needed to sell his home or just move to a different place for a while with her. They both left that choice up to Wallace.

When Wallace returned to Geneva there was a letter addressed to him from his mother. He thought it was odd that she would write him a letter. She usually called him from the hotel phone. He opened the two-page letter. He knew something was up because she never wrote that much. She began by thanking him for all their visits to see their beautiful home and Eveline both at home and

Willard. She mentioned Frank and how impossible he continued to be. When Wallace got to that part, he thought she was going to tell him she was leaving him or she was going to kill him. He never knew where they were in their marriage. Still, it was never good. The next part began with a mention of a visit from Mr. and Mrs. Lounsberry. Wallace thought that was strange they would visit for no reason. They arrived to discuss how they felt about Eveline's condition. Alice had mentioned to Wallace that she blamed herself for her mother's behavior by having an affair with a black soldier. Wallace thought he assured her she should not put such blame on herself. Alice felt she ruined her family by knowing the truth about her father and mother. The Lounsberrys told Alice that they felt Eveline had a breakdown because she could not handle the brown skin baby. Even though she does not know why the baby was colored, she was not raised to be in such a controversial environment. They thought Eveline lost her mind about certain people that were part of the family that caused such a birth. Mr. and Mrs. Lounsberry placed the blame on Alice. When Wallace read that he could not believe they would think such a thing. Something must have happened. Everyone had gotten along for years and now when they should all be working to make her better, there was a family division. Wallace remembered the time when Eveline told Frank that she never liked him and that Wallace looked like him. That was one of the first times they visited her. Maybe there was some truth to the idea that Eveline is worried about what her parents are thinking and that has caused her to mentally eliminate people. Wallace was the closest to her and he did look something like his father. The letter ended with a sad note that the Lounsberrys thought it was best they do not affiliate with Alice and

Frank any further. Alice was beside herself and she told Wallace that Frank was delighted they wanted to end their relationship with them. Now, he could be himself again. Her life was as miserable as it had been when she was a young woman before she worked for the Women's Club of Rochester. She apologized over and over and hoped he did not feel the same way. Wallace was upset and angry and was not sure who he should talk to about this situation. After he reread the letter to make sure he had all the facts in order, he decided the best person was Samuel because he was their doctor and needed to know what was said.

As Wallace was going to Samuel and Rose's, he saw Rudolph walking home from work. He asked Wallace why he was out so late and if he was tired from all the discussion today. Wallace decided to let Rudolph know about the letter. After all, he was the person closest to Eveline other than himself. Rudolph thought that was a preposterous letter and sounded to him like the Lounsberrys may attempt to take her away to a different place to live, maybe back to Canada. Wallace had not thought about that and he worried for his mother and the possible reason Eveline might have thought the way she did. Rudolph offered to go to the Haynes' to help if Wallace wanted that to happen. Wallace was actually grateful to have him come along. When Rose answered the door, she looked like she knew something might be wrong. She called Samuel and they sat down to listen to the letter. Since everyone knew one another, it was hard to believe the family could be so at odds. Samuel thought it was interesting that the blame was being shifted away from the Lounsberry family including Eveline and on to Alice and her parents. He understood the reason, but was concerned about their plan for Eveline that seemed possible by the tone of the accusation. Samuel did mention that there were different methods used in Canada for patients who have suffered a shock. Wallace wanted to know if they could take her away. Samuel smiled and said, "Probably if they kidnapped her." Rose piped up and said, "After all that has happened in the world, people being bought and sold and killed, little children transported to a new country for sale, why couldn't they take her off to Canada." When Wallace heard this, he felt himself blushing as he thought of how Occidental was transporting humans. Samuel thought the best thing to do was continue planning a new residence for Eveline and inform her parents of the plan. He would be willing to draft a letter explaining what the next steps would be. They left and Wallace told Rudolph not to mention this to anyone, especially Winston. He was acting put out lately because he and Wallace were not as close as they once had been. Rudolph wondered what happened. Wallace told him that Winston had no desire to improve himself. Winston was upset that Wallace was meeting new men who were motivated and successful. Rudolph liked what he was hearing until Wallace mentioned Mike, the salesman from Stark and Baker. He wondered why Mike was so important. As it happened, Wallace and Mike had been confiding in each other and had become close friends. Winston felt like he was put second place in their friendship. Rudolph wanted to know what that meant. Winston wanted Wallace to himself and was jealous of any one man or woman that liked him. Wallace was happy with that when they were in school, but Winston was still at a high school mentality. The men Wallace liked now were smart, successful and appealing to him. Rudolph waited to hear more. Wallace used to be attracted to the rough and casual part of Winston. He was wild and fun to be with. Wallace liked that but knew there was more to a relationship than that. Rudolph laughed and admitted he liked the rough and casual part of Winston too.

The next day when Wallace woke up he decided he was going to look into properties that were available in the area. He went to the lawyer who drew up his will and inquired if he knew of any property along the lake that might be for sale. Before he told Wallace anything, he was shocked that he would be considering a move from such a unique home. Wallace told him he was not selling the house but he wanted to buy another one. The lawyer smiled and told him a place on South Main Street was going to be for sale. Wallace wanted to know more details. It was 775 South Main Street. It was large mansion overlooking the lake. It was in need of renovation. Wallace liked the idea already. He asked if he could see it. The lawyer told him that it was empty and that they could see it that day. Wallace thought this was like a dream that a house was so available. There must be something wrong with it or maybe it is a shack. They walked down Main Street and the lawyer explained that the family that lived there felt it was too large to maintain, so they left. Wallace liked the idea more and more. They stood in front of the property. It was a multilevel house. They went through the front door to a large staircase and in the back was a library with a massive fireplace with circular windows overlooking Seneca Lake. The parlor was the entire half of the main floor. The dining room overlooked the front yard. There were a number of large bedrooms on the second floor. The kitchen and preparation area was in the basement with a dumb waiter for delivery of food to the dining room. The servant's quarters were in the basement. Wallace knew this could be a grand home. He asked the lawyer what the conditions of the sale were? It would take a good amount of money to redesign the house to be more to Wallace's liking. The lawyer told him he would find out the price and discuss it with him tomorrow.

The Ford Maxwell was ordered and would be available in April. Wallace was excited about the car. He knew it would be a great new piece of machinery. He told Winston about the car. He was not nearly as excited as he thought he might be. Rudolph thought it was about time he caught up to his size car. Wallace remarked about how easy it would be to sell his red car. Winston spoke up and thought maybe the circus would want it for the clown car. Wallace did not think that was too funny. Rudolph realized the tension when he heard that remark. Wallace was correct that Winston had a different attitude. The new car would have to be picked up in Buffalo. Rudolph wanted to know why. Apparently, that was the delivery point for the Maxwell cars. A driver would be hired to bring it to Geneva. Wallace wanted to be the first to drive the car. Rudolph was not surprised about him wanting to be the first driver. Wallace explained that his red car would go to an auction in Buffalo after he picked up his new car. Rudolph asked if he wanted him to ride along. Wallace told him that he wanted to do this by himself. When Winston heard that he wanted to know why he was not asked to go. Wallace looked at him and said, "I wouldn't want you to be seen in a clown car." Winston realized what he had said earlier and apologized. Wallace explained about the house he saw and that the lawyer would have all the details for him. Rudolph knew why Wallace was talking about it, but Winston looked confused. All Wallace said was, "It might be time to move to a bigger house." Winston asked, "Why?"

The lawyer got in touch with Wallace to discuss the details of the 775 South Main Street home. The owners were glad that someone was interested in the mansion. Wallace offered $12,000.00. They accepted it with no conditions attached. He could have possession of it immediately. The paperwork would be ready by the end of the week. Wallace did not worry about the Washington Street property. He would remain there until the renovations were completed. When he moved to Main Street Eveline would move in with him and Sable would be residing with them. He may have to make a very attractive offer to get Olitha back full time. The house was larger than the Washington Street house and would require full time help. Rudolph reminded him that Mrs. Preston was the one he needed to make the big offer to. Wallace smiled and said, "She's easy. Money talks. Mr. Preston told me so." April would turn out to be a month of big changes. He heard the old saying that things come in threes. Now, there were three new things to look forward to, a new car, a new house, and Eveline coming home. He must ask Samuel if he should bring her to see it as it was being worked on. He hoped he would think it was a good idea. He remembered how she acted when they were choosing things for the Washington Street house. Even though she could be irritating, he missed her.

Wallace contracted with Mr. Nigel to do the reconstruction of the property. He took him to see what needed to be done to make it into a modern style home. He wanted big windows to replace the smaller ones. The house was to be open and airy so the breezes from the lake would blow through the house. Mr. Nigel thought the work would take about a month to complete. When Wallace thought about it, that was his birthday. What a great present; a new house, a new car, and a wife that returns home. There's the big three. He told Mr. Nigel to start immediately. Samuel offered to go with Wallace to see Eveline during the week this time instead of the weekend. Wallace wanted to know why. Samuel wanted to see how Eveline was during the week when there are only the residents around and no guests. They would go tomorrow. If she was doing well, maybe they would take her for the day to see the house. They needed to prepare their story line. Samuel thought that Wallace needed to tell her they were staying in Geneva. He thought that since she liked the atmosphere at Willard, he would buy them a house on the lake. Samuel would then remind her that she wanted to come home and he thought a new place would be a great way to begin. After they saw her reaction, they could offer for her to help decorate and choose accessories. Wallace was sad to think that the house he planned for so many years ago was being put behind him. He knew he must move forward; that had been his motto for life. He planned to make the Main Street home similar to the Washington Street home but only on a larger more elaborate scale.

They arrived at Willard and found Eveline in perfect spirits. She even recognized Wallace. They met in the reception area and had a coffee. While they were discussing things, Samuel mentioned that Wallace was interested in a new home. When he said that her eyes lit up. She looked at Wallace and said, "I'm glad you are getting rid of that house. My parents never liked it." Samuel found that interesting since he knew what her mother told Alice. Wallace did not respond to the Washington Street house comment. She asked when she could see it. Samuel asked her if she was ready today. She stood up and said, "Let's go." Samuel and Wallace took her by the hand as they walked to the car. On the way to Geneva, Eveline was asking all types of questions about the house but never a word about Washington Street. As they were going by Samuels' building, Rose was outside. She waved and Eveline yelled for her to come along. They stopped the car and she got in. Rose was happy Eveline was looking forward to their new home. Eveline did not react to the comment of "their new home." Wallace thought that was good. They pulled up to the front of the house. There were men all over working on the windows and the roofline. Eveline got out of the car and starred up at the size of the building. She looked at Wallace and said; "Now this is a house. I cannot wait to show my parents this one. Maybe now they will stop tormenting me." Samuel stood quietly as she talked. Wallace was glad he was not the target for her rage. Samuel was thinking that her parents had been the problem all along. He hoped that she saw a future in a new beginning. She looked at Wallace and said, "My Wallace will never let me down." He wanted to hug her but instead stood still. Then she nudged him and asked if he heard her. He laughed and said, "I sure did." Rose wanted to cry and Samuel wanted to cheer that finally the fog was taken away. She figured out that it was not Frank or Wallace that it was her father and she was afraid to break away but instead broke down to get away. After they walked through the house Wallace asked when they could spend time selecting decorations and lighting fixtures? Still there was no reference to Washington Street. Wallace thought better to let it go. On the return to Willard, Rose was chatting a mile a minute about how nice it would be to have her around so they could enjoy all the freedom the 19th Amendment would give women. When the men heard that, they made a face of disgust. They knew there was no more discussion because it was to be ratified to the Constitution on June 4th. Eveline asked if there was going to be a party then. Rose told her that if there was not they would sure make one. Wallace told Eveline that he would be back to take her to see the progress on the new house. She was happy to hear that and waved as they drove off.

Samuel told Wallace that they needed to deal with Eveline's parents. Now that the real issues were surfacing, the way they presented it needed to change. Samuel thought they needed a few more visits to make sure Eveline was moving forward in understanding who actually pushed her to the breaking point. They would approach her parents and discuss the findings. Samuel had a feeling that they would deny any such idea. They would have Eveline tell them what she thought. It should be done at Willard. Wallace agreed to let Samuel do the planning because he was the doctor. When he told Rudolph about all that had happened, he was overjoyed. He hugged Wallace and told him they needed to celebrate a new beginning in business, friendship, and pleasure. Wallace elected pleasure first. They laughed and went to the YMCA. When they arrived back to Washington Street, Winston was in his room. Wallace wanted to tell him about Eveline. Winston wanted to know why Rudolph had to be around all the time. Wallace told him there was some good news about Eveline. Winston was barely interested. Wallace told him anyway. There was something very wrong with him. Maybe Samuel would need to examine Winston. Wallace would tell Samuel about Winston's sullen behavior. Rudolph left for the evening and Wallace tried again to talk with Winston. Wallace explained that he was concerned about him and wanted him to know that he still cared about him. Winston turned and with fire in his eyes said, "You have never cared for me the way I hoped for." He told him to get out of his room. Wallace left but the thought crossed his mind that he had just been thrown out of a room in his own house. Winston seemed to be on the verge of a breakdown. Wallace went to bed and enjoyed thinking about all the pleasures of his day.

The next day, Wallace spoke to Samuel about Winston's behavior and outbursts. Samuel mentioned he had seen a difference in his behavior recently. He told Wallace that unless he came to his office there was little he could do. He thought Wallace should stay out of Winston's affairs; he had Mr. and Mrs. Lounsberry to deal with. Samuel went to Willard to visit Eveline. He went alone to evaluate her thinking without any one else there. Wallace understood and went to work. Lately, he had been so involved with his personal life that he was behind with his advertising and business affairs with the Goodwin Printing Company. He decided to go to Goodwin after he caught up on his work at Standard and Safege. It was the end of March and there was new advertising that needed to be completed for the spring and summer line of eyewear. When he got to his office, an associate of his told him that he saw Winston roaming the streets that morning. Wallace thought that was strange because he saw him last night. He knew he was not in good spirits but realized he did not see him this morning either. He would go to Goodwin when he finished his work. Winston would probably be working. As he walked to the Goodwin Company, Wallace noticed how the stores were decorated and a parade was advertised for tomorrow. The city was honoring the men and women who fought in the war. The Geneva Daily Times had a Welcome Home Edition with a centurion pictured on the front page. The figure was pictured with only a cloak falling off his body and boots on his feet. He thought how daring the front page of the newspaper had become, quite a visual to victory. He passed by the YMCA and remembered he had a meeting with the board that evening. For the first time he felt like he had too many things to do. He reminded himself that things would return to normal after the moving was over. When he reached the office, he was told that Winston never showed up for work. He left no message as to his whereabouts. Wallace decided not to worry; he was able to take good care of himself. He would see him tonight and discuss things then. This year, Wallace's birthday was less important than last year. He was not interested in it since there was a lot to look forward to. He did receive a card from his mother wishing him a happy 38th birthday, no mention of Frank though. That was another disappointment to him but he knew there was little he could do for their relationship. Winston was not at home when Wallace arrived. Sable left him a note telling him that Winston said he was leaving and was not sure when he was coming back. Wallace knew there was definitely something going on. He was glad to know that his assistant was able to keep the Goodwin operation going in Winston's absence. Maybe he needed a break away from everything; it would have been nice to be told. He needed to find out what Samuel was planning with Eveline's parents because that was top priority

Mr. and Mrs. Lounsberry were invited to meet Samuel, Wallace, and Eveline at Willard. They received the letter from the director explaining that Eveline's conditions had changed and they needed to meet and discuss the status of her recovery. They were to meet on Wednesday at 11AM. Wallace and Samuel went earlier to see how Eveline was doing and to discuss why her parents were invited. When Samuel told her that she was well enough to move into the new house on South Main Street, she needed to have the conversation with her family. She knew for a long time that she was controlled by her parent's attitude toward everything she did in her life. After Wallace and Samuel heard this, they were satisfied that she was ready to confront her parents. They arrived exactly at 11AM. They seemed uneasy when they realized that they were the only ones present. Samuel began by explaining that Eveline had a long but successful recovery from the shock of her pregnancy. She had regained most of her recollection of past events and people. He looked at Eveline and gave her the gesture to begin her story. She took a deep breath and began telling them that she was happy doing what she wanted. She explained that she realized she did many things not because she wanted to but to satisfy them. When she mentioned the word satisfy her father said, "We knew you would satisfy us." At that, Eveline continued and told them it was always under their conditions, not hers. Her mother tried to interrupt but Eveline told her it was her turn to talk and they needed to stop being first. Eveline wanted them to know that she was happy doing it her own way and if they did not like the choices she made, that was their problem not hers. Her father told her she was out of line for saying such things after the proper upbringing she had. Eveline went on to tell them that was why she wanted them to stop meddling in her life. She admitted she tried to kill her baby because she was afraid of what they would want to do with her and her child. Then Samuel decided it was time to expose the letter that Alice received suggesting it was Alice's families' past that was at fault for her having a brown skinned baby and her ultimate breakdown. When Eveline realized her mother sent such a letter threatening to take her to Canada for more invasive treatments, she told them that they were underhanded and deceitful. Wallace sat and watched as Eveline continued to tear into them for being so controlling and overbearing. Samuel interrupted and asked if she was okay. She looked at him and told him she was doing just fine. She said, "I've had a long time to think things over. I'm glad I figured out that it wasn't Wallace who I saw as dead, it was my father." Her mother started crying and Eveline told her to get over that act. Samuel and Wallace remained quiet and watched Eveline finally take charge of what had been the trouble to her most of her life. Finally her inner mind came out. When Eveline paused, Samuel asked if there was anything more. Eveline said, "Yes, one more thing. You are to apologize to Alice for being so vicious." Her mother acted like she was just reprimanded. She agreed to talk with Alice. Samuel spoke about the timeline for Eveline to return to Geneva. When Mr. and Mrs. Lounsberry heard about a new residence, they asked where it was. Wallace explained that it was a mansion on South Main Street. He was having it renovated and it would be ready to move into shortly. He told them that Eveline and he had been choosing decorations, lights, and accessories for the house. Her parents seemed surprised that she had been doing so much. Eveline smiled and said, "I'm not as sick as you may have thought. I have things in better order now." The meeting ended and as they were leaving, her mother and father both apologized for their treatment and attitude. She accepted. Eveline thought that she would never quite believe the apology though. When they were getting into their cars, Samuel asked if they were all right. They told him they were surprised their daughter spoke up to them.

Samuel wanted to know if there was a reason it had to take this long for that to happen and under such conditions. Neither of them made an effort to discuss the issue any further. Wallace told them that they would be invited to the new home when they were settled.

On the way back to Geneva Samuel asked if he had seen Winston. Wallace told him that it was funny he asked because Winston had not been at work in a few days. Samuel mentioned that Winston did not make an appointment to see him and hoped he was okay. Wallace thought maybe he went to Rochester. He could not imagine why though. If he did not appear soon he would need to look into his whereabouts. When Wallace arrived home there were two letters for him. One was informing him that he was to finish paying for the house and he could take possession of it on April 8 and the other was a note from Winston. It was postmarked from New York City. Wallace had a strange feeling Winston went there to find out about things he was told never to discuss. The note only said, "Took a trip to New York because I need to find out more about Occidental." Wallace was afraid of what he would find out. The closing on the new house would be taken care of at the bank. Wallace would be the sole owner for now. When Eveline was settled and things were back to normal he would sign it over to her as he had with the Washington Street house. He made arrangements for the movers to have things taken to Main Street on the 9th. Mr. Preston told Wallace that Olitha was free to return to their employ. His wife realized what a strain they have been under that she could easily employ another colored woman from New York. Wallace cringed when he heard that especially when he wondered what Winston was uncovering at that very moment. He hoped Winston was not trying to punish him for the lack of lifetime companionship he accused him of the other night.

Time seemed to be moving very quickly in the last few days. The house was complete and looked perfect. He knew Eveline would fall in love with it. Rudolph saw Wallace and asked when he could see the completed project. Wallace told him anytime. They went that afternoon. Rudolph was impressed with the grandeur of the house and that the view was breathtaking. He asked if he had seen Winston. Wallace told him that he received a letter from him saying he was in New York. Rudolph looked puzzled and asked if there was a reason for his trip. Wallace told him no, but knew there was more to it than he wanted to discuss. Rudolph wanted to know about the new car. Wallace explained he had to go early next week to Buffalo to get his car. He told Rudolph about getting both Sable and Olitha to work at the new house and showed him where they would reside. He thought the kitchen and living quarters for servants was perfect in the basement. Wallace told him that Eveline would be coming to 775 Main Street after the place was settled. Rudolph offered to stay with her when he went to Buffalo. Wallace thought this might be good and Rose might want to be there too. Rudolph said, "It will be like old times." Wallace mentioned the meeting with Eveline's parents. He told Rudolph how Eveline stood up to them for the first time in her life. Rudolph smiled and told him he should see her at a rally. He referred to her as a cat ready to scratch the life out of things. Wallace laughed and was happy he did not see that side her.

Moving day was the day after Wallace signed the papers for the house. The man at the bank asked him where his wife was. Wallace wanted to know why. He said,

"We were all waiting for her to squeal and tell everyone in the bank how lucky she was." Wallace laughed and told him she was busy moving into the house. The bank officer smiled and thought how lucky they were to avoid the noise. Wallace drove to Willard with Samuel to sign Eveline out for the last time. Wallace told Samuel that he never thought this day would come. For the longest time he thought she would never regain her memory. Samuel told him it was faith and the support he gave her even when she thought he was dead. Eveline was packed and ready to go when they arrived. She wore a spring hat and a sporty dress and matching jacket. She asked them if they thought she was ready to go. Wallace told her she looked perfect and he was ready to take her away. Samuel smiled and followed them to the car. Samuel explained to her on the way home that she could call him anytime she wanted to. She laughed and said, "I'm glad you have a telephone in your apartment. Rose and I were tired of her talking on your office telephone." Samuel reminded her that she was under his medical supervision. She made one of her nose raising faces but thanked him for all he had done. Wallace felt like the last months were a nightmare but now she acted like she used to. He still wondered how the whole story could have gotten so twisted in her mind. When they drove up to the front of the house, Olitha and Sable were waiting to greet them as they walked into the main hall. Wallace informed all of them that when his new car was there he had hired a driver. His name was James. He would chauffeur them around town. Eveline thought that was nice but was more interested in what the house looked like decorated. She walked from room to room. She stood in the library and stared at the lake. She looked at Wallace and told him she was glad she was on this side of the lake and not at Willard. He hugged her and agreed. While they were touring the rooms to make sure all was well, Wallace told her he had to go to Buffalo to get the new car. He explained that Rudolph and Rose were going to stay with her while he was gone. She liked the idea and was looking forward to being like they used to be when they were at rallies.

Wallace was in big rush to leave for Buffalo. It was a typical spring day, which was rainy, damp and dreary. He forgot to take a raincoat and proper weather gear. He was excited about getting the car and coming back to Geneva to get on with his life in the new house. He stopped to speak with Samuel to tell him about Eveline and how she was doing. Samuel asked him what he was planning to do with the Washington Street house. Wallace wanted to know why. Samuel told him that Rose wanted him to buy it. He told her not to mention a word of it when she was there with Eveline today. Wallace had not thought about the house. It was empty and he would deal with it in a few weeks. Samuel reminded him he wanted first right of refusal. Wallace agreed he would have first choice to buy it. Wallace made very good time getting to Buffalo. He arrived and they took his car to the auction house. He waited until they brought the new car to him. He remembered how he felt the first time he picked up his first little red car. He thought about how silly he must have looked when he tried to drive it for the first time. The dealer directed Wallace to where the car was parked. He saw it and was surprised at how large it was. The dealer told him they are being made bigger and better every year. Wallace took his time leaving Buffalo. It was raining and getting dark. He decided it might be smart to stay in a hotel and start out in the morning. During the night he woke up thinking about

Winston and what he was doing in New York City. He hoped that he would be back when he returned. While he was driving he began to feel like he was getting a cold and a fever. He figured he caught it running around Buffalo in the rain without a coat. While he was driving he kept feeling sicker and sicker. He had a flash of worry when he thought about the influenza epidemic. It had slowed down and was not as much of a danger as it had been. He hoped this was not the remnant of that epidemic.

He had a difficult time getting back to Geneva. The weather was bad and his body felt worse as the hours passed. He arrived home before dinner. Sable had prepared a special dinner to celebrate the new house, the car, the return of the help, and Eveline. Rudolph and Rose were included as was Samuel. When Samuel saw Wallace he told him to go to bed and rest. He examined him and told him he was on fire with fever. Wallace apologized to them but went directly upstairs. He assured Eveline that he was overtired and probably caught a cold in the rain. The dinner was one of Sable's best. Everyone enjoyed it and spoke of how good it would be when Wallace was feeling better. James the new driver came into the main hall and announced that he had cleaned and dried off the car. He parked it in the garage and it was a beauty. When they all heard that they went downstairs to the garage to see what it looked like. It sat under the light and shone like a star. The finish sparkled and the wire wheels made it stand out. Rudolph said, "That's an example of what Wallace and I have worked hard to attain." Eveline said under her breath, "I hope we can enjoy it." When Samuel heard that he remembered Eveline's remarks about Wallace being dead or dying. He hoped she was not having a premonition of his death.

Chapter 57

WALLACE'S CONDITION WENT FROM a cold and fever to pneumonia. Samuel came to examine him daily. During one of Samuel's visits, Wallace discussed other options for treatment. He mentioned that there were specialists in New York City that might have more knowledge about how to treat him. Samuel admitted to him that he was not able to recommend any other treatments. He thought that having another opinion was a good idea since this could be an offshoot of the influenza that ravaged the country. Wallace told Rudolph to place a call to Mr. Wellington at Occidental and have him get in touch with the specialist that they knew who was familiar with the illness. Samuel was there when he explained that this doctor was known for his treatments of pneumonia related illness. Rudolph made the call to New York. When Rudolph identified himself to Mr. Wellington he mentioned that Winston Spaulding had just arrived in his office. Rudolph explained the problem that Wallace was having. He told Mr. Wellington that Wallace wanted him to call to schedule a specialist to come by train to Geneva. Mr. Wellington knew whom Wallace was asking for. He explained that the doctor had good success with pneumonia patients and any related illness. The company would pay his expenses to get him to Geneva as quickly as possible. Rudolph wanted to know if Winston mentioned why he was in New York. Mr. Wellington told him he would call him after he arranged for the doctor to leave for Geneva. Rudolph understood that he could not speak while Winston was standing there. He thanked Mr. Wellington and told him he would wait for him to return the call.

Eveline was handling Wallace's illness better than Samuel expected. His room had been quarantined and no one except Samuel was allowed in to see him. When Samuel went to see Wallace he wore a mask and gloves. He was not sure how contagious Wallace was. He suggested that he go to the hospital. Wallace refused. He felt more comfortable at home with Eveline and his friends. Eveline was certain "her Wallace" would feel better soon, especially with a specialist coming from New York City. While they were waiting the telephone rang. The operator said a Mr. Wellington was calling for Rudolph Williams. Rudolph thanked him for returning his call so quickly. According to him, Winston was questioning the imports that he remembered coming from the Orient. Rudolph asked why. He told him that Winston was talking with someone in Geneva who was familiar with part of the operation. It was called the TOE&TIC operation. Rudolph asked if a name was mentioned of the person in Geneva that Winston spoke with. All Mr. Wellington heard that it was a woman who had just received a colored domestic servant from the TOE&TIC program. Rudolph surmised it might have been Mrs. Preston. She was trying to fill Olitha's position when she went back to work for Eveline. Rudolph asked what he told Winston. Mr. Wellington told him that he did not have to tell him very much. Rudolph wanted to know why. Winston remembered Mr. Ling and his secretive methods with people. When he worked there he remembered some of the people that would appear from nowhere and then were taken to be domestic servants. They were always colored women. Winston wanted to know if they were smuggled into the country. Mr. Wellington told him no but thought Winston knew more about the program than he let on. Rudolph asked if Winston questioned anymore about the smuggling issue. He told him that Winston left in a huff when he heard the discussion about Wallace's condition. All Winston said was, "I'll be on that train to Geneva with the specialist." Rudolph was not sure what TOE&TIC meant either. All of these things seemed to be a mystery. Rudolph thanked him again and hung up.

Rudolph wanted to know more about the mysterious information he received from Mr. Wellington. He asked Samuel if he could see Wallace about a call he received from New York. Samuel agreed to prepare him to go into his room. He told him to begin with the news that the doctor was coming from New York and would be here by morning. Rudolph did as Samuel suggested and then asked Wallace about the TOE&TIC operation in New York. Wallace was getting very weak but told him that he thought that was why Winston was in New York. Rudolph still was not sure what this strange title meant. Wallace knew he had to tell Rudolph in case Winston arrived and announced inaccurate information. Rudolph waited while Wallace finished coughing. The cloth had blood on it. Rudolph knew that he was in worse trouble than Samuel let on. Wallace told Rudolph to never tell anyone about what he was about to tell him. He admitted it was the worst thing he had ever gotten into. It was never meant to turn into the operation it now was. He explained about the human transfers from the Orient. Rudolph listened.

Wallace continued with the additional part that was the most troubling. He explained, between coughing up blood, that the program expanded into transporting and selling infants and children. Rudolph tried not to react. He told him that surrogate mothers who were colored women cared for these children on their trip to America. After the children were placed then these women were sold into domestic service. Rudolph asked if Sable and Olitha were some of these women. Wallace nodded his head. Wallace told him that he never wanted small children to be sold into slavery, prostitution or physical abuse. He was told that they had a better chance in the United States than where they were coming from. He pleaded with Rudolph to never tell anyone and to do whatever it took to keep Winston quiet. Rudolph told him he would do his best. He told Wallace that he spoke with Mr. Wellington and that Winston had spoken with a woman in Geneva who was inquiring about a domestic servant. Wallace agreed it had to be Mrs. Preston. She had no reason to know about where these women came from, only that they were available for work. Wallace asked for Samuel because he was feeling like he could not catch his breath. Rudolph called for Samuel and he left the room. Eveline wanted to know what he thought about Wallace. He told her that he was resting and hoped that the doctor got there soon. She knew something was going to happen. She told Rudolph, "I knew he was going to die." Rudolph tried to change her mind but she looked at him with fear in her eyes.

Samuel stayed with Wallace through the night in hopes the doctor would arrive sooner than expected. Everyone sat in the library. Sable offered refreshments throughout the night. No one said much of anything. At 4AM, there was loud coughing and gagging sounds coming from upstairs.

Soon after, Samuel came into the library and announced that Wallace had passed away. Eveline began crying and screamed, "I knew he was going to die." Samuel went to calm her down. He was afraid she would go into another shock. She sat down and Samuel gave her an elixir, which settled her down. Samuel told everyone that they needed to get some rest and they would deal with the arrangements later in the morning. Rudolph remained with Eveline. He now was in charge of everything. The things Wallace told him before he died were almost unbelievable. Now he knew why there was so much trouble in New York and why all the murders. Mr. Wellington knew the whole history of the events that led up to the trial too. Wallace was more deeply involved in all types of business than anyone would believe. He hoped he would never be asked to divulge the information he had just learned. Winston was a challenge yet to be conquered.

The doctor arrived from New York at 7AM and Olitha took him into the library. Rudolph was there and Samuel had not arrived yet. He explained to the doctor that Wallace died at 4AM. He took him to Wallace's room. The doctor wanted to examine the body. He explained that he could determine what actually caused his death. Rudolph left him and went downstairs. While he was waiting Samuel arrived and went to be with the doctor. There was a knock at the door, Olitha went to see who it was. She opened the door and saw Winston. He announced that he met the doctor who was called from New York. By that time Rudolph was with Olitha. He told Winston that the doctor was examining Wallace. He did not lie to him but told him now was not a good time for visitors. Winston looked at Rudolph and asked, "Have you talked to Wallace?" He probably hasn't told the whole story about his New York City operation." Rudolph acted like he did not know what he was talking about. Winston turned and walked away yelling, "I'm going to let everyone know what I found out about Wallace and his undercover dealings." Rudolph closed the door; Sable overheard Winston and appeared nervous. He asked if she was okay. He knew why she was upset but he was not to tell anything. Sable knew that Rudolph and Winston figured out how and why she and other women arrived in Geneva.

After an hour the doctors came to the library. Eveline was there and Rose was called to be with her also. The doctor ruled that his death was from pneumonia. The record would show that as the cause of death. He actually died of blood suffocation. It was a form of the influenza epidemic that was mostly over with. Had he gotten medical assistance the very day he felt bad, they might have been able to keep his lungs clear until his body got stronger. The doctor explained that he saw many people his age die a slower death than what the actual flu was like a year ago. He was sorry that he did not get help when he was in Buffalo. He told them that it was no ones fault, it was a sudden and fast illness. He recommended that when the body was taken away that the room should be sanitized with a strong disinfectant and to open the windows to let the air blow through. Eveline looked at Rudolph and said, "That's why Wallace wanted such big windows. He didn't know they would be used so soon."

A horse drawn hearse pulled up to the front of the house to take the body for funeral preparations. Rudolph made arrangements for the lawyer to read the will the next day. He called the Seneca Powers Hotel and asked his manager to have Alice call him immediately. Eveline called her parents and explained what happened and the details of the funeral. Wallace's wishes were to be in his new home for the wake. It would be in two days. Olitha and Rose offered to be in charge of flowers and to have the main room set for the funeral. Eveline was glad to have all the help she could get now. Samuel watched her closely in hopes she would not need too many elixirs in the next few days. She had no idea of what was in store for her with the funeral and all of Wallace's business dealings. Samuel told her that Wallace mentioned a few things to him. He thought she would need time to sort out all the affairs. She acted as if she was not hearing a word he said to her. Early in the afternoon the telephone rang and the operator asked for Rudolph Williams. It was Alice. She listened to Rudolph explain that Wallace's condition had worsened overnight. The doctor from New York City did not arrive in time. He died at 4AM. He heard sobs from the other end of the line. He explained that the wake would be held at the new home at 775 South Main Street. Alice said, "What an awful way to see his new home." She told Rudolph that they would come by train since Eveline's parents were angry with her. He did not question that remark. He was not ready to deal with that issue, even though he knew the story. Rudolph told her that they could stay at the Washington Street house if they needed to. She thanked him and hung up. Rudolph asked if Eveline was ready to go to the newspaper office to set up the obituary and notice of funeral times. He explained to her that Wallace had discussed all these things with him a long time ago. She seemed surprised. He explained that when she was at Willard he had a will drawn up and he was there when that was done. He was also asked to be the trustee and assist her in any way he could. She smiled and said, "Of anyone I know, you would be my choice after Wallace." He told her that he would do as Wallace requested. The newspaper would have two announcements of Wallace's passing. Rudolph organized the first announcement. It read, "Wallace Paine was one of the most alert, active, and eager American businessman to every degree. He possessed those qualities that enabled him to grasp whatever opportunities came his way and had the vision to judge and act accordingly. His interests were manifold and his energies were sufficient to permit him to maintain everything without slighting anything. Still a young man, he was regarded as one of the ablest financiers of the city and had acquired a reputation that was becoming national." Rudolph then included Wallace's past life in Buffalo and his advancements in Rochester as a young person. He listed the companies he was affiliated with. The obituary filled half the page in the newspaper. The funeral notice stated that calling hours were at his home at 775 South Main Street on May 2 from 11AM to 1PM and the funeral service would follow. His burial would be at Mount Hope Cemetery in Rochester at 4PM the same day.

The next day Eveline and Rudolph were meeting the lawyer to have the will read. The lawyer began with the date the will was signed and made official. Eveline realized it was a year ago when she was still at Willard that he wrote the will. She was the executrix and Rudolph was named trustee. All debt and obligations owed to Wallace by his family were forgiven. His brothers, sisters, and parents were each to receive $500.00. Eveline was to receive the major portion of the estate. Wallace stated in the will that he could never repay her for her faithful co-operation, help, and sacrifice for so many years. Any stocks and companies owned by him and Rudolph Williams were to be held for five years after which time were to be given to his wife. After the will was discussed and arrangements were made for the monetary exchanges, Eveline mentioned the house on Washington Street. Rudolph wanted to know what she was talking about. She told both of them that Rose Haynes always admired that house and I told her that she could buy it after we were settled in at our new home.The lawyer made a note of that and asked her what the selling price was going to be. Rudolph thought it was too soon to be making such decisions. Eveline told him that she wanted to get rid of it as soon as she could. She wanted $7,000.00 for it.The mortgage was for $6,500.00. The extra $500.00 would pay for extra expenses she might have. Rudolph was amazed she was so on top of the business aspect of that house. She looked at Rudolph and winked and said,"I might have looked like I forgot things, but when it comes to money, that's the last memory to go."The lawyer's eyes went up and he said,"Good business woman here." Eveline shook her head. Rudolph was speechless. As they were going back to 775 Main Street, Eveline looked at Rudolph and told him she was very happy he was the trustee. She thought they had a grand future in store for themselves.

Sources

Brooks, Allen. *The Prairie School.* W.W.Norton & Company, 2006.

Buffalo & Erie County Library

Geneva Public Library

City Newspaper Rochester, Restoration of the Frank Lloyd Wright House, 2010.

Geneva Daily Times, 1900-1920

Grant, Kerry L. *The Rainbow City.* Canisius College Press, 2001

New York Times, President Shoot at the Buffalo Fair, September 7, 1901

WGBH Boston, American Experience, 1918 Influenza.

Website Searches

Alice Paul, Wikipedia.com

Larkin Story, Bottlebook.com

Burlesque, Wikipedia.com

Clowns, Wikipedia.com

Darwin Martin House.org

Fireproof House, Wikipedia.com

Ford Model A, 1903-1904, Wikipedia.com

Mauve Decade, Wikipedia.com

Music, Buffalo.edu

Pan-American Exposition, Wikipedia.com

Patent Medicines, Wikipedia.com

Ragtime, Wikipedia.com

Vintage Victorian.com

Vintage Views.org / *Timeline 1881-1910/ Flower City, Rochester, NY*

Acknowledgments

I could not have completed the writing of this book without the generous support of many people. The research, organization and writing of the book took nearly five years.

Thanks to the staff of the Geneva Public Library's microfilm department for being helpful while I read 20 years of newspapers and the Buffalo&Erie County Library's research department on the history of Buffalo, New York. The staff at the Mount Hope Cemetery in

Rochester, New York was supportive of me in the search for the burial plots and the history mentioned in the book. Special thanks goes to Marsha Houser my editor for her generous help, support, and insightful reading of the manuscript. Her questioning me on parts of the book helped me to create a clearer understanding of the people, events, and places throughout the book.

Thanks to Shirley Wharton and Jack Mulvey for accepting the challenge to read the drafts and offer honest and generous feedback. A hearty thanks and laugh goes to my many friends and colleagues that patiently listened to my persistent discussion of writing this book.

Finally, to my mother Dorothy Allen, a giant thanks for suggesting the title. Before any words were written on paper, she thought of the title when she saw the house and heard what the theme of the book was going to be. Lastly, thanks to me for being so persistent and focused on the writing of *The House of Many Windows*.

<u>Disclaimer</u>

The House of Many Windows

by John Robert Allen